PRAISE FOR *BENEATH DEVIL'S BRIDGE*

"The suspenseful, multilayered plot is matched by fully realized characters. White consistently entertains."

—*Publishers Weekly*

"If I'm lucky, maybe once in a blue moon, I read a book that leaves my mind reeling, heart aching, and soul searching. One that haunts me long after The End. *Beneath Devil's Bridge* is one of those books."

—*Mystery & Suspense Magazine*

PRAISE FOR *IN THE DEEP*

"Convincing character development and a denouement worthy of Agatha Christie make this a winner. White has outdone herself."

—*Publishers Weekly* (starred review)

"This page-turner is tightly written with a moody sense of place in the small coastal community, but it is the numerous twists that will keep readers thoroughly absorbed. A satisfyingly creepy psychological thriller."

—*Kirkus Reviews*

PRAISE FOR *IN THE DARK*

"White (*The Dark Bones*) employs kaleidoscopic perspectives in this tense modern adaptation of Agatha Christie's *And Then There Were None*. White's structural sleight of hand as she shifts between narrators and timelines keeps the suspense high . . . Christie fans will find this taut, clever thriller to be a worthy homage to the original."

blishers Weekly

"White excels at the chilling romantic thriller."

—The Amazon Book Review

"*In the Dark* is a brilliantly constructed Swiss watch of a thriller, containing both a chilling locked-room mystery reminiscent of Agatha Christie and *The Girl with the Dragon Tattoo* and a detective story that would make Harry Bosch proud. Do yourself a favor and find some uninterrupted reading time, because you won't want to put this book down."

—Jason Pinter, bestselling author of the Henry Parker series

PRAISE FOR LORETH ANNE WHITE

"A masterfully written, gritty, suspenseful thriller with a tough, resourceful protagonist that hooked me and kept me guessing until the very end. Think C. J. Box and Craig Johnson. Loreth Anne White's *The Dark Bones* is that good."

—Robert Dugoni, *New York Times* bestselling author of *The Eighth Sister*

"Secrets, lies, and betrayal converge in this heart-pounding thriller that features a love story as fascinating as the mystery itself."

—Iris Johansen, *New York Times* bestselling author of *Smokescreen*

"A riveting, atmospheric suspense novel about the cost of betrayal and the power of redemption, *The Dark Bones* grips the reader from the first page to the pulse-pounding conclusion."

—Kylie Brant, Amazon Charts bestselling author of *Pretty Girls Dancing*

"Loreth Anne White has set the gold standard for the genre."

—Debra Webb, *USA Today* bestselling author

"Loreth Anne White has a talent for setting and mood. *The Dark Bones* hooked me from the start. A chilling and emotional read."

—T.R. Ragan, author of *Her Last Day*

"A must-read, *A Dark Lure* is gritty, dark romantic suspense at its best. A damaged yet resilient heroine, a deeply conflicted cop, and a truly terrifying villain collide in a stunning conclusion that will leave you breathless."

—Melinda Leigh, *Wall Street Journal* and Amazon Charts bestselling author

THE PATIENT'S SECRET

OTHER MONTLAKE TITLES BY LORETH ANNE WHITE

Beneath Devil's Bridge
In the Deep
In the Dark
The Dark Bones
In the Barren Ground
In the Waning Light
A Dark Lure
The Slow Burn of Silence

Angie Pallorino Novels

The Drowned Girls
The Lullaby Girl
The Girl in the Moss

LORETH ANNE
WHITE

THE PATIENT'S SECRET

A NOVEL

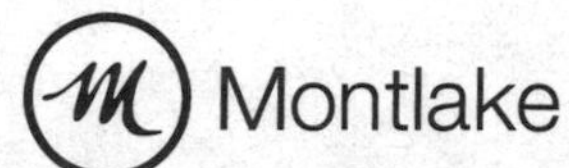

Montlake

Published by Montlake, Seattle

www.apub.com

ISBN-13: 9781542034067
ISBN-10: 154203406X

Cover design by Caroline Teagle Johnson

Printed in the United States of America

THE PATIENT'S SECRET

PREFACE

The inspiration at the heart of this work of fiction is a true crime—heinous and shocking—that occurred in a quiet neighborhood on the Canadian prairies. The events of that day made criminal history in Canada, and they have been covered extensively by the media, as have the subsequent trials. While the backstory in *The Patient's Secret* draws directly from some of the true facts of this crime, what is spun around it is fictional.

HOW IT ENDS

It's best not to resist the change the "Death" tarot card brings. Resisting will make transition difficult. And painful. Instead one should let go, embrace the necessary change, see it as a fresh start. The Death card is a sign that you need to draw a line through the past in order to move forward. It says: Release what no longer serves you.

—*Artist's statement.* Death. *36 × 48. Oil on canvas.*

It's darker in the woods than she thought it would be. The old-growth trees sway and twist in the wind. Rain drives over the canopy in waves. The cliff trail is narrow, slippery with mud. Mist sifts across her path, bouncing back the weak beam of her headlamp.

She runs deeper into the forest and fear rises in her belly. She should have searched properly for her phone before exiting her studio. She shouldn't have gone out at this hour. But she was forced into the night, into the teeth of the summer storm, by the voices that have begun in her head again. She's desperate to outrun them. On another level she knows she will never flee them. Not now. The Monster is not out there circling her. It's not someone else. It's inside her head. It is her.

I . . . stabbed . . . got . . . blood on me . . . couldn't stab again . . . too young to die . . . pleading . . . not to kill . . . heard the gurgling . . . once it started, it couldn't stop. It had to be finished.

A silent scream swells in her chest. The sound comes alive. It pierces her ears. Tears sting her eyes. She pushes harder, faster, craving escape. Her breath rasps in her throat. Her chest heaves. Sweat dampens her T-shirt beneath her waterproof running jacket.

An image slices through her brain—the gaping, leaf-shaped wounds. The gouge in the eye socket. Blood . . . so much blood. Splattered and spattered and sprayed over the walls, across the ceiling, on the lampshades, the television screen, the exercise bike. The hallway carpet saturated and sticky with it. She can smell it again. Hot. Meaty.

I'm sorry. I'm so, so, so sorry . . . I was another person. I don't even recognize that person. It's like it wasn't real, it wasn't me.

She sees the glint of the blade. She hears screams. She moves her legs even faster.

I killed . . . I killed . . . I killed. I didn't want to—

Lightning cracks above the canopy and thunder booms. She stumbles in fright, almost going down. Shaken, she stops, bends over, and places her hands on her hips. She sucks in big gulps of air. Her heart slams against her rib cage. Her exhalations explode in ghostly puffs in the beam of her headlamp. Thunder grumbles again and rolls out over the ocean. She can't see the sea, but she can sense it, a surging, empty blackness below the cliffs through the trees to her right. And now that she is still, beneath the drumming noise of the rain, she can hear waves churning and clattering the pebbles at the base of the crumbling sandstone cliffs.

Things have gone so wrong.

She had a plan, but it flipped on her. She doesn't know what to do now, or how to even be. Or what her purpose is.

Something moves among the trees. She tenses, flicks her gaze toward the shapes in the forest to her right. As she moves, her beam shivers in the mist, and shadows dart and lunge. She swallows, peering hard into the darkness between the trunks and ferns.

Lightning flickers again. The thunder crash is almost instant. The storm is directly overhead. Rain pummels down harder, and the wind swishes through the treetops with the sound of a rushing river. In her peripheral vision she glimpses a hooded figure in the trees. Then he's gone.

Her pulse quickens. Her mouth goes dry. Panic licks in her belly.

She needs to get out of these woods. She glances back along the trail. It would take longer to return than to continue forward. If she presses onward, within minutes she will pop out into an open expanse on the grassy bluffs. She'll be clear of the woods. Beyond the grassy area lies a parking lot, and behind the lot is a street with lights. It'll be brighter. Safer. She can run home along the roads, under the lights.

She begins to run again. Lightning flares. She moves faster, stumbling over roots, sliding in mud. Pine cones, small branches tear loose from the trees, and the debris bombs down. A flying cone narrowly misses her head. She ducks. Her abrupt movement makes shadows leap and scurry. She stops again. Panting, she spins around and sees the hooded figure once more, lurking between the trees. His face is in blackness, as though masked. Fog thickens, and he's gone. A claw of fear grabs her throat.

She takes off fast now, legs powering her forward, her shoes slipping. She stumbles. Windmilling her arms, she manages to right herself, then tries to go even faster.

Another bolt of lightning. For a second the trail ahead is starkly illuminated. She sees the hooded figure again. Now with a flashlight in his hand as well as a bright headlamp on his head. A faceless Cyclops. Her body freezes. Her brain is paralyzed. She can't breathe, can't move. He comes toward her, closer, closer. Her beam hits the reflective strips on his pants and jacket. The light dances back, making the strips gleam like silver blades, like a skeleton costume at Halloween.

I . . . stabbed . . . got . . . blood on me. She has no cell phone. No weapon.

He suddenly moves quickly toward her. She ducks off the trail into dense undergrowth between the trees. She crashes through brambles and berry scrub, tripping and falling over logs and rocks and roots, her arms flailing, branches snapping back across her face.

He comes into the bushes after her, his two beams of light punching powerful tunnels through the mist, illuminating trunks and leaves and making the rain shimmer silver. Thunder cracks again. She whimpers. Tears burn her eyes. Another branch whips back and slices across her cheek. Rain—or blood—wets her face. She can hear him. Coming. Like a big animal crashing through brush, getting closer. She hears his breathing. She falls again, scrambles on hands and knees through the mud, cutting her palms on brambles and thorns.

She whimpers again as she crawls under a low branch. She switches off her headlamp and tries to be still. But the lights come closer. She sees the search beams illuminating the ground. He's almost upon her and she can't take it.

She screams, bolts up out of her hiding place, and staggers forward like a wounded deer. Suddenly she's out of the trees and there is black emptiness before her. She's reached the edge of the forest. The cliffs. The ocean. She spins around, but he's right there. She's trapped.

"What . . . what do you want?" she gasps, her voice hoarse.

He raises his hand with the flashlight, like a weapon to strike her. He's saying something, but she hears only a mounting roar of noise inside her head. He lunges for her and grabs her arm.

She screams, struggles, and squirms out of his grasp. She's now right at the cliff edge. Panting. He crouches in front of her, swaying, primed for her to dart, ready to dive to block her flight. She feels loose stones beneath her feet. She's right on the crumbling edge of the sandstone cliff.

He yells, but his words are snatched by the roar of the wind in the trees and the sound of waves below the cliffs. He lunges for her again, and she scratches and claws at his face, his neck, screaming. Her fingers catch fabric, and his cap and hood come off. In another flash of lightning, she sees his face.

Everything in her brain stalls.

You?

But the moment of shock costs her. Her assailant's hand goes high into the air, and he brings his flashlight down hard across her temple. She staggers, momentarily blinded, and she feels his push against her chest as the ground simultaneously gives out under her legs.

She hurtles backward into air. Arms flailing, she realizes she's going over the cliff. A scream surges from her chest as she falls and spins and spirals downward in the lashing rain and driving wind. Lightning pulses. A growl of thunder swallows her cries.

Her shoulder slams into a rock. She bounces off it. Her head smashes into another rock lower down. Her body cartwheels out into the void again, and farther down, she crashes her ribs and face into a ledge. She feels her neck crack, her back break. When her skull strikes the next jagged rock on her fall toward the pebble beach far below, her world mercifully goes blank.

The voices—finally—go silent.

LILY

NOW
June 20. Monday.

CHART NOTES: **TARRYN**

Patient, 15, presents in the aftermath of being arrested for shoplifting. Reports she does not require therapy, she's "not crazy," but her parents are forcing her to attend for a "few sessions" to meet restorative justice requirements.

The morning has dawned dark with heavy clouds. Wind gusts, and rain streams down the windowpanes of Dr. Lily Bradley's home therapy office. The thunderstorm that broke over their neighborhood barbecue yesterday has not let up. Lily fears the ancient poplar growing over the shed in the corner of their yard will come down in this onslaught of wind, and it could crash into their house. Specifically, onto her eight-year-old son's attic room. She tries not to think about it right now. Or why her husband, Tom, left for a run at 5:30 a.m. In the dark of the storm.

She tries not to think of their horrendous fight yesterday. Neither she nor Tom has fully processed what happened yesterday, or how their lives will change now. Lily is just trying to focus on getting through her appointments. She knows it's a form of denial. But routine is also her method of survival. "Stacking" her habits to build a perfect life is what gives Lily control over her world. She *needs* routine. She needs to feel in control.

Tom leaving for a run in the dark of a storm is *not* part of the Bradley family routine. She saw he was gone when thunder crashed and lightning flared early this morning, forcing her to sit bolt upright in bed. In the flash of light, she saw the duvet thrown back on his side of the bed. The mattress was cold. She went downstairs and found a note on the kitchen counter.

Gone for a run to clear head.

She tries to concentrate on her job, on her patient, Tarryn Wingate, who sits on the oatmeal-colored sofa in front of her. Lily's chair is made of wood and soft, buttery leather. Ergonomically designed. It cost a fortune. But she uses it for at least eight hours a day while counseling her clients, so she needs to be comfortable. She wears tailored but loosely fitted linen pants, a cream sweater. Simple pearls. Her golden-blonde hair is twisted into a gentle knot at the nape of her neck. Wisps hang free. Feminine, but neat. Professional. Classy. Yet approachable. Her sartorial choices are also part of her routine, her definition of who she is, and they're aimed to inspire confidence and, above all, trust.

Trust is key in psychotherapy.

Her office is similarly designed. Ordered yet comfortable. A safe and sheltering space. Like the name of her business, Oak Tree Therapy, signifying a solid yet growing organism that can endure the pressures of time, something with deep roots.

Today she feels anything but safe.

Her roots have been exposed. Her insides are raw. She is terrified that their whole life, everything she has worked so hard for, is about to come crashing down.

A notepad rests in her lap. On the top of the page she's written, *Tarryn, 7:30 a.m.*

"Thank you for coming so early, Tarryn," she says.

"It's not early, not for me," replies the fifteen-year-old. "I told you last time I'm usually at the pool by five thirty a.m. for swim squad training, before school."

Tarryn wears no makeup. Her jeans are a designer brand, as is her sweatshirt. Her brown hair is shoulder length and pulled back into a jaunty ponytail. Athletic build. Clear eyed. She's still hostile. She doesn't trust Lily yet.

Lily forces a slight smile and says nothing. She waits for her young patient to lead. She can tell a lot about someone in the spaces between the words. And in their body language.

Tarryn, uncomfortable with Lily's silence, shifts on the sofa. "So how many more times do I have to come back? I've already told you I stole that pink sweater, and I was arrested. And I told the store owner I am sorry."

"Do you feel sorry, Tarryn?"

Outside thunder grumbles. Rain lashes afresh at the windows. Lily's thoughts boomerang back to the fight. *Why is he not home yet?* She tries not to glance out the window at the poplar bending dangerously in the wind. She told Tom last summer they should cut it down. He insisted on waiting until the baby raccoons nesting in the tree matured. The raccoon family is fully grown now, and still living in the tree.

"Does it matter?"

"If you don't actually feel sorry, then why did you tell the store owner you were?"

"Because I had to. As part of the restorative justice program."

Lily nods. Waits.

Tarryn looks down, picks at the fraying hole in her carefully ripped designer jeans. "I'm not crazy," she says. "I just don't know how this is supposed to go. Or how long it's going to take."

"You also told me you do have money, Tarryn, that you could have bought the sweater if you wanted. But you haven't told me why you chose to steal it instead."

Tarryn glances up slowly. "What if I don't want to talk about it?"

"Well, it's really up to you. We can talk about whatever you want. This is your time, your space. And it *is* a safe space, Tarryn. It's private. Like I said before, whatever you say in this room stays in this room. Client confidentiality is paramount, which means that your relationship with me is also something you choose to define. Again, like I explained in our first session, if you happen to run into me outside of therapy, it's completely up to you whether you want to even acknowledge me or not, and I will take the cue from you."

A sly smile curves Tarryn's mouth. "Like you just ignored me, pretended not to know me at the pool the other day, when you brought your son for swimming lessons?"

"That was the cue you chose to give me, so yes. Some of my clients don't want it known that they're in therapy. Others are completely fine with it."

"So you really won't tell my mother what I say in here?"

"As I said, this time is yours."

"Even if she's paying?"

"No matter who is paying." Lily jots a note on her pad. *Mother? Control issues?*

"But you're writing down what I say."

"They're just my personal chart notes. If it makes you uncomfortable, I don't have to do it."

She eyes Lily. Suspicious. Thunder growls again. Tom should have returned by now.

"I don't want you writing it down."

"Okay." Lily sets the notepad and pen on the small table beside her chair. "Shall we go back to why you decided to steal the pink sweater even though you had money to buy it?" She observes her patient carefully as she speaks. Being a therapist is like being a detective looking for clues to solve a mystery, to find the reasons underlying the "presenting problem," which in this case is the shoplifting. The presenting problem is what propels someone into therapy—the person has reached a critical inflection point in their life. But while the presenting problem might be obvious, why it occurred is often hidden, even from the patient themselves, buried deep in the unconscious. Lily's job is to coax the underlying forces out of the unconscious, making them conscious, where they can then be examined and dealt with.

Tarryn shifts on the sofa. "Yeah, it's not like I'm poor. My parents make loads of money. Tons of it. My dad is a partner in his law firm, and they have offices in multiple cities. They're, like, the top criminal law firm. And my mother is a town councillor, and she also owns a real estate business that my grandfather started. So we're rich. My mom is going to run for mayor next year."

Lily knows this, of course.

The Bradleys live in a wealthy oceanside enclave on the outskirts of Victoria on Vancouver Island, a stone's throw across Juan de Fuca Strait from Washington in the US. But it's still a tight-knit community. Everyone knows everyone's business. Everyone is connected in one way or another. It's a fine line to walk as a therapist. Tarryn's mother—town councillor Virginia Wingate—has built her platform on maintaining law and order and cleanliness in Story Cove. Tarryn's father, Sterling Wingate, is a partner at Hammersmith, Wingate & Klister. And Dianne Klister is one of Lily's closest friends. So Lily has a pretty good idea just how much Daddy Wingate is worth, and what he's like. She also knows that Tarryn's parents are in the process of divorcing.

Lily waits. Thunder rumbles.

Tarryn clears her throat. "I . . . just wanted to see if they actually watched the security cameras, you know? A friend of mine from school said she took stuff all the time, and . . ." She trails off.

"And?"

"My friend was caught."

"So you wanted to get caught, too?"

"That's ridiculous."

"So you *didn't* want to get caught?"

"Of course not."

"You wanted to challenge the system, then? See if you were special? The one who *could* get away?"

"You're twisting things. Look . . . I don't think this is going to work. I gave the fucking sweater back, okay? I didn't even like it. And I *told* the manager I was sorry, like I was supposed to." She surges to her feet and reaches for her backpack.

"What happened to your friend after she was caught, Tarryn?"

The teen hesitates. "The store manager held her until the police arrived. And then she was arrested. There was a big fuss—she had to go to group meetings, do community service. And she had to give up her dancing lessons in order to do it." A pause. A defiant look creeps into her eyes. "Stacey's parents don't have the power that mine do. Her dad works in a supermarket, and her mother is just a stay-home mom. Her mom was always at Stacey's dance rehearsals and stuff. And *that's* why Stacey is not rich—her parents don't put in the time." Tarryn slings her pack over her shoulder and goes to the coatrack near the door. She grabs her jacket off the hook.

"How did you get here today, Tarryn?"

She wavers for a moment, then turns to face Lily. "What's that got to do with anything?"

"I was wondering whether you have someone to pick you up since you're leaving early."

The girl's gaze locks on Lily's. Belligerent. But it's a belligerence born of fear. This kid is vulnerable. She's crying out for help. For the love and attention of her parents.

"This is a safe space, Tarryn," Lily reminds her softly. "I need you to understand this. I'm just trying to get to know you a little better, but we don't have to talk about the sweater. We can talk about whatever you want. Or you can in fact leave whenever you want."

Tarryn inhales deeply and looks away. Lily catches a glimmer of tears in the kid's eyes.

"My mom," she says finally. "She's parked in the lane out back. She . . . she's taking time off work to bring me to my therapy sessions."

Lily nods. "Would you like it if your mother was more like Stacey's mom?"

"You mean poor?"

"I mean, does your mom take you to your swim practice every morning, like Stacey's mother takes Stacey to all her dance rehearsals?"

Tarryn glowers at Lily.

"How do you usually get to swim practice?"

"My dad drops me off on his way to work."

"Does he wait for you to finish swimming, then drive you to school afterward?"

"No. I get the bus to school afterward. My father needs to put in the work."

"Your father goes to work at five thirty a.m.?"

She breaks eye contact and stares at her boots. "You don't get to be anyone without putting in the work."

"Is this what your father says?"

"Everyone knows that."

"Like swim training? You need to put in the work before school?"

"I was an Olympic hopeful. That's what my coach said. *That's* why I was training five mornings a week. That's why I spent every weekend traveling to swim meets and going to trials."

"You say you *were* an Olympic hopeful. What changed?"

Slowly Tarryn returns to the sofa. Deflated, she sinks down onto the edge of a cushion, still clutching her jacket and backpack. "I didn't make the trials, because I had to do the restorative justice program. And I had to do it or I would get a criminal record. Besides"—her features suddenly harden and her eyes turn to flint—"Coach has a new and better protégé, anyway. Someone younger and prettier."

"Does being pretty give one a better shot at the Olympics?"

Tarryn's gaze lasers into Lily's. Her mouth flattens, and she doesn't reply. Lily thinks of the man she saw with Tarryn and the swim squad at the pool when she took Matthew for his lesson. A big, macho dude with sandy-blond hair. Lily has seen him several times at the pool and working out in the gym. A guy with an eye for the ladies.

She makes a mental note to circle back to "Coach."

"How do you feel about no longer being an Olympic hopeful?"

"Duh. How do you think I feel?" She sits silent for a while. "My mom . . . she thinks I stole something to get arrested on purpose."

Lily hears the yard gate slam. *Tom. He's back.* Her stomach tenses. She forces herself to keep her focus on Tarryn. "How so?"

"Because I'm a perfectionist, and my mom believes I put too much pressure on myself, and she thinks I was scared that I wouldn't make the cut at the trials, so I sabotaged myself to give myself an excuse."

"Do you think she's right?"

Her jaw juts out and her cheeks flush red. "That is so fucked up! Why would I do that? My dad believes me—that I didn't do it on purpose. I want to go and live with him, but my mother doesn't want to expose me to his 'lifestyle.' He was having an affair, and she kicked him out. But I don't blame him because my mother is a total bitch."

"Your parents are divorced?" Lily wants to hear how Tarryn frames it.

"They will be. They're separated now. My mom says I should see this restorative justice program as an 'opportunity'"—Tarryn makes air quotes—"to finally 'quit this swimming thing' and focus on schoolwork. That's what she calls my Olympic dream: a 'thing.' But she's the one who's the perfectionist. She's always trying to be 'perfect' in this 'perfect' town. She's the one who was so busy being perfect that her husband left her for another—more perfect—woman."

"And have you met this woman?"

She swallows and looks down at the carpet in silence. Finally she says, "My mother is the one who stuck me in that stupid private Catholic school. Apparently the school that *your* son and daughter attend is not good enough for me."

Lily's stomach tightens further at the mention of her daughter. She knows Tarryn is obfuscating, trying to redirect, to mess with Lily by goading her. Her mind whips back to the terrible personal row about tween girls at the barbecue yesterday.

Focus.

In her peripheral vision she notices the light in the shed flare on. Lily steals a quick glance, sees Tom's silhouette moving in the shed. With shock she realizes he has no shirt on. There's a strange urgency to his movements.

Struggling to project calm, Lily says, "Uh . . . you mentioned that your father feels differently to your mother?" The light goes off in the shed.

Lily hears the back door of their house slam—her office is attached to the house. It's an old building. She hears Tom thudding up the wooden stairs. He's moving fast. Unusual. Tension winds tighter. She glances at the clock on the wall. The session with Tarryn is almost over.

"My dad gets me. He knows what it's like to have a dream, and to go for it. He's, like, the only one in the world who loves me."

"The only person in the entire world?"

She rubs her knee. "And Coach."

"So . . . your coach—he's one of the only two people in this world who love you?"

"Well, not *love* love. It's more . . . he cared about me."

"'Cared'? Does that mean he no longer does?"

Tarryn's eyes narrow. "I didn't make the team cut, right? So . . . he's busy. He's focused on those who need to get ready for nationals now. But he was the one who always traveled with me to the weekend swim meets out of town. The other kids have parents who drive them, and who travel with them on the ferries, and who overnight at the motels and stuff. My parents can't manage entire weekends away from work."

Lily hears a siren rising and falling in the distance. The mist is thickening outside, the rain still coming down heavily. There must be a traffic incident on the roads.

"My parents are not like the other parents. Other mothers bake things for the fundraising sales, but my mom . . . she just writes a check or whatever. She doesn't have time for that shit."

The siren grows louder—a plaintive howling in the wind and rain. Lily cannot abide sirens. They hurtle her back to a dark place. They make her think of a terrible time in her childhood, when she lost her parents and sibling. When she became an orphan. Sirens trigger a primal and physical response in her body that is quite apart from her mind. It's something she cannot control. As a therapist Lily knows that trauma lives in one's body and that the body keeps the score even if the mind has no narrative for what occurred. Even if the event is completely compartmentalized in the unconscious.

It's partly why she became a therapist—she knows personally, intimately, what debilitating long-term effects trauma can have on a child and how shocking events can shape a teen, and an adult. Her goal in life is to help others cope with mental adversity, to show that one does not have to be irreparably destroyed by horrific actions of the past. Her goal, hourly, daily, weekly, monthly, yearly, is to show, again and again, that a person *can* make a choice to change the narrative, to overwrite the patterns of history. That a person does not have to be defined by the past. Or by genetics. People *can* change.

It's her life calling. Her purpose. And everyone needs a purpose.

Lily glances again at the shed outside. This time Tarryn's gaze follows. Lily can see her patient is also listening to the sirens. They're being joined by more. A wailing, rising-and-falling chorus, growing louder. Banging sounds upstairs. Through the walls she hears Tom yelling for their daughter, Phoebe. Her heart hammers. She feels hot. Her gaze darts again to the clock on the wall. Just a few minutes left in the session. She needs to see this through.

"Tarryn, can . . . we, ah . . . can we return to something you mentioned earlier? About your coach's new protégé?"

She exhales heavily. "You mean the new girl with the 'most potential'?" More air quotes. "It's Sally-Ann now."

The sirens grow very loud. It sounds as though they're coming down their street. Lily's throat tightens. Her skin prickles. She can barely think.

"So . . . so you need to be pretty to have Olympic swimming potential?"

"What?"

"You said she was younger and prettier."

"Fuck you."

Lily blinks. The sirens grow even louder.

"Besides, Coach didn't actually say that. Sally-Ann told me he said it. And she's probably lying. I reckon she's in love with him. Which is so fucking idiotic. How can you fucking be in love with your coach and think it's going to get you onto some world-class team?"

The sirens are right outside the house. Red and blue lights suddenly strobe through the blinds on the narrow window that faces the street, and the glow pulses over Lily's office walls and ceiling. She surges up from her chair and hastens to the window. Parting the blinds, she sees two marked police cars come to a stop right in front of their yard, light bars pulsing. The sirens go quiet. The cruiser doors swing open. Three uniformed officers exit into the rain. But the lights keep flashing in silence. Lily hears Tom yelling for Matthew now.

"Besides, Coach is married, and he's not interested in juveniles," Tarryn says, coming up beside Lily to see out the window.

Lily's pulse races. She's unfocused. She hears the front door of their house opening.

"Like marriage even matters," says Tarryn. "I saw Coach with a woman who is definitely *not* his wife, and who is definitely not a 'juvenile.' He was kissing her around the back of the rec center."

Lily sees Tom rushing down the driveway toward the approaching cops. He wears an orange rain jacket—not his usual red one—over his running pants with reflective strips. His hair is soaked—plastered to his skull. His running shoes are caked with black mud.

"Jesus, is that your *husband*?" says Tarryn. "What are the police doing at your house?"

MATTHEW

NOW

Matthew Bradley hears the wooden gate in the yard slam. He thinks it's the wind.

Still in his pajamas, he clambers onto his knees on his bed and peers out the dormer window of his attic room. The entire attic area is his space. His turret, his control tower. It has dormer windows that look out on three sides—over the backyard, down into the street in front of their house, and onto the lane that runs along the side of their property, where his mother has two parking bays for her patients. He's king in his turret. The observer and recorder of all things. It's summer, and tomorrow is supposed to be the solstice—the longest day of the year—but on this stormy morning, it looks dark as winter out. The fog is thick, and the rain comes down in sheets. Water streams down his small windowpanes. As he looks out, he sees a branch snap off the poplar. It whirls down to the yard, gets momentarily snagged on the washing line, then tumbles to the grass.

That's when he notices his father crossing the lawn, heading for the shed.

His heart quickens. He leans closer to the window. His dad is wearing waterproof running pants with reflector strips, but his head is bare, and his hair is wet. He's got no rain jacket. Matthew clearly saw his dad leaving with his rain jacket and a flashlight this morning. He saw the flashlight beam bobbing down the lane through the mist, and he thought it was super cool that his father was heading out in a storm. His dad's long-sleeved white running shirt is now sopping, sticking to his skin.

The motion-sensor light over the shed door flares on. Matthew sees his dad more clearly now. His father, struggling to unlock the door, shoots a glance over his shoulder. He seems . . . nervous?

Matthew leans so close to the window his nose presses against the glass. There is a big dark stain on the front of his dad's shirt. Mud? Maybe he fell. His father disappears into the shed. The door shuts behind him. The shed light goes on.

Matthew frowns. His wild imagination is leaping. The stain on his father's shirt seemed more red than brown. *Like blood.*

He scoots out of bed and scurries over to his desk. He yanks open a drawer, grabs his digital camera. Matthew could use a cell phone to take photos, but he's going to be a famous reporter one day. Like an investigative journalist. Or a detective. Or an undercover cop. Or one of those officers who wears a white Tyvek bunny suit with a hood, like on TV, who shoots pictures at crime scenes. He's only eight, and most of the kids at school think he's weird and "stalkery," but he likes to watch people when they don't know they're being watched. And he likes to take photos of the other kids when they don't think anyone's looking. *Candid.* A new word for him. One he learned from Mr. Cody, who lives down the street next to the forest, and who is Fiona and Jacob's father. Mr. Cody is a watcher and a photographer, too, but Mr. Cody watches birds. He told Matthew his photos showed "real talent." That they were "great candid shots," and he explained what the word meant. He also taught Matthew some clever tricks with the camera. Matthew shoots his candid photos of adults in his neighborhood, and he prints some of the images out on his printer, on photographic paper his mom bought for him at Walmart. And he's created binders with different subject headers like Backyards. Swimming Pool Habitats. People at the Beach. The Cricket Club. The Yacht Scene. The Mall Life.

"Case files," he calls them. Among his collection are young girls in bathing suits. Lovers kissing. People rifling through the garbage and recycling bins on the streets at dawn, or walking dogs, or arguing. Or sitting in cars. Sometimes he sneaks right up to houses and peeks into the windows. If he goes when it's getting dark, he can see everything inside quite clearly—like little stage sets. He sees the old man who passes out in his chair daily with a whiskey bottle at his side. And the lady who knits while her cats sleep on the back of her sofa. And the trendy couple down the road in the new house with lots of glass who like to serve fancy drinks to a variety of very interesting-looking friends. And the moms who do yoga with their babies watching. And the lady one block over who hides bottles from the liquor store in strange places. And the father who meets someone else's mother in the park. And the kids from school who drink and smoke and kiss in a clearing deep in the woods, or in the cave down on Grotto Beach.

Matthew has a whole mental map of his neighborhood and who lives in it, and what they do. Sometimes he will decide to target a particular subject and follow them for a week or so. Reconnaissance. And he'll make a special case file for that person, taking notes about what time and day they do certain things. Habits. Patterns. Just as Mr. Cody might watch and study birds, or a scientist might observe the habits of weasels. Matthew is like the *National Geographic* eye on Story Cove, the safe neighborhood with hidden secrets. He is the diviner and keeper of those secrets in his surveillance turret on top of the Bradleys' heritage home.

Matthew generally doesn't tell anyone about what he sees. He prefers to keep his information locked in the compartments of his brain. But just knowing—it makes him feel special. Like he has a superpower. Like he's part of a league of secret superheroes who fly over Story Cove with a big seeing eye. Occasionally he might share a snippet of something juicy with Harvey Hill, who is a chess champion and Matthew's only real friend. Besides, Matthew's mother would kill him if she discovered he takes photos of her patients, too, as they enter and leave her practice downstairs. He hasn't told his mom and dad about the Shadow Man, either. The Shadow Man sometimes watches the Bradley house at night from the shadows across the street. The Shadow Man is tall and dresses all in black and wears a face mask under his bike helmet. The Shadow Man has a bike with a reflective streak on the crossbar, and he doesn't know Matthew spies back at him from up in his dark attic window.

Matthew clicks a photo of his father's silhouette in the lighted window of the shed. He aims, clicks again as his dad takes off the wet, stained shirt. Matthew clicks, capturing an image of his bare-chested father. His dad then moves out of view. Matthew's attention drifts to the lane on the other side of the fence. A silver car is parked in the bay, engine running. There's someone inside. There's also a square glow of light on the grass, coming from his mom's downstairs office—she must have an early patient. Someone must be waiting for the patient in the silver car.

His dad suddenly exits the shed and hurries shirtless through the rain toward the kitchen door.

The door bangs downstairs. For a moment things are quiet. Matthew stills and lowers his camera. He feels a bit scared for some reason he can't explain. He hears his dad thumping up the stairs.

"Phoebe!" His father's voice booms on the second floor. "Get up—time for school!"

Closet doors slam in his parents' bedroom. A tap runs.

Matthew hears a wailing of sirens in the distance.

"Matthew!" his dad calls up the attic stairs. "Time to get dressed!"

His father thuds heavily down the stairs.

The sirens grow louder. They're coming closer. Something is happening. Suddenly Matthew sees red and blue lights flashing outside. He rushes to the front window that looks down over Oak End.

Two cop cars, black and white, light bars flashing, screech to a stop right outside Matthew's house. His hands begin to shake with excitement. He aims his camera out the window, shoots, *click click click*, as three uniformed officers get out of the cruisers.

Another car—metallic brown—arrives. It, too, has flashing lights. But inside, along the windows, not on top. An unmarked car. *A ghost car!* Matthew is beyond excited. It stops across the street, under the gnarled cherry tree where the Shadow Man usually stands.

He sees his father hurrying toward the uniformed officers. His father is wearing a rain jacket now.

His mother suddenly comes barreling out of the house behind his dad.

His mother grabs his dad's arm. His dad turns to face his mom. He says something to her, and her hand goes over her mouth. She looks scared. His father's face is very, very white. One of the officers touches his mother's arm and appears to ask her to step away from his dad.

Matthew slowly lowers his camera.

Something terrible has happened.

LILY

NOW

Lily shrugs into her jacket as she runs out the front door into the rain.

A woman in a black coat is getting out of an unmarked vehicle across the street as three uniformed cops approach Tom.

Lily reaches her husband, grabs his arm. "What's going on?"

He turns to face her. His complexion is bloodless. Fear strikes a hatchet into her heart. "Tom?" she whispers, casting a nervous glance at the uniformed Story Cove PD officers. Their faces look grave. She grips his arm tighter. "Tom, what in the hell is going on?"

He lowers his head, says quietly, near her ear, "There's a woman's body on the beach. I found her on my run."

"What?" she demands.

Before Tom can say anything further, one of the SCPD officers touches Lily's arm. "Can you please step back, ma'am?"

"Why? What on earth is going on?" Then she sees what the officer is looking at—a smear of red down the side of Tom's neck. Blood? And more smears on the backs of his hands. Her breath chokes in her throat.

The uniformed officer asks, "Are you the one who placed the 911 call, sir?"

Tom drags a trembling hand over his wet hair. "Yes. I'm Tom Bradley. I . . . I was out for a run, very early, along that trail that starts at the end of our cul-de-sac, over there—" He points down the road. "It goes through the Spirit Forest Park. I came out the other end of the woods onto Garry Bluffs, and I walked to the lookout platform to catch my breath, and that's . . . that's when I . . . saw a body, on Grotto Beach, feet almost in the water."

Lily glances to where Tom is pointing, toward the forest trailhead. The sirens are silent, but the light bars still pulse in the morning mist. The rain is letting up. Dog walkers are gathering across the street, neighbors coming out of houses, others peering through windows. The woman in the black coat approaches Lily and Tom. She has brown skin, arresting angular features, and full lips. She wears combat boots and a black police cap. Her curly black hair is pulled back in a severe bun at the nape of her neck. Her eyes are inky and unreadable under long, false lashes.

Lily stares at her. She's seen this distinctive-looking Black woman on television. She's the detective from the homicide division who provided press briefings on the three deadly sexual assaults on female joggers—one killed along the Elk Lake trails last year, and two brutally bashed to death along the Goose Trail the year before. All the assaults occurred on the Saanich Peninsula, all within a twenty-minute drive of the nearby city of Victoria. The media dubbed them the Jogger Killer attacks. Words refuse to form in Lily's brain.

The detective casts her gaze quickly over Lily, then turns to Tom.

"Detective Rulandi Duval," she says. "You were the one who placed the 911 call?"

"Yes, I . . . I just told the other officers. I'm Tom Bradley. Dr. Tom Bradley. This is my wife, Lily."

Lily expects the detective to reach out to shake her hand, but the cop sticks both hands into her trench coat pockets and fixes her attention on Tom.

"I found the woman when I was out for an early run. She's on Grotto Beach."

"You were running? On Grotto Beach?" Her voice is husky, calm, measured. Her features give nothing away.

Lily feels a bolt of raw fear. Nothing makes sense. No one can *run* along Grotto Beach. It's a thin strip of stones that are the size of tennis balls, and they're slimy with algae and sharp with barnacles, and the beach is littered with driftwood and giant logs. Grotto Beach lies beneath sheer sandstone cliffs. It's barely even visible at high tide. The only way down to the beach is from the bluffs, via a rickety staircase of wood and iron.

"I was running the cliff trail through the forest, and when I was catching my breath on the bluffs, I saw her down on the beach," says Tom. He glances at Lily. "She . . . she was just lying there, unmoving, limbs at odd angles. It looked as though she'd fallen down from the cliff. And there was a . . . Crows were hopping around. So I climbed down the stairs, and . . ." He starts to cry.

Lily's erudite, distinguished husband, her man of academia, is actually crying in the rain on their front lawn. A horror, a disgust, a bewilderment, swells inside her chest. She's suddenly hyperaware of the people watching from across the street, of her neighbors seeing her and Tom like this. She notices a silver sedan stopped on the corner where their lane joins Oak End. It's Tarryn's mother. Councillor Virginia Wingate, who is running for mayor. She's observing them closely from behind her windshield. Virginia was parked off the lane earlier, waiting for her kid. She would have seen Tom entering their yard through the back gate, possibly without his jacket. Maybe she noticed the blood smears on him.

Lily's gaze flares back to Tom. Who is now in his orange jacket. A clean, fresh jacket he doesn't usually wear because he doesn't like the color.

Detective Duval glances down the street. She stares at the dark wall of forest, the tall trees swaying in the wind. She turns slowly and regards the Bradley house.

"And then you ran all the way home, to here." It's not a question. More like an observation. "And you called 911. From here."

"I . . . For Pete's sake," snaps Tom. "How can you all just stand here asking me these questions when she's lying down there? Being pecked at, eaten, by crows, scavengers!"

"The coroner and a forensics team are already en route to the location, sir," says the detective. "My partner is also on his way to the site." She tilts her chin toward the house. "This is your home?"

He wipes his mouth. Lily can't take her eyes off the blood smears on the back of her husband's hand.

"Yes. I . . . I didn't have my cell on me. I usually run with it, but I plugged it in to recharge in the kitchen last night. I usually recharge it overnight next to my bed, and because it was in a different place, I . . . I forgot it."

Phoebe opens the front door. "Mom?" she calls from the doorway.

Lily hears panic in her child's voice. "Go inside, Phoebe," she yells.

"What's going on?"

"Now!"

Detective Duval regards the Bradleys' twelve-year-old daughter with her pink hair and heavy eye makeup. Lily sees the cop's gaze move over their pretty heritage house again, going to the bronze plaque on the gate post that reads Oak Tree Therapy, L. Bradley, PhD. Lily sees this homicide cop with the inscrutable face and combat boots look up at the dormer windows in the attic. Lily feels a punch in her belly as she notices Matthew's little white face in the window, staring down at the events unfolding on their front lawn. Hot anger spikes through Lily's fear, and it fires quickly into a kind of protective rage.

Her precious children. Her beautiful house. Her perfect life. She feels it all sliding, crumbling away like those sandstone cliffs into the sea. Bile surges into her throat. She wants to flee. She also wants to stand her ground, dig in her heels, stop—fix—everything. Defend her family and her life to the death. Because they're all she has. They're all she knows now.

She's also frightened this cop will find out about last night.

The detective says to Tom, slowly, as if she's dumb, as if she didn't get it the first time around, "So you ran from the bluffs, through the forest, up this street here, and in through that front door there?"

"No. I . . . went in around the back. Through the gate from the lane."

"That lane over there?" She points to where Virginia Wingate's sedan is still idling.

Why in the hell won't that Wingate woman get moving? Bloody vulture-istic voyeur. Scavengers, all of them. Standing around gawking, watching hungrily for pieces of gossip they can snatch and spread all over town within the hour.

"Yes, that lane," says Tom.

"Not the most direct route?"

"Front door was locked," says Tom. "I don't take a key when I run, so I leave the back unlocked. The kitchen door."

"So you ran into that lane, entered your backyard through the gate at the rear of your property . . . What time was that?"

"Can't you tell from the 911 call?" Tom's frustration is returning heat to his cheeks. He's standing more erect, shoulders more squared. More defensive. Combative.

"What time would *you* say it was that you entered your house and placed that call?" Detective Duval asks.

"Christ," he mutters. "I don't know. What does it matter? There's a woman dead on the beach."

"Is this about the Jogger Killer?" Lily asks quickly, because she wants to steer things away from her family.

The detective's gaze ticks to Lily's.

She swallows. "I . . . I've seen you on TV," Lily says. "The joggers—that's your case, isn't it? Is this why you were called in? Is it another jogger attack? On Grotto Beach this time?"

"I tell you what," says Detective Duval to Tom, ignoring Lily. "Why don't you take us back along that trail? You can point out where you were running, where you came out on the bluffs, where you stood on the lookout platform, and how you first saw the body. And then you can take us through, step-by-step, what you did next. Okay?"

"Yes, yes, that's fine," says Tom. "I can do that."

Lily says, "I'll just get my—"

"You need to stay here, Mrs. Bradley," Detective Duval says.

"*Dr.* Bradley," Lily counters.

Detective Duval does not respond.

Blood thuds in Lily's ears as she watches her husband walk down the street with the homicide investigator and two of the uniformed SCPD cops. The third cop gets back into his vehicle. He talks on the radio with his door open, one leg out. Mist swirls around them, blurring everyone, like it's all a fiction of her imagination, like this isn't really happening.

A woman comes running across the street toward Lily. It's Hannah Cody, Lily's friend who lives in the house at the end of the cul-de-sac.

Hannah reaches Lily. "Oh my God. What's happened? I heard there's a body on the beach. Was it Tom who found her? Is everything—"

"That's the detective from the Jogger Killer investigation," Lily says in a monotone that doesn't quite feel like her own voice.

Hannah stares at her. "Do they think it's connected to those *sexual assaults*?"

"I . . . I don't know." Tears fill Lily's eyes. "I don't know what to think," she says softly.

Hannah turns to watch Tom and the cops disappear into the woods. "Who is it? Who's dead?"

"I don't know."

Hannah glances at Lily. "It must surely be murder," she says softly. "Why else would they send homicide?"

RUE

NOW

A cold breeze blows off the sea as Detective Rulandi Duval picks her way over the rocks toward the body.

Two media vans are already parked on top of Garry Bluffs, behind a perimeter of yellow crime scene tape that flaps in the wind. It didn't take the scavengers long. They sense a kill a mile away. A small crowd is also gathering farther along the bluffs, local residents watching as forensic techs in white boiler suits sift like ghosts through the mist as they scour the beach for evidence.

Pathologist Fareed Gamal—from the coroner's office—is already hunched over the decedent, taking liver temperature. When a heart stops, a body begins to cool at an average rate. Although air temperature, air movement, clothing, body dimensions, rain, and posture all remain variables, the algor mortis does help determine time of death, and Fareed still uses it.

A police photographer has already captured images of the dead woman and the immediate surroundings. As she nears, Rue sees that the decedent is wearing black leggings, a dark-pink rain jacket, and black running shoes with a white swoosh on the sides. The seawater has reached the shoes—the tide is rising. They'll need to move her soon. The woman's limbs lie at awkward angles. Like a broken doll's.

"Hey," Rue says as she reaches the scene.

Fareed glances up. Rue catches sight of the woman's head. Shock rattles her. The skull has been split like a watermelon, exposing shiny pink-and-gray brain matter. The decedent's hair is dark brown, shoulder length, wet and matted. A puddle of blood glistens beneath her skull. Her face is mashed beyond recognition. Rue can't even tell whether the woman has eyes in the blood-filled sockets. Beach lice and other critters are already crawling inside the open wounds. Near the woman's head lies a crumpled red rain jacket. It's covered in blood. More blood gleams beneath the woman's right thigh. The fabric of her leggings is ripped, exposing a deep gouge in her flesh. A shattered tibia protrudes lower down her leg.

"Jesus," Rue whispers.

"Massive blunt force trauma," says Fareed. "The kind you see in vehicular accidents. Might be difficult to determine which particular injury caused her death." He looks up at the cliff towering behind them, and then his gaze goes back to Rue. "What are you doing here? You think it could be one of the JK's?"

"First responders are on high alert for incidents that could be related to the other jogger deaths," she says. "Story Cove PD saw it was a female in running gear, similar in age and circumstances to the other victims—we got the call right away."

"No overt signs of sexual assault on this one, though."

Rue runs her gaze over the decedent again. Her leggings are still on. A key difference. The others were naked from the waist down.

"What can you tell me so far, Doc?"

"Well, she's a white female. Like the others. Midthirties to midforties. Given rigor and livor mortis, I reckon she's been dead about eight to twelve hours. The blunt force trauma is consistent with a fall from the height of those cliffs."

Rue bites her lower lip and studies the crumbling sandstone cliffs. "So . . . she could have fallen from up there . . . sometime last night?"

"Yeah, I reckon she's been down here most of the night." He begins to pack up his gear. "I'll know more once we get her up onto the slab." Fareed clicks his bag shut and comes to his feet.

"Is that the guy who found her?" he asks with a tilt of his head toward the base of the stairs that lead up to the bluffs. Tom Bradley stands there with Rue's partner, Toshi Hara. Bradley is wrapped in a silver survival blanket.

"Yeah," she says.

"And that's his red jacket that was covering the decedent's face?" He nods to the bloodied garment near the decedent's head.

"It's what he says. He claims he saw her from the lookout platform on the bluffs, then he climbed down via those stairs, came over here, dropped to his knees on the rocks beside the body. And then he says he kind of lifted her body, like this"—she motions with her hands—"cradled it, in order to attempt to resuscitate her, but then he realized she was dead."

Fareed raises his brow and glances at the decedent's mashed head. "He was going to resuscitate that? Like how? Mouth-to-mouth? You can barely even see where the mouth is with that trauma."

She shrugs. "He claims he then took off his jacket, covered her face to protect her from the rain, and then ran home to call for help."

Fareed's gaze locks with Rue's. Quietly, he says, "Like the others were covered."

"The others' faces were covered with branches and forest debris."

He nods slowly. "But still, covered."

"That fact remains holdback evidence, Doc, the face covering. Keep it to yourself."

"Feels personal," he says, looking at the decedent's face again. "Like there was remorse. Guilt. Shamed by what was done. Hiding her face like that."

"Yeah, Bradley's story is not adding up. Will you let me know when you can fit her into your schedule? I'd like to observe."

"Sure thing. I'll give you a call."

"Thanks."

"Consider it a date." He grins. "It's the only way I'm going to get one with you."

"How many times must I remind you I'm a happily married woman, Doctor?"

"Until you aren't." He chuckles and begins to make his way over the slimy rocks, carrying his bag toward the stairs beneath the bluffs.

An uncomfortable sensation sinks into Rue as she watches Fareed moving carefully over the rocks. She's had to work harder than most, being a woman, and one of color, to get where she has, and she keeps her private life private. There's no way anyone could know of her marital strain. Yet Fareed's words cut close to the bone. Much too close.

A gull cries above, and Rue glances up at the cliffs again. A raven watches from a dead branch poking out of the rock wall. Much higher—far above the towering tops of the old-growth trees—an eagle circles. Mother Nature, like the media, knows there's carrion down here.

Rue crouches down to examine the body more closely. A tiny purple crab scuttles over her boot. Moisture drips from the bill of her cap. The beach stones make clicking and knocking sounds as the tide continues to push in.

She mentally catalogues the woman's clothing. The trail runners are a well-known brand. Fairly new. About a size eight. The treads are gnarly—specifically designed for off-road trails. Black mud is caked between the lugs in the soles. Same color as the mud on the forest trail that Tom Bradley brought them along. The woman's leggings and jacket appear water resistant from the way little beadlets have formed on the fabric like jewels. A tiny logo on the left sleeve of the jacket shows the garment is a common brand of outdoor wear. The jacket is zipped over what appears to be a T-shirt. Rue's gaze moves up the body. A chain with a silver medallion rests at the woman's throat. With a gloved hand, Rue carefully moves some of the woman's gore-matted hair aside to get a better look at the necklace. Her movement exposes a tattoo on the side of the woman's neck—an image of a mythological-looking creature with a lion's head, the body of a dog or maybe a goat, and a tail with a snake's head at the tip. Tongues of flame come from the lion's mouth. Strange, incongruous parts that don't belong together.

A glint of light in the facial gore catches Rue's attention. She leans forward slightly. She can see a small crystal in the mashed flesh. Nose stud? But the face is too damaged and bloody to tell for sure.

Rue moves her attention down to the decedent's hands. Bloodied and wounded. Several fingers obviously broken. Ripped nails. Dark matter beneath the nails. Three silver rings on her left hand. Without moving the jacket cuffs, Rue can see eight bracelets of white metal on the left wrist. Some are bent. She's wearing a watch that does not appear to be a smartwatch.

Rue is about to reach into one of the jacket pockets when she notices something green trapped between the bent fingers on the decedent's right hand. She edges over and leans in to see better. A broken strand of tiny plastic beads in shades of green and orange is entangled in the fingers. It seems oddly familiar.

She carefully tries to extract the strand.

"Hey, boss."

She jumps and overbalances. Rue catches herself and steadies her balance by bracing her gloved fist on a rock. "Jesus, Toshi, don't the hell sneak up on me like that."

"Didn't mean to spook you." He falls silent for a moment as he stares at the body. He clears his throat. "Bradley wants to know if he can go home. Says he has some important meeting on campus."

"Campus?"

"He's a psychology professor at Kordel University."

Rue's gaze shoots to where Tom Bradley still stands at the base of the cliff stairs, wrapped in the silver blanket.

"He's shivering like a bloody leaf," says Toshi. "He's been outside in the wet and cold since early. I reckon he's going to be heading into hypothermia territory, and he's probably in some degree of shock."

"Get someone to take him back to the station and give him something warm to drink," she says. "But first I want his clothing and shoes. I want him photographed. I want swabs taken from that blood on him. See if he'll agree to give us a DNA sample while he's still rattled. Unless he shows signs of medical distress, hold him. Otherwise take him to the ER and keep watch on him there. I want to question him again myself, on the record. There's no way that Bradley saw this body from where he claimed he was standing on the lookout platform. The sight line doesn't work. Plus the visibility was poor."

"Yeah, something is definitely off with him."

"Let him stew awhile."

As Toshi leaves to deal with Tom Bradley, Rue reaches into the right-hand pocket of the pink jacket. She pulls out a small key ring with a metal fob. There are three keys on the fob. One looks as if it belongs to an old Volkswagen vehicle—it has a distinctive VW pattern in the metal. She turns the fob over. Her pulse quickens at the sight of the logo.

The Red Lion Tavern. An "old English pub" near the Story Cove marina.

A memory slices through Rue's brain. A dark, slick street. A woman exiting the doors of a pub with a Tudor facade. Wind ruffling her dark, shoulder-length curls.

Her gaze snaps back to the woman's gore-matted hair.

It can't be.

But another part of her brain says, *It is her. It's got to be her. How could you not see it right away?*

Her pulse races.

Very carefully Rue replaces the keys in the jacket pocket—they will be entered into the chain of evidence at the morgue. She reaches into the left pocket and removes a crumpled gas receipt. She opens it carefully. The gas was bought at a station on Story Cove's Main Street, and it was paid for with a credit card. This will help in identifying the woman and her movements. Also in the left pocket, Rue finds a stick of lip balm. And a folded business card.

She opens the card.

It shows a Kordel University logo across the top. In the center is a name.

Tom Bradley (PhD), Dept. of Psychology.

Energy and relief crunch through her body. Tom Bradley knew this woman? The professor is now squarely in her sights.

And this has nothing to do with Rue's personal life.

LILY

NOW

Lily's kids sit white faced at the kitchen counter. They stare at her. She can't think what to say to them. The words she screamed at Tom yesterday evening rip through her brain.

How could you lie to me? Betray me, deceive me like this? Our marriage, our entire life, it's all built on a lie.

Yesterday changed everything Lily had once held to be true about her relationship with her husband, about her life, about herself as Tom's wife. Now this.

Gutted, confused, she reaches for the kitchen counter to steady herself.

She desperately wants to tell herself that "this" is nothing. Tom simply went for a run in a storm at 5:30 a.m. and found a dead woman on the beach. Then he returned with smears of blood on his hands and neck. And now he's simply showing a homicide cop investigating serial killings where he found a woman's body. It's probably some stranger lying dead on Grotto Beach. No one they know . . . She suddenly notices the muddy footprints leading across their white tile floor from the kitchen door to the stairwell, then up the stairs. More muddy prints track from the staircase to the front door. He didn't change his shoes, yet he went upstairs. To get a clean jacket? Because Lily definitely saw him in the shed without his shirt or his customary red rain jacket.

She can't even begin to explore the possibilities that might be unfolding, unraveling beneath her feet today. Her gaze goes slowly to the kitchen counter. Tom's phone is not there.

I . . . I didn't have my cell on me. I usually run with it, but I plugged it in to recharge in the kitchen last night. I usually recharge it overnight next to my bed, and because it was in a different place, I . . . I forgot it.

"Mom?" Phoebe asks. "What's going on?"

Lily clears her throat and goes to the fridge, avoiding her children's probing gazes. "Everything's going to be fine. Your dad came across a woman who got injured while out running this morning, and he called it in to the police. Now he's helping to show them where to find her."

"Is she dead?" Matthew asks.

Lily's throat constricts. "No—I . . . uh . . . I don't know. The police will find out everything they need to know."

"Who is it?" Phoebe asks.

Lily yanks open the fridge door. She stares blindly at the contents. "They don't know yet, honey. You guys need to finish your breakfasts and brush your teeth." She thinks of homicide detective Rulandi Duval talking about the Jogger Killer on TV. She thinks of a woman lying dead. If she was murdered, whoever did it must still be out there. "I'm driving you both to school this morning."

"I like the bus," says Matthew.

"I'm taking you. No arguments." She reaches into the fridge for lunch meat and mayonnaise. She still needs to pack their lunches. Routine. Order. It's what holds Lily's life together. Sticking to habits will also protect her children from whatever horrible thing is happening. Her kids are her world. She will do anything to keep them safe. She knows this to be true of Tom, too. Tom has always put family stability above all else. Despite what she learned about him last night. Or perhaps that underscores it. Tears suddenly fill her eyes as she tries to see what else she needs for the lunches.

Focus.

One tiny step at a time, and she will get where she needs to be. Meanwhile, just the act of moving forward with familiar tasks will hold her together. This is what she often tells patients in crisis. But Lily knows it can be easier to identify problems in the lives of others than address one's own. It's easier to dig the secrets out of her patients than pull back the curtain on her own protective behaviors. She doesn't want to admit even to herself what her fixation with routine and order really hides.

As Carl Jung said, "People will do anything, no matter how absurd, in order to avoid facing their own souls."

Lily knows from her patients—and from personal experience—that while nothing is more desirable than to be released from an affliction, it also holds true that nothing is more terrifying than to be divested of a crutch.

"Mom?" Phoebe says again. "Are you okay?"

She smears a tear from her face. "Yes. Of course. Do you want ham or salami on your sandwiches?"

Phoebe scowls. "I *told* you, like a hundred times, I'm vegetarian now. What is your problem? Christ. It's like talking to a wall. You listen to your patients all day, but you never seem to listen to what *I* am trying to say."

A dart of anger spears through Lily. She snatches a jar of organic peanut butter out of the pantry and slams it down on the granite counter. She struggles to open the seal. The peanut butter is sugar-free, and it's unhomogenized, so the oil has separated and is layered on the top in a goopy mess. Which is why she hates making peanut butter sandwiches. She first has to stir in the oil and it spills everywhere. She grabs the bread and begins the autopilot process of making sandwiches.

"Do you think it's someone we know from around here?" Matthew asks, spooning cereal up from his bowl and speaking around a mouthful.

"Maybe not." Lily butters the bread.

"But it *could* be someone from Story Cove," says Phoebe. "In fact, it's probably more likely to be someone from this neighborhood than someone who came running from elsewhere. A lot of people from here like to jog in the morning. Who do we know who likes to run in—"

"Can you guys eat up already?" snaps Lily as she slaps peanut butter onto bread. "We need to get moving. We're going to be late."

"And who wants to be late, or screw up their routine while their father leads police through the woods to find a dead body, right, Mom? God forbid."

Lily flicks a hot glance at her daughter. Phoebe glares back. Her eyes are ringed with black eyeliner. She wears dark-purple eye shadow that makes her eyes look like holes in her head. Her face is pale from a powdery makeup that Lily hates, and her child's dark-pink hair hangs lank about her face. An old memory erupts in Lily's brain. Another girl. Black eye makeup. Dyed black hair. Goth clothes. Her hands freeze. She can't think for a moment. Sounds go distant. Fear rises in her throat.

"Why did Dad go running with his flashlight instead of his headlamp?" Matthew asks.

Lily is jolted back. "What?"

"I saw him leaving the house early this morning with a flashlight in his hand. And he had a jacket and cap on but he came home without his jacket and cap, and without his flashlight."

"Are you sure?"

"Yeah." Matthew shoves the last spoonful of cereal into his mouth. Milk dribbles down his chin as he chews and speaks. "Dad went into the shed, and then came out without his shirt on."

"What? Dad was outside with no shirt?" says Phoebe. "In the rain?"

Matthew nods, wipes his mouth, and pushes his bowl away.

"That's nonsense," says Phoebe. "Why would he do that?"

"Of course it's nonsense," Lily says crisply. She carefully places the top of the bread on the sandwich filling, making sure the edges line up perfectly. Focused on the sandwich in her hands, she cuts it across the middle as she says to her son, very quietly, "You didn't take any photographs, did you?"

Matthew hesitates. "I . . . uh . . . no."

"Are you certain?"

He wavers again, but before he can speak, the doorbell resounds like a gong through the house. They all still and look up.

"It's the cops again," whispers Matthew.

Lily grabs a dishcloth and hurries to the door, wiping peanut oil off her hands. She opens the door.

"Hannah! I . . . I thought it was—"

"Honey, hey. Is Tom back yet? Is he okay?"

"He's . . . fine. Listen, Hannah, I'm in a bit of a rush. I need to get the kids ready for school."

"Oh, I just came to offer them a ride. I'm driving Fiona and Jacob." Hannah gestures to her Mercedes, which is idling out front, her two kids visible inside. Lily realizes one of the police cruisers is now parked on the opposite side of the road. There's a cop inside, watching their house.

"I thought it better than letting them all walk to the bus with . . . you know." She leans forward, lowers her voice to a barely audible whisper. "With a sex killer maybe running around."

"We don't know that yet, Hannah. It could just be a terrible accident. And thank you for the offer. It will be a great help." She calls over her shoulder, "Phoebe! Matthew! Hannah is going to drive you guys. Go brush your teeth. Get your things."

As Lily's kids thump up the stairs, Hannah says, "Does Tom know who it is?"

Lily's throat closes. She can't seem to speak, so she shakes her head. At the same time she notices the phone on the hall table, below the mirror. There's a smear of red on the receiver Tom held when he called 911. She feels sick. She cannot wait for Hannah to leave with the kids.

As soon as they've gone, she shuts the door, leans against it, and takes in a deep, shuddering breath. She feels herself decompress. A little.

The hall clock strikes the hour and the cuckoo explodes out the doors. *Cuckoo!*

Lily's heart almost stops. Her pulse skyrockets and begins racing again. She curses, then peers through the blinds. Hannah's car is gone. The cop is still there. Lily is sure he can't see around the back of their house from where he is parked.

She grabs her shoes and hurries outside into the backyard and makes for the shed. The motion light above the shed door switches on. Again she jumps, then hesitates, glances back toward their house. Upstairs is Matthew's window. It has a clear view of the shed door.

Lily finds the door unlocked. She opens it, enters slowly, and reaches for the interior light. She switches it on. The door swings slowly shut behind her.

A cool scent of dampness and soil fills her nostrils.

She scans the interior. It's neat. Ordered. Like everything else in their lives. Garden tools hang on racks, lined from big to small. Bags of potting soil and clay pots rest on shelves. A workbench stands beneath the window. Storage bins are lined beneath another bench along the back wall. Lily recalls Tom's silhouette in the lighted window and how he seemed to go to the rear of the shed. A ball of tension tightens in her stomach as she makes her way to the back of the shed. She pulls out a storage bin.

It contains a hose.

The next bin contains coils of wire for her tomato plants.

Lily pulls out the third bin, and her breath stalls.

Inside is her husband's white running shirt. She bought it for him last Christmas. It has a big, round Ocean Motion logo on the back. It's bundled into a wet ball. And the front is soaked through with . . . *blood.*

TOM

NOW

The camera flashes in his face. Tom blinks. He's beyond exhausted. Cold. Shivering.

"Can you turn around, please, sir?" says the uniformed cop.

Tom slowly turns his back to the cop. He now faces the detective sitting on a chair watching him. Detective Toshi Hara. A third cop stands next to Tom holding paper evidence bags.

"Extend your arms out to your sides, please," says the cop with the camera.

He stretches out his arms.

Click. Flash.

The staccato punctuations of sound and light are an assault on his brain. These policemen make him feel like a criminal. He can't think straight. Lily's words slice through his mind.

How could you lie to me? Betray me, deceive me like this?

"I just went for a run," Tom says. He doesn't recognize his own voice. Everything feels surreal, as though he got out of bed at dawn and slipped out the door into a storm of alternate reality. Or perhaps the storm started four months ago. Or fifteen years ago, when he first laid eyes on Lily. If he really thinks about it, the storm now breaking around them all started thirty-three years ago.

Maybe he will wake up. And things will be normal again.

But Tom knows nothing can ever be normal again. Perhaps it never was. Normal is a construct. A story people tell themselves. It's what everyone does—feigns some concept of normalcy. Stories people tell themselves are the only reality humans know. Tom is keenly aware of this. So is his therapist wife.

"Turn around to face me again, please, sir," says the cop with the camera.

Tom faces the photographer.

"Can you extend your hands toward me—palms up?"

Tom obeys.

Click. Flash.

"Palms down, please."

Click. Flash.

Tom stares at the blood smears on his skin. *Her blood.*

"Can you take off your jacket and shirt, please?" says the cop with the camera.

Tom removes his jacket. The third cop holds open a large paper evidence bag. Tom drops his jacket into it, then pulls his shirt up over his head. It's the clean one he put on upstairs in his house. Tom drops the shirt into another paper bag held out for him. His whole body is shaking. His teeth are chattering. He doesn't know if it's just the cold or shock. Probably both.

Click. Flash.

"Turn around."

He's facing Detective Toshi Hara again.

Click. Flash.

Hara sits silent, watchful. The man's features are impassive. A cop's poker face. Not a spare bit of fat on the man. Lean and mean. His hair is thick and shiny black and impeccably cut. His skin is a pale beige and is smooth and unblemished. He wears a crisp white shirt and deep-burgundy tie. His pants are tailored, his shoes tan leather. Trendy. Not the hard-boiled, disheveled detective of television series. Difficult to tell how old he is. Maybe late twenties. Tom imagines Detective Hara lives a bachelor's life in a high-tech designer apartment. Small, and far too expensive for his cop's salary. Tom imagines Toshi Hara has ambition and plans. He probably dates stunning women.

Click. Flash.

"Can you tuck your chin in so we can see the back of your neck properly?"

Tom tucks his chin in. The camera moves closer behind him. *Click. Flash.* The cop takes more photos of deep fingernail scratches down the side of his neck. Another of the smear of blood on the other side of his neck.

"Pants and shoes off, please."

Tom tenses. He glances at Detective Hara. The man nods.

"I don't have to do this," Tom says. "Do I?"

"You touched the body," says Hara. "You said you cradled her. Like this." He makes the rocking motion that Tom showed the cops earlier.

"Yes, but that's—"

"That's why we need your clothes, sir. We need to understand what happened to the deceased woman you found. Evidence on her might have transferred onto you. It could be something that will help us find who did this to her. You would want that, no?"

"You . . . you don't think it was an accident?"

"We're looking at all options."

Tom feels trapped. Claustrophobic, suddenly. His gaze shoots to the door.

"We'll get you into something dry as soon as we get this over with," says Hara. "And then we'll find you a hot drink. Is that okay?"

"I need to make a call."

"That's fine, that's okay. You can do that. If we could just get your pants, underwear, and your socks and shoes first, please," says Hara.

Tom stares at him, his brain racing. "My underwear?"

"Please."

He swallows. If he refuses, it makes him look guilty of something. An innocent man would surely want to do everything to help the police.

Tom removes his shoes. They go into a brown bag. Next come the socks. He then slides his black, waterproof joggers with reflective strips down over his hips and legs. He steps out of them. The cop with the paper bags reaches with a gloved hand to take the pants.

Tom inhales deeply, then removes his underpants. The cop holds out another paper bag.

Tom stands with his hands covering his groin. He's never felt so exposed, so . . . violated, in his life as he does standing naked and shivering under harsh fluorescent lighting in front of these three fully clothed men, two of them visibly armed. Men with the constitutional power to rob him of freedom, to lock him away.

The cop with the evidence bags goes to a table. He writes Tom's name on the side of each bag, along with the time and date and a description of what is inside.

Hara comes to his feet. He's much shorter than Tom, but he has an imposing aura.

"Just need to take samples of that blood on your neck and hands, okay?" Hara snaps on a pair of blue latex gloves, reaches for a kit on the shelf. He rips it open.

Tom closes his eyes as Hara swabs the blood. The detective seals the swabs in containers and hands them to the evidence guy, who labels each one. Hara then hands Tom a pair of fleece drawstring pants and a fleece top in a matching navy color. Tom imagines this is the clothing they give suspects before transporting them to a remand facility.

"Sorry, but we don't have shoes. These will have to do." Hara gives Tom a pair of crime scene booties.

Tom stares at them.

"Oh, one more thing," says Hara. "Will you provide us with a DNA sample?"

"What?"

"A DNA sample. Simple, quick swab from inside the cheek. It will help us in eliminating any DNA you might have left at the scene."

Tom stares at Hara. His pulse races. He feels a bolt of terror. He's being pushed into a corner. He tries to swallow, but his throat is tight. If he refuses, it will fuel suspicion. It could make things harder for him. He thinks of why he went running this morning. He thinks of what happened yesterday and the fight with Lily. He thinks of what happened at the barbecue at the Codys' house, and he clears his throat.

"Sure."

Hara snaps on a fresh pair of latex gloves, reaches for a different kit on the shelf. He rips it open. "Take a seat."

Tom sits on the chair that is pushed toward him.

"Can you open your mouth, sir?"

Tom opens his mouth.

"A little wider."

He obeys. Hara sticks the swab inside his mouth and scrapes the lining of his cheek. It's a physical intrusion, this man's gloved hand and the swabbing tool moving inside his mouth.

Hara removes the swab, inserts it into a container, seals the container, and hands it to the evidence cop, who again marks it with Tom's details and the time. The evidence cop leaves with Tom's DNA, the blood samples, and the brown bags containing his clothes and shoes. The camera guy exits the room, too.

Hara smiles and extends his arm toward the open door. "You can make that call now, if you like."

"I . . . I don't have my cell with me," says Tom.

"We can provide you with a phone. This way, please, sir."

Tom follows Detective Hara into a white room with no windows. Inside is a coffee table in front of a small sofa, an armchair, and a chair on wheels. Tom glances up at the ceiling. A camera in the corner watches him.

"Wait here, please." Hara shuts the door.

Tom thinks he might throw up.

RUE

NOW

Mist sifts through the dripping old-growth conifers as Rue walks slowly back along the trail through the Spirit Forest Park. She examines the ground carefully as she goes. Water drips everywhere and mud squelches beneath her boots. A police perimeter has been established, and forensic ident techs work in a grid pattern along the cliff above where the woman's body was found.

The trees around her are monstrous. They loom like cathedral arches over the narrow trail, muting light from above. The understory is dense with berry scrub, primordial-looking ferns, devil's club plants with tiny, sharp spines.

"Over here," calls a tech who is waiting farther up the trail for Rue. When she reaches him, he points to an area of broken and crushed vegetation just off the jogging trail.

"Prints leading off the path here match the decedent's size-eight Nike trail shoes," he says, careful to steer Rue clear of stepping on top of any tracks. "The prints head into the woods this way." He points to depressions in the ground with his tracking stick as she follows him. "The subject wearing the Nikes appears to have been moving in a highly erratic pattern toward the cliff edge, and then she went through there."

He aims his stick at an area of squashed and broken foliage. Tiny damaged branches show cat's eyes of freshly weeping sap.

"Just the one set of tracks?" Rue asks.

"Three sets."

She glances sharply at him. *"Three?"*

"Come, I'll show you. Careful to stay right behind me."

"It's all been marked, photographed?"

"Yeah. And impressions have been cast."

He leads Rue farther into the dense undergrowth and points to more tracks in the black mud. Rue crouches down among the ferns and studies the marks. "Those triangle shapes"—she points—"they're indentations made by the lugs in the woman's Nike trail runners?"

"Affirmative. I'm betting mud samples in her shoe lugs are also going to match the soil samples we've taken from up here and from the edge of the cliff. There's a second set of prints made by someone who appears to have left the trail and come after her into these bushes. See over there?"

Rue moves over and pushes some berry branches aside. She studies the ground where her tech is pointing.

"This is a really clear one," he says. "A chevron pattern on the sole. Size-eleven shoe."

Rue studies the print.

"Male?" she asks.

"Definitely someone bigger and heavier than the Nike subject. Broader feet."

Rue's mind goes to Tom Bradley. Toshi will have taken his shoes.

"These larger chevron prints land on top of the Nike prints in places, indicating whoever made them came after her. The pattern of indentation in her depressions indicates she was moving fast, running in places, falling, crawling at times on hands and knees. And the person behind her was moving more methodically."

Prey and hunter, thinks Rue, studying the marks. One fleeing, one taking his—or her—time.

"And both sets lead to the cliff edge?" she asks.

"I'll show you." He takes Rue deeper into the woods. "Like I said, she left the main trail and appears to have been running in an erratic fashion, not following any clear path. She fell here." He points. "She scrambled on her hands and knees—see the handprints under those leaves there? The knee marks there? She took flight again. Fell again. And then she crawled into this patch of devil's club there." He shows Rue a grove of prehistoric-looking plants with leaves the size of dinner plates. The plants stand almost four feet tall.

"*Oplopanax horridus*," he says. "Terrible stuff. You don't want to get into a patch like this. Both the stems and leaves are covered with fine, brittle spines that break off easily in skin. They're toxic, and can cause severe allergic reactions in some individuals. If this was your decedent cowering in here, you'll find evidence of those spines on her body and clothing."

"And where's the third set of prints?" asks Rue.

The tech leads her closer to the cliff edge. "The third set of tracks comes in from a northwesterly direction, along what appears to be a small wildlife trail. They start to follow, then parallel the other two sets over here." He points his stick.

Rue drops to her haunches again and studies the new set of prints. "Looks like these were made by boots."

"Yeah. Size ten. Whoever made these arrived sometime after the first two individuals." He leads Rue to the cliff edge. "Signs of a struggle—marks in the ground here." He points. "Stones and rocks loosened. Blood trace on the crushed fern leaves and wildflowers there. And some more blood back there." His gaze meets hers. "And the ident techs found a headlamp and cap."

"Where?"

He takes Rue to the items, which lie on a patch of stony ground right near the crumbling cliff edge. They've been flagged with yellow crime scene markers. She drops into a crouch and studies the black cap.

It has a gold Kordel University logo above the bill. She thinks of the business card in the dead woman's pocket.

Tom Bradley (PhD), Dept. of Psychology.

The headlamp near the cap is a Petzl. Blue and white with a strap in matching colors.

"We should be able to get some DNA from the cap, and possibly off the Petzl strap," the tech says. "There's also this." He gestures to another crime scene marker on the ground.

Rue moves over. The tech is pointing to a few tiny plastic beads. Bright green and orange against the black soil. Her stomach tightens as her mind goes to the broken strand of beads in the dead woman's damaged fingers.

She nods, inhales deeply, and pushes back up to her feet. She goes to the edge of the cliff and peers cautiously over. Her stomach swoops. She's directly above the location of the body. Rue's gaze drifts to the ocean. Fog is still dense over the sea. On a clear day from this vantage point, one would be able to see the snowcapped Olympic range in the US. She turns slowly and surveys the wall of forest behind her.

If either the woman or her assailant was wearing this headlamp, it must have been dark. And it was stormy. Misty.

Judging by the prints and tracks, someone chased the woman off the trail and toward the cliff. Whoever followed her struggled with her right near the edge of the cliff. Given the blood trace, one of them was injured, possibly during the struggle. Then the female jogger went over the cliff. The headlamp and cap might have been knocked off during the struggle. And the decedent could have ripped the green and orange beads off her assailant, given that the broken strand was still tangled in her fingers.

But what of the third person?

"We need a drone," Rue says, reaching into her pocket for her mobile. "We need to scan the face of this cliff, see if there's any other evidence, anything else that might have come off her body in the fall."

She places the call.

LILY

NOW

Maybe it's *not* blood on her husband's shirt, yet another part of Lily's brain knows it is. For some reason Tom hid his shirt in here before calling the police. He lied to them about his phone, too.

Even as Lily is trying to acknowledge some terrible unfolding reality, her brain is screaming to find alternate explanations. More comfortable explanations.

People will do anything, no matter how absurd, in order to avoid facing their own souls.

Wind gusts outside and debris clatters onto the tin roof. She tenses and thinks of Councillor Virginia Wingate, who was parked outside their back gate in the lane, waiting for Tarryn. She thinks of what Matthew saw from upstairs. She thinks of the cop sitting in his vehicle watching their house.

Lily reaches into the bin, then stops herself. Fingerprints. She can't have her own fingerprints in the blood on this shirt. She glances around the shed. She sees her gardening gloves—yellow with tiny pink roses. She pulls them on, then takes a small garden refuse bag out of a container. She reaches into the bin for Tom's shirt and gingerly drops it into the refuse bag.

Now what? What is she even trying to do? She hears another siren begin to wail in the distance. Panic kicks her in the gut. Hurriedly, she rips off her gloves, sticks them into the refuse bag with her husband's bloody shirt, and opens the shed door. She peers out, glances at the next-door neighbor's house. No one is watching from the windows. She hastens into her own home through the kitchen door.

For a moment she stands inside, holding the bag, her mind suddenly numb.

A bang sounds on the dining room window. Lily gasps, spins, and drops her bag. It falls to the floor and opens, exposing the bloody shirt as she stares at the window. There's a man outside. He bangs his fist on the glass again, mouthing something.

It takes Lily a second to register the features of her patient—Garth Quinlan, a firefighter, husband, and father of three. Garth points at his watch. *Shit.* Lily checks her own watch. She lost track of time. She completely forgot her session with him.

She makes a motion for him to wait two seconds, bends down, and shoves the bloody shirt back into the bag. Lily hesitates, then scoots the bag under the dining table with her foot. She rubs her face, smooths back her hair, takes in a deep breath, then goes to open the rear sliding door. Her heart beats fast.

"I rang the buzzer for your office," Garth says. "And I knocked. But there was no answer. I tried to call, and it went to voice mail. Then when I went back to my truck in the lane, I saw over the fence that the lights were on in the shed, and I saw you going inside your back door, so I came around."

Anger explodes in Lily's chest—another coping mechanism. Anger blots out fear, so Lily grabs hold of it and doubles down on it. It gives her control. She's Dr. Bradley again. And Dr. Bradley has rules. Patients are *not* permitted to intrude on her personal life. Her family. And this side of the house is strictly private. She makes this clear at the outset with every new intake. But there are always one or two patients who try to push boundaries, who attempt to enter her personal space for various reasons, who try to learn more about her and her family. Garth should not have come around to her personal quarters, and she tells him.

"I apologize, Garth," she says crisply. "I meant to cancel. But something terribly important has come up. An emergency. And please don't ever come around to this entrance again."

He regards her intently. There is a strange look on his features. Quietly, he says, "What kind of emergency?"

"A family emergency. I really do apologize. Please forgive me. I'll call to reschedule as soon as—"

"Is that blood?"

"What?"

"Blood."

"Wh—where?"

"On your hands, and on your face."

Lily's gaze drops to her hands. She stares in horror at the red on her fingers. It must have gotten onto her when she shoved the shirt back into the bag. So much for trying to use gloves.

"It's on your face, too."

Lily realizes she must have transferred it when she rubbed her face and smoothed back her hair.

"Did someone get hurt?" Garth asks. "Is that the emergency?"

The landline in the hallway begins to ring.

"Is there anything I can do?" he asks.

The phone shrills again, and again. Two more rings and it will kick to voice mail.

"I . . . I need to go. I'll reschedule." Lily slams the door in Garth's face and runs for the phone. She grabs the receiver on the last ring. As she does, she catches her reflection in the hall mirror and sees the streak of blood down her cheek and the blood on the backs of her fingers holding the receiver. *The dead woman's blood.* For a moment she can't speak.

"Lily?" Tom's voice jolts her back.

"Christ, Tom. Where are you? What's going on?"

"Lily, I . . . I'm at the station. I need—"

"Station? *What* station?"

"Police station. Downtown."

She stares at her pale face in the mirror with the blood smear from her husband's shirt, which is now in a bag under the dining room table.

"Lily?"

"Yes," she says quietly.

"I need you to do something. Are you listening? I need Dianne. Get Dianne."

"Dianne?"

"Dianne Klister."

Her friend Dianne. The highly priced and infamous criminal lawyer. Hadn't she just thought of Dianne? Yes, when Tarryn reminded Lily that her father was a partner in the same law firm as Dianne. Hammersmith, Wingate & Klister.

Her mind spirals backward in time—to a day recently when she met Dianne for drinks at the Ocean Bay Hotel. Where Lily got the weird note and was forced to confess to Dianne that she was being followed, watched, by some kind of stalker, and Dianne regarded Lily as though she had lost her mind.

"Lily, are you there—are you hearing me?"

She feels as though her brain is mired in thick syrup. She can't make it work.

"You . . . need a *criminal* lawyer?" Her voice comes out hoarse.

"For God's sake, yes, Lily. The police are trying to question me in relation to this woman's death. They've got me stuck in some interview room and they've taken all my clothes. It's beginning to look weird. I need counsel. And I need you to bring me some clothes."

Her gaze goes to the dining table, the bag with Tom's shirt under it.

"They took your clothes?"

"Yes."

"Why? I mean . . . why don't they think it was an accident?"

"I . . . can't talk. There's cameras in here and this is not my phone. Just get Dianne down here, and bring me a change of clothing."

"Who—who was she, Tom? *Who* did you find on the beach?"

The line goes dead.

LILY

NOW

Lily dials Dianne's office. As the phone rings, her attention is drawn to the framed photos of her family on the hallway wall. Her favorite is a beautiful shot of the four of them in Aruba, laughing in sunshine on a sugar-white beach fringed by a turquoise sea. Another image shows Lily and Tom on a glamping trip in Clayoquot Sound, taken to celebrate their wedding anniversary. They're smiling, arms around each other. Emotion blurs her vision. Another photo is of the four of them on safari in Botswana. It was taken by their guide on the day they saw three of Africa's "big five"—a rhinoceros with a baby, a herd of elephants, and a leopard in a tree with a kill.

"Dianne Klister's office, how can I help you?"

She's jerked back to the present. "I—ah, is Dianne in?"

"Ms. Klister is presently unavailable, would you like to leave—"

Lily slams the phone down. With fumbling fingers she dials another number—Dianne's mobile. Her gaze is pulled back to the photos as the phone rings. She stares at another image shot on their Africa trip. It's of her, Tom, Matthew, and Phoebe waiting to board a boat for a shark tour in KwaZulu-Natal, the surf pounding behind the pier in the distance.

"Lily?" Dianne's voice comes through the receiver.

"Hey, I . . . uh . . . I . . ."

"Lily? You okay?"

"You sound like you're on speaker," Lily says. "Is . . . there anyone else listening?"

"I'm in my car, driving. I'm alone. What's going on? You sound strange."

She squeezes her eyes shut. "We need your help. Tom . . . Oh, God—" Her voice cracks. "I don't know how to say this. I don't even know what this is."

"Okay, listen, I'm pulling over. I'm stopping." Lily hears the sound of Dianne parking. "All right, take it slowly. You've got all my focus. Just say it as it comes to you."

Lily swallows, wipes her mouth, then remembers the blood on her hands. Her gaze rockets back to her reflection in the mirror. Horror fills her. She now has a streak of the dead woman's blood across her mouth. Her eyes are wild and glassy. Her hair is drying in a mess after being wet in the rain. This is not the woman she is. She's supposed to be the woman—the mother, the wife, the therapist—whom her friends envy for being in control, for always being perfectly turned out, no matter the occasion. The woman who has no skeletons in her closet.

"Lily?"

"Tom's at the police station. He's being questioned in connection with . . . with a dead person. He found a dead jogger on the beach this morning, and homicide detectives are going to be asking him questions. They've taken his clothes, Dianne. He needs counsel. Immediately. Can you help us?"

A heavy pause, then: "Which station?"

"Downtown. The main one. Dianne—" Lily hesitates, reality dropping like a heavy, cold stone through her bowels. "The cop, she's the officer who was on TV. A homicide detective. The one on the jogger murder cases."

"Sergeant Rulandi Duval?"

"Yes."

"Listen closely to me—are you listening, Lily, are you focused?" Dianne's tone has changed. Lily's friend now sounds sharp. All high-powered efficiency. Like another woman entirely.

"Yes, yes, I'm listening."

"Do not say anything. Not one thing. To anyone. Got that? No. One."

She nods. "Okay."

"Say it, repeat it back to me."

"I must not say a thing. To anyone."

"Remember that. For Tom's sake. For your sake. And get this into your head—neither Tom nor you are compelled to answer any questions from the police. This is your right under law."

"He didn't do anything, Dianne."

"Whether or not Tom did anything, if he's being questioned by homicide investigators, if they've taken his clothes, this is not going to play well for him in the media. We need to think immediately about mitigating fallout, protecting his job. And your job. Insulating Matthew and Phoebe."

Lily feels bile rise in her throat.

"First," Dianne says crisply, "arrange for someone to pick up the kids when school gets out, preferably someone who can take them to their own home, and someone who will shield them from the news for the time being. And cancel your appointments for the day. I'll head straight to the station now. Meanwhile, you get some clothes ready for Tom. Something smart, respectable. And make yourself presentable. Then come to the station. I'll meet you there." There's a pause. "Whatever is going on, Lily, Tom needs you now. You must pull yourself together for him, and for your family."

"But if Tom's done nothing wrong—"

"He's being questioned by a high-profile homicide detective who is on the case of a serial killer who violently rapes and then bludgeons to death female joggers. Just let that sink in, Lily. The Jogger Killer is currently terrorizing women who are now too scared to go out running alone. And Rulandi Duval is a pit bull with a chip on her shoulder. She's a woman in a position of power in a traditionally male environment, and she's got something to prove. You and Tom also ooze privilege. You live in Story Cove. You own a boat. It's moored at an exclusive marina. You belong to a country club. Tom works in academia with young female students. You work with people who need to trust you, and who want the fact that they are in therapy to remain private. Duval will give you both a rough ride just because she can. The public will not go easy on you, either."

Lily is going to throw up. She needs to go to the bathroom. Her stomach has turned to water.

"And again, Lily, I cannot stress this enough: do not talk to anyone, no matter how friendly they seem, until I understand what's at play here. We'll work out strategy from there."

Dianne kills the call.

Dazedly, Lily hangs up. She goes to the dining table and retrieves the bag with the bloodied shirt. She hesitates. She has to put it somewhere. Or better, wash it. Quickly she goes to the laundry room down the hallway. Lily empties the bag into the top-loading washing machine and turns the dial. Water starts filling the machine tub. She adds detergent. Then she stares at the water. It's turning pink as her garden gloves and her husband's shirt begin to swirl back and forth in the suds. Then it strikes her—what if the cops ask where the shirt is that Tom wore earlier?

I was just doing the family laundry, Officer.

She hurries upstairs to the second floor, gathers an armload of dirty laundry from the basket in the bathroom. She rushes back down to the laundry room, and she adds the other clothes to the pink and foamy water. She shuts the lid, then glances at the refuse bag she dropped on the laundry room floor.

She gathers it up. It has blood evidence inside it. Where should she put it?

What am I doing? Why am I even trying to hide this stuff?

Because her husband was trying to hide it.

And there *has* to be a good reason Tom put the shirt in the shed in the first place, before calling 911. And when she learns the reason, it will make sense. It *has* to make sense. She trusts Tom—doesn't she?

She thinks of their fight again, and it's like a physical blow to her body.

She doesn't trust Tom.

He lied to her.

He's been lying to her for their entire married life.

But then, Lily had sort of been lying to him, too. Or rather, she'd buried her own secrets so deep she could almost forget they were there. It was as if they belonged to someone else. Someone who was not Lily Bradley, mother of two wonderful children. But then the stalker appeared. Then the notes came. Then her patients' issues started mirroring her own. Slowly, little by little, Lily began to unravel.

She goes into the kitchen with the bundled-up bag and comes to a halt in front of the fridge. She saw something on TV once—a true crime show where a woman hid a bag containing human blood trace inside a freezer. But first the woman put raw meat in it.

Lily yanks open the door of their massive side-by-side fridge-freezer. She removes three packs of organic, grass-fed ground beef. She rips off the packaging, then tosses the frozen lumps of meat into the refuse bag. She wraps the bag up tightly and stuffs it back in the freezer. She puts the ground-beef packaging into the garbage bin beneath the sink. She's about to head up the stairs to change when a movement outside the window catches her eye.

She spins to face the window, her hands fisting. But there's nothing there. Just branches swaying in the wind. For a moment she stands, numb, watching the branches. The sound of her cuckoo clock ticking loudly—*tick, tick, tick*—filters into her brain. She jerks herself back into action and runs up the stairs. She turns on the shower, then rips off her cream sweater, her neatly tailored but loosely fitted linen pants, her camisole, her underwear, and she pins up her hair. She steps under the stream of steaming water and scrubs the dead woman's blood off her hands and face.

Lily towels off and dresses hurriedly. Jeans, a white T-shirt, a soft pink hoodie. She ties her hair back neatly and applies lip gloss.

You need to look like you're in control. You are *in control.*

But the glassy-eyed woman looking back at her from the mirror is barely recognizable to Lily.

She packs a bag of clothing for Tom, then remembers something else. His phone.

I plugged it in to recharge in the kitchen.

She unplugs Tom's phone from the charger on his side of the bed, then goes down to the kitchen, where she plugs her husband's phone into the charger on the counter to match his story. She takes one more sweep around the house, then reaches for her purse. The mere thought of going to the police station is terrifying for Lily. She has a fundamental unease with cops that is hardwired into her body because of her childhood. Yes, she knows that the police protect civilians. Yes, they keep neighborhoods like hers safe. But law enforcement is also inextricably twisted into the horrendous memories of what happened to her family, and even though Lily is able to rationalize her innate fears, even though she's dealt with her past in extensive therapy, it doesn't stop her from feeling them. And now compounded with those fears is a rising, fresh terror that some kind of relapse into the darkness of her past could occur.

She heads to the hall closet, removes her nice raincoat, and listens once more for the sound of the washing machine chugging safely away down the hall. She shrugs into her coat, reaches for her car keys, and picks up the bag of clothing for her husband. A loud banging sounds on the front door, followed by the gong of the doorbell. Lily stalls. Her heart races.

"Mrs. Bradley? Can you open up? It's the police. Open up, please."

Blind panic immobilizes her.

HOW IT BEGINS

THEN
April 20. Wednesday.

Two months before she dies.

The stalker stands in deep shadows beneath a gnarled cherry tree, watching the house across the street, gloved hands fisted around the handlebars of a bike. It's dark. Cold, despite the fact that it's spring. A damp fog creeps up the streets from the ocean a few blocks away, forming eerie halos around streetlights. Panniers on the sides of the bike hold a wet bathing suit, a towel, running shoes. The stalker's breath steams out through holes in a balaclava worn beneath a bike helmet. Droplets of moisture roll like beads off the watcher's waterproof clothing, glistening as they catch refracted light.

It's a safe neighborhood. Established. Streets lined with character homes, each fronted by a little green patch of lawn. Some with picket fences. Others with no fencing at all. Old trees—magnolia, cherry, oak—line the sidewalks. Story Cove. A romantic name that hearkens back to the man who founded the town in the 1800s, an Englishman called Simon J. Story. And the English tradition lives on here, just north of the US border. The Britishness oozes from the quaint pubs, from the fish and chips and pie shops, the afternoon tea with scones and clotted cream sold in cafés. It can be heard in the crack of cricket bats on the lawns of the Windsor Country Club, where rugby is also played by the men of the neighborhood, and where the cost of a membership could feed a small country.

A few blocks away, halyards chink against yacht masts in a pretty marina. Story Cove is a place with garden arbors and rambling roses, a place where deer graze on the nearby golf course, where children still laugh and play in the streets, and where masked raccoons are the only real bandits of the night as they slink through the darkness, checking through the rich folks' neatly sorted recycling and garbage.

Given the geography of Story Cove, the way the town is situated on a peninsula that juts into the Salish Sea, it might as well be a gated community. There is no reason for riffraff to pass through. Those who enter Story Cove live here. Or they come as help. Which is why the stalker has taken care to learn how to blend in.

The home under observation belongs to the Bradley family. The walls of the house look black in the night, but in daylight they're a deep eggplant purple with fresh green trim along the eaves. A brass plaque on a gate reads OAK TREE THERAPY, L. BRADLEY (PHD).

The stalker has learned much about the Bradleys over the months. And in various ways. Theirs is a life of routine. Which means their movements are predictable. It makes things so much easier.

The stalker knows what yoga and Pilates classes Dr. Lily Bradley takes, and where. What pastries she buys on what days. Where she has her hair cut and colored. Who her girlfriends are, how much she weighs, how many carbs she tries to limit herself to each day, which of her friends drinks too much wine, how fiercely protective she is of her children. The stalker knows what organic juice little Matthew prefers, and how much he loves his camera. The stalker is aware that Phoebe is a gothic fashion acolyte and that Professor Tom Bradley works at the university and habitually imbibes too much at the Red Lion Tavern on Friday afternoons, where he meets with a group of academics for a regular happy hour. Sometimes Tom Bradley and his mates straggle down to the yacht club afterward and drink more on one of their boats.

Tom and Lily appear to have a pretty perfect marriage. A storybook family in this Story Cove neighborhood of privilege. But it's an illusion.

All of life is an illusion.

People don't live in nicely painted heritage homes in pretty neighborhoods. They don't live in modern high-rise condos, or rustic cabins in the woods, or homeless shelters under concrete bridges. People live in the six inches of real estate between their ears—in that three pounds of fat and protein that is the human brain. They live inside their heads. That's where reality resides.

That's where every single human constructs an individual narrative of their life.

That's where they tell themselves who they are, and what they can and can't be. And no person's reality can ever be the same as anyone else's. The notion that there is one objective truth out there—that's the biggest illusion of all.

And always hidden beneath the narratives are the secrets. Deep and dark and primal. Everyone has them.

And the more you watch someone, the more you begin to see how hard they are working to hide the dark secrets that drive them.

Downstairs in the eggplant house, the blinds have not yet been drawn, and the lights inside throw a bright gold square into the night. Like an illuminated stage set. A vignette for the audience of one that lurks beneath the cherry tree.

Clearly the occupants feel safe, exposed like that. But this is about to change.

Someone moves into view from the kitchen. The stalker tenses. It's the husband. Tall. Dark. Dressed in black jeans, a black turtleneck sweater. How very academic. How befitting a psychology professor who studies deviant minds from the distance of his ivy-clad ivory tower. A privileged man, born into generational wealth. The kind of wealth and breeding that can protect people from paying for the terrible, twisted things they might do.

Professor Tom Bradley wears oven gloves as he carries a steaming pot to the dining table. His wife suddenly steps into the golden vignette. Dr. Lily Bradley. All buttery blonde and impeccably coiffed. Nice breasts. Hips trim from expensive workouts with her personal trainer at the gym. Lily Bradley sets a bottle of wine on the table. The husband fetches an opener.

The wine is uncorked, poured. The wife picks up a wineglass, says something. He laughs. She laughs, too, throwing back her buttery hair and exposing the smooth column of her throat.

A bead of need coalesces deep in the stalker's belly. Fists tighten on handlebars.

The wife married up. Her husband is fifteen years older. She's his second wife. He came with the money.

The need in the stalker's belly blossoms into a fierce, hot, and dangerous longing. It rises to the heart. And with the raw, aching desire comes something more sinister—a need to destroy what lives in that eggplant house.

All the stalker wants from the Bradley family . . . is everything.

Suddenly the wife stills. She glances toward the window. The stalker tenses. The wife says something to her husband, then walks directly to the window with her glass of wine. She cups the windowpane with her free hand and peers into the night, looking directly at the cherry tree. The watcher holds stone still, doesn't even breathe. Dr. Lily Bradley reaches for a cord and drops the blinds.

Show over.

The stalker smiles. It's working. Lily Bradley has sensed something watching, prowling at the edges of her life. She's felt a vestigial flicker of awareness.

Game on. Time to move to the next stage.

But as the stalker mounts the bike, a crack of yellow light slices into the darkness. The stalker's gaze shoots up to the attic window. The drape in the small dormer window upstairs is slightly open, exposing a band of light. *The boy.*

Every muscle in the watcher's body freezes until the drape is finally dropped back into place, and the yellow light is snuffed.

The watcher is edgy now. There's always a crack. A crack in everything. That's how the light gets in. Or how the dark gets out.

The stalker waits a while longer. Cold creeps into bones. Hands go stiff in gloves on the handlebars.

A faint breeze stirs. Droplets plop down from the gnarled branches, and an ambulance wails in the distance, the sound swelling and dying as the sirens bypass Story Cove en route to some tragedy.

The watcher cycles down the street, just another shadowy, helmeted figure sifting into the suburban night.

LILY

NOW

Lily steels her spine and opens the front door, expecting to see the uniformed officer from the cruiser parked across the street.

It's a man in a suit. Asian heritage. Good-looking, and impeccably attired.

"Mrs. Bradley, I'm Detective Toshi Hara." The man shows Lily his ID. "I'm with the Integrated Homicide unit and I work with Detective Rulandi Duval—I'm her partner. I believe you met her this morning?"

Lily glances at the cop car across the street. Shock crashes through her as she notices a media van is now parked behind it. The big red logo on the side of the van says CITV News. Like some blatant, flashing sign in front of their house. The band of tension across her temples tightens as she realizes how visible the name of her therapy business is on the plaque near the driveway. Any photos the media take of their house will show her therapy shingle. Her name.

"What can I do for you?" She's beginning to shake. She realizes this is suddenly about so much more than a dead female jogger on the beach. It's triggering her childhood trauma, making her relive what happened after the cops showed up on that terrible day. A buzzing noise begins in her head.

The washing machine starts to spin, and it makes a clunking noise. Detective Hara looks past Lily into their hallway. She moves into the center of the doorway to block his view and keeps silent, waiting for him to answer.

"Is that your machine?" he asks. "Do you want to attend to it?"

"It's faulty. Been meaning to fix it. It's fine."

He regards her.

"What do you want?"

"I'd like to ask you a few questions. About this morning."

"My husband is at the station," she says.

"It's not your husband I want to speak with. It's you. I just have a few questions. It's procedure. Can I come in?"

The washing machine noise goes louder.

"I'm just leaving." She hooks her purse over her shoulder, grabs Tom's bag of clothes, and steps out the front door, forcing Hara to move backward. She pulls the door firmly closed behind her and locks it. "My husband, Tom, has asked me to bring him some clothes, since you've taken his, and I'm about to leave, so—"

"Can you tell me where you were yesterday, up until this morning?"

She stalls. "Me?"

His dark eyes hold hers. He waits. Lily glances at the media van. The doors are opening. A woman in a skirt and a man with a camera are climbing out. Tension whips through her.

"Is that when she—the woman—died? Yesterday sometime?"

He waits.

The reporter and her cameraman are crossing the street. Lily's brain races. The police must have asked—or will be asking—Tom the same questions. She cannot contradict Tom. Perhaps this is why Detective Duval has sent her partner over, to head Lily off and question her before she can speak to her husband, before she and Tom can agree on a common narrative of the day and confirm each other's alibis.

I cannot stress this enough: do not talk to anyone, no matter how friendly they seem, until I understand what's at play here.

"I'm sorry." Lily pushes past Detective Hara as the reporter hits the end of her lawn. "Our lawyer is Dianne Klister. You can speak to her." She hurries toward her BMW, parked in the driveway. She beeps her lock as she nears.

Detective Hara shouts after her, "She's your husband's lawyer, Mrs. Bradley. Not yours. She's going to be working for him, not you."

Lily yanks open her car door, throws her bags inside. As she climbs into the driver's seat, the female journalist comes at her with a mike, and the camera guy starts shooting.

"Dr. Bradley!" yells the reporter. "Why has your husband been taken to the downtown station? Why is he being questioned by homicide police?"

Lily slams her car door shut and starts the engine. She can hear the reporter shouting outside the window. "Did your husband know the victim, Mrs. Bradley? Is this related to the other jogger cases?"

Lily grits her jaw, firms her fists around the wheel, presses down on the gas, and pulls out of her driveway too fast. She spins her wheel as she turns onto the street, and her tires hit the road with a snick and a screech. She guns the gas and speeds down the quiet cul-de-sac. She comes to an abrupt halt at the stop sign. Her heart hammers. Sweat pools under her arms. She's breathing rapidly. The reporter's voice reverberates through her skull.

Did your husband know the victim, Mrs. Bradley? Is this related to the other jogger cases?

It's followed by the echo of Dianne's voice.

Whether or not Tom did anything, if he's being questioned by homicide investigators . . . this is not going to play well for him in the media.

As she drives to the station, she tries to pinpoint when she first became aware that something was going wrong. It was in the early spring, when she began to feel watched.

And then came the notes.

LILY

THEN
April 24. Sunday.

Just under two months before she dies.

"It's time to go, guys!" Lily calls up the stairs.

It's Sunday, and Lily is taking the kids to Mass at the little stone church near the water. She attends the Our Lady of the Peace Catholic church with Phoebe and Matthew every Sunday morning. Tom used to come with them, but while Lily needs the religious tradition as a bookend to her week and to keep herself on track, her husband has drifted away from organized faith. He prefers to go on his long runs on Sundays. He claims exercising and the outdoors are his church, and on Sundays he always tries to incorporate some kind of nature trail into his mileage, either through a forest, along the water, or along one of the mountain hiking routes.

Going to Mass is also a way for Lily to hold her parents and her little brother in her heart. When Lily was young, her mom and dad used to take her and her baby brother to church. The therapist in Lily also sees value in the Catholic tradition of confession, although she knows well that some secrets can never truly be told to a local priest who lives and shops and exercises in the same small town. Just as she is aware that some of her patients hold secrets back from her. She has methods for coaxing them out, though. The human body is not terribly well designed to keep secrets. It creates incredible stress. It can be exhausting. It comes out as problematic behavior.

Cops know this, too. The relief when a bad guy finally gives in and confesses is physical, and visible. A criminal will often fall asleep in the interview room once he has released his secret.

Phoebe and Matthew come clattering down the stairs. Anger spurts through Lily as she sees what her daughter is wearing.

"Phoebe, go and change."

"Why?"

"You can't wear that to Mass."

"Because it's black? Because it's goth?"

"Because it's not suitable. Move it—hurry up and change. We're going to be late."

Phoebe stands her ground, glowering at her mother with fierce kohl-rimmed eyes, and the tension that explodes in Lily's belly awakens something much, much deeper. It stirs a memory of when she was twelve, when her own mother confronted her about her appearance and her choice of boyfriend, and when her mother forbade her to see him. She cautions herself to tone it down. To pick her battles with more care. She knows intimately how terribly wrong things can go, and just how vulnerable this age can be for a girl, even for a child who seemingly has it all, who appears well adjusted at home, who has caring parents and friends, and who is doing fine at school. Until suddenly things are not fine.

"Okay," Lily says. "We can talk about it later. Let's just go."

"I don't want to go to church anymore," Phoebe says.

"You must," quips Matthew. "Or God will smote you."

"It's *smite*, you little idiot. And Dad doesn't go. I asked him why, and he said it wasn't for him. He said I can make my own decisions. I think Buddhism is a better fit for me, quite frankly."

Lily bites her tongue and counts backward slowly from five. "We'll talk about it all when we come home, okay? We can all have a family discussion with your dad included. Deal?"

Phoebe inhales and marches toward the door. "Fine," she calls over her shoulder.

Matthew runs after his big sister. Another bolt of memory slams through Lily as she watches her son's little legs. For a moment she can't move. It's happening more and more frequently—these memories. Perhaps it's the ages of her children. Or just this time of year.

Or something more sinister.

For the last couple of weeks, she's begun to feel that she's being watched. Stalked. At first it was just a sense, a kind of awareness. An edginess. Then she began to see movement in shadows when she looked out the window at night. And she's sure someone followed her to the supermarket, and that someone was watching her from across the parking lot when she came out of the gym. A guy on a bike with a balaclava.

She's also pretty certain she saw the same figure across the street when she was getting her hair done at the salon, and again on the day she met Hannah for coffee at the French Bakery Café and they sat at a table on the sidewalk.

Lily tries to banish those thoughts from her mind as they drive to church. The world looks beautiful today. The streets are full of cherry blossoms. Fallen pink and white cherry petals cover cars and line the sidewalks like spring snow. Flowers are blooming in gardens, and Matthew spots a big buck on the bright-green golf course.

After Mass they exit the church into a brisk sea breeze, and as they near the car, Lily sees a piece of pink paper flapping under her windshield wiper.

She beeps the locks and lets the kids into the car before she reaches for what she thinks is a ticket or some kind of marketing flyer. But at the same time, she's suddenly edgy and hyperaware of her environment.

She slides the piece of paper out from under the wiper, then glances around, eyeing the churchgoers, looking for a sign that someone is watching. Her gaze settles on a man near trees, smoking a cigarette. Then her attention moves to a woman who seems to be staring at her, before Lily realizes the woman is waiting for someone else, who comes running over. She swallows and unfolds the flyer. She goes cold.

Printed in black are the words **YOU CAN'T HIDE FROM SATAN IF SATAN IS INSIDE YOUR HEAD.**

RUE

NOW

Rue enters the interview room carrying her "prop box" and finds Tom Bradley seated on the sofa waiting for her. He's dressed in PD sweats and crime booties, and he's pale and fidgeting with his fingers.

"Hello, Dr. Bradley. Thank you for waiting."

He doesn't reply.

She sets her prop box on the coffee table and seats herself on the desk chair with wheels. She faces Tom across the small table. Behind her on the wall is a corkboard. A surveillance camera near the roof feeds into a monitoring room, where her superior and other members of her team are watching and taking notes. She anticipates that from time to time, one of the other detectives might knock on the door, call her out of the room, and suggest either stopping a certain line of questioning or doubling down on another that, in their view, seems to be working.

The interview room is designed to feel comfortable. The last thing they need is to get to trial and have some lawyer declare to a jury that they mistreated a suspect. It doesn't go down well. Everything Rue's team does right now is with a view to a successful prosecution down the road. Although, ideally, they would rather not go to court at all. They'd prefer a confession and a guilty plea.

"How are you feeling?" she asks. "A bit warmer?"

Tom flicks his gaze up to the camera. He rubs his knee. "I have an appointment. I need to get to work."

"Hopefully we won't be long." She presses a button on her digital recorder and sets it on the table between them. "This interview is being recorded. I'm Sergeant Rulandi Duval. The interview is with Tom Bradley, of 2112 Oak End, Story Cove." She states the time and date.

"Am I under arrest?" Bradley asks.

"No. You're free to go and you are free to remain silent, although your cooperation will be helpful, because a woman is dead. You found her, and you're in the best position to assist us in understanding what happened. Can I call you Tom?"

He swallows and nods.

She takes a file folder out of her box, opens it, scans the page on top, and says, "You work at Kordel University?"

"Yes. I'm a faculty member at Kordel. Psychology Department. My areas are neural and abnormal psychology."

Rue purses her lips. "So . . . here's the thing, Tom." She leans back in her chair, projecting ease, acting as though she has all the time in the world. "There are a few things that are not quite adding up with respect to your account of events this morning, and we'd like to run through the details once more, just to clear up some questions."

A sharp knock sounds at the door. It swings open to expose a woman.

Rue's pulse quickens as she recognizes Dianne Klister. A notorious criminal lawyer in this town, and a media whore. Klister is in her mid-forties, with thick auburn hair cut to swing at her jawline. She's dressed in a trademark designer suit with heels that probably cost more than Rue's Subaru Outback. She wears chunky gold neck jewelry like battle armor and carries a leather briefcase for which some crocodile or snake probably gave its life.

Not only has Dr. Bradley lawyered up, he's engaged one of the city's top, hard-core crime sharks. People don't hire lawyers like Klister when they have nothing to hide. This woman's fee would send average folk into bankruptcy, or at the least force a second mortgage. The fact that Klister is standing here right now sharply piques Rue's interest, and it slides Rue further along the scale toward seeing Tom Bradley as a key person of interest. And there is no doubt in her team's mind that the Grotto Beach jogger met with foul play.

"Ms. Klister," Rue says.

"Sergeant Duval," says Klister, remaining standing in the doorway. "I'd like a moment to confer in private with my client."

Rue crooks up her brow and glances at Bradley. "We were just officially running through Tom's account from this morning—"

"In other words, a fishing expedition," Klister interjects.

"We have some lingering questions about Dr. Bradley's version of events this morning," says Rue.

"And what else do you have?"

"A Kordel U running cap found at the scene. And a headlamp. Signs of a chase and a struggle, plus blood trace on the cliff above where the decedent was found." Rue's drone operator also discovered a second headlamp snagged on a rock on the cliff face, along with a dark-pink running cap caught halfway up the cliff on a dead branch. "And we have footprints at the edge of the cliff. Same brand and size as the trail shoes your client was wearing." This has since been confirmed. Rue pauses a beat, letting it all sink in, then says, "Plus a business card in the decedent's jacket pocket with your client's name on it. And the dead woman's blood on his hands and neck. And your client's bloody jacket left at the scene. And a witness who saw your client entering his yard this morning wearing a bloody shirt, which he was not wearing when we arrived at his house following his 911 call."

Klister doesn't even blink. But Tom Bradley stiffens on the sofa, and his eyes widen.

Rue silently thanks Toshi for grabbing Bradley's DNA sample when he did, because there is no way in hell Klister would have allowed it.

Rue also sent Toshi to question the wife before the couple got a chance to align their stories or alibis.

"Are you charging my client?" asks Klister.

"No. We're—"

"Come, Tom, we're leaving," says Klister, her hand on the door handle.

"I do need to ask your client where he was yesterday. If he could account for his movements from yesterday morning to the time he found the body—"

"He has nothing more to say. Tom, let's go."

Bradley gets to his feet.

"Did you recognize the decedent, Dr. Bradley?" Rue asks. "Do you know who she is?"

Tom Bradley crosses the room toward his lawyer. Rue can see the professor wants to talk, wants to explain himself, and she silently curses Klister. If Rue had had a few more minutes alone with him, she'd have gotten something. She's certain of it.

"Why did you cover her face, Dr. Bradley?" Rue asks.

"We're done here," says Klister.

But as Bradley and Klister begin to exit the room, a female officer steps into their path and motions to Rue. "A word, Detective?"

"Can it wait?" Rue's words are crisp.

"There's a teen out front. Joe Harper. Says his mother is missing. He lives with his mom in Story Cove. In Oak End, right next to the forest trailhead. He says his mother's running shoes, her cap, rain jacket, phone, and her headlamp are all gone from their house. He last saw his mom at a barbecue across the cul-de-sac yesterday, and he heard about the body on the beach. He says he knows the man who found the body. Tom Bradley is a neighbor on their street, and Bradley and his wife were also at the barbecue yesterday."

Rue's gaze snaps to Bradley. He's gone sheet white. Bradley and his counsel exchange a hot glance.

Before Rue can speak, Klister places her hand on Bradley's arm and says to Rue, "It's been good seeing you again, Detective." The lawyer flashes a false smile, then turns and leads her client down the corridor, expensive heels clicking.

As Rue watches the criminal shark and the professor leave, she says quietly to the uniformed cop, "What's the name of the teen's mother?"

"Arwen Harper. She worked at the Red Lion."

ARWEN

THEN
May 6. Friday.

SIX WEEKS BEFORE SHE DIES.

Arwen Harper sets a third tarot card on the copper bar counter. She's doing a quick three-card spread for Red Lion Tavern manager Dez Parry—the woman who hired Arwen six days ago.

It's the Death card.

"Oh great," says Dez, who is polishing a beer glass. They're in a brief slump between lunch and happy hour, and after seeing the tarot deck poking out of Arwen's purse, Dez asked her new server to do a reading for her. "Does that mean I'm going to die?"

"Of course you are." Arwen looks up and meets Dez's gaze. She smiles slowly. "We're all dying. Some just faster than others."

"Well then"—Dez sets the glass on the shelf and picks up another from the rack—"what's the takeaway?"

"You need to interpret the cards in relation to one another, and in relation to yourself, and in the context of your particular question," says Arwen. "You said you have a conundrum—you don't know whether to put all your savings into a down payment on an apartment, because while it would offer a secure future, it will also lock you down. Or you could use the money to travel the world, but then you'll have nothing to fall back on. So—" Arwen spreads the three cards farther apart, her rings catching the bar lights. She taps the first card. "This card represents your question, your current situation. This second card here represents your feelings around it, and this third card is the outcome."

Dez stills her hands. "My outcome is the Death card?"

Arwen grins. "It's not a bad card. It symbolizes the end of something, as in a major transformation, a passing from one cycle to another. A *necessary* transformation. It's a sign that you should perhaps release what no longer serves you. Or it could be something new ahead, like a marriage, a business opportunity, a baby on the way, a big move—something that will require letting go of old ways, losing the old self in order to become the new person. But if the card lands upside down, like this one, it can mean a delay, significant challenges in accepting or adjusting to the required change."

"And that second card—the Fool—is that how I feel about my conundrum?"

"The Fool is the part of you that is tripping along the road of life with indifference, carrying your load like a bundle on a stick, but not stopping to think, just going with a flow. But the Fool in context with this first card, the Sun, it tells me you're questioning this way of being now. You want more meaning in your life journey. The Sun here represents a triumph over the matter in your life. More control."

Dez snorts and grabs another wet glass. "Cheap tricks, Arwen. Cheap tricks. Hocus-pocus. I basically told you all that myself."

Arwen laughs. "Think of it like therapy—the patient holds the answers all the time anyway. The cards are like a therapist's way to tease the truth out of your unconscious. Sometimes the tarot is even used in therapy."

"Therapy is the last place you're going to find me."

As Dez speaks, the tavern doors swing open. Both Arwen and Dez glance up.

Four males enter. One is taller than the others—dark hair with a distinguished gray streak at his temple. Good-looking. Broad shoulders. Bit of an athletic swagger, which is offset by a chic wool coat and scarf and the leather satchel slung over his shoulder.

Bells clang in Arwen's head. *Jackpot. Bingo.* A frisson of excitement crackles over her skin as the men unwind their scarves and hand their coats to the hostess. They head for the big round table in an alcove of windows by the fire.

Humans are creatures of habit, and the doctor of psychology is no exception. Almost right behind the group of men, a gaggle of six women enter, all laughter and shrill chatter. Nearly all blonde. Expensively attired. Middle aged. They're here for Friday wine hour before their kids and husbands come home and the weekend gets rolling.

"Showtime," says Dez as she reaches for a stack of menus and calls for the barman, who is in the kitchen eating a late lunch.

"Mind if I take the guys?" Arwen asks as she scoops up her tarot cards, her bracelets tinkling as she moves.

"The Kordel profs?"

"Is that what they are?"

"Friday happy-hour regulars. Like clockwork. The tall, dark one is Tom Bradley. Psychology. The slightly shorter guy with brown hair is Simon Cody—philosophy. The South Asian–looking guy is Sandeep Gunjal. He teaches economics. And the skinny, deathly pale, balding dude with the big forehead is Milton Timmons, English lit." She eyes Arwen. "Are you sure? They're not big on the gratuities. Those women, however, are super-big tippers if you play them right," Dez says.

"I never play women like them right."

Dez grins, taking in Arwen's neck tattoo, her crazy-wild curls, her armfuls of bracelets, her long skirt, her overt sense of simmering sexuality. "Your loss."

Wrong. My win, thinks Arwen as she collects four menus off the stack and heads over to the group of men.

"Afternoon, gentlemen. My name is Arwen. Can I get you anything to drink while you take a look at the menus?" She smiles, making eye contact with each individual as she hands out the menus. And she carefully catalogues each male now that she's up close, assessing prospects, noting wedding bands—they each sport a ring. Arwen figures Simon Cody works out with weights and is vain, and he thinks he's a ladies' man. His hands look strong. His eyes are green and intense. Milton Timmons's eyes, on the other hand, are woeful. The English professor has long, delicate fingers, and his high-domed forehead gives him a cerebral look. Sandeep Gunjal has a warm aura, liquid, smiling eyes. Sartorially, he's the most fashion conscious of the bunch. Tom Bradley is talking to his friends, and he doesn't even look at her face as he reaches for his menu. Arwen holds on to his menu, forcing him to tug slightly. And when she doesn't relinquish it right away, he glances up into her eyes.

She smiles. He holds her gaze, instinctively curious, and Arwen notes that up close his eyes are a deep blue. His hair is nicely cut and windblown. She laughs as she notices a few errant cherry blossoms on his head. "You have petals on your hair," she says. "Like you've been through a wedding."

He laughs in return and dusts off his hair. "The wind is ripping those blossoms off and blowing them all over the place like a bloody blizzard today."

Arwen can imagine him in his long wool coat, striding through the windswept blossoms. Or along a stormy cliff. Like a Heathcliff on the moors—a character befitting a role in a Gothic mansion. She's further intrigued, allured, by the fact that he's a student of "abnormal" minds. Tom Bradley is definitely the most attractive of the bunch to Arwen.

He takes the menu, and his gaze lowers to the name tag on her chest.

"Arwen. Thank you." His voice is deep, warm. A playful twinkle enters his eyes. *Poof* goes the image of the devoted husband.

Sorry, Lily Bradley, but your Dr. Tom Bradley is a typical male with a stroke-able ego, and he's just opened the door to me.

A door to his own trap.

And to your trap.

Arwen returns Tom's warm and inviting smile, feeling a rush of excitement, nerves of anticipation. *The game is on.*

"Your parents *Lord of the Rings* fans?" he asks.

"Excuse me?"

The skinny man interjects with a theatrical voice, "'For I am Arwen, daughter of Elrond, half-elven.'"

She pulls a face. "You've lost me. My name comes from my mother's lineage. Welsh background. So, what can I get you guys? Anything to drink while you decide what to eat?"

The guys order a selection of craft beers on tap, and she leaves them chatting by the warmth of the fire as she goes to the bar to place her order with Hank, the bartender.

As Hank pours the beers, he says, "They always start with the beer, but if they get on a roll, we'll be cracking out the top-shelf single-malt Scotch later." He sets the glasses of beer on her tray. "Friday night like clockwork, those profs. Sometimes they bring others, but usually it's always that core four."

"So I hear."

It's precisely why she applied for the job at the Red Lion. Professor Tom Bradley has a happy-hour habit, while Dr. Lily Bradley has a Friday night book club habit, a.k.a. wine night with the girls. The Bradleys bookend their weekends by balancing these booze-filled habits with a running habit and a church habit on Sundays. Clearing their heads and cleansing their sins.

Friday nights also see young Phoebe Bradley left at home to watch over her little brother, Matthew. Phoebe busies herself on her iPad and Matthew holes up in his attic while their parents indulge.

Arwen carries the tray of drinks over to the men's table.

Friday nights present Arwen with maximum opportunity.

RUE

NOW

The teen waiting for Rue in the reception area is tall and of Asian heritage.

"My name is Joe Harper," he says in a shaky voice. "And my mom is missing."

She takes him into an interview room with a table and two chairs, and she closes the door.

"Take a seat, Joe. Take your time. Can I get you anything, some water, tea, coffee?"

He shakes his head and seats himself at the table. His hands are trembling. Rue's heart immediately goes out to him. He's around her son's age.

Rue takes a seat, and Joe pushes his iPhone across the table toward her. The screen displays an image of a woman.

"This . . . this is a recent photo of my mom," he says.

Rue takes the mobile from him, and her breath stalls. Her skin goes hot.

It *could* be her—the woman Rue followed to the Red Lion. She never did get a clear look at her face, but there is something disturbingly familiar about Joe Harper's mother. She breathes in slowly, deeply, steadies her mind, then glances up and meets the teen's gaze.

He doesn't look anything like the woman in the image. His mother has very pale skin, and her dark-brown hair has an auburn glint. Light-blue eyes. Like a sky on a hot summer's day. In the image the woman's head is thrown back and she's laughing. The long, pale column of her throat reminds Rue of a graceful swan. And plain as day, on the left side of that swan neck, is the tattoo—the mythological creature with a lion's head and the tail of a snake that Rue noticed on the body of the dead woman. In the photo she is so alive, leaning against a giant, upended tree that has weathered to a pale gray. Her loose mop of curls blows in the wind. Her arm—which she's holding up—is full of bracelets. Rue uses her fingers to zoom in on her face. She sees the wink of a nose stud.

She wonders if Joe Harper might be adopted, as she herself is. Rue looks nothing like her own parents. It took years of searching, of following clues, and two visits to Southern Africa to learn her bio mother was of mixed race and Malaysian heritage and grew up in Cape Town, South Africa. Her bio mom, now deceased, apparently spoke Afrikaans primarily. All Rue knows of her bio dad is that he was Black and lived for a time near Maputo in Mozambique, once a Portuguese colony, and that he spoke both Portuguese and Makhuwa.

"And your mother's name is Arwen?" she asks quietly.

Joe nods, rubs his mouth. "Arwen Harper."

"When did you first notice your mother was missing, Joe?"

"I haven't seen her since yesterday, when we went to a neighborhood barbecue across the street at the Codys' house—the Codys live right across from us."

"And you live at the end of Oak End?"

"Right beside the trail that leads into the Spirit Forest Park, yes. I left the party before she did. I . . . I wasn't into it."

"So you don't know what time your mother left the party?"

"I . . . I really don't. I should've made sure that she came home okay, and maybe she did, but I just went to bed." His eyes fill with tears. He swipes them away. "She often works in her studio all night, so it's not like I expect to see her at night. She sleeps in her studio, too. It's like a bedsit. But we always have breakfast together, especially on school days. That's her thing, her one rule, her commitment to me—that we are together at that time . . ." His voice catches. He stares at the table for a long moment, trying to gather himself. "We often don't have supper together, or see each other during the rest of the day, but she *always* makes an effort for breakfast. It's her time to check in with me, make sure I'm eating properly. I . . . I'm sorry," he says as he swipes at his tears again.

"It's okay. Take as long as you need."

"When she didn't come in this morning for breakfast, I went to check on her in her studio, and she wasn't there. That's when I saw her running stuff was also gone, so I figured she was out for a run, which would be unusual at that time on a Monday morning. So I tried her cell phone, and it just went to voice mail. Then . . . then I heard the sirens, and I saw everyone in the street, and the police cars up the road, and I heard that a body—a woman's body—was found on the beach."

"Does your mother usually take her cell phone when she goes running?"

He nods. "Especially if she's running alone." His gaze bores into Rue's. The look in his eyes is beseeching. "Is it her? Is the woman on the beach my mom?"

Rue thinks about the fact that no phone was found on the body. "We're not sure yet who the woman is, Joe," she says softly. "Is there any identifying mark that—"

"The tattoo." He points to her neck. "She has that tattoo on her neck. It's a chimera. She also has ink on her hip. An image of the Greek goddess Apate."

Gently, Rue says, "You mentioned her running gear was missing from your house. What does your mother usually wear when she goes for a run?"

He rubs his eyes, hard. "A dark-pink jacket—she calls the color fuchsia. She's an artist. She always uses fancy names for colors. She paints with oils mostly. And . . . her shoes are Nike. Trail runners. She has black leggings."

"What about headgear? Headlamp? Any kind of flashlight?"

"A . . . a pink cap to match her jacket. And a Petzl headlamp she bought from Mountain Equipment. She takes the lamp if it's dark out."

"So she does run in the dark?"

"Well, dusk sometimes, and it can turn dark before she gets home."

"What color is the headlamp?"

He looks scared, his eyes glassy, wild. "It—it's orange and white. Is it her?"

It matches the description of the headlamp located on the cliff face by the drone.

"Do you have another parent around, Joe? Or a close next of kin nearby?"

"It's just me and my mom. I don't have a dad. I mean, I never met my bio dad. I don't even know his name, or who he was. I had a stepfather for a while. Peter Harper. He adopted me when he married my mom. But they split some years ago, and then Peter died. It's just been me and my mom since."

Rue thinks of the battered body she saw on the beach. A single mother. This child alone.

"Your mother has no significant other, no partner?"

He glances down and hesitates, as if embarrassed or shamed by something, then shakes his head. Very quietly he says, "She does have a lot of male friends, and sometimes they stay the night, but—" He clears his throat and meets Rue's gaze again. "No one special."

Rue nods slowly, watching him. "How old are you, Joe?"

"Sixteen."

She feels a clutch in her stomach. He's two years younger than her own son. She thinks of the woman she followed to the Red Lion and wonders if she might need to declare a possible conflict of interest in this case. She also doesn't want to. She needs to know where this is going now; she needs control of it. And she isn't certain yet that this is the woman her husband was seeing.

Rue takes her phone from her pocket and brings up an image. She shows it to the teen. "Do you recognize these keys, Joe?"

"Yes. Yes, those are hers. We have a VW bus. We drove it across Canada to move here. We sort of lived in it along the way, and one time we drove it all the way down through the States to Mexico, and . . ." He chokes on tears and his voice dies. He weeps silently.

Rue goes to find a box of tissues and a bottle of water. She returns and gives them to Joe. He blows his nose and takes a deep drink. When he seems a little more composed, Rue shows him another photo. "And this fob—do you recognize it?"

He nods. "It's from the tavern where she works. Her . . . her painting doesn't provide a steady income. I mean, she sells her art and stuff, but it's never been her main source of income, and she needs to earn money while she's working on her special project."

"What kind of project?"

He stares numbly at the photo of his mother's fob.

"Joe?"

He looks up.

"What kind of project, Joe?"

"I . . . I don't know. It's a book. Nonfiction. She wouldn't tell me what it's about. She just said it was a special project, and when it was done, it would be our big break. It's why we came west and moved here. She said it was for research, and that it was going to take a while to get all the details she needed."

"When did you arrive in Story Cove?"

"We moved into Oak End on the last day of May. We were closer to the city in an apartment before that. We arrived on the island in early March."

"Where did you live before you moved to the island?"

"A town called Oakville, outside of Toronto. My mom worked with a television studio, doing investigative research and reporting, and writing for various programs."

"Investigative work?"

"Like, undercover stuff, mostly for consumer programs. There was one series she worked on for CBC where she went undercover to a bunch of dentists to expose the fact that some would claim she needed fillings and a whole lot of expensive work, while others said her teeth were fine. She helped expose a financial con artist one time. And some dating racket, and someone who was scamming seniors. She's also worked on true crime shows . . . but the art, the painting, her tarot cards, she says that's how she processes stuff. Her art is like therapy, and it's an outlet for her. She . . . she needs it." He hangs his head down and sits silent for a long while. Rue senses a lot more. She senses a troubled mother. A very lost teen.

"It's her on the beach, isn't it?" he says very quietly, without looking at her. "She's the body lying beneath the cliff. My mom. It's my mom."

"Joe," Rue says, "we still need to make an official ID, but it does sound like your mother."

His entire being goes still. For a long while he says nothing. "Can . . . can I see her? To be certain."

"There will be an autopsy. This happens by law if there is a sudden death. The postmortem will help the coroner's office, and us, determine what happened to her. And then, yes, we can let you see her body. The coroner's office will want a scientific identification—either from DNA or dental records. So it will help if you can provide the name of your mother's doctor or dentist. And we'd like to come to your house, to take a look around, and also to collect something like a hairbrush or toothbrush that contains some of your mother's DNA."

"I don't think my mom has been to see any doctors or dentists here, but I know where she has some medical bills from back home."

"That will help. Do you have someone you can stay with?"

"I . . . I don't know. Maybe the Codys across the street."

"Okay, I tell you what—my partner and I will drive you back to your house, and you can locate those medical details for us and take us through your home, maybe point out anything unusual. And we can meet with the Codys. I'll also connect you with someone from victims' services, and they'll be able to put you in touch with any social services or anything else you might need. Is that okay?"

He nods.

"Can you share this photo of your mother to my phone?"

Joe AirDrops the image to Rue's phone.

"Thank you. I'm going to ask an officer to wait with you while I print out a copy of this photograph. I'll be right back, okay?"

He nods.

Rue gets up and is about to leave the room when Joe says, "I hear it was Dr. Bradley who found her."

Hand on the door, Rue stills. "You know Dr. Bradley?"

"Yeah. He . . . I'm sort of dating the Bradleys' daughter, Phoebe."

PHOEBE

THEN
June 1. Wednesday.

EIGHTEEN DAYS BEFORE SHE DIES.

Phoebe Bradley sees him for the first time in early summer, when the school year is almost over.

The trees are full of fresh green leaves, and gardens are blooming. It's a clear day, shimmering with promise and a warm sea breeze as she makes her way to the school bus stop. She rounds the corner, and her attention is immediately snared by the new guy—how could it not be?

He's tall—taller than most of the kids clustering with their backpacks and books on this balmy morning. His hair is black as pitch and shiny. High and angular cheekbones. He's athletic-looking, but definitely not a jock—he's got a studious, aloof air. His hair is shaved short on the sides but is longer on the top, and his bangs flop almost into his eyes. Neat and narrow sideburns. An earring in one ear. Phoebe is a manga fan. She's so enamored with manga and anime and the culture around them that she's started to teach herself Japanese and plans to take it as a course next year. Whenever she can, she doodles in the manga style on her iPad, on scraps of paper, on notebooks . . . and he's like a perfect, smoldering manga hero. She's in love. Like on the spot. She can't stop glancing at him.

"Who *is* he?" she whispers to Fiona Cody, who is in her grade. The Codys live down the road, and Fi's mom and Phoebe's mom are good friends. Fi's dad also teaches at the university—Simon Cody is a professor of philosophy—and he's friendly with Phoebe's father. There are quite a few people in their neighborhood who work at the university. Academics with money, or "generational wealth," as her dad calls it. And when he says it, he laughs, because everyone knows that professors don't make a ton of money from teaching. Most of the other faculty and staff live in a more artsy and slightly more run-down neighborhood to the north, or closer to the actual campus. Her mom calls that area "eclectic."

The Cody and Bradley families often get together for barbecues in the summer. And on those long, warm nights, Simon Cody and Phoebe's father like to sit in the garden around the firepit and talk for hours while they drink. And then one or the other—depending on whose house they're at—will wobble home along the road, calling goodbyes, laughing, talking so loudly that Phoebe is sure all the sleeping neighbors wake up.

Fi also has a little brother. Jacob. He's far less annoying than Matthew. Jacob and Matthew don't really get on, but then Matthew doesn't really get along with most kids his age. Matthew and Jacob catch a different bus to the elementary school.

Fi whispers, "He just moved in across the cul-de-sac from us."

"*Our* street? Oak End?"

"Yeah." Fi's gaze goes to the new guy. "The house with the cottage and the studio in the backyard."

"The Americans' house?" They all refer to it as "the Americans' house" because the owners are from the States and are seldom here. The main house stays empty most of the year, but they rent out the small garden cottage and adjacent studio year-round. The cottage has been empty since the old man who lived there had a stroke and had to go into assisted living. "When?" asks Phoebe. "Why didn't you tell me?"

"It just happened. Him and his mom."

"No father?"

"Just the two of them. My dad helped them carry stuff inside, and my mom went over with a zucchini loaf to welcome them to the neighborhood. She's an artist or a writer or something."

Artist.

This appeals to Phoebe.

She stares at the hot new guy. Her smoldering manga dude. In her mind she's already drawing him, and she's adding herself to the image as his love interest. She's a "dark magical girl" in gothic attire—moody and the opposite to a "sweet magical girl." She's not a bad character; she just needs to be understood, and she needs for someone to love her. Like him. She pictures herself with pitch-black hair, thick bangs hanging in her eyes. Nah. Scratch that. Silvery lavender hair. Side part. Wearing a lacy, black, cropped top. Or . . . rather . . . dark-pink hair. Yes. That image fits better. And she's wearing a long coat over her lace top, fitted at the waist, open, and flaring out slightly at her calves. Boots—combat boots right up to her knees, long laces. Her coattails flap out behind her in the wind when she walks or runs. Fingerless gloves.

He glances at her. Phoebe freezes. The images in her mind shatter like smashed mosaics. She can't breathe. He holds her gaze a fraction longer than is necessary, and Phoebe's cheeks get hot. He turns away, and her stomach tingles. She's excited, dry mouthed.

It's two days later—when Fi has an early dentist appointment and doesn't come for the bus—that Phoebe has an empty seat beside her when her manga guy boards the bus.

He comes down the aisle, and as he nears her seat, he says, "Hey. Okay if I sit here? Or is it taken?"

"No. I mean yes. Uh, it's not taken." She blushes and scoots over slightly. Her heart, her blood, her whole body is racing. She looks out the window, but she *feels* him beside her, his warmth. His presence. She can't even begin to think of what to say to him, or even if she should say anything at all.

The bus pulls into the street. The noise of the kids rises into a mad cacophony as someone throws an apple at someone else. The bus driver yells a warning for everyone to calm down and remain seated.

"So, you live up the street from me," he says.

Surprise ripples through Phoebe. *He noticed.*

"Yeah." She glances up at him. He's looking down at her. He's so utterly perfect. She can't believe he's real and sitting beside her, talking to her. His complexion is a pale khaki color. His eyes are pools of mystery.

After noticing him the first time, she went home after school and began to draw a storyboard where he is a captain fighting for a force of righteousness, and she's his dark and devilish sidekick who uses magic and is not always up to good, and for a moment Phoebe feels as though he can see right into her mind, that he sees her secret images, her desires and dreams, sees the box of dark-pink hair dye she plans on buying from the drugstore this weekend, which she will use next Friday maybe, when her mom and dad leave her to babysit Matthew. Perhaps Fi will come and help her.

"My name's Joe," he says.

"Phoebe," she replies as the bus bumps and rumbles on, and the kids' voices rise to a shrill.

"I thought maybe you'd be in one of my classes, but I guess not."

Her face goes warmer. He, like so many others, has mistaken her for being in her midteens. She already knows that Joe is his name. Joe Harper. And that he's in grade ten. Which means he's around fifteen or sixteen. She's only twelve. She's in the seventh grade, and she's one of the youngest kids in her class. Her birthday just made the cutoff. But Phoebe can easily look fifteen or sixteen, especially with makeup. She also knows now that Joe actually started at their school in March. It's only since he moved onto their street and started taking this bus that she noticed him, though.

"So where do you come from?" She steers the subject away from age and grades.

He laughs and it sounds a bit rueful, which piques Phoebe's interest. She regards his eyes as she waits for him to answer.

"You mean most recently? Because we move, like, at least every two years."

"That is so cool."

"No, it's not. It's . . . I don't know. I've had enough of it. I wanted to stay in the last place we lived. In a town not far from Toronto. I liked the school. I had friends. But my mom said we needed to come west for some work she was doing. We only just recently moved into Story Cove, though. We were living closer to downtown, and I was busing into school from there. But our apartment lease was short term and we were going to be forced into a smaller one, until my mom met some guy at her work who helped organize the cottage at the end of Oak End for us." He laughs and repeats, "End of Oak End. Sounds like it's really the end." He falls silent, then says, "I hope so. Would be nice to stay in one place at last."

Phoebe laughs, too, and it feels so good. Like they're sharing something intimate.

"The cottage comes with a studio, which is great for my mom's art."

"She's an artist?" Phoebe already knows, of course, that she is.

"Well, it's not her job, although she does sell pieces."

"So where does she *work* work?"

"At the tavern on Main, waiting on tables."

Phoebe stares at him. Most of her mom's friends are things like therapists, or lawyers, or doctors, or they own businesses like wool shops or coffee shops, or they're stay-home moms who hover over their kids and go to yoga and to the spa for deep tissue massages and mani-pedis. None of them would *ever* wait on a table.

He reads something in her face and smiles. "I call her Renaissance Mom, a.k.a. Super Mom."

He's not embarrassed. No fucking stupid pretensions. This is so incredibly romantic. She's read about starving artists and all that—famous people needing to wait tables until they score a big break. Her heart swells. The way he talks about his mother seals the deal—Phoebe Bradley is now 100 percent sold on Joe Harper.

"I'd like to be an artist, too," she confesses. "Well . . . I do art, but not painting. Mostly digital on my iPad."

He glances at her lap, where her iPad rests on top of a fat fantasy novel she's reading.

"You have any on there I can see now?"

Her face goes hot again. If Joe sees her manga drawings, he might realize right away that she's depicting him. She is rescued by the students erupting en masse from their seats as the bus pulls into the school driveway.

Phoebe and Joe join the throng of kids and coats and backpacks and noise jostling down the aisle and tumbling like jelly beans out of the yellow bus.

"Hey," he hesitantly calls after her as she heads for the school entrance. She stops, turns. A breeze blows her hair back, and the students part like a sea around Phoebe and Joe as the kids continue their surge toward the school entrance. He comes up close, hesitates. "Wanna go to that pizza place on Main after school?"

Phoebe is momentarily lost for words. She has chores. She has to babysit later. She will also have to ask her mother, and then Joe will want to know why, and it will come out that she's only twelve.

"I have a late-afternoon shift there," he offers. "Plus it's Friday." He smiles. "I also get discounts."

None of the kids she knows have part-time jobs, or worry about discounts for food. She suddenly develops a desperate desire for pizza.

"They have vegetarian?"

"Of course." His grin deepens. "I'm a veggie, too. So is my mom."

Phoebe melts. And everything that is Joe Harper and his single mother who live in the garden cottage with the studio down the road is exactly what she wants in her life.

"Sure," she says.

"Good," he says.

"Well . . . I should go." She gestures with a tilt of her head to the school doors.

"Yeah, me too. My first class is in the shop, though. Auto mechanics. So I'm headed that way."

She smiles, then turns and heads up the stairs. At the top, she glances over her shoulder.

Joe is watching her, and he gives a small, self-conscious wave, which strikes her as both macho and terribly sweet.

LILY

NOW

Lily waits on a plastic chair in the reception area of the police station with the bag of fresh clothing on her lap.

Each time the door swings open, she tenses, thinking it's Tom.

When it finally swings open again and she sees Dianne and Tom, Lily is slammed by shock. She knew her husband's clothing had been taken, but she didn't expect him to look like this, like a prisoner, in a navy sweat suit with crime booties as temporary shoes. She realizes too late she forgot to pack shoes for Tom. She was distracted by the arrival of Detective Toshi Hara—she didn't think about bringing footwear.

She rises from the chair, clutching the bag of clothing tightly to her stomach with both hands.

"Tom?"

His complexion is bloodless. Stubble shadows his jaw, and his hair sticks up where it dried oddly. He looks exposed, vulnerable. Crumpled. Worst of all—Tom looks shamed. And scared. Which makes her frightened.

His gaze meets hers, and Lily also reads something deeper and far more complex in his eyes. Her attention shoots to Dianne. Her friend in contrast is all spit and polish, shoulders squared, spine straight as an arrow, chin held high, and her eyes are . . . angry?

Lily has known Dianne for fourteen years, ever since they first met at the gym and learned they shared a personal trainer. At the time, Lily and Tom had just moved as newlyweds into their Story Cove house, and Lily was preparing to launch her own therapy practice.

Lily has always been able to confide in Dianne, the woman with whom she drinks a little too much, usually at the Ocean Bay Hotel overlooking the sea. But right now Dianne Klister seems a stranger, and Lily realizes she's seeing her girlfriend in full-fledged work mode for the first time ever. And she appears every bit as formidable as the press has always made her out to be. Detective Toshi Hara's words surface in her mind.

She's your husband's lawyer, Mrs. Bradley. Not yours. She's going to be working for him, not you.

Lily recalls the confidences she confessed to Dianne the last time they drank at the Ocean Bay Hotel, and her blood chills. "Is . . . is everything okay?" she asks. But it's not. Clearly nothing is okay.

Dianne says crisply, "We'll talk later. Are those Tom's clothes?" She tilts her chin toward the bag Lily is clutching.

"There are media vans and reporters outside the station," Lily says as she hands the bag to Tom. "And out front of our house."

"Get changed in the washroom," Dianne tells Tom. "There's a men's room at the end of the hall. I'll speak to someone, see if I can get you guys out via the basement service entrance at the rear of the station. It leads into a small lane. I'll call for a vehicle to pick us up there." She digs in her purse for her mobile while Tom makes for the men's room with his bag.

When he returns he looks a little more normal, apart from the crime booties still on his feet, which make him shuffle a bit. A uniformed cop takes them all through the reception area and into a stairwell. They hurry down the stairs. Dianne ushers them through an underground parking garage and out into an alley lined with dumpsters. Lily reaches for Tom's hand. His skin is dry, cool. They're like fugitives as they stand in the drizzle, waiting for Dianne's driver.

A black sedan with tinted windows pulls up. Dianne hustles Lily and Tom into the back seat and climbs into the front passenger seat.

The driver wears glasses and a blank expression. He drives up the ramp and turns into a back lane behind the station. He proceeds down the lane, windshield wipers squeaking as drizzle comes down. They turn into a larger street, where Lily is relieved to see there are no media vans or reporters. They drive toward Oak End, furtive in their own little town, and Lily feels as though they have entered an alternate reality.

"They've identified the body," Tom tells her quietly.

Her gaze rockets to Tom's face. The look in his eyes is like a physical punch to her stomach.

"It's Arwen Harper," he says.

Lily's mouth opens.

Dianne swivels sharply in her seat to face them and says curtly, "We'll talk later."

Silence falls. Lily's heart pounds. They travel familiar streets, yet everything looks different. The narrative—the actual reality of their lives—has in fact changed. A memory fills her mind. She hears Arwen's voice in her head.

You think you know him? You think anyone can truly know their partners? He's been aware all this time what you are . . .

Lily extracts her hand from Tom's and angles her body away. Her eyes burn.

The vehicle turns into Oak End. She sees two media vans now, plus a white SUV with a radio station logo on the side. All parked in front of their house. Farther up the street a dark-blue sedan is parked under a cherry tree. It has aggressive bull bars and it screams *ghost car.* Lily suspects the cops might be staking them out until this is resolved. Until one of them—either she or Tom—slips.

"Okay," Dianne says, turning around in her seat. "When we exit the car, just look ahead and go directly into the house. And hold hands. Say nothing." She meets their gazes. "I mean nothing. Not to anyone. Not to your children. Not to your neighbors. No one is your friend right now, understand? And I don't want you saying anything to each other in front of me, either, or you lose any spousal privilege you might have should this get to court."

Lily's jaw goes tight.

The sedan pulls into their driveway. Reporters who until now were keeping out of the rain clamor out of the vehicles and come running with mikes. Cameras flash. Lily, Tom, and Dianne exit their vehicle and make for the front door. Lily and Tom hold hands tightly.

"Ms. Klister? Ms. Klister, are you defending Professor Bradley? Has he been charged with anything? Professor Bradley, did you know the victim? Dr. Bradley, was the victim ever a patient of yours?"

Dianne spins around to face the gaggle. "This is private property. Trespass, and your employers will not be impressed with the legal action that will come down like a ton of bricks on you all."

Another flash from a camera. As soon as they get inside and shut the door, Lily whirls to face her husband.

"*Arwen?* My God, Tom. How . . . how did this happen?"

"*You* tell *me*!" Tom barks at her. "You think *I* know what happened? What the fuck—"

"Lily," Dianne interrupts quickly as she places her manicured hand on Lily's arm. "Could you give me and Tom some time alone? I need to consult with him in private."

"Why alone?" Lily asks.

"We need to go through some things," Dianne says. "In private."

Lily's brain reels. "I don't understand. Why can't I sit in?"

"It's best that you and Tom do not discuss anything in front of me."

"She's my wife, for God's sakes, Dianne," Tom snaps. "You and Lily are *friends*. You're *our* lawyer."

"I'm *your* lawyer, Tom."

Lily stares at Dianne. A terrible cold sinking sensation slides through her gut.

"What did you mean, 'should this get to court,' Dianne? There's no chance Tom is going to be charged for anything . . . is there?"

"Let me talk to Tom. And let's see what the detective appears to feel so cocksure about, okay? And we can respond to that. No matter what anyone did, it's not our job to prove Tom's innocence. It's up to the police to prove guilt. They will have to provide irrefutable evidence beyond any reasonable doubt that he did something. And given that Tom hasn't been charged, clearly they don't have that right now."

Lily feels her jaw drop. "I—I can't believe this is happening," she whispers. She looks at Tom. She thinks of his bloody shirt. His lie to Detective Duval about his phone. She thinks of the barbecue and the terrible fight in the pool house, and of her and Tom's earth-shattering argument when they got home. She feels faint.

"Why can't you be lawyer to both of us?" she asks quietly.

"If this does end up going to trial, Lily, a prosecutor can subpoena you to testify against your husband. Right now, anything Tom might have told you in private could be protected by marital privilege, but other things are fair game. It's a bit of a fossil of a rule, but helpful. However, if Tom confesses anything to you in front of me, that privilege is gone."

Tom says, "I haven't done anything."

Lily says, "Do *I* need a lawyer?"

Dianne eyes her, and Lily knows her friend is recalling the confidences they shared over martinis—Lily's suspicions about Tom. She's acutely aware of how concerned Dianne became over what she perceived as Lily's growing paranoia. Or psychosis, even. Lily wonders if Dianne could—or would—use any of those confidences against her in her defense of Tom, just to demonstrate to a jury that someone other than Tom had motive, or opportunity, or means, to kill Arwen Harper.

Someone who was possibly even emotionally, or mentally, unstable. And worse. She could find out worse—Dianne's company uses sophisticated detectives.

"It would be a good idea to be prepared, just in case," Dianne says. "I can recommend someone if you like. Or if you'd prefer, I can find someone else for Tom, and I can represent you. But it's Tom who's under police scrutiny for murder, Lily. Not you."

Lily stares at her girlfriend. Her intimate drinking buddy, to whom she has revealed secrets. Would Dianne throw her under the bus just to win? Lily already knows the answer. Dianne is a legal shark who chases cases that can become causes célèbre. She *wants* cases that will play out in the media and in the courts of public opinion, and the more controversial the better. She will do *anything* not to lose. Dianne *is* her reputation. Dianne doesn't know how to be anything else. Lily just never thought she might end up on the wrong side of her friend's drive.

Before Tom can take Dianne into the study, Lily pulls him back, draws him aside. She whispers in his ear, "Whatever you do, Tom, whatever you say, remember the kids. Do it for the kids. They don't deserve this." Her gaze holds his, and the memory of the argument pulsates tangibly between them.

He cups her face. His eyes pierce hers. "I love you," he whispers. "I've always loved you. It'll be okay. Please trust me."

But all Lily can think of is how Tom has broken her trust.

LILY

THEN
May 20. Friday.

Four weeks before she dies.

Lily finds Dianne at "their" table on the terrace overlooking the pool and the ocean beyond. It's Friday, but book club has been canceled because Hannah has an appointment and the others decided to take a rain check. Since Lily considers Friday evenings "me time," she called Dianne to suggest a cocktail. Or three.

"I got started." Dianne grins, holding up a half-empty martini glass as Lily drapes her purse over the back of a chair and takes a seat.

A male server arrives almost instantly with a fresh round of drinks and a plate of oysters in their shells.

"I took the liberty of ordering for you, too," says Dianne, unfurling a white linen napkin as the server sets a martini in front of Lily.

Lily reaches hungrily for her drink. "You look pretty pleased with yourself this evening. What gives?" She takes a deep sip of her drink, relishing the alcohol burn through her chest.

"Won a big case."

"Congratulations. Cheers." Lily raises her glass. "I haven't seen anything in the news."

"You will tomorrow." Dianne reaches for a wedge of lemon.

"You mean the television exec? The one accused of raping six women?"

Dianne smirks and nods as she squeezes lemon over a raw oyster. "Verdict came in. Not guilty." She slips the oyster into her mouth and sucks the juice from the shell.

Lily lowers her drink and regards her friend. "He's guilty as fucking sin."

"Prosecution screwed up. I didn't. Hey, don't look at me like that, it's what I get paid the big bucks for—getting the law right." She reaches for her drink and leans back in her chair. "I'm no arbiter of morals. I just work within the letter of law."

"Is there anything you wouldn't do for a win, Dianne?"

"Nope."

"Ever feel . . . I don't know, dirty?"

"Oh, don't go trying to analyze me now, friend. You keep that in your office. Besides, we all have our dark places. Even you." She points her martini at Lily.

Lily laughs, but it sounds off to her own ears. The light has changed. The breeze feels cooler. She reaches for her sweater. As she drapes it around her shoulders, Lily uses the moment to survey the other patrons at the tables on the patio. Her sense of being watched is making her twitchy and hypervigilant. Her gaze is drawn to a man under the trellis. He's obscured partially by a pillar. Alone. Dark hair. Black shades. Dark jacket.

She returns her attention to Dianne, but the sensation of being observed spreads like cold in her stomach. Her mind drifts to the note left on her windshield outside the church.

You can't hide from Satan if Satan is inside your head.

That note was real. It was *not* her imagination. She's not being paranoid. Maybe she should tell Tom. She is also terrified of telling Tom, because then he'll ask why the words in the note are so upsetting to her, why they hold so much power.

"So how's Tom?" Dianne asks, as if reading Lily's mind.

Lily can't help what comes out of her mouth next.

"I . . . I think he's having an affair." Perhaps she says it to divert Dianne's attention, but now that it's been voiced, it hangs in the air like a tangible thing, and Lily realizes how much this notion has been eating at her.

Dianne lowers her drink. "What?"

Lily's cheeks heat. "I don't know why I said that. Forget about it." She reaches for her glass and swallows the rest of her martini in two big gulps. She raises her hand and motions to the server for another round.

Dianne continues to stare at her. "What makes you think this, Lily?"

"It's just . . . little signs, you know?"

"You mean you're being paranoid?"

"No. I mean Tom goes for longer and longer runs on the weekends. And he goes farther afield, like to the Elk Lake trails. He's also staying out later and later on Friday nights—he goes to the yacht after. I've smelled perfume on his shirt. He seems . . . distant. And Hannah said she saw Tom last Sunday running with a dark-haired woman when she drove past the bluffs. When I asked him about his run, he said it was just the usual, nothing different." The new round of drinks arrives, and Lily promptly takes a gulp. "He's also taking extra care with his appearance. New shirts. More time working out with his weights. Wearing aftershave. That sort of thing."

"Doesn't mean it's anything other than some midlife crisis. How old is Tom now? Isn't he, like, going to be sixty next year? That's a milestone that would mess with my head."

Lily gives a shrug and then forces a big, fake smile. "Probably. It's just in my head."

"Why don't you just ask him, Lily?"

"Maybe I'm afraid he'll say yes."

Dianne helps herself to another oyster. "And if he did say yes? What would you do?"

Lily swallows and looks at the sea.

"Probably kill her."

Dianne doesn't smile, because there's something in the way the words came out of Lily's mouth, a certain tone, that makes it seem as though she means it.

"If it was me," Dianne says, slowly, sitting back in her chair, "I'd get even. Have an affair myself."

"I'm not you." Lily reaches for her glass and finishes her second martini. The drinks are strong and she feels heady, surreal. "I have far too much invested in my marriage and my kids to do that." She feels a squeeze of emotion, and it catches her throat. "In truth, if he was being unfaithful, it would devastate me. I like my life the way it is, Dianne. Or the way I *thought* it was. I guess I've felt horribly smug for the last few years. I began to believe our marriage, our family, was pretty darn perfect." She pauses. "You have no idea how hard I've worked to make it so." Her voice fades. "No idea."

The server arrives with two more martinis.

"Oh, we didn't order more," Lily tells the waiter as he begins to set the glasses on their table.

"They're from the gentleman under the trellis," says the server. He places a white envelope next to the drinks. "He sent a note."

Lily whips around in her chair. The man she saw earlier has gone. Her heart beats faster.

"Which man?" she calls after the server. "Where is he?"

But the server disappears through the glass restaurant doors.

Dianne reaches for the envelope, opens it, and removes a white card with a single line of text.

Lily's mouth goes bone dry. She thinks of the note left on her windshield outside the church.

"What does it say?" she demands.

Dianne frowns. She shows Lily.

Enjoy the drinks. From someone who knows.

Lily snatches the card from Dianne's hand. It's been typed. The bottom right corner of the card is embossed. Lily runs her thumb over the raised embossing. It's in the shape of a goat's head. A goat with big horns. In the center of the goat's forehead is a pentacle—a five-pointed star. A noise begins in her head. She can't breathe.

You can't hide from Satan if Satan is inside your head.

"Lily?"

Dianne's voice sounds as though it's coming from far away, through a long tunnel.

"Lily!"

She shakes herself, tries to focus. She tastes bile in her throat as memories slice like shards of a broken mirror through her brain. She tries to make them go away, but everything inside her brain feels like a sharp kaleidoscope of disjointed images in a carnival house of horror.

"Are you okay, Lily? Are you unwell?" Dianne's hand is on Lily's arm. "Lily, look at me. Focus. What's going on? What's upset you?"

"That . . . that's the sign of Baphomet," she says, her voice hoarse.

"Of what?"

"The embossing. It's in the shape of Baphomet—the sabbatic goat. A pagan idol conflated with Satanism."

Lily lurches up. Clutching the card, she stumbles hurriedly over the patio in her high heels. She enters the restaurant through the glass sliding doors. She spins to her left, then her right, in search of the waiter who brought the note. She can't see him. She stops a female server. "The waiter who served our table, the one closest to the pool over there—" She points through the glass with a trembling hand. "Where is he?"

The employee looks startled by the intensity in Lily's voice.

"He clocked out for the day, can I perhaps help you?"

But Lily is already marching over to the bar.

"Who did this?" she calls out to the barman as she slaps the card onto the counter.

He comes over, glances at the card. He frowns. "Who did what?" he asks.

Lily jabs her fingers onto the card. "Who just bought two dirty martinis and had them sent with this card via our server to that table out there?" She points.

"Oh, right." The bartender glances around the establishment, searching for someone. "I can't see him. He must have left."

"What did he look like?"

"I was busy, I . . . didn't really take a good look. Average height. Dark hair. Thin face. Black jacket, black jeans. Excuse me—" He goes to attend to a customer at the far end of the bar.

Lily stares after him.

Dianne comes hurrying up, carrying Lily's purse. She hands the purse to her and puts her arm around Lily's shoulders. Gently, Dianne escorts Lily through the restaurant and out the front door of the hotel. When there is no one around, she says quietly, "Hey, what in the hell is going on?"

Lily's gaze drops to the card still clenched in her hand.

What sick game is this? This . . . If someone knows, it could destroy everything—my family, my marriage, my life. Everything.

Emotion pricks into her eyes. She inhales and looks away from Dianne.

"Lily, talk to me. What spooked you?"

"Someone printed text onto a card and came here and bought us drinks. It was premeditated."

"Look, you need to calm down. It's just a note from a guy who bought drinks for two women who probably looked to him as though they hadn't had a good lay in months."

"And how would he know I haven't had sex in months?"

"Oh, honey, I . . . Is this part of why you think Tom is seeing someone else? You think he's lost interest in you."

Tears fill Lily's eyes. She swipes at them. "It's me. I . . . I just have no libido right now, and I don't know what's going on. And I think I'm pushing him to look for sex elsewhere."

"Come here." Dianne gathers Lily into her arms and hugs her. She smells of expensive perfume and vodka, and slightly fishy from the oysters. She smooths a fall of hair off Lily's face and studies her friend's eyes. "You're in a bad way, my girl. And you're a little drunk. You and me both. How about we plan to get away from our families for some spa time in the next few weeks? And we can talk about stuff. Properly. You can tell me what's going on with you and Tom. Or . . . have you considered talking to a professional?"

"You mean therapy?"

"Even therapists need therapists, right? You're the one who always tells me that. Aren't you actually required to do that as part of your licensure because of the emotional impact of the work you do? You might have compassion fatigue, letting everyone dump on you all day. I bet you need a break—everyone else's trauma is getting to you. There's only so much a person can take in."

Lily breaks Dianne's gaze and sucks in a deep breath. Maybe she is losing her mind. But the note at the church was real. And this note in her hand with a satanic symbol is real. And in conjunction with the words *From someone who knows* . . . "I'm fine. Really. It's just . . . I . . . You're right. It's just stress. My patients' issues are weighing me down. I'll talk to someone."

Dianne frowns.

"It's fine. I'm fine. Honest." Lily fumbles in her purse for her phone. "I need to call a cab. Do you want me to call you one?"

"My driver is parked around the block." Dianne reaches for her own mobile and fires a text to her driver.

Dianne's car arrives first. She hesitates. "Are you sure you're okay?"

Lily forces a smile. "Of course." She makes a sign with her finger near her head. "A few too many strong martinis and a few too many crazy clients, that's all. Just need a break."

Dianne doesn't seem so sure.

"Go. Go," Lily says. "It's not like I'm going to go off killing anyone. Go. I'm fine."

As Dianne's car drives off, Lily curses.

"Killing anyone"? What in the fuck possessed me to say that?

Lily's cab arrives, and she gets in. "Can you take me to 2112 Oak End, please."

As the cab pulls out of the circular hotel driveway, her phone pings. It's a text from Tom. She reads it in the back of the cab.

Going to be late tonight. Don't wait up.

She types back quickly. Just heading home after drinks with Dianne. She hesitates, then types more. Are you going to the yacht club happy hour?

She hits SEND.

Waits.

A few moments later, a reply pings back.

Probably. Don't wait up.

Lily puts her head back and feels emotion expand like a painful balloon. She's even more convinced now that Tom is seeing someone. It's a really bad kind of growing feeling. Like the feeling of being watched. Gut instinct should not be underestimated, thinks Lily. The shrink in her knows that gut instinct is a very real phenomenon. Sometimes humans pick up micro clues, tiny subliminal signs that the conscious mind doesn't even register.

She quickly types another text to Tom.

Who with?

The reply bounces back instantly.

The usual.

She types:

Just the boys?

No reply comes. By the time the cab draws up outside the Bradley house, Lily's text to her husband still appears as unread.

RUE

NOW

Rue glances in the rearview mirror at Joe Harper, who is seated in the back of her unmarked vehicle. Toshi is in the passenger seat. They're driving Joe back to his home on Oak End.

Joe is motionless, staring out the window.

"You mentioned you were 'sort of' dating Phoebe Bradley?" Rue says as she turns into a side street, noting the location on the GPS.

Joe clears his throat. "Well, we're good friends. Close friends. But new friends, also. I only met her when we moved into Oak End."

"Which was when?" asks Rue.

"Last day of May."

"So, like, almost three weeks ago?" Toshi says.

"I guess."

"Do you know the rest of her family?" asks Rue.

"I've been to their house once, where I first met Mrs. Bradley briefly." He wavers, then says, "She kinda threw me out."

"Why?" asks Toshi.

Joe sits silent for a moment. "She feels I am too old for Phoebe. Mrs. Bradley—she was actually really furious about it. Phoebe told me later."

"How about your mother—she know the Bradleys well?" Rue asks.

There is silence in the back seat. Rue flicks her gaze up to the rearview mirror again. "Joe?"

He swipes tears from his eyes. "Phoebe might only be twelve, but she's much older in so many ways than the other girls in my grade. I . . ." Joe's voice chokes on emotion. "She gets me. But neither my mom nor Phoebe's mom got us. Mrs. Bradley tried to forbid Phoebe from seeing me, which just made Phoebe more rebellious. My mom and Mrs. Bradley had a big fight about it."

"When?" Rue asks.

"At the Codys' barbecue yesterday. I . . . I guess it's going to come out anyway that they had a big row in the Codys' pool house last night. A couple of people heard them, and Mr. Bradley and Mr. Cody went in there to stop them, and we all heard the yelling. Everyone was talking about it."

Rue and Toshi exchange a glance.

"And you know for a fact the fight was about you and Phoebe?" Rue asks.

He hesitates briefly. "Phoebe texted me when she got home. She said she thinks that's what started the fight. Her parents were still fighting at home."

"Did Phoebe say what else they argued about?" Rue asks.

He shakes his head.

"You mentioned you left the barbecue early, Joe. That was after the fight?" Toshi asks.

"Just after. Mr. Bradley took Mrs. Bradley home. Phoebe told me her dad came to fetch her and Matthew a little later. The younger kids were all in the recreation room downstairs in the main house, playing pool and listening to loud music and stuff, when the fight happened. I told my mom we should also leave, and she said she'd be dammed if she was going to let . . . 'that shrink woman' ruin her evening, and Mom was . . . she was drinking a fair bit, and she wanted more to drink. Most of the adults still at the party were pretty wasted by that time."

"So you left without your mother," Rue says.

"Yeah. I was mad at her. I . . . I was embarrassed for her. She was making a fool out of herself."

Toshi says, "And you didn't see her again?"

His eyes fill with tears, and he shakes his head. "I should have insisted. I should have *made* her come home with me."

"It's not your job to look after your mother, Joe," Rue says as she turns the vehicle onto Oak End.

"It sort of is," says Joe. "It's been like that for . . . My mom sometimes needs someone to watch out for her. She—she gets drunk, high, does stupid things."

Rue enters the circle at the end of the Oak End cul-de-sac and pulls up outside the address she programmed into the GPS. "This is your place?"

"Yes," says Joe.

She puts the vehicle in park, and they all get out. The rain has stopped. The sky is clearing and the breeze is turning warm again. Rue can smell the sea. They're parked right beside the trailhead where Tom Bradley led her into the forest this morning. She regards the trailhead, reframing the death in context of the presumptive ID they now have. Arwen Harper. And the fact that the dead woman lived right here and had argued with the wife of the man who found her body. And her son is dating the man's young daughter.

"Is that the Cody house?" Toshi asks, pointing at the large two-story across the cul-de-sac.

"Yeah," says Joe.

Rue's attention goes to the house. A figure moves in front of the attic window. Then, just as quickly, it's gone. Rue gets a strange feeling in her gut as she studies the window. She's learned to trust her gut.

They follow Joe through a gate on the side of the property, and Rue catches sight of an old blue VW van painted with huge white snowflakes parked under a carport. It has an Ontario registration.

"Is this the van you and your mother drove west, Joe?" she asks.

"Yeah. The cottage entrance is around the side of the main house, over this way." He leads them along a little path lined with rosebushes.

Rue casts a backward glance over her shoulder. The figure is back in the attic window across the street, but standing just to the side of the window, watching them, as if not wanting to be seen.

LILY

NOW

"What did you tell Dianne?" Lily asks Tom.

She and Tom face each other in the kitchen. Their kids are still at school, and Dianne has just left the house. Media vans are still parked outside, and a cop car lurks down the street.

Her husband's gaze bores into hers. The tension is cold and thick and hangs like something physical between them.

Slowly, quietly, cautiously, Tom says, "I told her that I—we—knew Arwen. That she lived down the road, worked at the Red Lion, was our regular server at happy hour, and that Phoebe was very friendly with her son." He pauses. "I told her there was an argument in the pool house at the Codys' last night."

She stares at him. Numb.

"The cops are going to find out, Lily. Dianne doesn't need surprises. I also told her I was with you all day yesterday, from after you went to church with the kids and I went for my run to when we all went to the barbecue. I told her you and I came home together, we drank some more, then you took a sleeping pill and went to bed, and I returned to the Cody house to fetch the kids. Then I went to bed." He breaks eye contact.

"And what else? What *else* did she ask you?"

"She asked if I was certain that you took a sleeping pill."

"What do you mean?"

"Like, was I sure you were knocked out cold by the meds."

"You told her I was, right?"

He swallows, nods. "Right. I think you were out cold."

Lily feels a shift. "Tom . . . this . . . this is what you told the detectives?"

"I didn't tell them anything. Dianne is just figuring if we can use you as my alibi."

The *we* versus *you* is a gut punch. Slowly, Lily says, "If I was knocked out cold, it could be argued I wouldn't have noticed if you got up and left the house."

"I was asleep the whole time," he counters. "I had too much to drink. I . . . I wouldn't have even noticed if *you* got up and left the house."

She stares at him. "I can't believe this is happening."

Tom touches his neck, where the scratch marks are red and inflamed.

"Did they ask about those?"

"I told Dianne they were from energetic sex. You and me."

Lily feels ill. She lowers herself onto the barstool, thinking of how she told Dianne she and Tom had not had sex in a while. She turns away, closes her eyes. "Why did you say that?"

"I just did. I got freaked out. I said it. If I take it back now, I look like I'm lying to her about other things, too."

"Why did you hide your shirt in the shed, Tom? Why is it full of blood? I found it and washed it, you know?"

He swallows. "I . . . saw her lying there on the beach, all broken, and I dropped to my knees, and sort of lifted her, to try and resuscitate her, and—but she was dead. So I ran home, and when I got here . . . I . . . I couldn't come inside our house with her blood all over me. I wasn't thinking straight. I was in shock."

"So you *knew* it was her when you saw her?"

"I . . . sort of blocked that possibility out of my mind at first."

"Where is your red jacket?"

"I took it off to cover her face."

Lily swears softly and rubs her face hard. "And your flashlight. Matthew saw you, you know? Leaving with a flashlight and jacket and returning without them."

"I dropped it when I fell racing home. It went into the bushes somewhere, and it had gotten light enough to run without it, so I kept going."

"So you left your jacket, lost your flashlight, ran home in a bloody shirt, and on the way into the yard, you passed Virginia Wingate sitting in her car outside the gate, then you unlocked the shed, went inside, hid your bloody shirt in a bin, ran upstairs shirtless in filthy shoes, and you got a new shirt and a jacket on before talking to the cops," she says, holding his gaze.

Silence.

"Why did you lie to them about your phone charging in the kitchen?"

He drops his face into his hands and scrubs his stubble. "I was hungover. Still fuzzy. After seeing her like that . . . I was confused . . . in shock. I was scared, okay? Given . . . given what happened in the pool house. It just came out when the cop asked why I called 911 from home."

"Jesus, Tom. Do you know how this looks?"

"And why did *you* go and wash my shirt, Lily?"

She glowers at him.

"Why?" he demands.

"Because *you* were trying to hide it, that's why. And I got scared, too. I didn't know what to do. There was a cop outside, and I was worried he'd come in and find it. I saw you going into the shed, and . . . I just got scared, Tom. I . . . I don't know what to think."

"You think I did it? You think I could have killed her?"

Silence.

He swears violently, drags both hands over his hair, then stills as something appears to dawn on him. Quietly, he says, "Tell me, on our children's lives, Lily: Did you leave the house after I fell asleep?"

Her heart begins to race. Her skin prickles with heat. She stares at her husband.

"Did you?"

She glances away.

"Lily?"

She inhales deeply, then meets Tom's gaze again. "We're each other's alibis, remember. We were here together all night."

Something changes in his face. He nods slowly and his mouth goes hard. And Lily can see what has entered her husband's mind, and she feels sick.

"You honestly don't think I could do something like that, Tom? Please, tell me you don't."

Emotion fills his eyes. "I don't know what to think anymore, Lily."

Mistrust, suspicion, blooms between them like a thick and tangible and shifting and growing thing, and Lily knows their life can never be the same again. The day Arwen Harper rolled into town in her blue VW bus painted with huge white snowflakes, with her sixteen-year-old son riding shotgun, was the day everything started to change. It was the beginning of the end.

Very quietly, she says, "Whatever either one of us thinks, Tom, or what either one of us has ever done—"

"I didn't do anything," he says.

"Regardless. Whatever happens now, we need to protect the kids." She holds his gaze. "Do you understand me? Can we agree on that one thing? Can you promise me that we will do *anything* to protect Phoebe and Matthew? To try to keep our family intact?"

"It might not be possible anymore, Lily," he says so softly she can barely hear.

"It has to be, Tom."

TOM

THEN
May 20. Friday.

Four weeks before she dies.

There is often a defining moment of trespass, and it's usually small, barely noticeable. Whether it's holding eye contact a fraction of a second too long, responding to a flirtatious text, or leaving a pub to go somewhere else when you've already had a little too much to drink. And once that fine—almost invisible—line has been crossed, it's like a plane at the instant of takeoff: It has no choice but to become airborne. Or crash. Tom knows on some level he's approaching this moment when Arwen says yes to Milton's suggestion they all repair to Simon's boat at the marina for a nightcap.

"How about you, Tom?" Simon asks as they all shrug into their jackets after a Red Lion happy hour that has already stretched well into drunken nighttime territory.

He hesitates.

"Oh, come on, Tom," says Arwen as she belts her coat. She's clocking out early tonight. She's accepted Simon's invitation, and her smile is bright, and her eyes crackle with fun and promise.

He glances at Simon, and he thinks of Lily, who went to meet Dianne for cocktails at the Ocean Bay Hotel. Lily will probably be home late. And Tom feels a fierce spurt of jealousy and rivalry when Simon places his big hand at the small of Arwen's back as they exit the tavern doors.

He reaches for his phone and quickly types up a text: Going to be late tonight. Don't wait up.

Lily's response is instant.

Just heading home after drinks with Dianne. Are you going to the yacht club happy hour?

Tom looks up from his phone and stares at the door, where Arwen has exited with Simon. He types: Probably. Don't wait up.

His phone pings.

Who with?

He types: The usual.

He pockets his phone and hurries after the boys, who are ambling down the road toward the marina with Arwen, her skirt and hair blowing in the wind.

The air outside is fresh. Clouds scud across stars, and a full moon rises over the water. Blossoms glow under the streetlights, and they carpet the sidewalk and the roofs of cars.

As he hastens to catch up with the group, his head begins to clear. He is reminded of the Sunday before last, when he went running and bumped into Arwen near the bluffs—also on a run. They laughed about how they'd just met the night before at the Red Lion, where she'd worked only a week. And they ran together for a while. Breathing hard, in perfect unison. It felt good.

Too good.

Because last Sunday he made sure he ran at the exact same time, hoping to encounter her again. And he did. There she was on the Garry Bluffs lookout platform, stretching her hamstrings, cheeks pink. They jogged together along the road that led to Manfred Hill, and together they powered up the twisting trail to the Manfred summit, where they laughed and caught their breath and marveled at the view.

An image of Lily shimmers into his mind.

Tom stalls. He thinks about his kids. His family. What Lily means in his life. How profound their bond. He sucks in a deep breath and jogs up to the group. "Hey, guys, I'm taking a rain check. Maybe next time."

They try to persuade him, but Tom waves good night and heads down the road. His home is not far, and he enjoys the walk. He feels solid about what he's just turned down.

A second later he hears footfalls behind him.

"Tom! Wait up."

He turns. "Arwen?"

"I figured you had the right idea. Walk with me?"

He wavers. "I—I didn't know you lived this way. I thought you told me that you drove to the bluffs to run on Sundays. I . . . thought you mentioned you lived nearer the city."

"I do. My bus stop is this way. Two blocks over."

"You don't drive to work?"

"Van is at the shop. Got some transmission issue." She smiles. The lamplight catches her throat. Creamy, white. Her tattoo moves as though the beast is alive. A gust of wind ruffles her curls. He feels a hot punch of desire low in his belly.

"I can call you a cab," he offers.

"God, Tom, you sound like you'll do anything rather than walk with me tonight."

Silence quivers into the air between them. A few blossoms fall.

"Of course not." His voice comes out thick.

"Besides, I actually like the bus. Especially at night—seeing different kinds of people. There's an appealing rawness to humanity the later it gets. I find it inspiring. For my art."

Tom studies her for a moment. Her eyes glint in the refracted light. He feels another uncomfortable yet deliciously delirious punch of desire. He clears his throat and begins to walk. She falls in step with him. He already told her on their last run that he lives on Oak End, just on the other side of the Spirit Forest Park from Garry Bluffs.

"Not enough base 'humanity' on display for you on Friday nights at the Red Lion Tavern, then?" he asks.

She laughs. A sound that burbles—yes, he thought that word, *burbles*—up from her chest. Infectious. He's drunk, he thinks. She's comfortable to walk beside. Her stride long and easy. It's like running with her. Her peasant skirt, the occasional sound of her bracelets. This fortune-telling, free-spirited artist-waitress. She's everything his life no longer is. She exudes energy, volatility. His life is routine. He's in a rut, really.

His thoughts turn to sex again. He tamps his desire down.

Yet there's something about Arwen Harper Tom cannot suppress. She's hooked him somewhere deep. He saw the scars on the insides of her wrists. He suspects it's why she wears so many bracelets. To hide or distract from the scars. Or maybe even to attract the eye to them. It intrigues the psychologist in Tom, the student of deviant human minds, the mental health advocate. And it sparks an innate compassion in him.

Arwen, a beautiful, sexual woman, has also flattered the baser side of Tom—the aging male whose wife is off sex for reasons Tom is still trying to figure out.

"I used to walk everywhere when I was a kid," she offers. "I lived in a small prairie town." A pause. "A safe town. Or it was safe once."

"Where did you grow up?"

"The early part of my life—a suburb of Medicine Hat."

Tom's chest tightens. "Oh . . . where?" He strives for a casual tone, but he hears the notes in his voice hitting false.

She glances up at him. "Do you know the area?"

Something in Tom says, *Be careful.* "Not really."

"It was a little place called Glenn Dennig."

Tom goes cold. A memory sifts through him.

"Do you know it?" she asks.

"Heard of it."

She falls silent as they walk, as though waiting for him to explain how he might have heard of a tiny neighborhood in the prairies called Glenn Dennig.

Instead, he says, "So is it far—I mean, the bus route to your house?"

"It's on a main artery into the city, so doesn't take long. And it's not a house that we live in. It's a tiny apartment with a bunch of university students as noisy neighbors."

"We?"

"I have a son."

Surprise spears through Tom. "I . . . had no idea."

"Why should you? I never told you. Joe. He's sixteen."

"Are . . . you—is his father around? I mean, does he—"

"I'm single." A beat of silence. "I'm a widow, Tom."

He stops walking. "Arwen, I'm sorry. When—"

"Just over two years ago. Cancer. We'd split up before he got ill, though. So . . ." Her voice fades. She clears her throat. "It—I guess it ultimately precipitated our move west. A fresh start for me and Joe." She starts walking again, and he hastens to catch up, to keep pace, because her stride has lengthened and quickened and seems fired by sudden emotion.

"Might have been a dumb idea," she says crisply. "At least for Joe. He's at that age—it's a transformative and difficult time where he seems to need the friends he left behind, and a sense of place—a sense of home, which he'd begun to feel. Sometimes I think he resents me every day. Especially now that we're being evicted."

"Evicted—seriously?"

"I don't joke about eviction."

This is the first time he's seen this side of Arwen. The real side, he realizes. The rest is facade. Being a smiling free spirit is hard work in reality, it seems. It runs contrary to nurturing a kid in a stabilizing home environment.

"I'm hunting for a new place. I saw something yesterday I might end up taking. It's awful, though, but it's all I can find right now. A basement suite with windows up high, like prison cells. It smells dank. And it's even smaller than what we've got now." She gives a forced-sounding laugh. "Joe will probably resent me even more. But the rental situation is tight. When we arrived I was in line for an apartment on Story Cove Main Street, just up the road from the tavern, which is why I took the job there. It's also why I put Joe into the Story Cove school system, but the rental fell through."

They reach the street corner where they will need to part ways. The moon filters through the trees.

"This is me," Arwen says. "Bus stop is half a block up. See you next week?"

"Wouldn't miss it."

She hesitates, then says, "Night, Tom."

He says good night, but she's already walking away.

"Arwen?" he calls after her.

She stops.

"There's a place available for rent at the end of our street. It's—"

"Oh, Tom, no—there's no way that would be in my budget. Oak End? Nice try—"

"It's a garden cottage, with a studio."

She angles her head. The moonlight hits her cheek.

"It's just come available," he says. "I mean, the old guy who lived there had a stroke last week and was moved into a care facility. I know the property owners pretty well—they live out of the country, and basically, the place is almost rent-free—a minimal cost for someone who'll keep an eye on the property, check the garden service comes and that the security system for the main house keeps functioning. If . . . I mean, I'd be happy to cover the basic charge for you if it would help. With your son."

Her mouth opens, then shuts. She glances away. Emotion glints in her eyes.

Without looking at him, she says softly, "Is this the place across the road from Simon's house?"

Surprise kicks his stomach. Confusion crumples through his brain. "Uh, it is. Do . . . you know about it?"

"Simon told me he thought it might become available soon. But I don't think he knows the owners."

Tom stares at her. His brain reels. Recent memories flash through his mind: Simon touching Arwen's arm. Simon saying goodbye after a night at the tavern, leaning too close to Arwen as he says something in her ear. Arwen's hand on Simon's shoulder as she laughs at something the guy said.

Has he just been played?

Has he offered to install a mistress for Simon across the cul-de-sac—a convenient place for his mate to screw their waitress almost under the nose of his wife and kids?

Jesus, stop it, Tom.

Arwen comes closer and touches his arm. He feels a curdle of sensation in his chest.

"There is no way on this earth I would take your money, but thank you for your generosity, Tom. And if you do have any influence with those owners . . . I cannot tell you how much it would mean to me.

And to Joe. Especially Joe. For him to be close to school, and for me to be within walking distance of the tavern."

And for Simon.

The appeal of Friday happy hour shifts toward something more nefarious. He feels the promise of pleasure with the guys leaking through his fingers. Tom feels a fault line chasing through the structure that underpins his friendship with Simon and the boys. The dynamic has changed. A woman has come between them.

And he's installing her on his street.

"I'll phone them tomorrow," he says.

She leans up on her toes and gives him a quick kiss on his cheek. He feels the soft brush of her lips across his skin. "Thank you," she whispers near his ear, too close, because it sends shivers down his spine and an erection presses against his pants, and he suddenly dislikes himself.

She steps back. "Maybe I'll see you on the bluffs this Sunday? Simon says he runs, too."

"Right. Of course."

"Night, Tom." She raises her hand and is gone into the moonlit darkness.

Tom stands there awhile. A breeze rustles through the neighborhood. A raccoon crosses the road, looks at him, then scuttles into the bushes. He wonders what he's done. Or is still about to do. What line has he crossed already, and just how far will he go?

How far has Simon gone?

And there's a more malign niggle, like a fingernail ticking on the glass periphery of his consciousness.

A little place called Glenn Dennig.

TAKEN

A True Crime Story

On Saturday, April 22, in 1989, a warm haze pressed down over Glenn Dennig, a sleepy prairie town located along the outskirts of Medicine Hat. To the residents of the suburb, the evening air felt unusually warm for early spring. They didn't mind. The warmth shimmered with the promise of a hot, dry summer. Soon the cactus plants on the semiarid prairie would be alive with flowers, and the scent of hot sagebrush would hang in the air. After the grip of a long, bleak winter on the western plains, a feeling of excitement mounted as layers of clothes were shed and dreams turned to new gardening tools, bags of potting soil, sales on barbecues and patio furniture and lawn mowers, and the lure of camping adventures in the deep coulees that harbored dinosaur bones and snake pits. Building a new greenhouse was topmost in Sergeant Mark Wozniak's mind as he patrolled the highway through town in his cruiser. He got the call at 8:58 p.m.

"I just knew it was going to be big—something we had not dealt with before. It was not going to be good,"

Wozniak told a journalist later.

The police dispatcher informed Wozniak that a male in Glenn Dennig had looked in through a neighbor's lit basement window and seen "a body with blood."

Wozniak immediately called in that he was responding. He engaged his sirens and sped to the address relayed by the dispatcher.

He was first on the scene.

His initial observation was of neighbors standing outside their houses on lawns, some in dressing gowns, pointing the way for him.

Wozniak screeched his cruiser to a halt in front of an average-looking Glenn Dennig rancher. The lights were on inside. He wasn't sure what he was dealing with—a possible domestic dispute, a homicide, a murder-suicide.

He exited his vehicle, went around the side of the house, and peered in through the basement window.

Nothing in his career had prepared Wozniak for what he saw through that window.

Waiting for him inside that brightly lit house was a scene that would forever stamp a dark and infamous mark in the annals of Canadian criminal history. And a scar deep in Wozniak's soul.

RUE

NOW

Rue and Toshi duck under an arbor thick with climbing jasmine as they follow Joe to his ivy-clad cottage. Behind the cottage the towering conifers of the Spirit Forest Park forest brood somber and silent. Water drips everywhere. Rue glances at Toshi. She can see he's feeling it, too—as if the forest is a presence, watching, waiting, rustling softly in an invisible breeze.

Joe unlocks the front door and shows them inside.

"It's only got the one bedroom, which I use," Joe explains. "My mom spends all her time in the studio over there."

The studio is across the lawn from the cottage, closer to the forest. It's a flat, rectangular building, concrete sides, much like a garage.

"As I said, my mom sleeps in the studio. And it has a kitchenette."

Joe still speaks of his mother in the present tense. It's understandable, thinks Rue. He hasn't seen her battered body, hasn't accepted yet that it is in fact his mom who was found dead on the beach.

The cottage is neat inside. At the entrance is a rack for shoes, coat hooks. An oval table stands next to an open-plan kitchen that has a counter with two stools. The living room area is the size of a postage stamp. A wood-burning fireplace looks as though it's been used recently. The scent of smoke still lingers in the air. Odd for summer, thinks Rue.

But then, the cottage in the shadow of the woods probably sees little sun, and it is cold.

"My bedroom is through the door behind the kitchen," says Joe. "And there's a small bathroom there." He points to a door.

"You mentioned your mother's running shoes were gone—did she leave them by this door?" Rue asks.

"Yeah. And her jacket usually hangs on that hook with her headlamp and cap."

"And you said she usually runs with her cell phone?" asks Toshi as Rue slowly scans the interior.

There are photographic studies of Arwen Harper on the walls. She was a beautiful woman, in a bohemian way. A ball forms in Rue's stomach. It feels like jealousy. And something more—a sick kind of gnawing, growing guilt over something she cannot dwell on right now. There is definitely a familiarity about this woman. But if she does turn out to be the woman Rue stalked, then she's already crossed a line, and with each second she's getting in deeper. She tells herself again that it can't be her.

"Yeah, like I said, I tried to call her cell, but there was no answer."

No phone was found with the body. Rue notices a canvas bag on the bench near the entrance. It's partially open, and a swimming towel and goggles are visible. The corner of the towel has a gym logo. WINDSOR PARK RECREATION CENTRE.

She stares at it, her chest going tighter. "Your mother's?" she asks.

"She likes to swim," says Joe. "She says water is a symbol of the unconscious, and she feels she needs to immerse herself in it in order to create. My mom has a bunch of weird ideas like that, including reading tarot cards." He shifts his weight and suddenly rubs his eyes, making them redder and puffier. The kid is exhausted. He looks like he's going to collapse.

"Is your mother a member at the Windsor Park center, Joe?" she asks gently.

He nods. "She works out in the gym there, too. And she likes running. I . . ." The air seems to suddenly punch out of him, and tears flood into his eyes. He swipes them away. "I'm sorry."

"You need to get some rest, Joe. If we can get those medical contacts for your mother, and if we could just take a quick look inside her studio, we can return later once we have a scientifically confirmed identification. Then we can all talk more, and we can get a team in here to take a detailed look around if necessary, if that's okay with you?"

He nods and goes to a chest of drawers. He opens the top drawer, rummages through it, and pulls out a few pieces of paper.

"Here." He hands over the papers. "They're medical bills she hasn't paid yet. And probably didn't intend to. We're always getting demands for delinquent payments and stuff. One of the bills is for her doctor in Oakville, Ontario, where we lived. And there's one from her dentist, and another from her therapist. Their contact details are all in there."

Rue glances at the invoice for the therapist. "Your mother was undergoing psychological counseling?"

He swallows and looks down. "Ah . . . yeah, she . . . she struggled with stuff. She tried to kill herself before I was born."

Rue and Toshi go quiet.

Joe looks up. "She never did anything like that after I was born. She wouldn't. I only know because she has scars on the insides of her wrists and I asked her about them."

Toshi glances at Rue. Rue didn't see the insides of the woman's wrists when she was on the beach—she never moved the cuffs of her jacket. The scars will also help to confirm ID.

"Was your mom seeing a therapist here, too, Joe?"

He shakes his head. "She said she was doing okay."

Rue hands the medical papers to Toshi. "Where can we find a hairbrush and toothbrush used by your mom? In her studio?"

"Yeah. I'll take you there now."

Joe goes into the kitchen, opens a small clay pot on the windowsill, and takes out a key.

They follow him outside and across the lawn to the studio. He lets them in, switches on the lights, and stands back.

In contrast to the cottage, it looks as if a hurricane has hit in here. As Rue enters she bumps a bike leaning against the wall near the door. It clatters to the tiled floor. Her heart jumps. She reaches down, picks it up, and places it carefully back against the wall. It has a pannier on either side of the rear wheel, and a reflective decal in a swoosh shape on the crossbar.

"She rides to the gym sometimes," Joe says.

Large paintings in various stages of creation cover the walls. A blank canvas rests on an easel near the rear window. Paint, bottles, jars, and brushes litter an old wood table next to the easel.

Rue and Toshi stare, transfixed by the dark paintings—bold, red slashes of oil paint streak like blood across black swirls with splashes of yellow. Others depict half-beast, half-human creatures like the tattoo on her neck. Another shows a figure with no face in a hooded cloak holding a scythe and standing on a bed of human skulls.

"Wow," says Toshi.

"My mom has a death fixation," Joe says quietly. "She painted those in Ontario. We transported them in the van."

Rue goes up to the painting. Pinned to the wall beneath it is a piece of paper with handwritten text that reads:

It's best not to resist the change the "Death" tarot card brings. Resisting will make transition difficult. And painful. Instead one should let go, embrace the necessary change, see it as a fresh start. The Death card is a sign that you need to draw a line through the past in order to move forward. It says: Release what no longer serves you.

"They're . . . disturbing," Toshi says.

"Mom always says art should come from the disturbed and disturb those who are comfortable."

Rue thinks of the invoice for the psychotherapist. She walks toward another painting. It shows a female face split into two disjointed parts.

"Mom calls that one *Apate*," says Joe. "After a Greek goddess. She also has a tattoo of this goddess on her hip."

"Who's Apate to the Greeks, then?" asks Toshi.

"She's the personification of trickery, of deception and guile," says Joe. "The goddess of lies. Apate was one of the evil spirits released from Pandora's box, and once she was free, she roamed the earth for millennia, sowing havoc wherever she went, using her gifts to deceive people. Mom says mostly people deceive themselves, that's why the face in her painting is split like that."

Rue crooks up a brow. She moves toward an odd-looking cabinet mounted on the wall in front of a table—essentially a giant corkboard behind doors that are open. Pushpins pock the board, and there are holes where there were more pins that have since been removed. Beneath some of the pins are tiny scraps of paper, as though whatever was stuck up there has been ripped off.

"What's this for?" she asks.

"For a project she was working on."

"What kind of project?"

"She was private about a lot of things, and this was one of them. Some stupid big-ass secret, so secret she locked it behind those doors whenever she wasn't busy with it. Big enough that we had to move across the country and come here so she could work on it. She claims it was going to be our major break."

"And she was hiding this from you?"

He inhales deeply. "I don't know what she was hiding it for." He stares at the board. "Sometimes I think she hid things from herself, so that she didn't have to look at them until it was absolutely necessary."

"So there was stuff pinned here?" Toshi asks.

"I don't know. I only ever saw it with those doors closed and locked. She had a laptop set up on this table in front of the board, but it's gone. I've looked everywhere. I can't find it, or her phone."

Rue and Toshi exchange another glance. No phone. No computer. All her electronics gone?

A knock sounds on the studio door. They all jerk around in surprise.

The studio door creaks open.

"Joe?" A woman appears. She sees the cops, and her eyes go wide. "Joe? Is everything okay?"

But Joe is suddenly sheet white. Silent. Staring at the door. As though he expected to see his mother walking in.

"I'm Hannah," the woman says awkwardly. "Hannah Cody from across the street."

ARWEN

THEN
June 7. Tuesday.

TWELVE DAYS BEFORE SHE DIES.

It's Arwen's day off from the tavern, and she is focused on her work in her studio.

She sits at a table positioned to face the corkboard "cabinet" she made herself. She can close and lock the doors in order to hide her board from prying eyes when she's not busy with it. The doors are now open, displaying what resembles the kind of crime investigation board that homicide detectives still use in television shows. Photos of four homicide victims are pinned at the top.

Arwen's laptop is on the table in front of her, its cursor winking on the screen. Her studio door is locked, and she's drawn the blinds. The interior lights have been dimmed, and her salt rock lamp casts a warm orange glow into the room. A cannabis joint burns in a saucer at her side. Next to it is a glass of pinot grigio with melting ice. Another bottle of wine chills in the fridge. Soft jazz rises from her Bluetooth speakers. Arwen is in her zone, and when she's embalmed in a mental womb like this, the outside world floats away. Reality becomes timeless.

She reaches for her joint, takes a drag. Inhaling deeply, she holds the smoke in her lungs for a few moments as she studies the old newspaper cuttings and photographs pinned to her murder board. Her gaze follows threads that link the victims to various locations, to family members, to police officers and timelines. She exhales slowly, and closing her eyes, she conjures up a scene from thirty-three years ago. It becomes a warm prairie day. April 22, 1989.

She imagines the prairie plains, the deep, winding coulees, the prickly pear cactus plants with yellow flowers, the tall outcroppings of sandstone being continuously sculpted by wind into haunting shapes.

She calls to mind Glenn Dennig near Medicine Hat.

Arwen opens her eyes, sets her joint on the edge of the saucer, and begins to type.

The first thing Wozniak saw was a woman's body lying on her back in front of a sofa, a blue nightgown crumpled up around her waist. She was naked from the hips down, her legs at odd angles. She was smeared with what looked like blood. Her shoulder-length brown hair covered her face.

According to official police records, Wozniak hurried back to his vehicle and radioed for backup. He did not know if there was anyone still inside the house, and if so, whether they might be armed, or in danger. He retrieved a tactical shield from the trunk of his cruiser, drew his sidearm, and waited for backup.

Within moments he heard sirens. Three more officers from his detachment arrived, screeching to a stop around his cruiser.

Eleven minutes after Wozniak received the dispatcher's call, the team of four officers breached the front door of the unassuming Glenn Dennig rancher using a stack formation.

The officers had no idea they were about to go down in criminal history as the first responders to one of the most shocking murders in this country.

Arwen reaches for her joint. She takes another long drag. She regards the photo of Sergeant Mark Wozniak on her board. The image was shot by a newspaper photographer more than three decades ago. Wozniak was just a patrol sergeant. Earnest-looking. His brown hair was thick, his face unlined. There was a freshness about him. Wozniak is still a cop with the Royal Canadian Mounted Police. His hair is now thinning and silver. His title is now inspector, and he's in charge of RCMP operations in Medicine Hat. His face is still strong. A good face. His eyes still kind, but they turn down at the sides now, and it makes him look tired. Those kind eyes witnessed terrible things that day. She exhales and stubs out her joint. She takes a sip of wine and begins to type.

Wozniak will never forget the chilling scene that hit him and his fellow officers inside the house.

"I've seen lots of bad scenes, dead bodies, over the years since," Wozniak told a reporter for the *Medicine Hat Standard* on the tenth anniversary of the killings. "But very few involving children, and even fewer with children left in that state. I . . . I don't understand it—an act of horror like that. The violence. I can't make sense of it, even now, all these years later."

Twenty years after he responded to the call at the modest rancher in peaceful Glenn Dennig, Wozniak said this on CBC television: "It was heinous, gruesome—something I never want to see again. It remains the worst scene I've ever had." He paused, and a strange look entered the man's eyes. He looked directly into the camera. "If there is such a thing as evil—it was there that day. Inside that house."

Arwen takes another sip of wine, calling to mind what Wozniak faced on that April evening. She types:

The first thing he noticed was blood—streaking the stairwell, the living room walls, more blood in the kitchen, on the floor, smearing the back door. Wozniak already knew what waited in the basement. He'd seen it through the window. Then the officers heard whimpering.

Arwen suddenly feels agitated. She scrolls to another location in her document. She wants to go back to the beginning and set more of the overall context, the color of the place. She hesitates, thinking, then types:

Medicine Hat is known as the "Gas City." According to tourism sites, the city boasts more sunshine per year than any other city in Canada—330 days on average—and while winter locks the prairie city in ice, the summers are hot and dry. When a natural-gas field was struck beneath the town in 1904, it was discovered to be massive—around 150 square miles. It supplied the growing city with so much affordable power that the streetlights burned both night and day because it was cheaper than hiring someone to turn the gas lights off.

The gas also fired giant kilns in the historic clay district. The kilns burned hot enough to bake red bricks impermeable to water, and the supply of bricks fueled the building of houses across the West. The beehive kilns also produced the famous Medalta pottery that was shipped around the world. But the near-constant flares from the gas wells and from the surrounding brick factories, where men toiled in punishing summer temperatures, lit the night skies with a perpetual orange glow. When Rudyard Kipling visited the city in 1907, it was this Dantesque scene that greeted him, and the online tourism sites love to mention it.

"This part of the country," he famously wrote, "seems to have all hell for a basement, and the only trap door appears to be Medicine Hat."

And it was indeed a scene from hell that greeted—

The door behind Arwen rattles. She spins around, knocking her wineglass flying. It shatters on the tile floor with a crash. Simultaneously the overhead fluorescent lights flick on. Heart pounding, Arwen blinks into the sudden, stark brightness, feeling confused and physically ripped from her faraway world of murder.

"Mom?"

"Jesus! Joe!" She lurches up from her chair, bumping it over as she hurries to her board and shuts the barn doors. Adrenaline shoots through her system as she spins to face her son.

"What in the *hell*, Joe. Get out of here!" She points to the door. "How *dare* you walk in on me like that? For fuck's sakes . . . you couldn't simply knock?"

Her son stands shocked. Arwen catches a glimpse of herself in the mirror on the wall. She sees her wild, unbrushed hair and is reminded she's still wearing a nightgown, blue and white, like the dead woman in her narrative, and it makes her furious. Because her son has seen her like this, and she hates it.

"I told you never to come in here. Never. Do you get that? What part about that did you not hear? This is my work space. This is my headspace. It's a private space. We share the cottage, not this space, Joe. Get out."

But Joe stands resolute, staring at the cabinet doors she has just shut, his mouth slightly agape.

Arwen dials it down a notch, worried now about what her son might already have seen.

"I'm sorry," she says more quietly. "Jesus, Joe. You really startled me. I . . . I was in the zone."

Her son's attention slides to her laptop, then to her pile of notebooks full of the scribbled notes from interviews she did before coming here. Joe's gaze goes to her file of old newspaper clippings, then to the old tape recorder and cassettes.

"I just came to ask if you wanted some supper," Joe says quietly. "I'm warming up that leftover pasta. I came to see if you wanted a bowl. I—"

"Our deal is breakfast, Joe. I will always be there for breakfast. But if I choose to work late, then I work through dinner. I have stuff in the fridge here. I have a microwave."

Her son is fully aware that she sometimes paints all night, noise-canceling headphones on, deep inside her own head, inside her psyche, inside her heart.

His gaze sifts toward the empty booze bottles on the counter, then to her wineglass, then to the joint still smoldering in the saucer, and Arwen becomes acutely conscious of the smell of marijuana and incense, and the smell of her own unshowered body.

"Yeah, Mom. I see you have . . . stuff."

Her mouth tightens. Her son is judging her. And in her boy's eyes she's falling short, again. Arwen's heart both hurts and tightens in defense. Sometimes she feels it was just the other day she was sixteen herself. She remembers feeling like a complete adult and a child at the same time. Sometimes she still feels she is sixteen years old, just a teen buried deeper inside an older and more desperate woman with a fucked-up head and sagging body—battered from her rounds in the washing machine of time. She doesn't have any right to be a mother.

She can't even live by her own codes of responsibility.

Whatever made her think she could do this—manage to raise a boy, and to live up to her son's standards? What did she do to deserve such a solid human being? Joe should by all accounts be a rebellious piece of shit in prison with a mother like her. Sometimes bad parents get good kids.

Sometimes good parents get the worst kind of children.

"Is that your project?" he asks with a nod toward the shuttered murder board. "Is that what we came west for?"

Arwen inhales deeply. "Yes, it is. How . . . much did you see? How long were you standing behind me before you put on the overhead lights?"

"What is the project, Mom?"

"I can't tell you, Joey. Not yet. It . . . I need to finish it first. I need to get all the information. I need to be sure."

"You mean, like, you need to get proof? Like with the other things you worked on for the television station?"

"Sort of. Yes. But this is bigger. Much bigger. It's going to take us places."

His gaze goes to her laptop. "Bigger than one of your investigative feature articles?"

"It's a book, Joey. I've been promised an advance. A really good one."

"As in money?"

She nods.

"Are you, like, working undercover at the tavern or something?"

Her pulse quickens. "That's—" She was going to say, *That's dumb*, but she never wants to call her son dumb. He's one of the smartest human beings she knows. Smarter than she is, that's for sure. "I'm waiting on tables so I can keep doing this."

"So how big is this advance?"

"Joey, please, not now."

"I don't understand why not now—why does it have to be a secret? Why from me? I can keep a secret, Mom. You owe me the truth. You uprooted me and forced me to move halfway across the country in our crapped-out van, into yet another new school. You made me leave my friends behind, and you won't even come clean with me about *why*?"

She inhales deeply and looks into her boy's eyes. So like his father's. She's denied him that, too—connection with his father's side of the family. A connection with his Japanese cultural heritage. She knows her son struggles with a need to belong, a need to feel rooted in something solid. But that window of opportunity is long gone now. She never told Joe's father she was pregnant with his kid. Arwen just vanished from the man's life. As she walked away from so many things that scared her. True intimacy, the fact that she was beginning to love Joe's father, simply became too overwhelming, so she fled. She now knows why. It's taken her most of her life to figure it out and to get this far.

"It's about a crime, Joey," she says quietly. "A true crime. A horrible crime. Long ago."

He stands dead still. He waits. Hope burns in his eyes. It hurts her. She's come closer to the truth than ever before.

"I got some inside information," she says. "About eighteen months ago. Something no one else has."

"Like, a lead?"

She nods. "I followed it, and it led to more, then I hit pay dirt. I'm writing a story about that crime."

"Is it a murder?"

"More than one murder."

His glance returns slowly to the laptop. He swallows. "So the murders—they happened here? In Story Cove? It involved people who still live here now?"

"That's all I can say right now. My . . . contract stipulates that I will deliver an exclusive, and until then, it's all terribly confidential. If I allow anything to leak, I could lose my edge, my advance, the whole deal."

"You're lying. You don't have a contract."

"I will, Joey. Soon. When I get enough written, and when it gets approval."

"And how long is that going to take? How damn long this time?"

For a moment she can't think what to say, because she doesn't want to tell yet another lie to her son.

He curses and makes for the door.

"Joe—"

He turns. He's still hoping for the truth.

Instead, Arwen says, "My studio door was locked. And you didn't even knock. You let yourself in with a key. Why?"

He glares at her. And Arwen wonders again just how much he saw of what was on her corkboard.

She holds out her hand. "Give me the key, Joe. I want all the keys to my studio."

He throws the key onto the table. It goes skittering across the surface and lands on the tile floor among the shards of glass and spilled wine. He exits the studio.

Arwen swears. She hurries to the door, slightly unsteady on her feet from all the wine and cannabis, but she can't write this story without first dulling the edges. She steadies herself by placing a hand against the doorjamb. She calls after her son, who is crossing the lawn as he makes for the cottage.

"Joe!" she yells.

He spins around and yells back, "I came to ask if you wanted to join me for supper because I brought a friend home from school, Mom. I thought you might want to meet her."

"Her?"

He continues to the cottage door.

She runs out onto the damp grass in bare feet. "Joey!"

He keeps walking.

"Joe! Who *is* she?"

He stops in the cottage doorway. "Her name is Phoebe. Phoebe Bradley. She lives down the street, and she wants to be an artist, too, and I thought it would be cool for her to meet my mom. But you know what? It was a fucking dumbass idea. Because you're an embarrassment."

"Joe!"

He goes inside and slams the door.

"No," she whispers. "Oh, Joey, no. Not the Bradleys."

RUE

NOW

"How well do you know Joe and his mother, Mrs. Cody?" Rue is speaking to the woman on the verge next to her cruiser while Toshi bags a hairbrush and toothbrush and keeps an eye on Joe as the teen gathers some essentials.

"I met them when they moved in here about three weeks ago. Simon—my husband—already knew Arwen from the tavern where she works. It was Simon who dropped Joe off at the station this morning to report his mother missing. Is it . . . I mean, is it her? On the beach?"

"We don't yet have an official identification, but we believe it is Joe's mother."

She nods. "I understand. We'll look after Joe while . . . for whatever he needs. He's got no one else, from what I understand. He's friendly with Phoebe Bradley, but . . ." Her voice trails off, and her gaze goes to the forest.

"But what?"

Wind gusts, and Hannah Cody holds a fall of blonde hair back from her face. "Lily was really unhappy with Phoebe seeing an older boy. But Joe is a good kid. He's friendly with our children. We have a son Matthew Bradley's age, and our daughter, Fiona, is best friends with Phoebe. I understand Lily's concern, but . . . I don't know. I thought she was overreacting. She has some kind of trigger issue with the age gap, and although I asked, she never explained why. I got a sense it was something from her own past . . . I can't believe it was Tom who found Arwen."

"When did you last see Arwen Harper, Mrs. Cody?"

"At our neighborhood barbecue yesterday. I didn't see exactly what time she left. The storm broke and sent most people home early. She was one who stayed."

"We're going to need a list of all your guests."

"Is that necessary? I don't want them—"

"It is necessary. We also believe there was some kind of altercation in the pool house, between Arwen Harper and Lily Bradley?"

Hannah blinks. She glances up the road. "I . . . I wasn't there. I didn't see or hear the fight. Simon did. He went down to the pool house after he saw Tom going in there. He says . . . he thinks they were arguing about the kids. I don't know what else. All I know is Lily and Tom left right afterward. Lily was in a rage. Arwen remained awhile longer and drank some more. She seemed . . . reckless to me."

Rue eyes the woman. She senses a lot more going on beneath the surface in this cul-de-sac.

"And your husband, Simon, he just left Joe outside the station this morning? He didn't come inside to assist Joe in making the report?"

Hannah swallows. "I took our kids to school and Simon had a class to teach. When Joe came into the street saying he couldn't find his mom, Simon offered to drive him to the station on his way to the university. He did ask Joe if he needed help, and Joe said he could manage alone. We knew the police would take care of him."

"Any other guests witness the pool house argument?" asks Rue.

"I don't think so. A few guests heard yelling. Swearing. Glass breaking."

"And where were Joe and Phoebe, and the other kids, during this time?"

"Well, when the rain started coming down, and the thunder and lightning, we all went inside, or under cover, and most of the kids went downstairs to the big rec room in our house. Or they went home with their parents. It's not like Lily to lose her temper, you know? She's always . . . so controlled. In charge. She's a therapist. She's accustomed to her patients losing their shit in her office day after day, hour after hour. She knows how to deal with it, but I guess this was just . . . personal."

"What about Tom Bradley? How well do you feel he knew Arwen Harper?"

Her eyes narrow slightly. She glances away again, as if debating how much to say. "Tom . . . I don't know. Like Simon, he knew Arwen from the tavern. Simon, Tom, and some of the other guys from Kordel gather every Friday afternoon at the Red Lion, for a so-called happy hour that often runs late into the night. Arwen was their regular server." She glances toward the cottage. "Tom got her that accommodation."

"What do you mean?"

"She was looking for a rental with a studio. This place became available, and Tom knows the owners. He called them and gave a reference for Arwen."

Rue nods slowly and digs her hands into her coat pockets as wind gusts again and more clouds gather. It feels like autumn again, despite the fact that it's summer. Typical of this rain forest climate.

"And where is your husband now?" Rue asks.

"He's at work. Like I said, he has classes. He's teaching a summer program this year."

Toshi and Joe exit the cottage. Joe carries a bag of clothing and a backpack. Rue says, "I'll need that list of everyone who was at your barbecue yesterday, along with contact numbers. And I might need you to come into the station later to make an official statement."

Hannah Cody pales. "Is—are you thinking it wasn't an accident?"

"We're treating the death as suspicious at this time."

Joe and Toshi approach.

"Thanks for your time, Mrs. Cody. And we appreciate you offering to take care of Joe. We'll be cordoning off the cottage and studio now, and we'll return later today to pick up that list of party attendants, so if you could have it ready?"

Hannah lowers her voice to a whisper as Joe comes closer. "Is his mother's death related to the jogger killings?"

"What makes you ask that?"

Her eyes are bright. "Just . . . because . . . Joe said his mom was jogging. Alone. Early, and in a wooded area. And now she's dead. And you were the lead investigator on the other Jogger Killer cases."

"Like I said, the investigation is ongoing," Rue says. Her gaze goes back to the Cody house, then up to the attic window. Simon Cody is next on her interview list.

RUE

NOW

"I didn't expect to see so many students on campus at this time of year," Rue says.

"We offer summer courses." Professor Simon Cody eyes her warily from behind his desk. They're in his office at Kordel. An evergreen hedge grows outside his window, and Rue can see students walking beneath chestnut trees.

Cody has a boyish face, a head of thick, brown hair threaded with strands of silver. Tall side of average, the build of a distance athlete. Rue guesses he's in his late fifties, maybe even pushing sixty, like his friend Professor Tom Bradley. Cody exudes a controlled energy, an arrogance that Rue finds often with older men who sit in academic towers and pontificate about the world and society's systems while living and operating quite apart from the reality of them.

The bookshelves behind him are stacked with works by Sartre, Plato, Descartes, Russell, Hume, Kant, Nietzsche, Marx, Locke, Foucault, and Machiavelli, along with a bronze-colored bust that declares itself to be Hippocrates, and on the wall is a classic painting of Sisyphus pushing his boulder up a mountain.

Another wall boasts stunning photographic studies of birds from ducks and swans to eagles to vultures pulling at a zebra carcass.

"Did you shoot those?" she asks with a nod to the images.

"I did. I'm a keen birder."

"And I see you and Tom are both marathoners." She smiles and tips her head to another photo, this one of Simon Cody with Tom Bradley in running gear. Both are holding up medals. "Looks like it's from the Boston Marathon."

"I have a class in a few minutes, Detective. What can I do for you?"

She takes out her notebook and pen and opens her notepad. His eyes dart to the notebook. His features tighten.

"Thank you for bringing Joe Harper into the station this morning."

"It's the least I could do. Hannah called to say it's most likely his mother who was found on Grotto Beach."

She holds his gaze. He doesn't blink.

"You knew Joe's mother fairly well?"

"So it *is* her?"

"We're working on the presumption it is."

He moistens his lips and nods. "She lived across the street, and she was our regular server at the Red Lion. It's devastating news. I am so sorry for Joe."

Rue waits, but he offers nothing more. His silence speaks loudly. She's not sure yet what it's saying.

"So you decided not to accompany Joe into the station to report his mother's absence?"

His eyes narrow. "I knew he'd be in good hands with you people. Look, I have students waiting. I need—"

"I need some questions answered, sir. We can always do this at the station if you'd prefer to come down and do it in person, on record?"

He inhales slowly, deeply. "If you could make it quick."

"When did you last see Arwen Harper?"

"At our house last night."

"What time did she leave?"

"I don't know. She might have gone home around . . . eight p.m."

"You saw her leave?"

"Yeah, I saw her go. She was one of the last to leave, and she'd had a lot to drink. We all had."

"I believe you witnessed an argument in the pool house?"

"Who told you that?"

She says nothing.

He rubs his chin. "I was in our kitchen. The storm sent us all scurrying indoors. Tom was peering out the kitchen window watching the lightning. He saw Lily, his wife, going into the pool house with Arwen. He said it looked like they were arguing. He got worried and went out to check. When he didn't return right away, I followed to see what was going on. And I heard the three of them yelling at each other."

"About what?"

"I didn't hear specifics. Just shouting. And breaking glass. I went inside. They . . . were all pretty heated. Tom grabbed Lily by the arm and told her they were going home. Both he and Lily—they were shaking. He wouldn't tell me what happened. He wanted to take Lily home right away, and he said he'd return for the kids—they were all in the games room downstairs. I poured Arwen another drink in the pool house, which she claimed she needed to calm down. But she was kind of . . . alive. Eyes bright. Excited-looking. I figured she was on something."

"On something?"

"Drugs. She took pills. I asked her what the fight was about, and she just laughed. And that was that."

"What do you think it might have been about?"

He regards Rue. She can almost see the wheels in his mind turning as he debates what to tell her.

Quietly he says, "This is not really my business, but Hannah told me Lily thought Tom might be having an affair."

"With Arwen Harper?"

"That's what Hannah said Lily thought."

Rue angles her head. "Tom Bradley is your good friend?"

"Yeah."

She purses her lips. "What do you think? Was your friend having an affair with Arwen Harper, your Red Lion waitress?"

"You'd have to ask him."

She nods slowly. "And it was Tom Bradley who secured the accommodation for Arwen Harper across the street from your house?"

"Look, if you don't have any specific questions for me"—he pushes his chair back and comes to his feet—"I need to get to my class." He gathers up his papers and begins sliding them into a satchel.

"Did you like her?"

"What?"

"Did you like Arwen Harper?"

He stills. "She—yes, we all did. She was fun. Easy to be around. She put new life into us old guys. I really am saddened by the news." He picks up his satchel. Then, as if realizing he should show more emotion, he says, "It was a complete shock to hear the news this morning. I . . . Do you know yet what happened? Hannah says it might not have been an accident."

"That's what we're trying to find out."

"Well, if you don't have any more questions for me"—Cody comes out from behind his desk and goes to open his office door—"I must get to my students." He waits with his hand on the door handle.

Rue slides her notebook and pen back into her cross-body bag, comes to her feet, and straightens her blazer. She glances out the window at the young female students walking down the path, the wind flirting with their hair and skirts. Cody does not appear terribly rocked by the death of his neighbor and friendly server who made them all happy. She exits the office, and Cody pulls the door shut behind both of them. He locks it.

"Good day, Detective," he says.

She nods and begins to make her way down the passage toward the building exit.

He calls after her, "Those woods—they're also full of homeless people, you know."

She stops, turns.

He comes up to her. "But you're probably keenly aware of that," he says, lowering his voice as two female students pass them. "It's been in our local news a lot. One of our town councillors who plans to run for mayor is making it part of her campaign to clear that forest of homeless vagrants. Virginia Wingate. You should speak to her. Or to the vagrants. Maybe one of them saw or did something. My daughter told me she and Phoebe Bradley saw one of the men the other day. Exposing himself."

Rue holds his gaze. "You reported this?"

"Not to the police. I did speak to Virginia, though."

"When did this occur?"

"Last Wednesday."

"And why didn't you officially report a man exposing himself to your daughter?"

He hesitates, then his face hardens quickly. "I am not interested in playing Whac-A-Mole, Detective. It's part of a bigger, systemic problem. Those woods need to be cleaned out."

RUE

NOW

Rue and Toshi are back in Oak End, parked outside the Cody residence, waiting for Hannah Cody to return from collecting her kids from school. Joe Harper is inside the house. When they knocked on the door, he told them where Hannah was.

A silver Mercedes pulls into the Cody driveway. Four kids inside.

"Bingo," says Toshi, reaching for the door handle. "She's brought the Bradley kids home from school with her."

"Probably to avoid the media camped outside their house." Rue opens her door. "It's always the poor kids who get caught in the cross fire when their parents screw up."

Rue and Toshi approach the Mercedes as Hannah gets out the driver's side.

Toshi murmurs under his breath, "She looks edgy."

"What is it, Detectives?" Hannah asks as they reach her.

A small boy with a heavy backpack climbs out the back door of the sedan. A girl with dark-pink hair exits behind him.

Rue recognizes the girl as the Bradley daughter she saw at their house early this morning. Phoebe.

With wide eyes the small boy says to Rue, "You're the murder detective!"

"No one said it was a murder, Matthew," snaps Phoebe. She's been crying—puffy eyes, mascara tracking down her face through powdered makeup. She's dressed all in black, nails painted black. Her T-shirt displays a human skull. A silver ankh hangs from a chain around her neck.

Goth is the word that comes to Rue's mind.

"She *is*," Matthew insists. "She's the officer who was on TV about the Jogger Killer. That's what the kids at school were saying—she *is* a murder detective."

Another girl and boy exit the Mercedes. The Cody kids.

"You little idiot," Phoebe snaps. "Have you thought about Joe? This is his mother you're talking about, asshole." Tears fill her eyes. She swings her backpack over her shoulder and marches toward the front door of the Cody house. Joe stands in the window, watching them, waiting for Phoebe.

Rue smiles gently at Matthew. "She sure sounds like a big sister."

He pulls a face, but his eyes remain bright as his gaze darts between Toshi and Rue.

"My dad found the body. I saw you this morning, from my room upstairs. My room is like Mr. Cody's room over there." Matthew points up to the dormer window on the top floor of the Cody house where Rue saw the shadow of a figure standing earlier. "Mr. Cody has the whole attic as his office, and it's like a control tower with a 360-degree view. He can also see everything that is going on from all sides, like me. He's been teaching me how to take good pictures of things I observe."

Hannah says, "Matthew, Fiona, Jacob, go inside. I'll talk to the detectives out here."

"And did you see anything from your 'control tower' earlier this morning, Matthew?" Rue asks, taking a bit of a chance.

"I totally did! I took photos, too! One day I'm gonna be one of those police photographers, or a foreign photojournalist. I saw my dad going for a run really early. In the storm. It was still darkish and he had a flashlight. And when he came back without his jacket and with no flashlight, he went straight into the shed, where—"

"Matthew!" Hannah grabs the kid's arm and yanks him away from Rue. "Your mother says you're not to talk to anyone. Not without a lawyer present. Go inside."

"Why not?"

"Because," Hannah says. "Just go inside. Please." She looks desperate. "Fiona, take Matthew and Jacob inside."

"We do have a question for your daughter," says Rue. "If that's okay with you, Mrs. Cody?"

Worry widens Hannah's eyes. "What kind of question?"

"Your husband mentioned that Phoebe and Fiona encountered a stranger in the woods," says Rue.

Hannah looks panicked.

"Fiona?" Toshi says. "Can you tell us what happened?"

Fiona shoots a glance at her mother.

Hannah says, "Jacob, Matthew, inside. Go."

The two boys slouch off reluctantly, and Fiona waits until they have gone.

"It was nothing," the girl says quietly. "Phoebe and I went into the woods last Wednesday and there was a guy lurking about the clearing, that's all." She looks at the ground, her face going red. "He . . . was watching us through the bushes."

Hannah gasps. "What? Fi, you never told me that!"

Fiona's face goes bloodred. "Because I knew you'd overreact, like now. And Phoebe said not to."

"This is important, Fi. This man could be dangerous." Hannah looks frantically at Rue, then Toshi. "I swear, if I knew this, we would have come in and reported it."

"Your husband was aware of an incident," says Rue, watching the woman carefully.

"I . . . I told Dad," Fi says.

Hannah looks stunned. For a moment she is rendered speechless. "Do . . . you think this man . . . do you think he had something to do with the . . . the accident this morning?"

Toshi gets out his notebook. "Can you describe this individual, Fiona?"

She fiddles with the strap of the backpack slung over her shoulder. "We didn't really see him. He had a dark hoodie on, and black pants. He ran away into the bushes when we yelled at him."

"What were you and Phoebe doing in the clearing, Fiona?" Toshi asks.

She swallows. "Nothing. We were just there."

"Fiona," Rue says softly. "It's okay if you were doing something that your parents might not like. Because this is far more important, and I'm sure they won't get mad, right, Mrs. Cody?"

"Of course. Of course it's fine," Hannah says quickly. "Tell them, Fiona. Whatever it is."

"Phoebe had a packet of cigarettes. And some strawberry vodka. We were going to . . . you know, in the clearing where kids go to smoke and make out and stuff."

"Christ, Fi," Hannah whispers. "Why didn't you tell me?"

"Because of the vodka and the cigarettes."

"But you told your dad."

She swallows. "He said he'd take care of it, and tell Councillor Wingate, who is going to clean up the woods, and he told me not to go in there again. He says the woods have become a bad place."

Rue and Toshi exchange a glance.

Rue says, "How old do you think this man was?"

"I don't know. Not, like, old. He moved fast. Thinnish."

"Hair and skin color?" Toshi asks.

"I think he was a white guy. I didn't see his hair."

"Have any other kids mentioned seeing him?"

She shakes her head.

Rue and Toshi thank Fiona, and Hannah gives them the list of the barbecue guests that she compiled. When Rue and Toshi get back into their vehicle, Hannah has gone inside with Fiona. They can see Phoebe and Joe both watching their vehicle from the living room window.

"Something is off about everyone in this place," Toshi says quietly.

"Tell me about it. We need to find a way to look at Matthew's photos."

"Not going to happen without a warrant," says Toshi.

As she reaches for her ignition, Rue's cell rings. Caller ID says it's Fareed. She connects the call on speakerphone.

"Hey, Doc," she says. "Got a time slot for us?"

"Eight a.m. tomorrow morning," Fareed says. "I can squeeze your jogger into my roster early if I move some things around."

"Thanks. I owe you."

"Promises, promises."

Rue kills the call and starts the engine. Toshi peers through the windshield at the trailhead at the end of the cul-de-sac that leads into the tall, dense trees.

"I know where that clearing in the woods is, where the kids go," Rue says. "We'll get a team in there before daybreak tomorrow to do a sweep north of the trail and question anyone found sleeping there."

TAKEN

A True Crime Story

The three additional officers who responded to Sergeant Wozniak's call for backup were Constables Harry Woollcott, Leon Conti, and Dal Manik. Conti had received special ERT, or emergency response training—the RCMP equivalent of SWAT training—and he organized the small group into a combat configuration. They moved as one unit up the stairs, and they breached the locked front door with a battering ram.

The officers entered with drawn weapons and thudding hearts.

Blood streaked the walls, and a whimpering sound came from downstairs.

Conti motioned quietly for Woollcott and Manik to remain on the main floor. He and Wozniak proceeded cautiously down the stairs to the basement.

They entered a recreation room.

A sofa faced away from the stairs. Behind it, near the base of the stairs, lay a male, about six feet tall. A screwdriver covered in blood lay on the carpet near him. He had dark hair, pale skin. Receding hairline. Thick mustache. A well-built man dressed only in boxer shorts. His torso was punctured with leaf-shaped wounds. His right eye socket was a gaping maw pooled with blood. His arms were raised, fists clenched as though he were putting up for a fight. But he was stiff with rigor mortis.

The whimpering sounded again. Both officers spun around. A small terrier whined and quivered next to the dead female Wozniak had seen through the window when he first arrived at the scene. The dog barked once, then whimpered again.

Wozniak tried to swallow. Emotion burned in his eyes.

The female's body—naked from the waist down—was also punctured with wounds.

Wozniak realized at that point that the carpet beneath his boots was saturated with blood. It squelched when he moved. A basement window was open.

On the wall was a large framed photograph of a family. It showed the dead man. The dead woman. Plus two children—a girl of around twelve and a younger boy of maybe eight or nine years of age. The same ages as Wozniak's kids. He thought of the blood streaking up the stairwell walls.

"The kids," he whispered. "Where in the hell are those two kids?"

RUE

NOW

Rue hits a key on her laptop, and the image of Arwen Harper that Joe Harper provided fills the monitor behind her in the conference room.

The group gathered around the table falls silent.

As the primary investigator on this case, Rue commands a core team of six—three corporals and three constables, all trained detectives. One of them, Constable Henry Hague, functions as an affiant who is assigned the role of collating the case documentation and ITOs—Information to Obtain warrants. Toshi calls Henry the Document Despot because he continually boots paperwork back to the officers so it can be redrafted to be more consistent.

Rue's superior, Sergeant Luke Holder, is also present for this briefing. At her disposal is the RCMP's forensic ident unit, the RCMP crime labs, and she can also draw on Story Cove officers as "task monkeys" since SCPD officers provided the first response and the body was found in their jurisdiction.

"We have a presumptive ID." She points to the image. "Arwen Harper, female, age forty-one. Single mother. Resident of Oak End in Story Cove. Harper, an artist, worked from her home studio and also as a server at the Red Lion Tavern. Her son, Joe Harper, age sixteen, reported her missing. No criminal record in the system. Her previous employment was contract work—investigative reporting—primarily for the CBC."

Rue gives her team a rundown of events since the 911 call came in from Dr. Tom Bradley. And she sums up her concerns about Bradley's account of events.

Holder folds his arms, leans back in his chair. "We keeping this case? Any reason to think it's connected to the Goose Trail and Elk Lake assaults? Or do we hand it over to another homicide unit?"

Rue tenses. She wants this one, Jogger Killer connection or not. For reasons she's not even ready to articulate to herself. She needs control of this investigation.

"My gut says we stay on it," she says. "The window between Arwen Harper's death and the last JK attack would be consistent with a cooling-off window for our unidentified subject, followed by a desire to assault and kill again. The weather conditions are also a match—heavy rain, low cloud. The location is a fit—a densely wooded area, isolated. The victim profile is also consistent—white female runner, alone, similar in physical appearance and age. The blunt force trauma to the head is consistent—"

"Could have been from the fall," says Toshi.

"The autopsy will tell us more, but yes."

"And no overt sign of sexual assault?" asks Luke.

"Her assailant could have been interrupted," Rue counters. "The jogger might have thrown him off by escaping into dense brush and hiding. It looks like she fought him at the edge of the cliff. She could have gone over the cliff before her assailant could follow through with his usual MO. And there's this—" She clicks another key on her laptop.

An image of the decedent lying with a red jacket over her head fills the monitor. She points. "The covered face, hiding the brutality of the head trauma—this detail is consistent with the JK assaults, and it's key because the covering of the faces remains holdback evidence from the other three murders. This detail was not released to anyone outside of this room." She pauses. "And neither was the fact that the JK took trophies. Locks of hair from each victim, plus an item of jewelry from each."

Luke says, "And Bradley says he did this—covered her face?"

"Affirmative," says Rue. "Bradley is also apparently a marathoner. There's a photo in his friend Simon Cody's office of both of them getting medals at the Boston Marathon. The Goose and Elk Lake trails could be familiar to him. They're popular trails for long-distance runners."

Toshi says, "That's something we'll need to ascertain—did Bradley frequent those trails?"

"I've sent Bradley's DNA to a private lab where techs can move on it faster," says Rue. "I also sent them a semen sample from the JK case, and if it's a match to Bradley's DNA, we've got our Jogger Killer. The private lab of course will not be able to run anything through the federal database—they don't have police access. But we'll get some early and fast results that will either rule him in or out, and we can build a case from there."

A tangible excitement rises in the room. Somctimcs that's all it takes—a lucky break, even if it comes years down the road. The killer makes a mistake, does something stupid, like striking too close to home. Or a victim fights back, and things go wrong. Tom Bradley could have slipped up.

"And what about this Simon Cody guy?" Luke asks.

"He remains on our radar," Rue says. "Arwen Harper was friendly with both men. As well as other males at the Red Lion Tavern. She was last seen at a barbecue at Simon Cody's house, where she reportedly engaged in an altercation with Tom and Lily Bradley in the pool house. The only other witness to their fight—or part of it—was apparently Simon Cody. Joe Harper said he last laid eyes on his mother at the Cody barbecue. However, Bradley has lawyered up and is no longer cooperating. Neither is his wife. We've obtained a list of the barbecue guests and have started a door-to-door canvass in search of more witnesses. Maybe someone—a dog walker, another runner—saw Arwen Harper heading out for a jog later that night. Or they saw Bradley going out. We already have a witness statement from Story Cove councillor Virginia Wingate. She was waiting in her car outside the lane gate for her daughter, who was in therapy with Lily Bradley. Councillor Wingate saw Bradley entering his back gate wearing a white shirt that was stained with something dark, possibly blood. She claims the shirt had a big round logo on the back—black. She thinks it might be an Ocean Motion logo. She can't recall seeing a flashlight in Bradley's hand. His head was bare. Hair wet. But when Bradley met me outside his house after placing the 911 call, he had on a blue shirt and an orange jacket, which we have taken into evidence."

"So he changed his clothes," says Constable Georgia Backmann, who is taking copious notes. She's one of the newer detectives on the team.

Rue nods. "Affirmative. If we can obtain reasonable grounds to secure a warrant, I want that Ocean Motion shirt." She reaches for her water bottle, takes a deep swallow. Replacing the cap, Rue says, "And I want the photos Matthew Bradley said he took of his father returning from his run."

Toshi takes over. "We're initiating a sweep of the forest north of the trail following reports of vagrants in the woods. Perhaps someone saw something. We're also looking for Bradley's missing flashlight."

"A vagrant or some Curious George could also explain that third set of boot prints found on the cliff," says Luke.

Rue says, "Meanwhile Tom Bradley remains our key person of interest, but like I said, he's lawyered up and is not answering any questions." She pauses. "He's engaged Dianne Klister."

"The *Blister*?" says one of the detectives. He whistles softly. "You're kidding me."

"If he's retained Klister the Blister," says Backmann, "my money's on him being guilty as sin. Innocent people don't hire counsel like the Blister."

Someone laughs.

"Okay, autopsy is at eight a.m. sharp tomorrow," Rue says. "Toshi and I will observe. Once our decedent's ID is scientifically confirmed, Toshi will take a team to conduct a search of Harper's residence, looking primarily for her electronics—no phone was found on her body, and her son says she always runs with her cell. I'll visit her place of employment, the Red Lion Tavern on Main."

Rue assigns tasks to the rest of the team, including running full background checks on Tom Bradley and Simon Cody and contacting and questioning all the Codys' barbecue guests.

"Whether the attack on Arwen Harper was random, opportunistic, or whether she was specifically targeted, victimology will be key," says Rue. "So let's find out who Arwen Harper was. Why she came to town, who her friends were. And what she was doing in the minutes, hours, days, and weeks before she died."

She pauses and meets everyone's gaze in turn. "Okay, let's all get some sleep, and hit this one running tomorrow."

RIPPLE EFFECT

NOW

Arwen's death is like a boulder that has been cast into the still waters of Story Cove, and ripples are fanning out in giant, concentric, multiplying circles, sending waves into every house, every life in this neighborhood, leaving none untouched.

This is the thought in Lily's mind as she sits next to Tom watching the news from the sofa in their living room. The reporter on the television screen holds a mike as she stands outside the downtown police station.

An image of Dianne, Lily, and Tom arriving at the Bradley house in Dianne's car fills the television screen. Lily stares with mounting horror at the outside of her own pretty eggplant-colored house with the green trim she selected for the eaves. The camera settles briefly on her therapy shingle.

Oak Tree Therapy, L. Bradley (PhD).

Bile rises in her throat. She glances at Tom now. And what she sees in her husband's features fills her with dread.

Tom breaks eye contact and changes the channel.

"Homicide investigators are saying little today about the body of a female jogger found on—"

He flicks to another channel.

Footage of Dianne's car pulling into their driveway fills the screen. A reporter's voice rises above the melee.

"Ms. Klister? Ms. Klister, are you defending Professor Bradley? Has he been charged—"

Tom's cell rings. Lily jumps.

He mutes the TV, takes the phone from his pocket, glances at the caller ID, swears softly, and connects the call.

He listens, and Lily tenses as the look changes on her husband's face.

Tom says into the phone, "But I haven't done anything. I just found her—" He listens, nods. Kills the call. He stares blankly ahead.

"Tom?" Lily says.

He clears his throat. "That was the dean. The board convened an emergency meeting and have decided it's best if I opt to take a leave of absence, effective immediately, until this is sorted out. She says maybe things can resume as normal come fall."

"Maybe?"

Tom says nothing.

"They can't do this. Can they? What happened to innocent until proven guilty?"

"She said it would make things easier if I made it clear it was my choice to step away temporarily. I'll continue to receive pay. They feel it's best for the reputation of the school." Tom pauses. His eyes go watery. "Someone will pack up and deliver my personal effects tomorrow."

Lily stares at her husband. The ripples are only just beginning. How long before her own patients start calling?

Almost on cue, she hears the phone in her office begin to ring.

"Tom," she says very quietly. "I think we need to let the kids go stay with your parents. Just until this goes away."

His gaze locks with hers.

They both know "this" is never going to go away. Not now.

Matthew sits quietly in the dark on the landing upstairs, listening to the television and to his parents downstairs. Most of the lights in the house are off because of the reporters camped outside. His parents want the press to think the Bradleys have all gone to bed or something. Matthew was feeling sort of excited earlier. Now he just feels tired. And scared. He didn't even get a proper dinner. Just pizza pops warmed up. And his parents aren't talking in front of him and Phoebe, and Phoebe isn't talking to him, either.

He peeked into Phoebe's room earlier. She'd been crying most of the day after they came home from the Codys' house. Now she's busy with her iPhone. When he knocked on her door, she told him to get lost.

Matthew feels tears burn into his eyes.

He doesn't know why the police took his dad to the station this morning. Or why the people on TV seem to be acting as if his dad could have hurt Joe's mom.

He doesn't know why his dad had blood on him when he returned from his jog, or why he left the bloodied shirt in the shed. Or why the people on TV are talking about other jogger murders.

When Matthew went to look for his dad's shirt in the shed a short while ago, he found nothing there.

Now he's terrified his mom and dad will discover that he told the murder detective he took photos.

Matthew begins to cry.

Down the street at the Cody house, Joe watches the same news with Simon. Hannah is busy in the kitchen. The Cody kids are upstairs in their rooms doing homework.

"And what are police saying about a possible connection to the Jogger Killer deaths?" the anchorman asks the reporter.

"Little to nothing at this time," the reporter in the field answers. "But the woman's death is definitely being treated as suspicious, and the homicide detective on the case is the same lead investigator in the JK cases."

Simon is quiet as he watches. An edgy energy rolls off him in waves. Hannah is trying to be nice, and she's sweet, but Joe feels empty. Numb. As if his legs and arms and fingers and toes belong to someone else. He can't even think.

The only thing that helps Joe is being able to text Phoebe. But even that digital discourse is now growing strained. Phoebe is increasingly worried about her father and is growing defensive. And Joe also feels his walls going up. This is his mother they're all talking about.

Another text from Phoebe pings through, and Joe's phone vibrates as the screen lights up. He reads the text.

> I know I said my dad drives me insane and sometimes I want to kill him but he'd never hurt anyone. I swear on my life. I don't know how they can say these things on TV and Twitter.

He can't do it—he just can't respond to her any longer. He lurches up and heads for the stairs.

"Joe—" Hannah hurries after him. She places her hand on his arm. "I'm so sorry. We shouldn't have had the news on. Come have some dessert. I made—"

"I'm not hungry. Thanks."

He goes upstairs to the spare room that Hannah has made up for him. He plops onto the bed and stares at the window. It's dark out. Stars speckle the sky high above the tips of the trees that loom behind their cottage. Emotion fills his eyes and he can't breathe.

He wonders what will happen to him now. That female detective called earlier to tell him the postmortem would be done at eight a.m. tomorrow.

He lies back, and a memory of what he read on his mother's laptop fills his mind.

Sergeant Wozniak and Constable Conti looked at the family photo, then at each other. Both feared the worst. They could deal with the whimpering dog later, but two children could be upstairs. Dead. Or alive and in danger.

They moved fast back up to the main floor. Constables Woollcott and Manik still waited with white faces and weapons drawn. Conti motioned silently for Woollcott and Manik to remain in place. Wozniak and Conti climbed the stairs, guns ready.

The carpet on the upstairs landing was also sodden with blood. Bloody footprints led into a white-tiled bathroom.

The officers glanced into the bathroom. A kitchen knife lay on the tiles in a pool of bloodied water.

Opposite the bathroom was a girl's bedroom. Decorated in soft pinks with teddy bears and a frilled pillow on the bed. There appeared to be no obvious signs of violence. Still, something about the room felt wrong to Wozniak. He sensed something. But Conti motioned for Wozniak to move with him to the next room.

The officers moved cautiously forward and into a boy's bedroom papered with *Star Wars* posters. What Wozniak saw on the child's bed never left him. A major bloodletting incident had occurred. A little boy lay on his back wearing only undershorts. His sightless eyes stared at a ceiling stickered with a galaxy of stars. His throat was slit, and he'd also been stabbed. A toy lightsaber lay near his bed.

Wozniak's first thought was, *Oh God, he tried to fight off this evil with his little saber.* His second thought was, *Please let him be alive.* But he could see the truth. The boy was dead and the attack had been violent. Blood was spattered and streaked on the walls, ceiling, bed, carpet, window, everywhere. This small boy had been killed on his bed. In his own room. In his own house. While his mom and dad were home and should have been able to protect him. In a good, peaceful, middle-class neighborhood. A space that was supposed to be safe. A noise made Wozniak spin. He faced the corner of the room, heart racing. A hamster scuffled in a cage and looked at him.

The two men exited the bedroom. Conti moved in front of Wozniak.

They entered the main bedroom. Wozniak could not breathe. Another little boy lay on the queen-size bed, unmoving. He wore pajama bottoms. His face was covered with a pillow.

Wozniak holstered his sidearm and removed the pillow.

The child was also about seven or eight. But this boy had lighter-brown hair. Freckles. His jaw hung open, showing missing front teeth. His throat had also been hacked open, and he'd been stabbed in the little torso at least four times.

On the wall above the queen-size bed was another framed photo of the family. It showed the same dead mother and father, plus the boy from the child's bedroom. And a pretty young girl with light-brown hair. So very much like his own daughter.

"So who's this boy?" Wozniak whispered, staring at the photo. He thinks of the drag marks in the kitchen, leading to the back door. "And where's the girl?"

Conti says, "She's been taken."

In a more cosmopolitan and grittier neighborhood to the northwest of Story Cove, Rue pours herself a vodka tonic. She carries it to the sofa on a tray with a plate of leftovers she heated in the microwave.

It's almost midnight. She's both tired and amped. The first hours on a homicide are critical. She'll eat, grab a few hours' sleep, and get back at it early.

Her husband, Seth, was already asleep in bed when she arrived home, and her son, Ebrahim, is busy on his computer in his room. Eb is in his first year at college and always seems to have loads of work.

She sips her vodka, reaches for the remote, and clicks on the TV. She finds the newscast she routinely records and hits PLAY. On the wall beside her is a photo of her mom and dad—her white adoptive parents—with Eb. It was shot last year, just before Rue took Eb with her on her second trip to Southern Africa to search for more of their biological relatives. She and Eb visited Maputo in Mozambique together, where they found a cousin of her biological father's. But they learned nothing more about what had happened to Rue's dad. After meeting with some more of her deceased bio mom's relations in Cape Town, Rue learned that her mother had died as a result of a stabbing incident in a sprawling township named Khayelitsha. There was never any memorial in her honor, so Rue and Eb had a plaque crafted and placed it in a memorial garden near the sea. Afterward Rue took Eb to the Okavango Delta in Botswana for a safari as a very special treat for them both. It was a much-needed respite and proved to be a wonderful bonding time for her and Eb.

The trip gave Eb some sense of his own roots on her biological side. Searching for her bio parents had always been a vague ambition while she was growing up and feeling she never quite fit anywhere, but it was only after Ebrahim was born that that drive grew hot and fierce in Rue. As she held her new baby in her arms, it had hit hard—it was the first time in her life she was looking at family who looked like her. And it made her think that there were more people out there of her blood. Her curiosity grew intense.

Eb has since asked more about his dad's heritage, so now they have dreams to visit Denmark, where Seth's mom was born.

Rue's thoughts turn to Joe Harper as she fast-forwards through a story on a flood. Joe, who looks nothing like his mother. Who doesn't know who his father is. Her heart hurts for the boy. She feels him.

She hits PLAY when she sees an image of the police station.

"The female jogger was found on Grotto Beach this morning by Dr. Tom Bradley, a member of the psychology faculty at Kordel University. Dr. Bradley's specialty is abnormal psychology—"

Eb enters the living room.

"Hey, I thought I heard you come in," he says, going into the kitchen, opening the fridge. Rue's son is a bottomless pit. He grabs a jug of milk, an apple, leftover cake.

"I guess you landed a big one, huh?" He brings his stash into the living room and plunks down into a chair beside her. He takes a bite of the cake. "You think it's one of the Jogger Killer's?" he asks around his mouthful.

Rue's gaze goes to her son's wrist. Her chest tightens. "We're keeping an open mind," she says. "How was school?"

He shrugs, takes another bite of cake. "Got a paper due tomorrow."

She hesitates. "What time did your father come home today?"

Eb stops chewing. "Why?"

"Just . . . wondering."

His eyes narrow slightly. "I don't know, Mom. I was in my room." He regards her oddly. "Mom, if this is about—"

"It's not."

But it is. It totally is. It's consuming Rue, burning the inside of her gut like smoldering tar, and the toxic smoke is fingering slowly through her body. Soon it's going to consume her mind, and she will no longer be able to control her simmering rage.

Eb glances down. He stares at his food and says, "Sometimes people are good people, they just aren't good for each other, you know?"

"It's okay, Eb."

"It's not okay. I know it's not. I . . . It's all right if you leave him."

Rue holds her son's gaze. The voices on the newscast blur. A buzz grows inside her head. And with it all, her heart swells. She loves him so much. He's her world.

"He's a good dad to me, but not a good partner for you."

Emotion threatens to betray Rue. If there is one person who can make her cry, it's her boy. Rue and Seth have stayed together for him. But as much as Eb might love his dad, Rue no longer believes she can make the marriage work. Seth has betrayed her yet again, after promising it was all over and that it would never happen again. And this time it was Eb who found him out and who told Rue.

"Let's not talk about this right now, okay?" she says. "It's been a long day."

Eb gathers up his food and his glass of milk, gets to his feet, then wavers. "Mom . . ."

"What?"

"I will do anything for you, Mom, you do know that, right?" A pause. "I want you to be happy."

His gaze tunnels into hers as he says it. And Rue can't ask about the little orange and green beads that are missing from his wrist. She just can't.

Not yet. Not now. She's certain everything will turn out okay, and then she won't need to ask at all.

RUE

NOW
June 21. Tuesday.

The autopsy suite is cold. Exposed pipes run along the ceiling, and fridges that hold the dead hum as they maintain temperatures low enough to halt bacterial growth and decomposition. Rue has attended her fair share of postmortems. She's familiar with the unique scent that hangs in the air of every morgue—a mix of tissue preservative, astringent cleanser, and death itself. But familiarity does not breed comfort in Rue. She chews cinnamon gum as she observes pathologist Fareed Gamal and his diener. Toshi stands at her side. They're both suited up in protective gear over their clothing. Fareed narrates his observations into an overhead mike as he goes.

The dead woman lies naked on the stainless steel table. Her head rests on a block that exposes her throat. The table is slightly tilted so her body fluids will drain. A grocery-style scale hangs at the foot of the table, awaiting her organs. At Fareed's side is a smaller table topped with a dissecting block and the urgent-looking tools of his trade—pruning clippers, a vibrating bone saw, large knives. These are not finely tuned implements designed for lifesaving surgeries. These are to cut bodies apart, crack open rib cages, saw through bones.

Fareed and his assistant have already weighed and measured the dead woman. An external examination has been conducted, and they have meticulously tweezed off fibers and debris and hairs and bits of vegetation. They then removed her jewelry and carefully undressed her, recording everything as they went. Each item taken from the body so far—whether a tiny fiber or a piece of clothing—has been marked and taken into evidence.

Rue stares at the tattoo on the decedent's arched neck. The dead woman has another tattoo on her hip that resembles the painting of the goddess Apate in Arwen Harper's studio. The ink is stark against her pale, translucent skin.

Rue forces herself to see the decedent objectively now. She needs to intellectualize, compartmentalize, or it will overwhelm her. From experience she knows that if she allows the emotion in, she won't be able to focus sharply on the small clues. She cracks open another tablet of gum and pops it into her mouth. Toshi glances at her. It's only his second autopsy. But he's a natural. She's not.

"She smells like she was drinking heavily sometime before she died," says Toshi.

Rue says around her gum, "Would be consistent with reports that she was highly intoxicated at the Cody barbecue."

"We die as we live," says Fareed, reaching for a ruler. "Our mental and physical traumas, our pasts, daily habits, lusts, desires, fetishes, addictions—it's all written into the body." He glances at them from behind his plastic face shield, which will soon be spattered with blood and bone gore when he brings out the saw. "Our bodies keep score even if we don't ourselves. Nothing left to hide once you're up here on my table. Death is the great equalizer when it comes to alcohol, too. Whether cheap vodka or Dom Pérignon, it's all ethanol. All toxic, and the human body metabolizes it to exude the same sickly-sweet smell, privileged or poor."

He leans forward to measure and study the neck tattoo. He describes it for the recording.

"Looks like a chimera," he says into his mike.

"Which is what, exactly?" asks Toshi.

Fareed glances up briefly. "From Greek mythology. A fire-breathing female monster. See? Front part of the body is a lion, middle is a goat, rear is a dragon. A tail is usually depicted, like this one, with a serpent's head on the end. These days a chimera is sometimes used to denote a fantastical idea or figment of the imagination."

"Her son said the tat on her hip is some Greek goddess," says Toshi.

"Apate," says Rue. "Goddess of deception."

Fareed turns over the decedent's left wrist, exposing the underside. "Deep wrist injuries on the insides of both wrists," he says. "Cuts are longitudinal in orientation."

"Self-harm?" asks Rue.

"Consistent with an old suicide attempt," Fareed says as he turns his attention to the torn nails. He begins to take scrapings from beneath them.

"She was seeing a psychotherapist in Ontario," Toshi says.

The scrapings go into evidence bags marked RIGHT and LEFT. Fareed reaches for forceps. He begins to extract the broken strand of tiny orange and green beads caught between her fingers.

Rue swallows. Her gaze fixates on the bead strand.

Fareed drops the beads one by one into a small metal basin at his side. They land with a plinking sound. It feels unnaturally loud in her head.

"Orange and green beads. Appear to be plastic. Round in shape. Two millimeters in diameter." He carefully tweezes another, bigger bead out from between the fingers. "Brown metal. Hexagonal shape. Ten by five millimeters. Flat surface." He frowns slightly behind his face shield and leans closer. "Imprinted with some insignia." He pauses. "Looks like a stylized rhinoceros head."

The buzzing grows louder in Rue's brain. Heat prickles over her skin.

Toshi leans closer for a better look. "It is a rhino head, yeah. At least it looks like one to me. There were some more beads found on the cliff. My guess is she ripped them off her assailant in the struggle. Before she went over."

Claustrophobia tightens a fist around Rue's throat. She thinks of Eb. She can't breathe. She feels faint.

Fareed drops the metal bead into a stainless steel dish at his side. It lands with a hard clink.

He reaches for his Wood's lamp—the size of a large flashlight—and his assistant turns off the overhead lights.

Fareed pans his Wood's lamp over the body, searching for semen, which fluoresces under ultraviolet rays. Blood and saliva do not fluoresce. Some lint does. And even though there is no overt evidence of sexual assault, as there was on the victims of the Jogger Killer, he's being meticulous.

An odd splotch of purplish light appears on the inside of the woman's upper left thigh.

Toshi flashes a glance at Rue. "It'll yield DNA," he says.

But before Fareed can begin the task of taking vaginal swabs, Rue feels her stomach heave.

"I . . . Excuse me . . . I . . . need some air." She hurries for the exit.

"You okay?" Toshi comes after her.

She raises her hand. "Just feel off. Need fresh air."

She hastens out the sliding metal doors, shame swelling inside her chest, along with a feeling of rising nausea. She runs down the shiny-floored corridor under the strips of harsh fluorescent lighting, making for the fire escape doors at the end. She bashes through the fire doors and races up the concrete stairs. Rue pushes out of a door and inhales the damp, cool outdoors.

Fuck.

She drags her hands over her hair and realizes she's trembling. She swears again before noticing a man in medical scrubs stands smoking a cigarette nearby.

Rue hasn't had a cigarette in months. And the man is looking at her as though he can see straight into and through her.

"Bad start to the day?" he asks.

"I guess. Can I . . . can I bum a smoke?"

He offers her his pack and she takes a cigarette. With a trembling hand she puts it to her lips and he clicks a lighter. She leans forward to take the light and inhales.

Coughing slightly, she says thanks.

The man leaves, and Rue stands smoking under the shelter of a concrete slab. She can't believe she actually asked the man for a smoke. A memory fills her mind.

It's hot. Dry. So hot that heat shimmers white over the African landscape.

She's outside a tiny gift shop at their lodge in Botswana, having a smoke in the sparse shade of a thorn tree while Eb is inside buying trinkets to take home to Canada.

Her son exits with two little plastic bags. In each is an African bead bracelet with a single bronze-colored bead stamped with the rhino logo of the Save the Rhino Foundation.

Eb smiles sheepishly. "One for me and one for Dad." He shows Rue. And she knows he bought them because their Motswana guide wore several on his wrist, along with a leather thong tied with bigger beads. Eb's admiration for the young, handsome, and muscular tracker who found them lions and showed them how to follow the prints of African wild dogs is bottomless.

She takes another terse drag on the cigarette as the memory sucks her deeper.

"Do you think your dad will wear it?"

"Doesn't matter if he does." A flash of his big smile, his bright white teeth. "I can wear both. And it's for a good cause. The foundation gets funds from every bracelet sold. It goes to stop poaching."

She inhales more smoke and coughs. Her eyes water.

Rue tells herself that her number-one job as a cop is to protect the public. And right now no one is at risk, or in danger, over her silence about Eb's beads. Or the fact that the dead woman *might* have been one her husband had an affair with. She also tells herself that pretty much everyone who goes to Southern Africa on safari returns with similar beads. Saving rhinos is a cause du jour, too. Those beads can be bought online by anyone anywhere in the world.

But as she stubs the cigarette out, Rue knows she's not just compartmentalizing—she's entering a slippery slope of denial. She tells herself that if it does become an issue, she will declare it, and her superior can judge whether she should be removed from the investigation. Besides, it's far more likely that the dead jogger met a bad end because she was in the wrong place at the wrong time and fell prey to an opportunistic predator, maybe even the JK. Or her death is linked to Tom Bradley or Simon Cody.

Or both.

Usually the most obvious answer *is* the answer.

She has worked so hard at getting her position with Integrated Homicide. She's aware of the rumors and snipes that she got the job only so the department could meet a diversity quota, and she's determined to prove herself worthy. She refuses to allow her pathetic marital affairs and personal life to get entangled with this. She guards her privacy and her vulnerabilities and her son like a lioness, and she point-blank refuses to let Seth and his philandering dick screw up her career. Or her son's life.

But as Rue reenters the hospital and goes back down the stairs to the basement morgue, her mind goes back to the day she followed her husband.

RUE

THEN
June 8. Wednesday.

ELEVEN DAYS BEFORE SHE DIES.

Rue is parked outside the Windsor Park Recreation Centre. She's been sitting in her personal vehicle for more than an hour now, watching the entrance. She's parked along the far edge of the lot, where her white Subaru is in shadow and partially obscured by a cluster of trees. As she keeps an eye on the rec center entrance, she listens to her Pimsleur learn-to-speak-Portuguese level-one audio. She might as well make use of the time and try to learn some of the language her bio father spoke—or maybe still speaks. It could come in useful when she and Eb visit Mozambique again.

She repeats after the instructor, "*Eu não sou daqui.*"

I am not from here.

Rue is experienced in surveillance. She knows how to follow and observe people without being seen. But watching her own spouse on her day off is not something she ever thought she'd use her training for.

She checks the time.

"*Onde é o aeroporto?*" says the instructor.

Where is the airport?

"*Onde é o aeroporto?*" repeats Rue, struggling with the accent.

Every time another person exits the glass doors of the rec center, she tenses. The doors open again, and two women walk out in designer leggings, carrying yoga mats and coffees from the coffee bar inside. Then comes a woman with two boisterous kids in tow. The kids have wet hair, and one is hitting the other on the head with a pool noodle.

Rue checks her watch again. He's taking his time today. Suddenly he's there, stepping out the doors. Her husband. She feels a kick to her stomach. He's powerful in every sense. Big. His Nordic genes define him. Sandy-blond hair.

He's alone. Behind him the door slides open again, and a woman exits.

Rue's fists tighten on her wheel. Keeping her hands on the wheel, she leans back in her seat slightly. Seth knows her vehicle, but it's one of many white hatchbacks in the fully occupied lot. And she's picked her location carefully. Seth's focus is also wholly on the woman he's with.

The world tends to narrow around those in love. Or in lust.

For a hot moment Rue utterly detests her husband.

Seth and the woman walk together past the swimming pool windows. Wind blows the woman's skirt and ruffles soft curls across her face. When Rue was a little girl, she would have killed for soft, loose curls like that. Her husband and the woman walk to the corner of the building, and as they go around the side, just before they disappear from Rue's view, her husband touches the woman's face. He leans in, pulls her close, and gives her a kiss.

Rue watches the woman's arm slide down her husband's back. The woman cups Seth's butt, drawing him a little closer as he appears to deepen the kiss.

Rage spikes through Rue. It curdles into her stomach with jealousy, anxiety, hurt, bitterness. How is one supposed to feel? Rue should know by now. It's certainly not the first time Seth has cheated on her. He promised it would stop. But it hits her particularly hard this time, because this time Eb knows. And now she feels that in her son's eyes—she's just a doormat.

She feels shame. Because clearly Seth doesn't care how deeply he is humiliating her.

He's not even trying to be subtle about it. Everyone here can see them.

Her eyes burn.

She wonders what the woman's name is, where she lives, whether she is married, as the last one was. She wishes she could see the woman's face.

The woman and Seth both get into his truck.

One of the young teens from Seth's swim team walks past the truck. Rue recognizes her as Tarryn Wingate. Seth rolls down the window and waves at his swimmer. Tarryn returns the wave, and Rue suddenly wants to kill him. Her husband is not only lacking in subterfuge, he's flaunting his affair in front of people who know her. And when they do run into Rue in the street, they'll know a secret about her husband. And they will think: *What a fool this detective is. What a loser. She can't even leave her cheating white husband.* And Rue cannot deny the ugly feeling surfacing deep inside her that he disrespects her because of her looks, the color of her skin. She's the outsider again. The girl who doesn't belong. The girl adopted by liberal white parents looking to do some good in the world, parents who never understood why their brown child couldn't just blend in.

Eu não sou daqui.

I am not from here.

Seth's truck drives out of the lot. Jaw clenched, Rue pulls out and follows them.

She has one singular focus: find out who *she* is.

If it weren't for Eb having told her that he'd seen his father with a woman, Rue would have believed Seth. She'd have been duped into thinking he meant what he'd said this time. And that he'd kept his promise. Because she so badly wanted to believe it.

When Eb told her about seeing his dad kissing another woman, he was embarrassed for his mom. He said he'd been afraid to mention it because he didn't want to hurt his mother, but he was far too angry with his father not to spill the beans, and he hated seeing his dad treat Rue like this.

The truck turns onto Main Street, which leads into the elite Story Cove area. Her rage tightens to a hot white point in the middle of her forehead, and she fists the wheel.

Jesus, Seth. A woman from this place? Story Cove? Probably a privileged wife married to an older husband with money.

His truck pulls into a loading bay outside a Tudor-style building with a swinging sign that says The Red Lion Tavern. It's about a block up from the Story Cove Marina.

Rue pulls in behind a delivery truck a few cars farther back. The woman gets out of the truck. Rue has a clear view of her now, but she has her back turned to Rue, who swallows, her gaze riveted. The woman wears a boho skirt, a white peasant top, armfuls of bracelets. She's a direct contrast to Rue, who is often told that she's rigid, too buttoned up, too controlled, that she should *lighten up and laugh a little*. Rue comforts herself by thinking it's a cop's discipline. She knows it's something deeper. A deep fear of letting go. A fear that she might lose what she has earned in life if she does loosen her death grip. A fear of seeing her family break up, because family is something she has fought hard for and always believed in.

Apparently she's lost this battle anyway.

The woman blows a quick kiss to Seth, and he drives off.

Rue remains in place, watching as the woman enters the tavern with its Tudor facade and red umbrellas outside.

The door swings shut behind the woman. Time ticks on. Rue stares at the sandwich board outside the Red Lion entrance. It advertises lunch specials and takeout deals.

For a while she just sits. Numb. Time passes. Suddenly she decides she desperately needs takeout.

Rue reaches into the back seat of her vehicle, finds a cap and a baggy jacket. She puts these on, followed by her shades. She pulls the bill of her cap low over her brow and exits her vehicle.

Rue strides toward the entrance of the Red Lion Tavern and pushes in through the doors.

RUE

THEN
June 8. Wednesday.

ELEVEN DAYS BEFORE SHE DIES.

As Rue enters the tavern, she removes her shades. Her eyes take a moment to adjust to the dim light inside. The interior is full of dark wood paneling, warm accent lighting, booths with benches upholstered in what appears to be green leather. The effect is old British, yet with contemporary accents. A bar counter runs along the far side. The top is made of beaten copper. A lone bartender polishes a beer glass.

The hostess stand is vacant. Rue waits a moment, then bypasses the stand and walks past the sign that asks guests to wait to be seated. She enters the restaurant area and carefully scans the patrons seated at the tables and in the booths.

"Good afternoon. Can I help you?"

Rue spins around.

A woman stands with a menu in her hand. "Table for one?"

"Oh, I . . . uh, just came for takeout."

"I can take your order, if you like. Or you can place it with Rahoul at the bar."

"I saw on the board outside you have a special on fried calamari."

"It's one of our chef's specialties." The woman smiles.

Rue guesses her to be in her midfifties. The name tag on her chest says DEZ.

"I'll have the calamari to go."

"Chips or rice with it?"

"Ah . . . chips." Rue is trying to see around the corner into another area of the restaurant, because she can't find her husband's lover.

"Anything to drink with that?"

"Perrier, thanks."

"Name?"

"Sue."

"Okay, Sue. It should take about fifteen minutes. You can sit at the bar if you like, I'll have Rahoul get started on your drink. Or you can wait in the reception area."

Rue makes her way over to the bar and props herself up on a stool. Rahoul sets a glass on a coaster in front of her along with a small bottle of Perrier water with a slice of lemon on the side.

"Ice?" he asks.

"No. Thanks." She pops the lemon slice into the glass, pours her water, then turns on her stool to survey the restaurant as she sips, because she knows that woman came inside here.

When her Perrier is almost finished, she catches sight of her quarry. Rue watches in surprise as the woman carries a tray of drinks over to a table and starts handing them out. She cannot see the woman's face, but the clothes and the hair are hers.

Seth is banging a *waitress*?

Not a high-society wife from the gym?

Rue cannot take her eyes off the waitress as she makes her way back to the kitchen. She manages only a glimpse of the woman's profile.

"Sue?" says a voice behind Rue.

The server disappears into the kitchen. The door swings shut behind her.

"Sue?" a woman's voice says more loudly. "Your order is ready, Sue."

Rue turns to see Dez holding her bag of food.

"Oh, I . . . I'm sorry. My mind was . . . far away." She takes the bag from Dez, then hesitates. "Was that Rebecca I just saw, going into the kitchen? It is Rebecca, right? We had her as our server the other day, and she was so great. I'm just hoping my husband left a big enough tip."

Dez's smile fades a little, and a frown creases into her brow. Rue is fishing for the server's name, but she realizes she's pushed a tad too far and it's time to cut out because this woman is getting suspicious. She holds up the bag. "Thanks. Smells good."

Rue steps out of the tavern, heart pounding. She puts her shades back on. She's rattled. What in the hell is she even doing?

Her husband is banging a boho chick who serves food in a tony tavern in Story Cove? Rue figures even though she's a waitress, she is still likely someone he met while working out in the gym after coaching his swim squad.

She gets back into her car and puts her bag of hot calamari and fries on the passenger seat. She starts the engine and pulls out of the parking bay, joining the stream of traffic. Eb will make short work of the meal.

Maybe she'll leave the bag with the Red Lion logo on the kitchen counter just to see how Seth reacts.

Either way, she can't take this anymore. She's going to have this out with him.

RUE

NOW
June 21. Tuesday.

Rue reenters the autopsy suite as the portable X-ray machine is being wheeled out. The technician pushing the machine gives her a smile as she goes past. Fareed and Toshi both look up and stare at Rue, questions in their eyes.

"Sorry," she says. "Something came up."

"Your food?" Toshi asks, amusement twinkling into his eyes.

She clears her throat and nods to the X-rays up on the monitor behind Fareed. "What do the X-rays say?"

Fareed regards her for a moment longer, then says, "Well, the X-rays match the dental records sent via email to my office early this morning." He points. "This healed lateral malleolus fracture is also a match. It's a common fracture—a break of the knobby bump on the outside of the ankle. Medical records indicate she received treatment for the fracture two years ago." He pauses. "It's her. Arwen Harper."

Toshi says, "The DNA samples from her hair- and toothbrushes will likely confirm this as well, when the lab results come in."

"Do her medical records show anything else?" Rue asks. An image of her husband kissing the dark-haired woman floods into her mind. She tries to shake it, tries to tell herself it wasn't Arwen Harper, Joe's mother, whom Seth was banging. Another part of her brain knows she's like a bug trapped in a carnivorous pitcher plant of denial, and she's going to be consumed one way or another.

"Harper's records show she was referred by her GP to a psychiatric institution after what appeared to be a psychotic incident six years ago. She was diagnosed and treated at the institution for schizoaffective disorder."

"Which is what?" Rue feels ill.

"I'm no psychiatrist," says Fareed, "but to the best of my knowledge, it's a condition described as a mixture of schizophrenic symptoms—aural or visual hallucinations, or both. Basically the patient loses touch with what is generally accepted as reality. It can manifest as a panic type, which presents with manic behavior. Or a depressive type, which involves depressive symptoms. And then there's the mixed type, which presents with both manic and depressive symptoms."

"You mean, like, bipolar-type mood swings?" Rue asks.

"Yeah, from what I understand. It creates an emotional roller coaster."

Rue stares at the dead body, the tattoos. Again the image of a woman with Seth floods her mind in vivid colors. She sees the woman's arm going down her husband's back, her hand cupping Seth's buttocks. She can't unsee it now. She suddenly very desperately wants Tom Bradley to confess to killing this woman, so she won't have to ask Seth about a woman named Arwen.

Or Eb.

"You sure you're okay, boss?" whispers Toshi.

"Yeah. Yeah, I'm fine," she says quickly as she shakes herself. "Must be coming down with something. Any idea yet on cause of death?"

Fareed frowns. He's also eyeing Rue oddly. "Still need to open her up. But . . ." His gaze returns to the body on his slab. "I'm guessing there's a chance we won't be able to pinpoint one specific blow that killed her. My ruling could end up being that she died of blunt force trauma. Which would be consistent with deaths resulting from the trauma incurred by jumping or falling from great heights, or blast injuries, or with the person being struck by—or striking—any firm object, such as rocks, fists, a crowbar, bat, ball, another vehicle."

"If that's the case, there's nothing here that would prove this is a homicide?" she asks.

"Like I said, I've still got work to do here, but yes, it could end up that way."

"But there *is* the evidence of a struggle on the cliff," Toshi reminds her. "There's the blood trace at the top of the cliff. And the footprints that followed her."

"*If* it's her blood on the cliff."

Toshi's brow creases. "Yeah, well, we should have DNA results soon enough, along with the semen DNA—"

"Which might or might not have occurred at the time of death—I mean, she could have had sex prior to going running."

"Why don't you let me finish up here?" Fareed says.

She nods curtly. "Toshi, can you hang in here? I'll go visit Joe Harper and inform him that we now have an official ID, and I'll get the ball rolling on a warrant for Arwen Harper's phone records and a search warrant for her residence, just in case. If someone took her phone, those phone records could help us locate him. I'll also initiate a press release now that we have a positive ID. Then I'll head to the Red Lion and speak with her employers."

"Do you want me to do that?" Toshi says. "You can stay, and—"

"I'm fine. I . . . need the air."

I need to handle the Red Lion interview. Alone.

"Thanks, guys. Later."

She exits the morgue, her blood pounding.

She can feel Fareed's and Toshi's eyes boring into her back as she leaves. She can feel their questions. She needs to get a grip. She needs to get on top of this, fast.

MATTHEW

THEN
May 25. Wednesday.

Three and a half weeks before she dies.

It's a school day, but Matthew has a cold, and although he's not terribly sick, his mother said he could stay home. He's always on top of his schoolwork anyway, and his mom doesn't mind letting him have days off now and then. He's happily playing on his iPad when he hears the front garden gate swing shut. That's his cue—another patient on the move downstairs.

He grabs his camera and heads to the front window of his surveillance turret. Matthew watches a woman arriving. She has red hair to her shoulders, and she is pushing a bike with a helmet hanging over the handlebars. He leans closer—the bike has a reflective swoosh sticker down the crossbar. Like the Shadow Man's bike? Energy crackles through him. He watches carefully as she enters through the front gate, making a bit of noise getting her bike through. His mom's therapy office has a separate gate and a pathway that leads off the front street and goes beneath a trellis to a door at the front of her office. The door opens into a small waiting area for her patients. They come in, press a button that tells his mom they are there, and then sit and wait until she calls them in.

But when they leave, they exit out a side door. It leads to the path and to a gate into the lane. His mom says she designed it this way so her patients don't have to meet each other face-to-face. Some people don't want it known that they go to therapy, she told him. And if they've been crying and stuff, they can exit out the back without anyone seeing their puffy faces. People seem to cry a lot in there. Matthew figures it must be pretty horrible to need therapy if it makes people so sad.

He has not seen this patient with the bike before. But he's usually at school at this hour on a weekday. His window is open wide, so he leans forward, just peeking his head and camera out. He shoots a few images. Like a stealth watcher.

A few moments later Matthew hears the side door shutting downstairs. He hurries to the window that looks over the lane. He spies a big man exiting the lane gate. He's full of muscles, and his sandy-brown hair is shorn super-short like a soldier in the army.

Matthew clicks his camera as the man goes to a big Dodge truck with a shiny grille. He's a firefighter. He used to have his appointments later in the afternoon, so Matthew has examined his truck before, while the man was inside getting his therapy. There's a small plate above the regular truck registration. It says Story Cove Fire Rescue.

Matthew can't imagine a firefighter crying into tissues downstairs. He can't imagine why a firefighter who looks as strong as this dude with the big truck would ever need therapy.

But his mother says you can't judge like that. It's not what the person looks like on the outside; it's how they're feeling on the inside. Because everyone has feelings. Of love, of hurt, of betrayal, or anger, rage, depression. And sometimes you can't see on the outside just how broken or unhappy people are inside. Every single person on this planet, his mother says, has their own private pains and longings. And they all have their secrets. Sometimes those secrets make them unwell, because they are hard to keep hidden, and they fester. And then the people end up downstairs.

Matthew likes this particular idea.

It means people go into that room downstairs where his mother works, and little by little she makes them tell her their secrets, and then once she has them out, it relieves them, and it changes how they feel, and then their whole world looks different to them. He clicks a photo of the firefighter just as he gets into his truck.

Matthew expects the firefighter to drive off. But he doesn't. He sits in his truck for so long that the lady with the red hair and her bike come out.

She puts on her helmet, pushes her bike out the gate, and cycles down the street.

Only then does the firefighter start his truck and drive down the same street, not far behind the lady with the red hair.

LILY

THEN
May 25. Wednesday.

Three and a half weeks before she dies.

CHART NOTES: **GARTH**

Patient—firefighter in his late fifties, husband, and father of 3 young children with a much younger wife—presents for help processing a terminal cancer diagnosis. Says he's been given 8 months to live.

"Did you write the letter to Rose?" Lily asks. Her patient is edgier than usual today, and it's taken him a few extra minutes to settle on the oatmeal-colored sofa.

Garth extracts a folded piece of paper from his shirt pocket. He holds it up. "I did."

He's been Lily's patient for almost two months now, but it took him four weeks to tackle the letter he may or may not leave for his wife to read when he is gone.

"Do you want me to read it out loud?" he asks.

"Would you like to?"

He scrubs his fingers through his short hair, as if trying to get rid of some itch that is more psychological than physical. "Okay," he says. "Okay, I'll do it."

He unfolds the piece of paper and clears his throat.

"My dear Rose—" Almost immediately he chokes on emotion. He swears as tears fill his eyes.

Lily pushes the box of tissues closer to him. She feels his distress. She's being affected by her patients more than usual. It's probably because of her own increasing paranoia, her sense of being watched, stalked, the cryptic notes, the embossed image she believes was a satanic goat symbol. The words: *From someone who knows.*

On top of it all—it's the empty bottle of strawberry-flavored vodka Lily found under Phoebe's bed this morning when she was looking for the cat. And when Lily bumped the bedcovers while fishing out the vodka bottle, Phoebe's tablet on the bed flickered to life, and her manga drawing showed on the screen. What Lily saw shocked her to the core. It was a murder scene, and violent, and Lily cannot get the image out of her head now. It's circling around and around in her brain like a swarm of ugly, sticky, black flies buzzing over a bloating corpse.

Garth reaches for a tissue, blows his nose, then pours himself some ice water from the jug Lily always leaves on the coffee table in front of the sofa. Garth swallows half the glass of water, swipes the back of his hand across his mouth.

"You know what I realized in writing this letter, Doc? It was that my biggest fear, my deepest worry, is that Rose will find another man after I die. And this new guy is going to move into *my* house, into *my* bed. He's going to make love to *my* beautiful wife, and become 'Daddy' to *my* boys and girl. And I will just be, like . . . wiped off the slate of their lives, like I never even existed on this earth. This me. This Garth. This firefighter who is a nice guy who just wants to help people and care for his family."

Lily sits silent.

He snorts softly. "Shallow, right?" He struggles with another wave of emotion. "But then I realized that if I truly love Rose and my kids, I actually need to set them free. I need to give my wife permission to not feel guilty if she meets someone new. I . . . It's the biggest thing I can leave behind for her. Peace. Freedom. So—" He clears his throat. "That's what this letter says. I tell her she has my blessing to live, really live, after I die." He folds it up again and replaces it in his pocket.

"You're not going to read it?"

"No. I'm not going to read it out loud here. I am going to leave it for her for when I'm gone. It's between her and me. But in writing it, I think I came to realize—to accept—that there is no way I can beat this illness into submission. And I have no right to attempt to control my family from beyond the grave. It will give them guilt and pain. What I can do is release them. But I realize something else: what worries me even more than Rose forgetting me is her finding out who I was before I met her, and what I did."

Lily feels a tightness in her chest. "What . . . do you mean?"

"Do you think people can change, Doc? I mean completely change?"

"Yes," she says too quickly, too forcefully. Her mind whips to the newspaper cutting she keeps locked in a little box secured in a safe in her office. Lily inhales slowly, carefully. "I do believe that people can change, yes. If others let them, they can become better—or even completely different—versions of themselves."

Garth's gaze tunnels into hers. She can't read his features. The room suddenly feels cooler. Smaller.

"But it's other people, isn't it, Doc? Society as a whole doesn't allow you to change if you've done something terrible, does it? There will always be reminders, individuals who cannot forgive, who refuse to let go, who want to pull you back and stamp it like some indelible scarlet letter into the center of your forehead. So others will see you coming, and know that you must forever be judged and punished."

Lily fights an urge to lurch out of her chair, get out of this room, away from these things he's saying. She forces stillness, and she watches Garth closely, and she waits, and she wonders what he has really done, and how terrible it could be.

"I mean, people pay lip service to the concept of justice and atonement. And closure. And all that touchy-feely shit. But really, deep, deep down, if they are aware of what someone did, they're always going to think it could happen again, given the right set of triggers, no? They believe it is in you, in your blood, or in your DNA." He pauses. "Right?"

"Do you want to tell me what you did, Garth?"

His gaze lasers hers. Silence swells. He swallows. "No," he says finally. "No I don't. And I really don't want Rose and the kids to find out, either. Not ever. Because even you, Doc, would look at me differently, as much as you might tout professional objectiveness."

Lily opens her mouth, but Garth raises his big hand, stopping her. "I know what you're going to say—that I will feel lighter if I get it off my chest. And that maybe if I talk about it, I will die easier. But that's a load of crock. The moment I tell someone, their whole perspective of me, their concept of who I am as a good person, a guy who saves people from fires and cuts them out of mangled car wrecks on the highway, the guy who volunteers to drive animals to the vet for shelters—all that vanishes. All they see is a violent man. A dangerous man. A heinous monster. But if they don't know what I did, then *I* can forget that part of myself ever existed. I can pretend that the sick fuck of the past was actually someone else entirely. I can bury him in my unconscious like a high-functioning serial killer who can compartmentalize the horror inside. *That* is the only way people can change. When no one forces them to wear a label. When society doesn't keep reminding them they are not who they are trying to be."

Lily shifts in her chair. "The serial killer—he eventually devolves, you know? Holding things in like this can be very tiring, Garth. It creates stress in both body and mind. It stops—"

"Stops people from living properly? Makes them paranoid? Feeds substance abuse, or makes them act out in other bizarre ways?" He laughs dryly. "I'm going to be dead within eight months, or so they say." He holds his arms out to his sides. "Look at me—hard to believe that right now, huh?"

Lily regards him. He still looks fit and strong. But she also knows how quickly that can change with the illness that is silently eating away at him even as he sits on her sofa.

"And this is how I want Rose and my kids to remember me. Strong. Good. Kind. Hero."

"And if they do one day learn about this thing you hide?"

"There is a chance, Lily, that they won't. There is a chance. If I do tell Rose now, there is none." He pauses, holding Lily's eyes with an intensity that is so hot it's tangible. "If I tell her now, she and the kids will reframe their idea of me. I will be a guy who did a heinous thing. A guy who caused untold and cruel suffering." He goes quiet again. "What would *you* do, Doc? Would you confess? To your husband? Would you tell *your* kids? Or would you die with the gamble that maybe they will live on in innocence?"

Lily is hit by a terrifying sense that he's asking her about her own past and that he can see into her. That maybe Garth is just a mirror being held up to herself. Maybe *he* is the *someone who knows*. Because Lily knows she would take the same gamble as Garth one hundred times over. She clears her throat.

"Look, I don't know what you did, Garth. So I can't say. And this is not about me. This is about you. Perhaps if you told Rose, and she forgave you, you'd feel free. And so would she. Spouses can surprise us, you know?"

He laughs. "You really think there is such a thing as forgiveness? I mean, really?"

A shadow crosses over Lily. She feels a dankness creeping out of the corners of her office, and its fingers are cold and coming for her throat. But it must be that the sun has moved behind the poplar.

"Forgiveness—true forgiveness—is more about *you* letting go of the guilt and shame that imprisons you, Garth."

He shakes his head and glances at his watch. His time is almost up. He says, "No. That guilt, that shame—it's what *drives* me. To be a selfless firefighter, to be the best dad possible. That guilt, that shame, Lily, is what makes me a good man. I see my time's up."

"Same time next week?" she asks.

He grabs his jacket off the coat hook. "I think we're done here, Doc." He shrugs into his jacket. "I'm as ready to get dying as I will ever be. Not much point in talking about it further."

Lily isn't so sure. "How about we take a break next week, then you come back for one more? We'll schedule it now, but if you truly feel fine, then call to cancel. Deal?"

He hesitates, then smiles. "Deal. Thanks, Doc." He disappears out the door.

Lily stares after him. He's rattled her. She sees the red light on her desk flare. Her new patient is waiting.

She inhales deeply, goes to her file cabinet, opens it, and unlocks the safe. She reaches into the back, and her fingers touch a smooth wooden box. Lily takes the tiny box out. She opens it carefully and removes an old newspaper clipping.

It's a photo of a girl. She stares at it, her skin going cold. A little pendant nestles in the hollow of the girl's throat. Baphomet. The sabbatic goat. The girl's goth symbol. Beneath the grainy black-and-white image is a caption in italics that says simply, *"Sophie McNeill, age 12, missing."* The image is from a newspaper that was published in New York. Lily lifts out the second clipping and reads the headline:

Massive Cross-Country Search for Abducted Child

The light on Lily's desk starts to flash red again. She jolts and quickly replaces the cutting in the box. She returns the box to the back of the safe and locks it. She goes into her small bathroom, rinses her face, and freshens her lipstick. She takes a drink of water, smooths down her pants, then goes to the door of her waiting room.

Taking in another deep breath and exhaling fully, she tries to let go of her previous patient's energy and her own negative thoughts.

She opens the door and smiles at a very attractive and chic-looking woman in high-end cycling gear. The woman, a redhead, sets down the magazine she was paging through and comes to her feet.

Lily extends her hand. "Hi, you must be Paisley?"

"Good to meet you, Dr. Bradley," the woman says as she takes Lily's hand.

"Feel free to call me Lily. Come on in."

TAKEN

A True Crime Story

Wozniak exited the rancher and found the male neighbor who had placed the 911 call standing on the lawn next door with his wife. They were seniors, and the wife clutched a little white dog in her arms.

"They're the McNeill family," the man told Wozniak. "My wife thought she heard screaming next door. I came outside to see, and something looked—felt—wrong about the McNeill house. I saw the lights were on in the basement, so I peered inside. And . . . I saw her. I saw Della . . ." His voice broke.

His wife said, "I can't believe what's happening. They're a truly lovely family. They go to church, so friendly."

"Do they have kids—what are their names?"

"Yes," she told Wozniak. "A little boy, Danny. He's eight. And a girl, Sophie. She's twelve. They . . . Are they okay?"

"Did you see anyone, anything suspicious outside the house? Hear anything other than screams?"

"I don't know if it means anything, but there's been a strange young man in a black hoodie lurking around the place for a couple of days. I saw him in a beaten-up brown truck parked down the street yesterday. He had a male friend with him. I think they were watching the house."

Wozniak hurried back to his cruiser and called in the name and description of the girl based on the photographs. It was a world before the so-called Amber Alert, but a BOLO went out—an urgent message relayed to all agencies across the country to be on the lookout for a twelve-year-old girl named Sophie McNeill. Long dark hair. Caucasian. Pretty. He mentioned the truck, too.

Wozniak reentered the house to wait with the other officers for the coroner, homicide detectives, forensic techs, and K9 teams. But as soon as he stepped back inside, he heard Conti yelling upstairs: "We found her! She's in here! Under the bed in the girl's room. She's alive. Get an ambulance, now!"

Thank God, Wozniak thought, his heart hammering as he called for EMTs.

RUE

NOW
June 21. Tuesday.

After breaking the news to Joe Harper about his mother's positive ID, Rue drives to the Red Lion Tavern thinking about him. The kid is devastated. She feels as though she has robbed him of what little hope might have remained. She left him in the care of Hannah Cody and a fellow officer who works with victims' services.

As she turns onto the main road into Story Cove, Rue's jaw tenses. She checks the time and calls Seth on speaker, using her personal phone.

He picks up on the third ring.

"Hey," she says stiffly. "You still at home?"

"Yeah, what's up?"

She stops at a red light. "I need to ask you. Where were you the night before last?" An old woman pushes a cart into the pedestrian crossing and moves slowly across the road. There is a small, geriatric dog in her cart.

"What do you mean?" Seth asks.

Irritation sparks through Rue. The light turns green, but the senior takes forever moving across the crosswalk. "Just tell me, Seth. Where, *exactly*, were you on Sunday from around noon to when you returned home and got into bed?"

A beat of silence. "Look, Rue, if this is about—"

"Just *tell* me." Her fists clench the wheel.

"Can we do this later, after work, when—"

The old woman reaches the sidewalk. Rue presses down on the gas. "Seth, listen to me, and listen well—" She slams her brakes suddenly as a cyclist veers out from in front of a bus. She curses, then says, "The dead jogger, the one in the news, the one found on Grotto Beach—" She inhales deeply, steadies herself, turns down another street onto Story Cove's main road. "Her name is Arwen. Arwen Harper."

Dead silence comes from her phone. Rue feels sick. She sees the RED LION sign ahead.

"Is that who you were screwing? Is that who I saw you driving to the Red Lion?"

"You were *following* me? For chrissakes, Rue. How dare—"

"So it is her? She's dead, Seth, dead. Murdered. Do you hear me?"

He breathes more heavily. When he speaks again, her husband's voice sounds thick. "Are . . . are you sure—are you *sure* it's her?"

"We're sure."

A curse. Silence.

"Seth, she's lying naked on the slab in the morgue, probably having her rib cage cracked open right now, and her scalp peeled off, and her organs cut out and weighed. You *need* to tell me where you were on Sunday before someone else comes asking. And believe me, they will. And it's not going to look good."

"What . . . what happened to her, Rue?" His voice is a rough whisper. "You . . . you can't think—you can't possibly think that I had anything to do—"

"You told me your screwing-around days were over. You said never again, no more affairs. You made a vow. And it was a lie. And you weren't even subtle about it. People have seen you with this woman, Seth, so you better tell me that you have a watertight alibi for Sunday night when I was working late. Start with where you were at noon on Sunday."

"I was with the swim squad, on the ferry, returning from the meet on the mainland."

"They will verify?"

"Yes, of course. I was with the team members and chaperones. I was chaperoning a kid myself. Sally-Ann. She'll verify. They'll all verify."

"What time did the ferry dock?"

"I don't recall exactly. I'd have to check. Sometime around three p.m."

Rue pulls up outside the Red Lion. "And then?"

"We drove back into town. I dropped some kids off, including Sally-Ann. Then . . . I went for a meal and met some friends, and hung around for drinks."

"This can be corroborated?"

A pause. "Yes."

"And then?"

"We had a few more drinks, and I came home late, and you were home and in bed."

She closes her eyes, inhales, counts backward from four, breathes out slowly. "So you don't know where Eb was on Sunday, before I got in?"

Another beat of silence. "What's Eb got to do with anything?"

"Just . . . wondering."

Because I want to know that my son has a goddamn alibi, and I don't dare even voice the question to him. An image of Eb holding his glass of milk and plate of half-eaten cake fills Rue's mind.

I will do anything for you, Mom, you do know that, right? I want you to be happy.

"I don't know where Eb was," Seth says. "But what I'm telling you about Sunday is the truth."

"When was the last time you saw Arwen Harper? When were you last at the Red Lion Tavern?" She's testing him.

He clears his throat. "I—it was probably two weeks ago. When I gave her a ride to her work from the gym. It was already basically over by then, Rue. Look, I honestly don't even know a thing about her. It—she came on to me at the gym, and . . . it was just a fling for two or three days."

She closes her eyes. He's lying. She knows he is lying.

"Rue?"

"It is over," she says.

"What?"

"I said it's over. You and me. I want out. Of our marriage. I want a divorce. And you need to move out. Now. I don't want to see you when I get home."

"Rue—"

She kills the call. Blood thuds hot in her ears. She's shaking. Her mind spins back to the night she waited in her car outside the Red Lion.

RUE

THEN
June 16. Thursday.

Three days before she dies.

Rue is back in her vehicle listening to her learn-to-speak-Portuguese audio, playing softly in the background. It's dark. Raining. She's parked across the road from the Red Lion Tavern. Seth's truck is parked higher up the road.

Seth called her earlier to say he was going to be home late, and Rue had a feeling he would be seeing the waitress again. On her way home from a late shift, on impulse, she turned into Story Cove. And when she drove slowly past the Red Lion, she spied her husband's truck parked outside the tavern in the rain. Empty.

She circled around the block and came back the opposite way down the road, and now she waits across the road from the tavern, watching the entrance. Although she can't see Seth through the windows, she's sure he's inside. Rue's camera rests on the passenger seat. Perhaps she's not handling this in the best manner, but she wants photographic proof. When she files for divorce, she plans to make it go her way.

It grows colder in her vehicle. The rain comes down more heavily. Even though it's June, the wind off the sea has a chilling effect, but Rue is reluctant to turn on the engine to warm the interior. She prefers to not draw attention to her vehicle.

More time ticks by. The rain beats down a little harder.

The tavern doors open and a couple exit. They're older—seniors. The man helps the woman put up her umbrella, and he wraps his arm around her shoulders as they walk into the wet night. Rue feels a pang of loneliness. Of regret. Of time wasted on a man who doesn't respect her. Why did she fall for Seth, anyway? Is there a part of Rue that doesn't respect herself, that doesn't trust someone could love her fully? Is it because a buried part of her feels rejected by her biological parents?

The doors open several more times, spilling warm light into the darkness as people enter and exit the premises, laughing, happy.

Her audio runs its course and falls silent. Rue wonders if she should try to learn Afrikaans, too. That's what her birth mother spoke. Afrikaans and some Xhosa. She huddles deeper into her coat.

The tavern doors swing open.

It's her.

Rue sits upright. Her pulse quickens.

She watches as the dark-haired woman exits the tavern doors pulling a raincoat hood over her head. The waitress goes to stand under an awning, just away from the entrance, and she looks up the street. Rue curses. She's desperate for a good look at her face. And for a moment Rue wonders if she's been mistaken about Seth—maybe he's not inside. The tavern doors open suddenly, and Rue recognizes the familiar shape of her husband. He joins the hooded woman beneath the awning and snakes his arm around her waist. He says something near her ear.

Rue swallows and reaches for her camera. She aims, zooms in, clicks as her husband moves in for a kiss. She clicks again as the couple hurry arm in arm through the rain toward Seth's truck. She clicks as they get into his truck.

The truck's headlights flare on. It pulls into the street.

Rue feels ill. She lowers her camera to her lap.

Of course Seth is not home when she pulls into their driveway. He's not home when Rue goes to bed.

She can't sleep, and she lies listening to the rain and to Eb's occasional movements in his room downstairs. The rain stops. The house goes quiet. Still she can't fall asleep.

At 2:00 a.m. she hears the front door downstairs open.

Seth comes upstairs.

She feigns sleep. He gets quietly into bed. He smells freshly showered.

Rue lies staring at the ceiling. She needs to do something. This can't go on.

LILY

THEN
May 25. Wednesday.

THREE AND A HALF WEEKS BEFORE SHE DIES.

CHART NOTES: **PAISLEY**

Patient, early forties, has been on my waiting list for 6 weeks. Presenting problem . . . ?

A new intake is always a mystery. Sometimes Lily knows the presenting problem up front because they've told her on the phone. And then comes the detective work, because the presenting problem is usually a surface symptom of something far deeper and more complex—something the patient might even have hidden from themselves in order to function. But it's the presenting issue that propels someone into therapy.

Her new patient is certainly enigmatic. A very beautiful redhead with pale skin and alive with a restless energy. She wears Lycra leggings and a long-sleeved cycling jersey of thin, patterned fabric that shows off every curve and muscle. Lily would kill for a body like Paisley's.

Her patient places her bike helmet on the sofa, then walks over to Lily's bookshelf. She runs her slender fingers along the spines of Lily's books, checking the titles. She touches Lily's trinkets—a pottery mug shaped by Matthew's little hands, a seashell found in Mexico, a small sculpture from Australia. She picks up a framed photograph of the Bradley family taken in Cape Town.

"Can I get you some tea or coffee?" Lily offers.

"No. I'm good." She sets down the photo and goes over to study Lily's Rorschach inkblot print set, which Tom gave her last Christmas. Each blot is framed, and they hang in neat rows on the wall. Paisley glances briefly at Lily, as though assessing something, then moves to the wall that hosts Lily's mask collection.

"It was Jung, right?" says Paisley. "He called it a persona—the mask that each of us wears, the face we choose to present to the world?"

"Are you familiar with Jung's work—his archetypes?"

She sits. Finally. Crossing her Lycra-clad legs, she smiles. And Lily can't help but feel there is something a little patronizing in the upturn of Paisley's lips, the angle of her head, the way her blue eyes hold Lily's.

"Well, there's Jung's persona, the self, the shadow, and the anima or animus. The persona is the mask we chose to hide behind. Like you—your persona, your mask is one of a doctor—when you wear your white coat or hang out your shingle, people expect certain things. They believe you to be wise, compassionate, and kind. They expect you to behave in ways a doctor or therapist would. Put on a cop's badge and pick up a gun—you are the trusted protector. You are brave and just. Don the firefighter's yellow suit—you're a hero. A savior. Drape yourself in a black robe and put on a wig of gray curls and you are justice, the bigwig, a sage arbiter of truth and right and wrong. Put on a hood and you are a hangman, but take it off, and the hangman can go home to your family with an untroubled conscience because he was just doing his job." She leans back on the sofa, recrosses her legs. "We all need a mask in order to function. But wear the mask too long and we forget who really lives behind it. Right? We forget our authentic selves."

Lily shifts in her chair, increasingly uncomfortable with this talk on the back of her session with Garth.

"Do you feel you have been wearing a particular mask too long, Paisley?"

"I don't know. Maybe that's the problem—wearing a mask so long you are no longer aware you're even wearing it."

"And if I were to ask you what mask you think you wear?"

She runs her tongue over her teeth. "Mother. Wife. I guess those are my main personas I present to the world."

"And what do those titles mean to you?"

She hesitates. "That I am supposed to be nurturing, someone who offers safe harbor for my children. That I am virtuous. Kind. In control. That I am attractive enough to my husband so he won't stray. That I am good in bed—a whore behind closed doors. That I eat right and have my weight and carbs under control. That I am an accomplished businesswoman and also bake nice cookies and volunteer at my kids' school and take my kids to swimming lessons and make sure they understand their faith." She stops, catches her breath. "That I am organized. That I offer routine."

Lily swallows, thinking of herself, of how she takes Matthew to swimming lessons. Of how she obsessively counts carbs and volunteers at her kids' schools. Paisley could be describing Lily. "It . . . it sounds exhausting," she says.

"It fucking is."

"How many children do you have, Paisley?"

The patient holds Lily's gaze. "Girls. Three. Aged seven, nine, and twelve."

"It's hard work being a good role model."

"Yeah. Hard work keeping the dark and deviant little devil locked inside."

A noise begins in Lily's brain. The inkblot behind Paisley's head suddenly looks like Baphomet with horns. Sweat collects in her armpits. She struggles to concentrate and to find her next question.

"Do . . . do you work outside the home, Paisley?"

"I'm a pharmaceutical rep. And I travel a lot. But I don't have to work. My husband earns a good living, and I married into wealth. I married up. An older man." She smiles slyly—or at least it suddenly looks sly to Lily. "But work does give me an outlet. Without my travel, I wouldn't be able to fuck around."

Lily blinks. "Meaning?"

Paisley leans forward. "You want to know what my problem is, Doc—"

"Please call me Lily."

"Lily. My problem—my real problem—is I screw around. Sex. Risky sex, unsafe sex. With strangers. The wilder and hotter the better, and the more married the men, the more satisfying. I am addicted to fucking, Lily. And I can't stop. I used to be able to space it out and be more careful, but I need it more and sooner in order just to *feel*." She pauses. "Last week, while on a business trip to Toronto, I was arrested. For soliciting and having intercourse in public. Yes, I took money for sex. Money I don't need. And I need it to stop before it unravels the good things in my life, like my family."

Lily stares. *So here we have it. The presenting problem. A dangerous sex addiction.*

"I mean, I have a good husband. I have three perfectly beautiful, clean, innocent daughters. I have everything people say they want. Which means I also have everything to lose. And it's like . . . I feel like this is this devil in me that is *trying* to lose it all. Because if I do lose it, if I am exposed, then I won't have to try so hard to keep on my mask." She flops back into the couch, as though exhausted by getting this off her chest.

"And your cycling gear," Lily says quietly. "Is that also a mask? Something you chose to present to me on your first visit?"

Paisley huffs and sits back up. "It's a false narrative." She smiles slightly. "Not for you, but for my family. It's my cover." She holds her arms to her sides. "This is how I hide from my family and my community that I am going to therapy. They think I'm training for an upcoming bike race, and Wednesday is my long-ride day. But really it's my therapy day. It's why I chose to come to you. You operate outside of my own neighborhood. Plus you have a nice discreet lane off a nice quiet and leafy cul-de-sac." Her smile deepens. "I do my research, Lily."

Lily swallows. It feels like a threat. On another level she knows that's paranoia. Dianne is right. She needs a break. She's letting things get to her, reading too much into everything. But again, those notes—they were real.

"Is Lily short for Lilith?" Paisley asks.

"Lillian."

"She was a demonic figure, Lilith. In biblical myth. Did you know that?"

"I . . . did not. But like I said, my name is derived from Lillian. Do you want to tell me more about your arrest, Paisley?"

She leaps up from the sofa, paces. Lily sits silent, patient.

"It was about two a.m. There I was, on the street, in a skeevy part of town. Wearing a short pleather skirt. Thigh-high heeled boots in shiny black. Halter top, shimmery sequins. Bloodred lips. And I was hooking. I was hungry to be screwed in an alley, or behind some dumpster, pressed up against a dank brick wall, and for someone to stick dirty money down the front of my bra." She waits.

Lily refuses to show shock. "And did you get what you wanted?"

She snorts. "I got arrested before the john could pull his dick out of me. I was remanded with a promise to appear. Which I have yet to do. But . . ." Her face changes. Slowly she sits again. She rubs her face.

"It's like I am two people." She sits silent for a moment. Then, quietly, she says, "I'm scared. I really don't want to lose my family. I don't like what I'm doing. I feel shame. I feel filthy. Until the need somehow starts rising again, and growing acute. And it takes all my conscious energy to plan the next encounter, and to hide the truth, and cover up what I do. And sometimes I just feel like I am going to die. Perhaps this is what it's really about—a death drive. Part of me is looking for a way to destroy myself." She pauses. "And now you are judging me. I can see it. In your eyes."

"This is a safe space, Paisley. You should feel free to say anything here."

"Like a confessional?"

Lily tries to smile gently. "Like a confessional." But even she knows there are some things one can never reveal to a priest. "Tell me something, Paisley: If I had to ask you how old this little devil inside you was—this little being trying to destroy you—what would you say?"

"That's a weird question."

"Not really. Our minds are mosaics, and the sense of being inhabited by warring parts is common. Sometimes exploring and befriending those disparate parts of ourselves—our managers inside—can be helpful. One way to do this is to name the various internal managers, see how old they are, and then take them out and have a conversation with them."

Paisley purses her lips. "I don't know how old the little devil is . . . Eleven. Maybe she's twelve."

Phoebe's age. Phoebe with the strawberry vodka bottle under her bed. Phoebe, who drew a female manga character slitting another character's throat with a knife.

"So it's a she?"

"I guess. The same age as my eldest daughter. It's a challenging age, isn't it?"

Lily swallows. "It is. Balancing on the cusp between childhood and womanhood is complicated, especially given society's mixed messaging and expectations."

Lily clears her throat. *Focus.* "Now I want you to close your eyes, Paisley, and I want you to imagine this girl, bring her clearly into your mind."

"That seems . . . weird."

"Just try it."

Her patient closes her eyes, inhales deeply. It takes a while before she says, "I think I see her. I . . . She's laughing at me. Taunting me."

"Just watch her awhile, feel her."

Paisley is silent, but she begins to breathe heavily. Color rises into her cheeks.

"What does she look like, Paisley?"

"Dark hair. Long, dark hair. Very pale skin. Dark lips."

"Can . . . can you give her a name, so we can call her out again when we need to?"

She breathes harder, and her hands fist on her thighs. "I think her name is . . . Jane. No . . . I . . . She tells me her name is Sophie."

Lily's mind goes blank.

Paisley's mouth begins to twitch.

"I hate her! She's a bitch. She wants to hurt me. She—" Paisley's eyes flare open. Her chest is heaving. Her face has gone red hot and sweaty. She's shaking, and tears glitter in her eyes. "I can't do this. I cannot do this. I don't want to do this."

Lily's throat is bone dry. "Why not, Paisley?"

She rubs her mouth. "Because . . . she's horrible, this dark-haired child who wants to kill me. She's got a knife and she wants to slice my throat to silence me—to kill the good me. The innocent part in me. She wants to take *everything* I love away from me—my family—and . . . I . . . I don't know why, or what I have done to incur her hatred. Or why she would want to do this to me." Paisley reaches for the water jug in front of her, and with a shaking hand she pours a glass. She drinks deeply. "I'm sorry. I . . . I don't know where that came from."

"That's okay. You did really well. We won't try to go any deeper in this session, but next time maybe we can call out that other internal manager you mentioned—the good you. And we can ask the good girl if she has anything to say about . . . this bad girl."

"About Sophie."

Lily feels ice in her veins. It's transference. It's projection. That's all this is. She just needs a break.

TAKEN

A True Crime Story

Earlier that day, on the afternoon of April 22, 1989, Harrison Whittaker, seven years old, found his mother at her sewing machine in the basement, where it was cool. She was making a costume for his older sister and her starring role in the school play. Chrissie was going to be Sandra Dee in *Grease* and had been practicing her singing until Harrison's head hurt.

"Can I go to Danny's house to play?" he asked his mother.

"No. We're going to the mall in an hour. You need new pants."

"I don't need new pants. I need to go play. Please. Danny's mom said they're having a barbecue later, with hot dogs and ice cream, and then a video. And he said I could come. His mom said we could do a sleepover, and make a blanket tent. Pleeeeeease."

"Harrison—"

"Please, Mom. I will do all my chores and everything. I promise."

He whined and cajoled. He'd been patient all yesterday. And the unseasonably warm weather had everyone restless. His mother glanced at the clock.

Sheilagh Whittaker was tired. Her husband was working long hours in the oil and gas industry, where he'd just been promoted. She was carrying the household load as well as trying to launch a new family business. She still had to collect the pamphlets for their fledgling company. She needed to pick her battles and ration her limited energy, and Harrison had a way of sapping it all with his ebullience.

"Okay, fine. Okay."

"Thanks, Mom!" He kissed her, and her heart melted and she smiled.

The last time Sheilagh Whittaker saw her son was in her rearview mirror as she pulled out of their driveway on the way to the mall with Chrissie. He stood with his best friend and neighbor, Danny McNeill, on the McNeills' lawn—four houses down from the Whittakers'—wildly waving goodbye. Harrison held in his arms their little rescue terrier, Pogo. He took Pogo everywhere with him.

If Sheilagh Whittaker had forced Harrison to come to the mall to get new pants, her son might still be alive.

He'd be about forty years old now.

Sheilagh might even be a grandmother. Maybe her husband, Jim, would still be alive. Maybe he'd not have descended into alcohol abuse over the brutal death of their little boy. Jim Whittaker was never the same again after that spring day in Glenn Dennig.

If Sheilagh Whittaker had not asked her daughter, Chrissie, to take over the meringue pie she'd bought for the McNeill family at the mall, Chrissie might have grown into a completely different woman. Sheilagh might still have contact with her daughter.

"It's the biggest regret of my life," said Sheilagh Whittaker to a television journalist covering the anniversary of the Glenn Dennig family massacre.

"If I had not been so exhausted, if I had not conceded to his whining. If . . . if I had just made one little different decision, Harrison might not have fallen victim to a psychopath. We might all have had different lives, because the nightmare didn't end with Harrison's murder. It did not end with the deaths of Danny McNeill and his parents. It had a ripple effect down the years." Sheilagh Whittaker paused and looked away from the camera, and her eyes gleamed with tears.

"A psychopath destroyed us. There's no such thing as closure, you know? It . . . A violent crime like that, it doesn't just end when a killer is caught. It keeps on giving. For years and years. Even the young jury foreman—the stress of the trial affected him so badly. He was dead from a drunk-driving accident thirteen months after the verdict, and I believe he'd be alive if this never happened."

RUE

NOW
June 21. Tuesday.

"I'm Dez Parry," the woman says as she extends her hand to Rue. "Red Lion manager. I also wait tables, hire and train staff. The general dogsbody. What can I do for you, Sergeant Duval?"

"Is there somewhere I can ask you a few questions in private?" Rue asks as she repockets her ID.

The manager looks nervous suddenly. "What's this about?" Her frown deepens as something appears to dawn on her. "Have . . . haven't we met before?"

"I've visited as a patron," Rue says quickly. She tends to stand out in a neighborhood like this. "But this is business, unfortunately. It's about one of your employees, so if we could perhaps talk in private?"

Parry ushers Rue into a small office and closes the door. "Please, take a seat," she says as she moves a pile of folders off a chair.

Rue notices a CCTV monitor in a corner on a shelf. It shows a grainy image of the area outside the front entrance to the Red Lion. Another part of the split screen shows the area just inside the doors where the hostess stands.

"You have an employee named Arwen Harper."

"I . . ." Parry stills. Her eyes widen suddenly. Her hand goes to her mouth. "That's where I recognize you from. Television. The woman found on Grotto Beach . . ." Her voice falls silent. Her eyes begin to water and her complexion pales. She looks as though she might faint. "Arwen didn't show up for her shift today. I . . . tried to call her mobile but it kept going to voice mail . . ." She lowers herself into the chair behind the desk. Stunned. Processing. "It's her, isn't it? I . . . saw on the news that Tom Bradley—he's one of our customers—he found the body and . . . Christ. He . . . Did Tom Bradley find *Arwen*? My God, that must have been . . . Oh God."

"So you do know Dr. Tom Bradley?"

"Of course, yes. He's one of our regulars. He comes in with a group of professors from the university every Friday for happy hour, and they often stay late into the night. Arwen became their regular server. She got to know them quite well in a short period of time."

"Can you give me the names of the men who routinely come in with Dr. Bradley?"

"I . . . suppose it's not violating their privacy or anything. Everyone knows the profs are here every Friday. The core group is Tom Bradley, Simon Cody, Sandeep Gunjal, and Milton Timmons. It was Tom and Simon with whom Arwen formed the closest bond. She told me it was Tom who arranged for her cottage rental across the road from Simon."

"Exactly how friendly was she with them? Anything intimate?"

"I . . . I guessed Arwen was on the hunt. I mean, not in a bad way. She is—was—a struggling single mother, an artist. And she needed money. But I never really pressed her on her past, or what she was doing. From when I first interviewed her for the job, I had a sense she was running from something, getting away. And . . . and I saw the scars on her wrists. Beneath her bracelets and smiles and her easygoing attitude, I think she was a very damaged woman." She pauses. Tears sparkle. "Are you certain it's her?"

"Yes. I'm sorry."

Parry reaches for a tissue and blows her nose. She sits silent for a moment. "I can't believe it." She meets Rue's gaze. "Was it not an accident?"

"The death is suspicious, Ms. Parry. Which is why my team has been brought on board. It could have been that Arwen was just in the wrong place at the wrong time. But we need to cover all our bases."

Parry blows her nose and nods. "What can I do? How can I help?"

"Is there any reason to think someone might have wanted to hurt Arwen? Did she ever express fears, concerns about anyone in particular?"

"No. Everyone liked her. Men particularly. I can't think of anyone who would want to hurt Arwen."

Rue clears her throat. "Is it possible that she was sleeping with Simon Cody or Tom Bradley?"

"It's possible. I suspected it might be the case. But she never said. They're married."

"Did their wives ever visit the Red Lion with the men?"

"Not for happy hour. Tom and Simon have brought their families in for meals in the past, though."

"Did Arwen ever mention the wives—talk of them being jealous?"

"God no. She was . . . You know, Arwen came across so warm, so open, but in truth she never spoke about anything truly personal. While I felt like I knew her quite well, I don't think I ever knew her at all. It was all . . . a facade. This happy-go-lucky bohemian image she conveyed—it was like a mask she wore."

"How long has she been working here?"

"I hired her at the end of April. One of my servers had just quit, I was short staffed and pretty desperate. She responded to the sign I put outside, and I hired her on the spot. She turned out to be one of the best employees we've had. I am so, so sad to lose her."

Rue waits as Parry blows her nose and gathers herself.

"Do you know of any other men in Arwen Harper's life? Anyone else ever come with her to the tavern?"

Parry casts her mind back. "There was one guy. I saw him only twice. He came to pick her up after work, and for a drink at the bar once. He appeared to be waiting for her to finish her shift."

Rue tries to keep calm. "She mention his name?"

"No. I'm sorry. I respected her privacy, as I said, and I didn't ask."

"What did he look like?"

"Built. Sandy blond. Bit of a jock. Late thirties, maybe early forties."

You effing asshole, Seth.

Rue clears her throat. "Can you tell me when Arwen worked last?"

"Saturday, June eighteenth. She took the Sunday off because she was going to some barbecue. She was scheduled to work today."

Rue takes out her business card and a pen. She circles her mobile number on the card. "Call me at this number if you remember the man's name. Or if any of your staff happens to know it." She hands the card to Parry, hesitates, then tilts her chin toward the CCTV monitor. "Would your security cameras have picked up this guy at the bar?"

"Not at the bar. For privacy reasons the cameras only cover the inside and outside entrance. But it would have picked him up arriving and leaving."

"How far back do you save footage?"

"It rewrites every seven days. We just haven't put a budget behind a more comprehensive digital storage solution, but the seven-day period works well enough for our needs."

"Can I have a copy of the footage that you do have backed up?"

"Sure, I'll copy it onto a drive for you now."

"Plus a copy of Arwen Harper's shift schedule."

Parry nods and turns to tap keys on the office computer.

When Rue exits the Red Lion, she has a thumb drive of the security footage in her jacket pocket. It was four nights ago that she watched Seth leaving the tavern with Arwen. Seth will be on that footage, possibly visible in the company of the dead woman, and Rue is not sure what to do about it.

As she nears her vehicle, her cell rings.

It's Constable Georgia Backmann. Rue connects the call.

"Hey, boss," says Georgia. "One of our canvassers got something. He spoke to a female senior who lives across the back lane from the Bradley house. The senior claims a Dodge truck arrived and parked in the Bradley parking bay off the lane just after Tom Bradley was taken in for questioning on the morning of the 911 call. The Dodge was a dark, metallic gray with a decal on the rear cab window—a silhouette of a snowboarder. The senior says she's seen the truck there often before, but never so early in the morning. It has a Story Cove Fire Rescue plate. The senior believes the driver is a firefighter and one of Lily Bradley's patients. The officer parked out front of the Bradley home didn't see him because he entered from the back side of the lane. He was there only briefly. Might be a witness, might not."

"I'll check it out myself," Rue says as she gets into her vehicle. "I'm near the fire station. I'll swing by now."

RUE

NOW
June 21. Tuesday.

Rue turns her vehicle into the Story Cove Fire Rescue Station parking lot. The building has a Tudor facade like the Red Lion Tavern. It's a theme in this part of town, and with the shiny, red fire engines parked in a line outside, it belongs in a children's picture book. It looks fake. False. A mask.

As she drives slowly through, she scans the cars and trucks parked in the lot. She spies a metallic dark-gray Dodge truck parked at the end of the lot in front of a blue spruce. Rue pulls into a vacant space near the Dodge and calls Toshi.

"Hey, boss," he says as he picks up. "Just finishing up at the morgue. Like Fareed figured, his preliminary finding is that Arwen Harper died from massive blunt force trauma consistent with a fall from the top of the cliff. If she incurred any injuries prior to the fall, it got covered up by the subsequent trauma she sustained going down. But debris samples from the wounds have also been sent to the lab. Now we wait for the tox and DNA results."

"You sent it all to the private lab?" she asks as she exits her vehicle and begins to walk around the Dodge. She sees the snowboarder sticker on the back window and the Story Cove Fire Rescue plate.

"Affirmative," he says. "They've got a rush on the lot. I'm heading to Harper's residence next. We've secured the search warrant in case Klister's gang raises issues down the line, alleging we coerced the dead woman's grieving teen into giving us verbal access. Also got the papers in for her phone records."

"Good. I'll meet you at the residence. We might have another witness—just checking it out first." She explains to Toshi what Constable Backmann told her. Rue ends the call, pockets her phone, and walks up to the garage bay, where several firefighters in shorts are washing and polishing one of their ladder trucks.

A man with a rag in his hand looks up. "Hey," he says, standing erect and coming over to her. "Can I help you?"

"Detective Rulandi Duval. Integrated Homicide." She shows him her ID.

He studies it. "What's up?" he asks.

She jerks her thumb over her shoulder. "Who owns that gray Dodge back there?"

His frown deepens. "Why?"

"We're looking for possible witnesses to an incident, and that truck was nearby. I'd like to speak to the owner."

A burly guy emerges from around the side of the ladder truck, wiping his hands on a rag. "That's mine. Why?"

"And you are?"

"Garth Quinlan."

"You were parked in a lane off Oak End yesterday morning, Mr. Quinlan?"

"Yeah." He hesitates, then says, "Shall we talk over there by my truck, give the guys here some space?"

She follows him back to the truck. He faces her. "I . . . It's personal. I'd like to keep it private."

"Keep what private, sir?"

He rubs his brow, glances away. "Look, I'm in therapy. Psychoanalysis. And before you go thinking I'm crazy, I'm not. I just don't want the guys—or anyone—to know I'm seeing a shrink. And I've done nothing wrong. I was at my shrink's house for an early appointment."

Interest rustles through Rue. "What makes you think I'm here looking to see if you've done something wrong?"

"I saw the news. I know my therapist's husband found a body on the beach just before I arrived at their house. I figured . . . that's why you're here. The dead woman." He's getting edgy.

Intrigue deepens in Rue. "I'm just interested in whether you saw anything relevant to our investigation. You entered the Bradleys' yard through the lane gate and left a short while later. I'm guessing you didn't manage to squeeze a therapy session into that window."

He drags his hand over his hair. Big, strong, scarred hand. Knuckles of a fighter.

"Okay . . . listen, I'm going to be straight with you because I don't want trouble. I've got a record. Way, way back in another life, I was convicted for assault. I put a man in a wheelchair for the rest of his life. He can't even piss or feed himself. My wife doesn't know. And it's why I didn't come forward when I saw . . . I didn't want any police scrutiny or involvement. I'm dying, okay. Aggressive terminal cancer. It's my punishment, I guess. In a few weeks I will probably no longer be up for this job as a firefighter. I don't have time to waste. And yeah, it's why I'm in therapy. To help me process end of life, and to deal with the frustration and aggression I felt when I learned I would not be able to beat this illness into submission."

"I am so sorry for this news, Mr. Quinlan. What is it that you saw?"

He moistens his lips, glances away, as if still trying to find a way to avoid heading fully down this path.

"I . . . I'd scheduled an early appointment. I wasn't going to go back for more therapy, because I thought I had things under control, but . . .

but I don't. And when I arrived, Dr. Lily Bradley wasn't in her office. The door to her waiting room was locked. But I did see her car in their driveway, so I figured maybe she forgot, or had the wrong time. I tried to call her from my truck, then while I was on the phone, over the wall, I saw lights go on in their garden shed. So I peeked over the wall. Lily was coming out of the shed with a small garbage bag. She hurried into their kitchen door. So I opened the gate, thinking I could knock on the back door and catch her. Like I said, I have a clock ticking on my life, and I had a shift coming up, and I really needed to talk to someone before work. I saw her through the dining room window, and I banged on the glass. She . . . looked shocked. Wrong. And . . . when she came to the door, she had blood on her hands and face."

"Blood?"

He nods.

"What happened then?"

"She was super nervous. She claimed there'd been a family emergency. Her landline started to ring, and she slammed the door shut in my face. I was puzzled, so I . . . I guess I hung back and watched through the window a bit. I couldn't help it. When she came into sight again, she was in the kitchen. She took something out of the freezer—meat. She unwrapped several packets of it, tossed the meat into the small refuse bag she was carrying from the shed. She wrapped it up and stuck it in the freezer. Then she put the old meat packaging into the bin beneath the sink."

Rue regards the man. "You saw all this?"

"Look, I'm not proud of the fact I spied on my therapist. But you develop a relationship with a shrink—someone you spill all your personal secrets to. And she gives you nothing back about her personal life. You become naturally curious. And what I was seeing unfold . . . I couldn't look away. Then I felt like shit. And nervous. Because when I drove away, I saw the police vehicle parked across from the Bradley house. And later, I saw the news . . . and I figured, whatever was going down, you guys were on it, and what I saw at the Bradleys' house wasn't going to . . . I didn't think it would make a big difference to the investigation. However, it was going to make all the difference to my life, my wife and kids, if I did *not* get tangled with law enforcement."

"And now here you are."

"Yeah. Now here I am. You found me. And I know it looks weird now. And that's why I'm telling you up front that I have a past, because you will probably go looking and find out anyway." He pauses and holds Rue's gaze. Wind rustles through the spruce branches. "Please," he says quietly. "For my wife's sake, for my kids'—if my record doesn't need to come out, please do not hurt them. What I did in my other life was ugly. I don't want it hanging around their necks." He swallows, emotion welling up in his eyes. "Do you have children, Detective?"

"I do. A son."

"You'd want to protect your kid, right?"

PHOEBE

THEN
June 15. Wednesday.

FOUR DAYS BEFORE SHE DIES.

Phoebe opens the front door for Joe and bows, rolling her hand like a courtier of old, and says in a theatrical voice, "Welcome to our humble abode, fellow pilgrim."

He laughs, and so does she. Joe walked Phoebe home from the bus today, and she decided to invite him in. To be honest, he's the first boy she's asked home—as in a boy she's totally attracted to. There have been other guys, of course, but usually her parents' friends' children, or neighborhood kids over for birthday parties or playdates or summer barbecues.

Phoebe wants to show Joe the progress she's made with her graphic manga novel about Dark Magical Girl, but she's having second thoughts suddenly. She hasn't known him long at all, and she's nervous now that he's actually inside her house. The whole place seems to shrink in his presence. She's also super edgy about what her mom might say—her mom has total knee-jerk reactions to anything Phoebe does. The first words out of her mother's mouth are usually: *No. Don't. You can't do that. It's not a good idea, Phoebe.*

Her mom also has not seen her fuchsia hair yet. She dyed it with Fi's help at the Cody house, and they already got into trouble there for staining the white counter in the bathroom pink.

Maybe Joe will buffer her against a negative reaction. Her mom might be so focused on the fact that she's brought a guy home that she'll be all over it before she even gets to griping about the hair.

Joe doesn't get far beyond the front door. He stops and studies the framed photos of the Bradley family in the hallway. Just standing there, looking. A distance growing in his eyes. His gaze moves from the photo of her mom and dad on their camping trip to the one of their family safari in Botswana to the four of them laughing on the beach in Aruba.

Anxiety bites. He's judging her. Judging her whole stupid, conservative, privileged, white family—she can see it, feel it.

"What are you thinking?" she asks quietly.

He turns, smiles. Warmth in his eyes. Her heart tumbles.

"My mom always says that: *What are you thinking?*" he says.

"I mean . . . I know it's a girl thing, but—"

"It's okay." He touches her arm lightly with his fingertips. "I was thinking how nice it must be to have, like, a normal family, you know?"

"Normal? Us?"

"Yeah. A mom, dad, a kid brother. A house you've lived in, like, forever. Good friends all over the neighborhood. Knowing everyone. Going on family vacations around the world. It's, like, a Hollywood movie family."

"It kinda sucks, really. Everyone knowing your business in a small community. I like the sound of *your* life—super exciting, lots of travel and, like, freestyle adventure."

"Well, I would like to know my own father—I mean, even just know who he is. And me and my mom have never been to Africa. Probably never will." He looks more closely at their safari photo. "This must have been so freaking rad."

Phoebe fingers the orange and green beads on her wrist that she bought to save rhinos, and she feels a pang in her heart. More than anything in this world, she'd like to go on a safari with Joe Harper. Their photo seems to have made him wistful. And Phoebe suddenly isn't sure that now is the right time to show him what's on her iPad. It feels trite.

The door to the passage that leads to her mother's therapy office opens, and her mom appears.

Phoebe goes wire tense.

Her mother enters the hallway, a strange look on her face.

Phoebe's heart beats faster.

Her mom is holding an empty vodka bottle. Strawberry flavor. The kind Phoebe takes to drink in the grove in the woods with Fi. It makes Phoebe think of the man who spied on them.

Her mother's mouth opens to say something, but she suddenly sees Joe, who steps around the corner into her view. Her mom stalls in her tracks. She stares at Joe, her mouth opening slightly.

"Hey, Mom," Phoebe says. "This is Joe. From my school."

Matthew comes clattering and yelling down the stairs. "Mom! Mom! Phoebe dyed her hair! It's pink! Dark pink! Fi helped her and Jacob says they got pink all over the upstairs bathroom at the Cody house."

"Shut your stupid little face," Phoebe snaps at Matthew.

"Hi, Mrs. Bradley," Joe says quickly, holding out his hand like some gentleman, or businessman. It throws her mom off balance.

"Joe is new at school, well, new in the neighborhood," Phoebe says.

"Mom is mad at you," Matthew chirps. "Did you see what she found under your bed?"

"Get lost," Phoebe says under her breath.

"Matthew," her mom says. "Go upstairs."

He doesn't move. Her kid brother is staring at Joe. Admiration or something dumb in his eyes. Joe smiles sheepishly at Matthew and gives a teensy shrug.

Matthew grins.

Joe says, "Look, I really should be going. I . . . just walked Phoebe home from the bus, and I . . . yeah, I was just leaving. So, see you tomorrow, Phoebe, maybe? Nice meeting you, Mrs. Bradley." He moves quickly toward the door. "No worries—I can see myself out." He puts his shoes back on, reaches for the door handle.

Phoebe expects her mom to say, *No, don't go on my account.*

But her mother says in a super-cold voice, "Good to meet you, Joe."

The door shuts behind Joe.

"What is *wrong* with you?" Phoebe demands. Attack is her go-to form of defense. Attack before her mom attacks her about the vodka bottle and hair.

"Me?" says her mother. "What is wrong with *me*? This is what's wrong with me." She holds up the empty bottle. "What in the hell is this, Phoebe?"

"It's another vodka bottle, Mom, Christ. Is this the kind of thing you say to patients like slutty Tarryn Wingate? Because Tarryn gets drunk and sleeps around all the time. Probably even with her swim coach. Bet you're nice to her."

"Phoebe, you do not mention my patients. Ever." Anger crackles in her mom's eyes. It's like electricity radiating off her skin. Her cheeks are red. Phoebe feels a little afraid. She hasn't seen her mom look this angry. "And how old is Joe?"

"What's that got to do with anything?"

"He looks like he's twenty, Phoebe. You're *twelve*. You're not even in your teens yet."

"So what if he is twenty? Are you going to forbid me seeing him because he's too old for me? Are you going to tell me I can't dye my hair the color *I* want because I'm a *child*? Because it doesn't fit *your* vision for me? Because you know what, Mom, I *will* see him. I'll do whatever I want regardless of your stupid decrees, because you're not the boss of me, and if I can't bring my boyfriend home, I won't. I'll just go to his house. Or run away with him." She stomps up the stairs.

"You're grounded, Phoebe!" her mother yells up the stairwell behind her.

Phoebe storms into her room, slams the door behind her, and locks it. She leans against her door and tears fill her eyes. Slowly she sinks down to the floor and wraps her arms around her knees.

LILY

THEN
June 15. Wednesday.

Four days before she dies.

Lily lights a candle in the stone church by the sea and kneels facing a statue of the Virgin Mary. She closes her eyes and clasps her hands in prayer.

She should be home making dinner, but Tom called to say he'd be late, and she is alone in her soul, in a deep and terrible way that her husband will not understand, not when it comes to their daughter, and how Phoebe can make Lily feel like a monster.

After her outburst with her twelve-year-old, Lily is frightened. Her fears are compounded by her recent sessions with Paisley and her inner little devil and with Garth, who asks if people can ever truly be forgiven and allowed to become someone new. Lily's fight with Phoebe felt like a confrontation with her own inner twelve-year-old self, and perhaps that's why she gets so irrationally angry with her daughter. Like Paisley, Lily has her own inner bad girl. Like Paisley's, Lily's inner devil is probably also a tween betwixt girlhood and adulthood, being buffeted by a patriarchal culture and confusing pressures. Phoebe perhaps has become an external embodiment of some unconscious thing inside Lily. At least this is what the therapist in her is beginning to believe.

She needs to fix it before she pushes her daughter too far away. Before she loses her death grip on her perfect life. Before she can no longer compartmentalize and keep locked away the horrors of her past.

She bows her head as Mother Mary watches over her. Judgmental.

Repent.

Lily kneels in silence for a few moments as she continues to examine her conscience, as she must before entering the confessional.

She needs to be a better wife. She needs to engage in sex again with Tom, so he is not forced to look to his neighbors' wives or to other women to meet his desires. Seductive, destructive temptresses like Paisley. *Lead us not into temptation.* She must separate her own inner child from her dialogue with Phoebe. She must work harder to withhold moral judgment of her patients. Like the mounting revulsion she felt for Paisley, who serially seduces other women's husbands. Paisley is hurting, too. She's unwell. Lily needs to uphold her oath as a therapist and remain empathetic. Compassionate. That's all everyone wants—to be loved. To belong. To be forgiven for their sins.

Amen.

Lily makes the sign of the cross. She is ready for confession. The green light outside the small booth is on. Father is ready for her, too.

Lily enters the tiny booth near the back of the church. She kneels on the low bench. She can see Father's shadowed silhouette behind the latticed wooden screen.

"Forgive me, Father, for I have sinned," she says quietly. "It's been a month since my last confession. And I . . . I . . ." Her words die on her lips.

"What is the sin you wish to confess, my child?"

Her priest is eighty-two years old. He calls everyone in his flock "child." And it unnerves Lily because she is already struggling suddenly with her own inner child. For a moment she can't speak. Or think.

"Child?"

It strikes Lily suddenly. She knows what is wrong.

"I fear you will not be able to help me, Father. I . . . I fear that I have committed the cardinal sin that cannot be forgiven." She inhales shakily. "I have committed the deadly sin of despair."

The priest is silent for a long moment. The weight, the history, the judgment of the church over the eons suddenly presses down on Lily, trapped in the little confessional box. Her heart begins to race. Heat prickles over her skin, and sweat pools in her armpits.

The image of Baphomet shimmers into her mind, and it will not go away. The goat "devil" with horns. A noise begins in her head. She sees the goat pendant with the pentacle shimmering at the throat of little Sophie McNeill in the old newspaper photo.

"Yet you are here, my child," the priest says. "If you despair that the Lord God does not have it in His capacity to absolve you of your sins, why is it that you have come to me to ask for His forgiveness? Why is it that you kneel before me now in His name if you cannot believe in His all-powerful mercy?"

Emotion burns into Lily's eyes. She begins to tremble deep inside her belly.

"Father, I have come before God on many occasions over many years, and I have confessed all my sins. And I . . . I don't feel He has forgiven me. I . . . I feel doubt growing in me. I feel fear. I feel . . . the presence of something that has come to rob me of what is good." She hesitates. "I feel there is evil in me."

"When you confessed your sins before, did you do your penance? Did you honor your acts of contrition with a pure heart?"

"Yes, Father."

"Then you must trust that the Lord God's compassion and power to forgive are infinite, and that He indeed has the power to absolve all sin. To despair is to not believe in Him, my child. Despair is contrary to God's goodness. It's a loss of existential hope. It's the one deadly sin that cannot be forgiven because it contravenes our basic understanding of God." He pauses. "Now are you sure that this is your sin? Or do you think that deep in your heart you still believe in Him?"

"I . . . I still believe, Father. I think I still believe."

"Then what is it that you truly fear if He can absolve you?"

Lily's skin goes hotter. She thinks of the horrible manga illustrations on Phoebe's iPad. The knife against a white throat. The empty vodka bottle. The older boy. She thinks of gaping wounds like bloody, red eyes watching her from white skin. She smells the blood.

The devil, she thinks.

I fear a little Deviant Devil who bears the sign of Baphomet. A devil who cannot be named.

RUE

NOW
June 21. Tuesday.

They're in the bullpen. Rue has returned from speaking to Garth Quinlan and is updating Georgia Backmann, Toshi, and Doc Despot Henry Hague, who sit at their desks, listening to her.

"Lily Bradley put *meat* in a refuse bag and then stuck it in the freezer?" asks Toshi. "What in the hell for?"

"We need to get into that freezer and shed, and we need that Ocean Motion shirt." Rue checks facts off on her fingers. "Virginia Wingate saw Tom Bradley returning with the stained shirt. Matthew Bradley claims his father went directly into that shed after his run. Matthew Bradley took photos of his dad. Garth Quinlan saw Lily Bradley remove something in a refuse bag from the shed. Quinlan saw her put the refuse bag with ground meat into the freezer. Lily Bradley then opened the door to Quinlan with blood on her face and hands."

"So Tom Bradley went into the shed before he even called 911," notes Georgia.

Rue nods. "Then, while Bradley took me through the woods to see the body, his wife went directly into the shed and potentially attempted to remove evidence. We have grounds for a warrant to search that shed and house. And while we're in there, I want Matthew Bradley's photos."

"I'm on it," says Hague, reaching for his phone.

"Toshi, what did we get from the search of Arwen Harper's residence?" asks Rue.

"No laptop. No phone. Which is suspicious, since her son said she was working on a secretive project on her laptop, and it was apparently the reason they moved to the island. And it's worth remembering she worked as an investigative reporter and sometimes went undercover—we need to find out what she was doing. She also had a ton of medication in her bathroom cabinet. Uppers, downers, antipsychotics—I've sent it all in to the lab. Substantial marijuana and alcohol stash, too. And there's also evidence of a lot of printed material—newspaper pages, glossy photographs, spiral notebooks—that were recently burned in her fireplace."

"As if someone was destroying something?" asks Georgia.

"It's possible," says Toshi. "Something just felt weird about the amount of ash in that fireplace that did not come from wood. And the fact her laptop is missing. Plus the fact that she had a pinboard that appeared denuded. Also, it appears the lock on the makeshift doors to the pinboard had been forced open."

"Potential motive for her death here?" asks Georgia. "Like this was not a random or a JK predatory-type attack, but a targeted killing?"

"We should keep an open mind," says Rue. "Toshi, did you show Joe Harper the photos of the jewelry found on his mother's body? Did he notice if anything was missing, as in any 'trophies' taken like in the JK cases?"

"He couldn't tell," Toshi says. "Joe claims his mother switched out her jewelry all the time, and had a lot of it, so he has no way of knowing if something was taken."

"Okay. We can't assume nothing was taken, then," says Rue. "In the three JK cases, the assailant took one jewelry item from each victim—the silver antique ring from the first, a small compass set inside a jade pendant shaped like a Maltese cross from the second, and a bracelet in a hexagon shape from the third. All very distinct items. Plus he took a lock of hair from each body."

"But no sign hair was taken from Harper?" asks Georgia.

"Negative. Fareed didn't find any indication of that. However, we need to consider that if this was the JK, and not a targeted attack, he might have been thwarted before being able to carry through on his MO."

"Anything from her Red Lion employer?" asks Toshi.

"Nothing that immediately stands out," says Rue. "Other than Arwen Harper was very friendly with Tom Bradley and Simon Cody and their happy-hour crew."

"Like, sexually intimate friendly?" asks Georgia.

"Her employers says it's possible, even likely. Which raises questions about the men's wives—possible rivalry, jealousy. Arwen Harper expressed no fears to her employer, however. She was reportedly well liked overall. A friendly but very private person. Never mentioned any enemies. The last time she worked was an afternoon shift—Saturday, June eighteenth. The day before the barbecue. The day before she died. I'll go through the Red Lion CCTV from the last seven days—that's as far back as they store the footage—to see if something jumps out."

"Want me to do it?" Toshi asks.

"No," Rue says a little too quickly. She dials it back. "I'm good—might as well keep busy with something I can drop as soon as that warrant comes through."

Toshi regards her in silence for a moment. Rue feels her face warm and is thankful her complexion does a decent job of hiding it. Toshi turns his attention to his computer, then swings back.

"Oh—I found something on those plastic beads and the rhino stamp. Look here." He pulls up a page on his computer. Rue and Georgia gather behind his chair.

"See that rhino stamp on the bronze bead in this image? It's the logo of the Save the Rhino Foundation of Southern Africa. The foundation sells these bracelets to tourists at curio stores, and online to buyers around the world. Proceeds help fund antipoaching efforts." He glances up. "If Arwen Harper ripped that strand of orange and green beads off an assailant during a struggle on the cliff, there is a chance the assailant wearing it visited Southern Africa."

"Or . . . he bought his beads online," says Rue, staring at the computer screen. "Clearly they make a ton of those. The Save Koalas Foundation runs a similar fundraising program out of Australia."

Toshi frowns. "Yeah, sure thing, boss. But it *is* something distinct, right? Our unidentified subject could have an Africa link—either visited, or has an interest in preserving African wildlife. It narrows things down."

Rue feels Toshi watching her as she returns to her desk. She angles her chair and monitor away slightly and begins to go through the CCTV footage from the Red Lion, but her pulse runs high. She forces herself to focus.

She finds the time-date stamp for Thursday, June 16, and begins to watch the grainy CCTV footage on the split screen. She needs to know if her own vehicle will appear as identifiable parked across the street from the tavern entrance. She flicks a glance at the others in the bullpen. They're all busy.

She returns her attention to the screen and fast-forwards until she sees Arwen Harper approaching the entrance with an umbrella. The time matches the start of her shift that day. Rue watches as Harper enters and appears to talk to the hostess. She removes her raincoat, then disappears from the screen. People come and go. Rain falls outside the tavern. It grows darker out. Nothing jumps out at Rue. She fast-forwards, then catches the familiar shape of her husband. Her stomach muscles tighten.

She watches Seth enter the Red Lion. He glances around inside, goes in the direction of the bar, then disappears from view.

Rue turns her attention to the outside footage. It's dark out now. Rain comes down and obscures visibility of the sidewalk and street directly outside. She sees her white Subaru pull into the parking space.

Shit.

She shoots another glance across the bullpen. Everyone is still focused on their tasks. She zooms in on the white Subaru. Rain gleams on the windows. Rue can make out a dark shape inside, but she can't tell that it is her. She can't see the plates, either. Possibly the image could be enhanced, and someone might identify Rue inside. She also knows that if this car becomes of interest, footage could potentially be found from nearby street or traffic cams that might have picked up her vehicle registration. Plus a clear view of the driver. Her heart beats faster.

Arwen Harper reappears in the footage. Rue notes the time stamp. It matches the end of her shift. Harper exits the tavern, then vanishes from the scope of the camera. Rue knows the waitress went to stand under an awning, but it's not within view of the CCTV camera.

Seth appears in the reception area, exits the tavern, then vanishes in the same direction as the waitress. A few moments later, the white Subaru pulls out.

Rue sits back, heart thumping. Her husband is not tied on camera to the dead waitress. And, potentially, neither is Rue. She releases air she didn't know she was holding in her chest. She reaches for the shift schedule Dez Parry gave her, and she rechecks the time of Arwen Harper's final shift. She then fast-forwards to that time-date stamp. She watches Arwen Harper arriving at work. Nothing else appears unusual—patrons coming, going. Harper appears occasionally in the reception area to stack menus. At 3:15 p.m. Harper reappears in the reception area. She talks to the hostess, then exits the tavern. She stands for a moment outside the Red Lion entrance, checking her phone, then proceeds to her right and disappears. Rue is about to sit back and relax, thinking there is nothing on here that presently warrants further investigation, and she's probably safe in keeping her family and her marital troubles out of this. But as she is about to file the footage, Rue notices a male standing across the street from the Red Lion. Her pulse spikes.

It's Eb.

With his bike.

Just standing there watching the Red Lion entrance.

Rue hurriedly rewinds, watches again, her heart in her throat. It's definitely Eb. He arrived at 2:46 p.m. And he stood there watching the entrance until Harper came outside and left. A sick feeling swims into Rue's stomach as she sees her son's head turn, and Eb's gaze follows Arwen Harper as the waitress slips out of view of the camera.

Rue can barely think. Can barely hear.

"Boss! Did you hear me?" It's Toshi. He's standing up, shrugging into his blazer. "We got it. Got the warrant. Let's go."

Rue hurriedly ejects the drive, hesitates, then slides it into a baggie. She stashes it at the back of her desk drawer. She will have to think about this later.

MATTHEW

THEN
June 15. Wednesday.

Four days before she dies.

Matthew eats a slice of delivery pizza at the kitchen counter alone. His dad is late, and his mom is gone. After the fight between Phoebe and his mom, Phoebe went upstairs and slammed her door. His mom ordered pizza, said she was going to church, and told him to eat when the pizza arrived.

For a few moments it felt cool to be left alone with a whole pizza. Until it didn't. Now the house feels hollow. Cold.

He hears Phoebe's door open. She comes downstairs and her face is fierce. She's removed all her goth makeup. She shoots him a hot look.

"Where are you going?" Matthew asks as his sister heads for the door and starts putting on her new lace-up boots even though it's summer and warm out.

"None of your business."

"You're grounded. Because of the vodka. I heard Mom say so."

"None of your damn business, you little freak."

Well, that was guaranteed to make Matthew *make* it his business. Business always got more interesting when it was not supposed to be his. And if he could get photos of his big sister sneaking out when she was grounded, he could use that for a super-cool blackmail tool. He's done it before, and she had to pay with candy and all sorts of stuff like not tattling on him. And he's up for more bribery.

He waits until the door shuts, then grabs his camera and follows Phoebe down the road.

She goes to the end of Oak End.

He stays behind the bushes and watches as his sister knocks on the cottage door. Joe comes out. They talk a moment, then Joe closes the door behind him, and they go into the woods behind the house.

Matthew sneaks along behind them in the woods. Wind blows in the treetops, and the rustling hides any noise he makes. He's in his element, using his self-taught super-stealth skills.

Phoebe and Joe sit on a log.

Matthew crouches down in the ferns, clicks his camera.

Joe turns round. "Did you hear something?"

They listen, and Matthew holds dead still.

"Just the wind, I reckon," Phoebe says.

They kiss.

Matthew's heart beats like crazy. He clicks and clicks. This he will be able to use to blackmail his older sister for all sorts of things. He's on a high.

When they come apart, his sister says, "You know those trips, the photos you were looking at in our hall?"

"What about them?" asks Joe.

"It didn't seem that great—the whole family-togetherness thing. It's like . . . I have this totally annoying little brother. And my parents are super controlling. And my mom . . . she's always on my case. And it's like she's getting more and more freaked out about everything. I really am sorry, Joe. I . . . She was so rude. And it's so embarrassing, and I hate that you had to see her like that."

"What did she say after I left?"

"Grounded me. For the vodka thing."

He nods. "I would still love to go to Africa. Family unit or not. It's like a dream. African safari. And to Asia."

"Is that where your dad is from?"

"I don't know where he's from. Like I said, I have no idea who he even is."

"You could search, you know? I'm sure there are all kinds of websites and things that would help figure out how to find him. I mean, if you want to."

"I do want to. Especially now, since we moved here. My mom is also . . . I don't know. She's unraveling. She's . . ." He stops.

"She's what?"

"It's nothing. She's just busy with something weird and being super private." He touches Phoebe's wrist. And Matthew clicks again, then lowers his camera. He's taken aback by the gentleness in big macho Joe's touch. His kindness. It makes Matthew feel . . . sort of emotional inside. Like he's seeing another side to his big sister. Someone who needs kindness and a gentle touch.

Phoebe takes off her Africa bracelet that Joe is touching. Matthew clicks as she hands it to Joe.

"Here."

"What?"

"I want you to have it. It's a Save the Rhino Foundation thing. That photo you were looking at of us on safari—it was taken at a curio store where proceeds go to antipoaching efforts and saving the white rhino and stuff. They hire these dogs and teams of local women. They're all-female squads from the little villages, and these 'mammas,' they call them—they go after these poachers with guns and tracking dogs. It's super cool."

"I can't take this, Phoebe. It's your memory. Your memento of a special time."

"I want to share it. You don't have to keep it. Just wear it a bit. Okay?"

He's silent for a while. His shoulders seem tight, and he bows his head forward slightly.

Phoebe touches his arm. "Joe?"

He swipes his eyes. When he speaks his voice is thick. "Thank you."

Matthew for the first time feels as if he shouldn't be here, shouldn't be spying. That maybe some things should be private. But if he sneaks away now, they might hear cracking brush. So he waits until they get up and leave. And when they are gone, he runs home as fast as his little legs will carry him, because he doesn't want Phoebe to know he was gone. He doesn't think he will use these images for blackmail. Not this time.

RUE

NOW
June 21. Tuesday.

As everyone heads toward their vehicles, Rue tells Toshi she needs to go to the bathroom quickly. He mutters, but she says sorry, can't help it.

She pushes into the washroom and checks beneath the stall doors. No one inside.

She calls Eb.

Pick up, pick up. She checks her watch. Everyone will be gathering outside, waiting.

"Mom?"

Emotion punches through her chest, into her eyes.

"Eb, listen, I can't talk, but I need to know—where is the bead bracelet you bought on our trip?"

"What?"

"Just tell me, dammit, quick." Rue hears voices outside. Female. About to come in. But another voice calls them, and they stop to chat outside the washroom door.

"Mom? What is—"

"Eb, *please*. Where is it?"

"I . . . don't know. I . . . lost it. It must have gotten torn off somewhere. The thread that those bead makers use is cheap stuff. They use women from the village, who—"

"And your father's beads?"

"I haven't seen him wearing them recently. Mom, is everything all right?"

Rue smooths her hand over her hair and catches her reflection in the mirror. She looks drained. The voices outside sound as if they're about to enter the washroom.

"It's fine. It's all fine, Eb," she says quietly. "I'll be late today—I'll talk to you later."

The door opens and two women enter. Rue pockets her phone, turns on a tap, rinses her face, grabs a paper towel, pats her skin dry, and rushes upstairs for the raid on the Bradley house.

But everything is not fine. Not even remotely. Her son was outside the Red Lion on the victim's last day of work. He appeared to be waiting for her. Following her. And he's lost his bead bracelet.

I will do anything for you, Mom, you do know that, right?

Garth Quinlan's voice echoes in her head.

Do you have children, Detective? . . . You'd want to protect your kid, right?

TOM

THEN
June 17. Friday.

Two days before she dies.

Tom and Arwen have outlasted the rest of the happy-hour gang. After leaving the Red Lion, five of them—Tom, Simon, Arwen, Sandeep, and Milton—repaired to the Bradleys' boat for a "nightcap."

Sandeep and Milton were the first to stumble off the boat, laughing down the gangway and through the moonlit marina parking lot in search of a cab. Simon followed once he'd finished a last glass of Lagavulin sixteen-year-old single malt.

Tom finds himself cocooned alone with Arwen in his cabin. Outside the moon hangs big and full and round over the gently surging ocean. His boat rocks softly on the swells. Halyards clink against masts, and docks groan as hulls nudge against them.

He sits on his bench sofa beside Arwen. He feels loose, and his thigh touches hers. Moonlight shines through the side window and pools in a silver puddle over them both. Anointing them, wrapping them in a gossamer bond. Her pinkie finger brushes against his. He does not remove his hand. Desire swells like the surging tide in him.

He inhales deeply, unsure whether he has already crossed a line from which he might not be able to return tonight.

She gets up and goes to his small galley bar and pours him another whiskey, and one for herself. She glances at a photo on the wall. Tom and Lily and the kids. Tom swallows. He can't see Arwen's eyes, can't read what she's thinking.

"You haven't told me your wife's name," Arwen says as she drops ice into their glasses.

"Lily. Dr. Lily Bradley. She's a therapist."

Arwen brings him his drink and settles beside him. Closer now. Her armfuls of bracelets tinkle as she moves. She smells wonderful—a faint scent of perfume tinged with whiskey and a whiff of incense from her clothing that makes Tom think of his youth. For a moment, on this moonlit night, suspended upon the swells, he's just this guy with this woman. Not a dad. Not Tom the professor and teacher. Not the doctor of abnormal psychology, the student of dark and deviant minds. Just Tom. Suspended in a bubble of time and space and moonlight where things are possible that are not ordinarily possible in his ordered world of habit and safe suburban routine. How did he get here anyway? He thought it was what he wanted—that family. The house. Kids. Routine. Safe. It *is* what he wants. He's just taking a little break, because sometimes everyone needs a holiday. He's drunk. He's not thinking through his usual filter. He feels . . . heady. He feels a little . . . devilish. Hungry. Rapacious.

"Did you put something in my drink?"

She smiles and looks distorted. Tom tries to shake the disorientation. It doesn't work. He feels like laughing. He feels fantastic. Happy. So horny.

"You did, didn't you?"

She laughs, throwing back her head and showing her white throat. The tattoo on the side undulates, coming alive, writhing. Without thinking, he touches it gently with his fingertips.

"A chimera?" he whispers. "Disjointed parts. Why?"

Her eyes turn momentarily serious, and Tom feels a spark of anxiety.

"Aren't we all just disjointed parts trying to look whole? The good parts, the evil parts, the people we could be or don't want to be, all trying to keep each other in check?"

"You sound like Lily when she gets going on Jungian analysis."

Arwen falls silent and turns her face away. Tom is instantly sorry he's put his wife between them. He's broken some magic. He thinks this is the wrong thing to think, then giggles, then tries to stop himself from laughing. "Jesus, what did you give me? It's fucking amazing."

"Where did you meet your wife?"

"Why?"

"Just curious."

"Ottawa. It was at a psychology convention sixteen years ago. I was a guest speaker, and she was young and beautiful and smart, and she approached me at one of the cocktail parties to ask questions." He smiles, recalling the memory. "A young and green psychologist, dreaming about private practice. She was twenty-nine. I was a middle-aged guy and, yeah, flattered by the interest of someone fifteen years my junior. I asked her to dinner. One thing led to another."

"A middle-aged guy—you weren't already involved with anyone when you met her?"

He falls silent. A discordant clang sounds in his brain. He becomes conscious of the swell beneath the boat, the rocking. The wind is picking up. The sound of the halyards on the masts grows loud, and the slap of water against the docks becomes insistent. He clears his throat.

"I was a widower in a way. My common-law wife had died some years prior, and I was just coming off what was supposed to be another fairly long-term relationship."

"How did she die?"

His gaze flares sharply to hers.

"I'm sorry. I . . . That was callous." Arwen takes his hand and laces her fingers through his. Silence fills the cabin. She studies him. Moonlight catches her eyes and winks in the tiny jewel in her nose. Seductive, yet a chill branches through his chest. She seems to be morphing. Like her chimera. Something cold and sinister is rising around her. It's in the intensity in her eyes and the sharp edge that has entered her questions. Tom senses a feral kind of hunger flowing from her. Part of his brain tells him to call it a night. Quit. Leave. Now. While he is still unscathed. Another part is thick with booze and something more confounding, and he says, "It's okay. It . . . it was a very aggressive ovarian cancer. I lost her before we could start a family."

"You never wanted to marry her?"

He gives a wry laugh. "I did. She didn't. She liked to think it was a feminist thing. She had a brilliant mind and was very respected in her field." He sips his drink, his mind sliding back in time. "She worked at a psychiatric institute in Alberta. I taught at the school nearby. It . . . wrecked me when the disease stole her. It took some years to process the loss. It was six years in total and another relationship before I finally met Lily. Sometimes . . . I think I don't deserve her. She gave me new life, new . . . meaning."

"Lily is from Ottawa?"

"Yes. She grew up there. Single kid."

Arwen sits up sharply and turns her head away.

Tom feels awkward now. Uncomfortable.

She sips her drink, not looking at him. "Which psychiatric institution in Alberta?"

"The Margot Javinski Institute."

She meets his gaze. "I told you I spent my childhood in Alberta, right? A small suburb called Glenn Dennig."

The temperature inside the cabin drops. A buzz starts around the edges of his brain.

Suddenly she takes off her blouse, and her breasts gleam white in the moonlight shining through the cabin window. Shock rockets through Tom. She gives a slow, sly smile, then leans forward and presses her mouth against his, opening his lips. Her tongue slides into his mouth. Her hand cups him between the legs. A groan escapes his chest, and he feels himself grow hard against her palm. He allows her to deepen the kiss. He's falling, falling, down, swirling into a hot, red abyss.

She murmurs over his mouth as she massages his erection. "See? You want me. And you want your nice suburban life, too. See, Tom—a chimera." She undoes his zipper and slips her hand into his pants. He moans softly. "But I know your secret, Tom Bradley," she whispers over his lips, her breath warm. "I know what you did all those years ago."

A fine blade of ice slices through his sticky, sweet desire. He struggles to interpret what she just said.

"What?"

She sits back. Swollen lips. Sultry eyes. A smile twists her mouth, and it looks evil. Or is his addled brain framing everything through a strange, drugged lens?

He battles to sit up, get clearer. "What . . . what secret? What are you talking about?"

"I know about your common-law partner's patients, Tom. At the institution." She traces her finger softly down the side of his face.

He stares.

She reaches for her blouse, pulls it back on, and slides her bare feet back into her sandals. She stands up, grabs her purse. "I should go."

He sits there, zipper undone, erection obvious, confusion pulsing through his head.

"I don't understand . . ."

"Oh, I think you do. Which means I know about your wife, too. I know what you both did."

She makes for the stairs that lead up to the companionway.

"Arwen . . . wait!"

But with a swirl of incense, a tinkling of bracelets, and a soft swoosh of her long skirt, she's up the stairs. Tom feels the boat tilt as she climbs off, and he hears her footfalls on the dock.

Panic whips through him. He lurches to his feet. His world spins as he lunges for the stairs and up onto the deck.

"Arwen!" he yells into the night.

He sees her reach the end of the dock. She's heading into the parking lot. Moonlight shines like wet ink on her hair. Tom disembarks and staggers along the dock after her, his bare feet thudding on the wooden planks.

"Arwen! Wait!"

She vanishes into shadows on the other side of the lot. Tom halts, chest heaving. Everything sways—masts, boats, the dock, trees in the breeze, shadows, him.

He sees a small flare of orange in the darkness, and he smells cigarette smoke, pungent in the clear night. There's a figure on the deck of a boat next to him, silhouetted against the moonlight. The cigarette glows again. It takes a moment for Tom to register it's Simon. Sitting in a chair on his boat, watching. In front of Simon stands a tripod with the professor's telescopic camera mounted on top.

"Simon?"

"Hello, mate. Having a spot of trouble?"

"What the—what in the hell are you doing there?"

"Shooting the moon." Simon takes another drag on his cigarette and tilts his chin to the sky filled with stars. He blows out smoke. "I saw it rising over the water when I left your boat. Remembered I had a camera on my craft. So I stopped to take some shots. Not often one gets an opportunity like this. Beautiful, isn't it?" Simon glances to his right, toward where Tom's boat is moored. He drags on his smoke.

Tom's gaze follows. From this vantage point Tom's cabin with the lighted window can be seen clearly. Everything inside is visible. Simon, if he was looking, would have seen Tom kissing Arwen. He'd have seen Arwen's naked breasts. His stomach churns. Anger twists into his chest.

Simon smiles in the dark. His teeth glisten. Tom feels surreal. Everything in his world is off-kilter.

"What made her take off in such a rush?" Simon asks, blowing smoke.

"Nothing happened," Tom says.

"Of course not, old boy. Your secret's good with me, Tommo." Another drag. "She's worth it, though, not so?" He makes a lewd gesture near his groin.

"Fuck you, Simon."

"Be careful." A pause, another drag. "She's damaged goods."

"What do you mean?"

"You think you're the only one in our happy-hour cluster she's taken to bed?"

"I told you, nothing happened. I—"

"Your story and you're sticking to it. Don't worry. I won't tell, Tommy boy." Simon gets to his feet, comes to the railing on his deck.

Tom recalls the words Arwen spoke on the night she walked with him to the bus stop, the night he offered to call the Americans about the cottage.

Simon told me he thought it might become available soon.

"I see . . . I get it." Tom's neck tightens. His head begins to hurt. "It must have been real convenient to have me install your little piece of ass across the cul-de-sac for you. Complete with a separate studio you can enter via the secluded woods so Hannah and the kids won't see."

"Now, now, Tom, buddy. This is not like you." Another smile. "Is it? Surely it's just the drink talking? Or perhaps it's the drugs she gave you. She likes to play with the mind-altering shit. She's a dark one, that Arwen."

Wind gusts and all the boats seem to rise, sucking in the air, swelling like a giant chest, coming alive, their little window eyes glinting in the moonlight, their masts *chink, chink, chink*ing with laughter. Tom hears Arwen's voice in his head again.

A small suburb called Glenn Dennig . . . I know your secret . . . I know about your common-law partner's patients, Tom. At the institution.

Maybe he dreamed it. It can't be real. It must be the drugs, the drink.

I know what you both did.

"Go home, Tom," Simon says. "Go back to your wife. And do up your zipper first."

Tom looks down in shock. He yanks up the zipper and returns to his boat. He finds his shoes and locks up, putting off the lights. As his mind clears a little, he grows more afraid.

I know your secret.

He leaves the marina with Simon still smoking on the deck. As he walks up the sidewalk, wind rustles through the oaks. He feels the trees whispering, a signal from one to another. He feels the shadows edge closer.

Nothing feels real. He did imagine it all.

Surely?

Lily always says that reality isn't a place out there; it's a narrative inside your head. That's all this is. A fiction. Sleight of hand. A drug-addled Lewis Carroll through-the-looking-glass fantasy.

Something scuttles in the bushes. Tom freezes. His heart hammers. He stares at the plants. A raccoon ambles out of the scrub and onto the sidewalk. It stops, looks at him. A masked bandit. Tom doesn't move. The raccoon crosses the road, and three little kits follow.

Family.

It hits him like a blow. If Arwen tells his secret, it will obliterate his family. Totally. His marriage. Lily. Everything.

He cannot let that happen.

HANNAH

THEN
June 18. Saturday.

ONE DAY BEFORE SHE DIES.

A beautiful June sunrise shimmers over the ocean. It's two days away from the longest day of the year, thinks Hannah. The occasion usually brings happiness, but today she's edgy as she spreads icing on the cake she baked for the barbecue.

Simon came home very late again last night, and she heard him bump over a garden chair near the pool. She looked out the window into the moonlight and saw his figure going toward the cliff and the stairs that lead down to his "man shed," as she calls it. She returned to bed and lay staring at the shadows on the ceiling for another hour before he crept quietly back into the house. He smelled heavily of alcohol. But it was a more sinister thread that twisted through Hannah's heart—a feeling she's had before, one she usually manages to bury.

When she woke this morning, Simon was gone. He left a note to say he was doing his long training run this morning because tomorrow was the barbecue and he wanted to be on hand to assist her with last-minute prep.

Hannah glances at the note still lying on the counter. The ominous feeling rises in her chest again. She blocks it out. She needs to finish the cake, then wake the kids. She'll take Jacob to his swimming lessons at the Windsor Park Recreation Centre, where she will see Lily, who brings Matthew for lessons at the same time. They'll discuss last-minute things for the shopping list, and then she'll go to the store and pick up the flowers. She dips her knife into a cup of hot water, then tries to smooth the icing. Her mind loops back to Simon.

That Friday happy hour is getting longer and longer, but it's not so much that. It's more. She found a receipt for a chocolatier in Simon's blazer pocket two weeks ago. And two red hairs on his jacket sleeve when she was hanging it up, and she's certain she could smell perfume in the tweed fabric. And while doing the wash two days ago, she believes she discovered a pink lipstick smudge on his white shirt collar.

That woman moving in across the street—Hannah thinks that's what really has her rattled. The happy-hour waitress. Far too friendly with Simon, and he just about fell over his feet to help her unpack that weird blue van painted with snowflakes. Hannah scoops more icing up with her knife and wonders if it was Simon's suggestion that the waitress rent the cottage across the street. She asked him, and he said it had been Tom's brain wave.

Hannah bends down and studies her icing at cake level. She smooths out a bump. A woman like Arwen Harper—Hannah finds her threatening. She's everything Hannah is not. She's free. Creative. A little wild. Unscripted. Sexual. She threatens Hannah's way of being. She challenges Hannah's preconceptions of how she should behave as a middle-aged housewife.

Hannah stands back and wipes her hands on a dishcloth. She studies her cake. Maybe it's Tom who is sleeping with Arwen. Not Simon. She'd like to think that it's Lily's issue, not hers. Perfect Lily. Maybe Lily's family is not so perfect.

But her brain loops around again.

What if Simon fell in love with the waitress? She couldn't bear to lose him. What would she do? He'd take the house. It was his property when she met him. What would the kids want? Would they go with him and his new, sexy wife? Who would want Hannah then? She's got new wrinkles. She's carrying extra pounds. Her face is sagging. She no longer turns men's heads. She's understanding now what women mean when they say females her age seem to disappear. Hannah thinks of Simon knocking over the chair by the pool and heading to his shed in the moonlight.

She's been in his shed only once, and Simon doesn't know it. It's built into the cliff wall at the edge of the property. It basically hangs over the sea and is accessible only by steep wooden steps with a rope railing. And because Hannah is terrified of heights—utterly phobic—Simon believes his shed is safe from her prying. But two years ago Hannah white-knuckled it down those cliff stairs with a key she'd found in Simon's sock drawer.

Her pulse begins to race as she recalls the day. She hurriedly carries the icing knife and mixing bowl to the sink and turns the water on full blast. She doesn't want to remember the photos she saw in there. Simon is a watcher, that's all. He's a watcher of women and birds, and he captures photos of them with his long lens. That is all. He is an observer and student of humanity. A philosopher who dwells on worldviews. He's sort of an Übermensch, in Nietzsche's terms, and does not believe in God. Simon thus holds that there is no inherent morality or intrinsic value in anything on this earth. He believes man makes the values, the morals, himself. Which means Simon would probably have an affair if he felt it added value to his life, and he wouldn't believe it wrong. He would say, *The meaning of life is that you die, so make it valuable, Hannah. Make it mean something to you.*

What if he beds Arwen in the cliff shed?

She feels tears well in her eyes. She slams the tap handle into the off position and unties her apron.

The shed.

Hannah is propelled down to the shed.

She takes her phone in case she falls or gets stuck or freezes or something terrible happens. Gulls cry and wheel along the edge of the cliff at the border of their oceanfront property. Trees whisper and conspire in a jostling wall along the forest edge.

Hannah holds tightly on to the rope railing. She goes down inch by inch. Sweat breaks over her skin. Time ticks. He will be back soon. Far, far below, the ocean sucks and swells. Hannah closes her eyes for a moment, struggling to breathe. She imagines herself losing hold, going over, spinning into the void, spiraling down, hitting rocks, *bump, bump, bump* all the way down to the water until she is dead.

Focus.

She tries to compose herself, and she inches down to the wooden building.

Hannah unlocks the door. Inside there is a faint scent of incense. The taxidermy birds watch her with glass eyes. So does a stuffed weasel. Hannah goes to the desk with the computer where she found the photos last time.

Shock rustles through her. Spread out on the desk are more photos, new photos, that Simon has printed out.

Of Tom. And it looks like Arwen. Kissing. Framed by the window of a boat. The Bradley boat. A thrill chases through Hannah. Using her cell phone, she snaps photos of the prints. A noise halts her.

She glances up.

It's just the breeze swirling a strange wind chime hanging in front of the window.

She takes a last photo and pockets her phone.

It makes her feel better.

It's Tom who is the problem. Not Simon. Irritatingly perfect Lily's life is not so perfect after all.

A surge of weird, hot joy rises in her chest as she relocks the shed door carefully. A wicked little part of Hannah wants to show these to Lily. Show them to everyone. If only just to deflect from herself, from her knowledge of things in her own marriage that terrify her.

And maybe she will.

LILY

THEN
Saturday. June 18.

ONE DAY BEFORE SHE DIES.

Lily sits beside Hannah in the plastic chairs at the pool, watching their boys swim.

The scent of chlorine, the kids' shrieks, the splashes, the warmth and humidity encompass her with a familiarity, but today it's not relaxing for Lily.

She watches Matthew dive in. He's getting better. He climbs out again, and water sheens on his little white body. A memory slams into Lily so hard and so suddenly it shocks the breath right out of her. In her mind she sees another boy. Same pale skin. Same age. A lifetime ago. Her little brother. And suddenly the chlorine smells like blood. Her vision blurs. She sees gaping wounds again. Inside her belly—deep, deep down—a quivering begins. She hasn't thought about him in so long. Blocking it out is her way of coping, of surviving. But her kids' ages, it's rousing things from her unconscious again, and they're rustling up into her other life, into her world of routine and order. Her patients of late are not helping. Their issues are all feeding the beast growing in her, fueling her paranoia.

Yes, she could be wrong about the embossed symbol from the guy at the hotel. It could be what Dianne said—that she's imagining connections that are not there.

But she did not imagine the words: *You can't hide from Satan if Satan is inside your head . . . From someone who knows . . .*

She did not imagine her patient calling her inner child Sophie. The patient who came for only that one session and never returned.

She did not imagine Tom coming home again late last night. Smelling of booze. And this morning he was . . . weird. Off. Uncommunicative. He seemed worried. And it scared Lily. She's always felt secure in his love. Something has changed.

"What about marshmallows?" Hannah asks, typing notes onto her phone.

"What?"

"Are you even listening to me, Lily? You're not listening, are you? I've added ingredients for s'mores to the list—chocolate, graham crackers." She pauses. "What else do we need? Simon has already picked up the liquor and the pop for the kids, sparkling water . . . I've ordered the stuff for salads, baked potatoes, garlic bread, coleslaw, burgers, sausages, chicken, steak. What else?"

"Uh . . . you got vegetarian?" Lily says absently, her attention still on Matthew. He's doing so much better at his swimming this year. He's still the smallest boy. He's splashing all the way across the pool. Love and pride and a painful protective instinct crunch through her chest. Matthew and Phoebe are Lily's raison d'être. She knows why she wanted kids so badly. Having children is a hopeful, redemptive act. It's not only a literal reinvention of oneself, it's a way to reshape the idea of one's self. And as a therapist she knows most parents are like her—they strive to make the world safer and better for their offspring. It's about controlling and shaping the future in order to validate one's own being, and to make sense of the past. It's an act of redemption.

She notices her young patient Tarryn Wingate near the deep end on the other side, talking to her coach. The swim squad has exclusive use of the far lanes this morning. Lily thinks of Phoebe's outburst.

Tarryn gets drunk and sleeps around all the time. Probably even with her swim coach. Bet you're nice to her.

"Who's veggie?"

"What?"

"Who's vegetarian?"

"Phoebe."

"Since when did she go vegetarian?"

"What's the last name of that swim coach again?"

"Lily?" She looks at her friend. Irritation crackles in Hannah's eyes. "It's Seth Duval. This neighborhood barbecue—you're not interested this year? Why not? You're always . . . I don't know. You usually want to run the whole thing. Control it."

"*Control* it?"

"You know what I mean."

"You think I'm controlling?"

"Listen to yourself, Lily. What's going on with you? You've not been yourself for . . . I don't know. For a while."

"Did Dianne say something—did she tell you?"

A look flits through Hannah's eyes.

"So she did. What in the hell did she say?"

"She just asked me if I thought you were okay, or if I knew what was going on with you."

Anger snaps through Lily. She suddenly feels too hot, and trapped in this chlorine bubble of humidity. Shame creeps into her face. She's the therapist. She can't afford to look as if she can't hold her own life together. She *needs* to be in control of her life.

"Hey." Hannah places her hand on Lily's arm. "You can talk to me, Lily. Even a therapist needs someone to offload on." But there's an odd gleam in Hannah's eyes. Or is Lily imagining that her good friend is relishing her unraveling? Actually feeding off it?

"Is it Tom?" Hannah presses quietly.

"What do you mean? Did Simon say something? Did he tell you?" If anyone knows, thinks Lily, it will be Simon. "What did he say, Hannah? And don't lie to me—not about this."

Hannah shrinks back slightly from Lily's verbal assault. Redness seeps up into her jaw and cheeks.

"He's having an affair. I knew it," Lily says. "I . . . I *knew* it."

"*Is* he?" Hannah asks.

"Isn't . . . isn't that what Simon told you? Isn't this what you're driving at?"

"No. Simon didn't—"

"Do not go covering for Tom. Don't you dare lie to me, Hannah. You need to tell me."

The kids are getting out of the pool, reaching for their towels. Matthew drapes his towel around his shivering little shoulders. "Hannah, quick. Tell me before the kids get here."

"Look, the only thing Simon said about Tom . . . is . . . they all went to your boat last night, after the tavern. Their waitress went with them. Everyone left before Tom and Arwen." Hannah's face goes redder.

"Arwen? That's the waitress's name?"

"I thought you . . . knew."

Lily stares at her friend. Matthew comes running over, wrapped in his towel like a little burrito. A kid yells. Another one bombs into the water.

"He also said it was Tom who organized the rental across the street for Arwen."

"Tom *what*?"

"In the Americans' cottage. She's an artist. She needed space for her studio, and her son."

"The waitress has a son?"

Hannah pales suddenly. "She's a single mother. You . . . I really thought you knew, Lily. She's one of the party guests coming tomorrow, and why wouldn't you know?"

"Know *what*, Hannah? Tell me."

"I mean, I thought you'd know from Phoebe. Your daughter is sort of seeing—well, she's very friendly with Joe—the waitress's son. Her sixteen-year-old boy."

Lily feels her jaw drop, and her world tilts.

"There's something you should see." Hannah reaches for her phone.

LILY

NOW
June 21. Tuesday.

It's two days since the barbecue, since Arwen Harper died, since Lily's life as she knew it fully imploded, since she learned of the unfathomable depths of her husband's deception. And now reporters are camping outside and the cops are circling in. She stirs a pot of bubbling Bolognese and glances at Tom in the living room. She's prepping supper while he's trying to focus on a psychology journal in the living room. The kids are still at the in-laws' and will remain there until this thing blows over.

Lily isn't at all certain it will blow over.

Her deep fear is that her husband has done something far worse than deceiving her. All she does know for certain—in some deep and raw and ugly part of herself—is that it's a damn good thing Arwen Harper is dead. It's better. Safer. For her. For her family. She's just sorry for Joe. But that's Arwen's fault. *She* did this to her son. This is all her fault.

The door gong clangs. Lily jumps. It clangs again, and banging starts on the door. Tom jerks upright. They look at each other. The banging sounds again.

"Police! Open up!"

Lily sees uniformed officers coming around the side of the house. The banging continues.

"Mr. and Mrs. Bradley! Police! Open this door!"

She hurriedly wipes her hands on her apron and takes it off. She glances at Tom again. He's frozen in his chair, the whites of his eyes showing. Lily hastens to the door, unlocks it, and opens it.

Detective Duval and Hara stand there. More uniformed cops behind them. Lily sees a police vehicle parked diagonally across her driveway, blocking her car. More squad cars in the road. A police van. Journalists shoot footage and take photos.

"We have a warrant to search your house and your garden shed, Mrs. Bradley." Detective Duval hands Lily some papers. Lily takes them with a shaking hand, but can't seem to read them.

"Please allow us entry, or we will use force."

"Tom!" she calls.

He's right behind her. She hands him the warrant.

"I . . . I'm going to call Dianne," she says.

"Step aside, please, ma'am," says an officer as he brushes past her.

Tom tries to focus on the warrant text, but he appears to be in shock. His hands tremble.

Three officers go thumping up the wooden stairs in their big boots with Detective Duval in tow. Two more officers go directly through their house and exit the kitchen door with Detective Hara behind them. They stride over to the shed. Lily shoots another glance at Tom. His face is white. The light inside the shed goes on.

A female officer in their kitchen opens their freezer. Lily feels faint as the officer takes out the garden refuse bag containing the ground beef. Another cop opens the bin beneath the sink. The officers in the shed exit carrying thc storage bin in which Lily found Tom's shirt. Two more cops descend the stairs carrying an evidence bag containing Lily's fresh laundry with Tom's washed and neatly folded Ocean Motion shirt on top.

Detective Duval comes down the stairs hefting a box that contains Matthew's "case files" along with his other folders of printed photographs.

"You can't take those!" Lily reaches out her hand, suddenly desperate. "My son will be devastated. Those are his."

"Stand back, please, ma'am," says another officer.

Lily steps backward and is bumped by a cop carrying boxes. Another officer takes Tom's cell phone off the kitchen counter.

"You cannot take that," she says.

"It's covered by the warrant, ma'am," says the officer. A violent rage swells in Lily's chest. Her peripheral vision turns red. Her chest heaves. Her fists clench.

She suddenly feels Tom's arm on hers. His touch is gentle, kind. "Keep it in, Lily," he whispers. "Don't lose it in front of them. Don't give them anything they can use against us."

She swallows. She wants to sob and lean into her husband. She wants Tom to fold her into his arms and comfort her, and she wants to beat her fists against his chest and to scream and kick and tear his hair out and . . . kill him. She doesn't know what to believe anymore. She can't trust him.

He did this to them. He and Arwen.

Detective Duval suddenly stops dead in the hallway. She turns to face the wall and leans sharply forward. She stares at one of the Bradleys' framed family photographs. Lily goes still. There's something intense and ominous about Detective Duval's reaction, and it scares her.

"Toshi!" Detective Duval calls. "Come see this."

Her partner joins her. Duval points at the photograph taken in Botswana. Detective Hara leans closer. He exchanges a hot glance with his partner.

Lily swallows.

Detective Duval turns to Tom and Lily. She points at the photo. "Where is this bead bracelet now?"

"What bracelet?" asks Lily.

"This strand in this photo, on Mr. Bradley's arm."

Tom grasps Lily's wrist. His gaze lasers into hers. His features are fierce. In his eyes Lily reads the words *Say nothing.*

"Take this photo," Detective Duval says to an officer. "Bag it."

It goes into an evidence box. Lily's heart races. She tries to read Tom's face, but she has no idea what's going on.

Just as Lily thinks the cops are finally about to leave, Detective Duval's phone rings. The woman answers, tenses. Her gaze flicks to Lily and Tom again.

"A match?" she says.

She raises her hand, calling her partner over again. She says something quietly to him. Detectives Duval and Hara approach Lily and Tom.

"Mr. and Mrs. Bradley, you both need to come with us," Detective Duval says, her voice crisp, cold.

"What—why?" says Lily, confused.

Detective Hara takes out handcuffs. Lily's heart kicks.

"What on earth are you doing? Tom! Call Dianne again. Quickly. They can't do this. You *can't* take us." Lily's voice is desperate. "Tom, tell her. Tell her what Dianne said. They can't detain us if they're not charging us with—"

"That's exactly what we're doing, ma'am." Detective Duval reaches for Lily's arm. "We have reasonable and probable grounds to detain you both for further questioning in connection with the death of Arwen Harper."

"*Me?* Why me?"

Detective Duval takes firm hold of Lily's arms, cuffs her hands behind her back, and ushers Lily to her own front door.

"Are you certain your children are in good hands, Mrs. Bradley?" the detective asks.

Tears flood into Lily's eyes. She bites her lip and nods. She should never have put that damn bag in the freezer. What on earth possessed her to do something so obviously suspicious? And how in the hell did they know? She recalls the feeling of being watched through the window, then thinking it was just trees. She remembers Garth Quinlan outside her back door.

Detective Hara brings Tom up in cuffs behind her.

Tom whispers quietly behind Lily, "They can't detain us for more than seventy-two hours without bringing us before a judge and laying charges. Do not say anything, Lily. Not without a lawyer. Get a lawyer, Lily."

The front door opens.

Lily winces into the twilight as cameras flash and reporters begin to yell. She turns her head away from the crowd, allowing her hair to fall over her face as she is marched to the cruiser.

RUE

NOW
June 22. Wednesday.

Rue and her core team are in the bullpen with a crown prosecutor. It's early morning, and Tom and Lily Bradley have been in the holding cells overnight. The clock is ticking on how long they can keep the couple.

"What have we got?" the prosecutor asks, seating herself at a desk and opening the file. She sips her takeout coffee as she scans the file contents.

"Neither of them are talking—not cooperating at all," Rue tells the prosecutor. "And the wife has now lawyered up. So far, the skin and blood scraped from beneath Arwen Harper's nails have come back a match to the DNA sample Tom Bradley gave us. We have photos of what appear to be recent fingernail scratches on Bradley's neck. The band inside the Kordel University cap found on top of the cliff is saturated with Bradley's touch DNA. His DNA is on the Petzl headlamp strap, which was also found on the cliff. Arwen Harper's blood trace was found on foliage nearby. Bradley's shoe size and brand of shoes are a match to the prints that follow Arwen Harper's prints to the cliff edge. The mud in Bradley's shoe lugs is a match from the trail through the forest. Bradley also had Arwen Harper's blood on him, and on a shirt he tried to hide, and which it appears his wife washed as soon as Bradley left his home to show me the body. When Toshi arrived to question the wife, he heard the washing machine going inside their house. Harper's blood was also found on Bradley's flashlight. We retrieved it from a homeless person following an extended sweep through the woods after the Codys' daughter told us about a peeping Tom. We got him. He's been camping in the woods—he admitted he's responsible for the third set of prints on the cliff. He claims he found the flashlight under a bush after he saw Tom Bradley crashing through the woods on his way to call 911. He also saw the blood on Bradley's shirt, and the logo on the back. Additionally, we've seized a family photograph of Bradley wearing a green-and-orange bead bracelet identical to the broken strand found tangled into the decedent's fingers, and to the beads found on top of the cliff."

"Motive?" asks the prosecutor, taking another sip of her coffee.

"Hannah Cody, a friend and neighbor, brought in these photographs early this morning." Rue clicks her laptop and brings them up onto the monitor in the room. "They were taken by her husband, Simon Cody, and clearly show Tom Bradley and the victim kissing on the Bradleys' boat just three days before he reported her dead."

"That could give the wife more motive than him," offers Toshi.

The prosecutor nods as she regards the photos. "Opportunity?"

"They both had it," says Toshi. "Husband could have left the house while his wife was passed out on a sleeping pill. Or she maybe didn't take that pill as she claims, and she could have gone out again herself."

The prosecutor sits back in her chair. She tilts her chin to the file. "It's compelling, but it's also circumstantial. Plus there is also touch DNA on the cap that is *not* Tom Bradley's, and which has not yet been identified. And there is semen on the victim's thigh that is also not a match to Tom Bradley's DNA."

Rue says, "The additional touch DNA on the Kordel cap and the semen DNA are from different donors—they don't match each other. Nor do those two extra profiles match to anything else we sent to the private lab for analysis. We've put in a request to have the two unidentified profiles run through the RCMP's DNA database to see if they match anything in the system. We should have those results soon."

"So what we've got so far," says the prosecutor, "is nothing that proves beyond reasonable doubt that Bradley killed this woman, or that he led to her falling off the cliff. His defense will argue that Arwen Harper scratched him possibly during the fight in the pool house at the Cody barbecue. Klister will argue someone could have borrowed his Kordel cap, because you can't necessarily tell from touch DNA which was left first, or last. Those bead bracelets—they're not unique to Tom Bradley. His shoe brand and size are very common for trail runners. Yes, the mud in his soles is a match to the trail, but that's because, yes, he ran along the Spirit Forest Park trail. His flashlight had traces of the victim's blood possibly because Bradley touched the decedent allegedly to resuscitate her, then he picked up his flashlight to run home. His shirt contained her blood because he 'tried to resuscitate her.' Same with the blood on his body. He covered the victim's face with his jacket because, yes, it *was* personal—he was having an affair with the decedent." She aims her cup at the grainy photos on the monitor of Harper and Bradley kissing. "Clearly he was intimately involved with her, and possibly even had deep feelings for her."

"So why didn't he tell us he knew who the woman was when he showed us her body?" asks Backmann, playing devil's advocate.

The prosecutor shakes her head. "I don't know. But Klister's team could argue he was in shock, denial. And panicking, which is why he took off his shirt before calling 911, yet he did nothing about trying to hide the blood still on his skin."

"Sounds like a stretch," says Backmann.

The prosecutor gives a half shrug. "Whatever it sounds like, it's not irrefutable proof he did this. And it could play with a jury. Klister is good. We'll need better."

Toshi says, "And what about the wife? She washed her husband's shirt and went to rather extreme lengths to hide this fact by sticking meat in a bag in their freezer."

"Again, defense could argue shock, panic. When a person panics, it overrides the logic center of the brain. Look, this is going to be a high-profile case. Media pundits from all over the place are going to be weighing in constantly. Arwen Harper used drugs. She had psychological issues. She was institutionalized for a period, according to these medical records. Klister will use this. And bottom line, all Klister and her team need is to convince a jury there is reasonable doubt. That's all. They do not have to prove innocence, but we *do* have to prove guilt beyond any reasonable doubt. What we need is a confession. We need a guilty plea. We need irrefutable proof. Something."

Tension clamps across Rue's chest. She'd prefer to charge Bradley now. Arraign him. Hold him while they wait for other DNA results and while they continue investigation. A part of Rue needs him to be guilty.

"Okay, guys," Rue says. "We've got more work to do. Let's get moving. Let's find something before we have to let the Bradleys go."

RIPPLE EFFECT

NOW

Joe lies on his back in bed. He's still in the Cody house, and he has no will to get up. Or to even live. He saw on Twitter that the Bradleys have been arrested. He needs to talk to someone. About his mother. About how she was trying to hurt the Bradleys. About what happened . . . But that would demolish Phoebe. He doesn't know what to do, which information would be worse for her. He knows Phoebe is only twelve, but he loves her. She's the closest thing to true love Joe has had in his life.

He thinks of what his mother wrote.

When the EMTs got the girl out from beneath the bed, she showed no signs of external injuries. But she appeared catatonic, unable to speak.

"She was in extreme shock," Wozniak told a reporter later. "Her injury was inside her mind. I thinks she heard everything, and maybe saw some of what happened across the hall in the little boy's room. I wondered that day if she'd ever be normal again, given what she witnessed in that house of horrors. I mean, how could anyone be normal after such evil?"

But there was one other thing Wozniak noted as the EMTs took the girl away.

One glaring thing.

The girl who'd been hiding under the bed was not the girl in the family photos.

The girl under the bed was younger, and looked completely different. She was not Sophie McNeill.

The BOLO still stood.

Sophie was still missing, presumed kidnapped, and in grave danger.

If she was even alive.

A text from Phoebe pings through to Joe's phone. He reads it:

My dad has been arrested. I don't know what to do.

Joe closes his eyes and drops his hand holding the phone to the bed. He cannot answer her text.

I don't know what to do, either, Phoebe.

Downstairs Hannah Cody puts a plate of hot steel-cut oatmeal in front of Simon. She feels sick. Maybe she shouldn't have taken those photos of Tom kissing Arwen to that detective early this morning. Simon doesn't know, and she is too terrified to tell him. But Tom did what he did—that was not her fault.

"What do you think is going to happen to Tom?" she asks.

Simon sets down his *Globe and Mail* and digs his spoon into his oatmeal. "Heaven knows," he says without glancing up. "What a thing." He spoons porridge into his mouth.

"Do you even care?" she snaps.

He looks up, then sits back. Slowly he swallows his mouthful, and his features turn hard. Hannah recoils, afraid of her own husband suddenly. She goes to the sink and turns her back on him. She starts washing the oatmeal pot.

"What if he didn't do it?" she says quietly.

"What if he did?"

She closes her eyes and just stands there, trying not to cry as she thinks of Lily in jail. What has she done to her friend? What will happen to Phoebe and Matthew?

Tom sits in his holding cell at the police station, his face in his hands. His only hope is Dianne now. She said that if they do charge him, he's unlikely to make bail. He'll be considered a flight risk, and the nature of the crime is awful. They'll hold him until trial, which could be months or years away. But she also believes that all the cops have is circumstantial. No proof that he did anything to hurt Arwen Harper.

The uniformed officer who brought him breakfast said, "It's all over the news. National news, even."

He prays his parents are keeping the kids safe.

He prays that Lily's lawyer doesn't try for a tactic that pits her against him. He hopes she remembers her own words to him.

Whatever you do, Tom, whatever you say, remember the kids. Do it for the kids. They don't deserve this.

Matthew sits on the bed in the guest room at his grandparents' big house in Lands End. Both his parents have been locked up in prison. His home is being hounded by reporters. He heard his grandparents talking. They said the police took photos from Matthew's room. And he knows he told the murder detective about those photos he took of his dad. This is all *his* fault. Because he knows his father would *never* hurt anyone. Tears fill his eyes. It's because of him that his dad is behind bars for killing Joe's mother, and for some reason they have locked his mom up, too, maybe for trying to protect his dad. Guilt is like a monster sitting on his head. A thought strikes him.

He still has his camera. And there is something in there that the police didn't get because he hadn't printed it out yet. Suddenly Matthew knows what he must do.

A drunk woman in the next cell over from Lily's has been yelling and screaming all night. Lily closes her eyes, leans her head back against the cold concrete wall. She needs a shower, couldn't sleep. Perhaps this is her lot. This is what she deserves.

Perhaps she did kill Arwen Harper.

If she really thinks about it, it is actually all her fault.

Her mind goes back to the shattering events at the party just before Arwen died.

LILY

THEN
Sunday. June 19.

THE DAY SHE DIES.

Lily, Tom, Phoebe, and Matthew walk as a family unit down the road to the Cody house at the end of the cul-de-sac. They feel anything but a unit.

Tension is thick between Lily and her husband, and their kids clearly feel it. Tom carries a case of beer and a bottle of good wine. Lily carries the bocconcini-tomato-and-basil salad she made. As they near the forest at the end of Oak End, wind gusts and the trees sway and groan and rustle as if warning all to stay at bay. Heavy clouds are also muscling over the Olympic Mountains across the sea. A big storm is brewing. Lily glances nervously at the cottage with the blue, snowflake-covered VW bus parked under the carport.

"What's the matter?" Tom asks quietly as they near the Codys' driveway and the kids run ahead.

"Nothing."

"Of course something's the matter, Lily. You've been giving me the silent treatment since you returned from church this morning."

"And *you* haven't been weird and preoccupied since you came home so damn late on Friday?"

A hesitancy flits through his eyes, then his face hardens into a mask Lily recognizes—he's drawing a line in the sand, and he's going to be difficult.

"I've been completely normal, and if you had an issue about Friday, you had all of Saturday to talk about it."

"No I didn't. I had to go to the store early, and then I had to take Matthew to his swim lesson." *Where I was forced to look at photos of you screwing your waitress on* our *boat.* "Then you went out and came home late again last night."

"It was you who chose not to come with me to my work function last night—you were invited," he says, coolly.

"I had a headache, Tom."

It was a lie. After seeing those photos of her husband kissing his waitress, Lily could not possibly go with him and smile sweetly at his colleagues all night. She needed to have this out with Tom before she could act normal again, if ever. She took a sleeping pill last night and was asleep when he returned home, and this morning he was gone early for his Sunday run and she had to get the kids ready for church. Now there is the barbecue. And Arwen will be here. The issue swings like a sword of Damocles in the storm wind brewing over Lily's and Tom's heads.

Lily isn't sure how she will react when she lays eyes on Arwen, but she also desperately wants to see just who it is her husband is prepared to jeopardize his marriage for.

The party is well underway as Lily and Tom come through the yard gate. Men cluster around the smoking barbecue, drinking and laughing, and the smell of burned meat carries on the wind with music from the speakers. Kids are playing a ball game on the lawn. A bar has been set up on the patio, paper lanterns sway on strings in the mounting wind, and red-and-white-checkered tablecloths flap. A handful of paper napkins catch on a gust and scatter over the bright-green grass that rolls down to the edge of the bluff. Beyond, over the sea, the clouds muster and roll closer, black and heavy over the seething gunmetal-gray water.

Tom makes his way over the lawn to join the men, and Lily goes into the house with her salad.

She finds Hannah and some of the women drinking wine in the kitchen. She sets down her salad and looks for a glass. Hannah comes to the rescue and pours her a fat glass of pinot grigio.

"Thanks, I need this." Lily raises the glass and takes a big sip. "Where is she? Where is Arwen?"

"Not here yet. Come, I need to talk to you." Hannah takes Lily's arm and leads her onto the patio. Quietly, out of earshot of the other women, she says, "Look, I'm really sorry, Lily. I should never have shown you those photos. I don't know what possessed—"

"You *had* to. If I learned you knew, and you hadn't told me, I would be devastated, Hannah. It's not your fault. It's Tom's. I . . . I just don't know why Simon took those photos in the first place. What was he going to do with them?"

"You cannot tell Simon you saw them." Hannah shoots a nervous glance over to the pool, where Simon is turning meat with tongs and regaling his men friends with some tale that has them throwing back their heads and roaring with laughter.

Lily's heart goes hard at the sight of Tom laughing with a beer in his hand. For a moment she hates him. She hates them all. The men. She feels they are laughing at her. She wonders if the other husbands know that Tom is screwing the waitress he installed across the road, if they all find this amusing.

"Why can't I tell him?" Lily says coldly.

"Because he doesn't know that I saw them."

Lily's gaze flicks back to her friend. "What do you mean?"

"I went down to his shed. With a key."

"You? Down the cliff stairs?"

Hannah swallows. Her cheeks go pink. "I . . . I just did, okay? And I saw the prints spread out on his desk, and I took photos of them."

Lily regards her friend. Thunder grumbles, and the first spits of rain hit the patio awning. "Why did Simon take them? Why did he print them out?"

"Oh, you know Simon." Hannah laughs lightly. "He shoots birds, women, everything. He's an observer. It's what he does."

Clouds suddenly blacken the sun completely. Wind blows more fiercely, ripping at the lanterns. One tears off the string and wheels over the grass toward the forest. A checked tablecloth lifts off the table and cartwheels in a cloud of paper cups and napkins. Lightning forks over the sea and thunder booms. Almost instantly big, fat marbles of rain bomb to the ground. The men hurry to gather up their drinks and take the meat off the grill, and the children squeal and run toward the house as thunder grumbles and growls into the distance.

"There she is—that's her," Hannah says. "Shit. I was hoping she might not come."

Lily sees a woman walking across the lawn near the forest. She's going toward the pool. Her skirt is a thousand colors and billows in the wind, and her dark hair ruffles. Her stride is confident and most definitely . . . sexual. She wears a white peasant blouse, and bracelets shimmer on both arms, and she doesn't seem to give a damn about the rain starting to fall.

Lily lowers her glass slowly. Her heart goes cold. She can't take her eyes off the woman in the distance. A crack of lightning flares brightly over the sea. Thunder claps again. The woman enters the pool house as the men scurry up the lawn with the plates of cooked meat.

Lily steps out from under the patio cover. Holding her wine, she walks through the rain directly to the pool house.

"Lily!" Hannah calls from behind.

But Lily keeps going. Her heart pounds. Simon runs past carrying a plate of charred chicken as rain comes down harder.

"Come up to the house, Lily," he calls. "We're all going inside. We'll eat in there."

She can't see Tom. She thinks he's in the pool house with Arwen. She walks faster.

Thunder crashes. The rain redoubles, soaking Lily's hair and clothes. Behind the pool house the forest bends and sways and sounds like a rushing river. Rain splashes into the pool and pocks the surface.

She enters the pool house.

Arwen has her back to Lily. She's alone. No Tom. Arwen is pouring a drink at the bamboo bar in the corner of the pool house.

Thunder explodes and the windows rattle. Rain clatters onto the tin roof.

Lily stands in the doorway, drenched, hair plastered to her head. She watches the woman for a moment, all sorts of feelings crashing through her, along with the memory of the photos Hannah showed her—the woman's naked breasts in the moonlight. The woman's mouth against Tom's, her fingers laced into Tom's hair.

"Arwen?" Lily says.

The woman spins around. "Well, hello, Dr. Bradley."

Lily's jaw drops. Shock is visceral. She reaches for the back of a chair to steady herself.

"Paisley?"

LILY

THEN
Sunday. June 19.

THE DAY SHE DIES.

"Arwen," says the dark-haired woman with a bright smile as she extends her hand to Lily. "Arwen Harper."

"What . . . what on earth are—"

"You mean what was with the 'Paisley' and red-wig thing?" She laughs, reaches for her drink, and sips. A tattoo moves on her neck. Her bracelets clatter and Lily's eyes are drawn to them. She notices a puckered scar along the inside of the woman's wrist. Lily's gaze ticks to Arwen's other wrist before she can stop herself. Another scar. Lily never saw the scars or the tattoo on her new patient. She realizes it was because "Paisley" wore a long-sleeved cycling jersey and a cycling bandanna around her neck. Her "patient" was hiding the marks from Lily's keen therapist's eye. Just as she was hiding her dark hair under the red wig. And "Paisley" wore no bracelets to therapy, no nose stud. She came across as a completely different woman because Lily saw what Arwen wanted her to see.

Lily feels faint.

Words, logic, flee as her brain explodes with questions. Lightning cracks in another fork to the ground outside. It flickers again as thunder explodes. The nearby forest roars and sways with wind, and pine cones bomb onto the metal roof of the pool house. Rain streams down the windows, obscuring the view of the Cody house dressed in party lights.

"Can I top you up?" Arwen asks, reaching for Lily's rain-diluted glass of wine. "More wine? Or . . . hmm, definitely looks like something stronger is in order." She takes the glass out of Lily's hand, sets it on the bar counter, and reaches for a fresh tumbler. She pours a triple serving of gin into it.

Dumbfounded, Lily moves a strand of wet hair off her face. She came down to the pool house ready to confront a waitress who was her husband's mistress, and now she's unsure what she's dealing with. "What . . . do you want from me? What in the hell game were you playing, coming to my therapy practice dressed like that?"

Arwen hands Lily a fat gin and tonic. "Surely it's not that unusual for your clients to use a fake name in therapy? I mean, at least for the early sessions, until trust is built. That's what cash payments are for, right? There's emotional safety in anonymity. One is better able to confess one's secrets."

"Some patients use a false name at the outset, or just their first name, but not a . . . disguise."

Arwen shrugs. "Maybe that's *my* peculiar pathology, Dr. Bradley. Or maybe I wanted to see *you* in your therapist world, without you seeing the real me, at least at first. Aren't we all just hiding behind a mask, or wig, anyway? You in your doctor coat sitting behind your shingle in your benignly decorated office. Tom wearing his professor hat and black turtleneck looking all academic in his ivory tower." She pauses, angles her head, and points her glass at Lily. "Do you truly know who your husband is, Lily? Does he really know you—who *you* are?"

Lily's heart begins to pound. She recalls "Paisley's" words in therapy.

I think I see her . . . She tells me her name is Sophie . . . Hard work keeping the dark and deviant little devil locked inside.

Lily's brain sparks off in several new directions as she assesses the potential danger of this woman and how much to fear her. Her mind loops suddenly back to the words on the anonymous notes.

You can't hide from Satan if Satan is inside your head . . . From someone who knows.

The scope of what she is facing begins to dawn on her. With a quiet voice that is beginning to quaver, Lily says, "So you came to see me as a fake patient so you could get inside my head." It's not a question. Lily is listing the facts out loud as a form of processing, of buying time to devise a plan.

"*Did* I get into your head, Dr. Bradley?"

"And you're sleeping with my husband—I saw photos."

Arwen looks momentarily surprised but collects herself quickly and simply smiles. Lily guesses Arwen did not know about Simon's photos.

"And your son is dating my daughter," Lily says slowly. "Was that orchestrated by you, too? As a way to mess with my motherhood? You took a job at the tavern, befriended my husband, then you moved in down my street—"

"*Your* street?" Arwen laughs harshly. "So the neighborhood belongs to you, too?"

"What in the hell game are you playing, Paisley?" Lily snaps. "Tell me what you want."

"Arwen." A fierceness enters her eyes. "My name is Arwen. Remember it, Lily. I want you to look into my eyes and *see* me. I want you to *know* me. And yes, I want—I *need*—to be inside your head, where you should have held me all along. Now say it, say my name."

Lily blinks as an inky tendril of awareness begins to unfurl low in her belly.

"Say it!" Arwen demands.

Lily's gaze darts toward the door. They're far from the main house. Isolated by the storm. Fear cloaks her shoulders.

"Say it!"

"Arwen," Lily says carefully.

Arwen smiles thinly. "Now that's better. How's your drink?"

Lily watches the woman's eyes, her brain racing.

"How. Is. Your. Drink? Taste it. Tell me."

Lily takes a tentative sip. "It's strong."

"Have some more."

"I'd rather—"

"Have. Some. More."

Lily takes another sip, her gaze locked with Arwen's over the rim. "It's been you the whole time, hasn't it? Watching my house, stalking me. You left the notes."

"Well, I did pay someone to deliver the note with the drinks at the Ocean Bay Hotel. I had a shift that evening." A slow, sly smile curves her pretty mouth. "I had husbands to seduce. Men can be so easily led by their dicks, don't you think?"

That tendril of dark awareness in her belly unfurls further, and like a vine of thorns, it snakes and curls and branches upward into Lily's chest as the impossible begins to lay itself bare. Lily realizes she must find a way to handle this woman before this woman destroys her life, and her family. She cannot let this woman leave the pool house. Lily lowers herself onto a bamboo chair. Her knees feel weak. She's woozy. Perhaps it's the drink. Maybe Arwen put something in it. Slowly, she says, "What do you want?"

Arwen regards Lily as rain clatters outside. Finally she says, "Everything, Dr. Bradley. I want to take it all. I want to destroy you and your fake family who live in that eggplant house behind a facade of privilege. You make me sick, Lily Bradley. And so does your husband." Arwen's face hardens, her eyes turn to flint, and it seems as though something evil has entered her body. "You do not deserve one bit of what you have."

"What are you talking about?" But Lily already knows. She just doesn't know how Arwen knows.

"Or should I say Sophie McNeill?"

Lily's hand begins to tremble.

"Yes, I know who you are." Arwen comes closer. She sits on a chair facing Lily, their knees almost touching. She leans forward. Her eyes narrow. "I know *you*. I know where you come from, where you lived. I know what happened." Her gaze lasers into Lily's. And in a murmuring sort of monotone, as though reciting something, she says, "On Saturday, April twenty-second, in 1989, a warm haze pressed down over Glenn Dennig, a sleepy prairie town located along the outskirts of Medicine Hat. To the residents of the suburb, the evening air felt unusually warm for early spring. They didn't mind." She smiles and says sweetly, "But then they didn't know what was going to happen. Did they, Sophie?"

Lily's mind slides back to that warm day in Glenn Dennig.

TAKEN

A True Crime Story

The girl under the bed was a child from four houses down the street: Chrissie Whittaker, age nine. It was her little brother, Harrison, age seven, on the queen bed in the master bedroom, his body stabbed, his throat cut, his head covered by a pillow.

Sophie McNeill was presumed abducted and in grave danger. Wozniak told a reporter later, "I hoped to God Sophie was at a friend's house. My next thought was, What was the poor child going to do when she learned her entire family had been killed? At least she didn't have to see it."

All law enforcement agencies were mobilized, and the scene at Medicine Hat police headquarters grew fraught. Roadblocks went up around the city and along main arteries leading out of the prairie town.

Police called Sophie's school counselor, asking for names of friends she may have gone to stay with. The police school liaison officer visited Sophie McNeill's Catholic school and informed the principal about the brutal murder of the family of one of their students. The liaison officer asked for a current photo of Sophie. It went out across the country.

Sophie's swim coach was contacted. He informed the police she was not with them.

The principal told the school liaison officer that students often taped the phone numbers of friends on the insides of their locker doors, or kept numbers in notebooks. Police could not legally conduct a locker search, but the principal had authority to enter the lockers.

Sophie's locker was opened for the liaison officer.

There were no numbers taped to Sophie's door. The officer began flipping through a notebook. A loose page wafted to the linoleum floor.

The officer picked it up—a hand-drawn cartoon strip consisting of four panels. It showed a family of stick figures named "parental unit with kids." The stick figures stood under a sun beside a barbecue with flames. They were shown holding hands, like the stickers people put on the back windows of their cars.

In the next frame, the girl figure was shown stabbing her family members with a big knife, blood spurting out. Words beneath the image said, "Die! Die! May all that you love be destroyed!"

The girl was then depicted laughing and running up a hill to a truck labeled "Vincent's truck." The male stick figure inside the truck waved at the girl.

The final frame showed the girl and boy driving off in the truck, the word "Hahahaha" in a bubble over the vehicle. The two occupants inside were shown laughing. A rainbow was drawn over the truck as it drove toward a setting sun. Beneath the final frame were the words "Now we can be happy. The End."

A classmate identified the writing and drawings as Sophie's. The classmate told the police about Sophie's twenty-three-year-old "goth" boyfriend, Vincent Ellwood, who lived in a nearby trailer park with his mother, hung out at the mall with the other goth kids, and sometimes sold drugs.

The liaison officer showed the cartoon to her superior at Medicine Hat police headquarters, and a tentative judgment was made. Up until now, police had feared for Sophie's safety. Now they feared—unbelievably—that the twelve-year-old girl from the Catholic school could be a murder suspect. Sophie McNeill might have killed—or helped kill—her own family and Harrison Whittaker. And now she was on the run with her older boyfriend, who was missing from his trailer home.

The officer in charge ordered the drawing and notebook returned to the locker and the locks changed. He wanted the locker sealed until he could get a proper warrant.

Two days later, a gas station attendant in a small town in Saskatchewan saw a dented brown pickup truck that resembled Vincent Ellwood's pull into his garage. The attendant compared the truck registration and the faces of the occupants to the missing and wanted posters. He called the police while the girl and her older boyfriend were eating burgers in the adjacent diner.

One hour later, Sophie McNeill and Vincent Ellwood were taken into custody in the small Saskatchewan town.

LILY

THEN
Sunday. June 19.

The day she dies.

"I was there, Sophie," Arwen says. "Under the bed. I heard every vile thing that happened in that Glenn Dennig house of horrors."

A slow, terrible reality settles on Lily. "So . . . you're her," she says quietly. "You're Chrissie Whittaker."

"Christine Arwen Whittaker." She gives a cold, false smile and raises her glass. "Cheers."

Lily can't move. She just stares. Wind gusts. Trees bend. A shredded paper lantern tangled in a branch rips free and whirls past the pool house window in a blur of bright yellow, a tattered piece of what was supposed to be a sunny party in the perfectly calm neighborhood.

"Oh, look, you need another drink, you dropped yours."

Lily's gaze falls to the tile floor, where she sees the shattered glass she hadn't even realized she'd dropped.

Arwen gets up and pours Lily a fresh gin and tonic. She holds the glass out to Lily.

Numbly, Lily takes it.

"Cheers," Arwen says again.

Lily can't seem to move.

"Cheers, Lily." It's an order.

Lightning flickers outside.

Lily lifts her drink with a shaking hand and clinks the glass against Arwen's.

Arwen waits until Lily sips deeply. Thunder booms again. Lily wonders where Tom is, whether anyone inside is even missing them. Tom cannot learn what this woman knows. No one can know. Another part of Lily is being sucked far, far away from Tom, far away from the Cody house, all the way back down into the cold abyss of the past, back to face the little twelve-year-old devil inside herself. Back to look into the mirror to see the fractured face of the child who dyed her hair pitch black against her mother's will. A child who was forbidden to see her older boyfriend. A child who rebelled and was grounded, and who just wanted her parents and little brother dead so she could do whatever she wanted to do.

TAKEN

A True Crime Story

It was early morning, and bags of breakfast sandwiches from a local fast food chain were delivered to the cells of Sophie McNeill and Vincent Ellwood after they'd been transported back to Medicine Hat. The cops hoped the food would feel familiar, and that it would increase chances of cooperation. They needed confessions. They had to pull every trick before lawyers got involved, and interrogating children was complicated. Police need to respect special youth laws in Canada.

Sergeants Dave Blunt and Peter Chalk were assigned to the interrogation. Blunt was a former drug detective with a special talent for gaining trust and digging secrets out of young adults and teens. Chalk was a veteran polygraph operator and an ace interrogator.

As court transcripts show, Blunt and Chalk opted for a "father-figure, cool-cop" routine on Sophie McNeill, who sat hunched over and crying at a metal table in the tiny, featureless interview room.

Chalk's fatherly concern, however, elicited nothing from Sophie McNeill. She simply refused to talk. The harder Chalk tried, the more Sophie whimpered and sniffled and wiped her running nose with her sleeve.

That afternoon the handsome Sergeant Blunt entered the room, all blond hair, blue eyes, and trendy shades. Exuding an air of urban cool, he introduced himself as Dave. He asked Sophie about punk and goth music and her favorite bands. He asked what she thought of hardcore lyrics, and he coaxed her into revealing how she'd gotten involved in the goth subculture. She told him how lonely she felt, how she stood out at her Catholic school, how she thought organized religion was stupid because God surely wouldn't let people suffer if He existed and Wicca made more sense. And the goth crowd at the mall—they were all outcasts and they made her feel welcome. And her parents didn't understand how much she needed her friends, and the more they tried to stop her seeing them and her boyfriend, the more she hated her parents.

She began to cry.

Blunt moved his chair closer. He smoothed her hair and rested his hand on the back of her neck. He said comforting things, like she was cool, and smelled nice, and he thought she was pretty.

Blunt's actions would cost him later in court, but he eventually got Sophie to tell him how she'd met twenty-three-year-old Vincent at the mall and how, when her parents forbade her to see him, she'd started sneaking out the basement window at night, and how over months they'd plotted to run away together.

"And where were you going to run to?" Blunt asked.

"To Europe, to live in a Gothic castle in Germany. Or Transylvania. But my parents—they would've come after us. They'd cause trouble. They'd never stop looking for me."

"Why?"

"Because . . . they . . . cared about me."

"They loved you?"

She stared at the table, said nothing.

"So what did you decide to do about that?"

Sophie said she and Vincent had discussed killing them.

"It was your idea?"

"He only killed them because he loves me. I didn't mean it to actually happen. I didn't think he would. He's kind. Really sweet. He would never have done it if he wasn't under the influence of mind-altering substances, and once he started . . . it was too late."

It was a breakthrough for Sergeant Dave Blunt. He tried to stay calm, keep his cool-guy, hip-cop demeanor.

"How did he do it?"

Sophie told the cop that on the night of Saturday, April 22, in 1989, she was sulking in her bedroom with her headphones on. Her little brother had a friend over, and they were watching a movie in the basement, and her parents were getting into bed. Vincent arrived and threw stones at her window. She looked outside and saw him. He had a knife, and he was pointing at the basement window.

"He was completely high—twitchy, like he'd been doing coke or ecstasy. Before I could tell him the boys were downstairs, Vincent went in through the basement window. I heard Danny and Harrison scream, and I heard them running up the stairs and my dad going downstairs. I heard my dad yelling . . . and my mom, she was going down, and . . . I heard it happening, and it was awful." She sat silent awhile. "I knew there would be lots of blood, and I wanted it to stop. I didn't want it to happen anymore, but it was too late," she said.

"What did you do when you heard your mom and dad in the basement with Vincent?"

"I don't remember."

"Come on, Sophie. I know you do. It's okay, you can tell me."

"I think I went down into the kitchen. No . . . I went . . . I think I went into Danny's room, to comfort him because he was crying and scared and asking what was happening."

"Where was Harrison then?"

"I don't know. I think he ran to my parents' room when Vincent came crashing up the stairs, bumping into the walls, and Vincent was bleeding and carrying a knife, and he was mad, like, wild and tweaking."

"Was there anyone else in the house?"

She looked surprised. "No, why?"

"No one else watching the video in the basement with the two boys?"

"No."

Sergeant Blunt realized Sophie and Vincent had no idea there'd been another child inside the home. At the time he thought Chrissie Whittaker must have escaped into Sophie's bedroom and slipped under the bed while Sophie and Vincent were with the boys.

"What was Danny doing in his bedroom?" asked the sergeant.

"Crying. Scared. I . . . I went to comfort Danny, because he's really sensitive. The plan was not to stab him. We were only going to smother him to death so he wouldn't feel any pain, because we couldn't let him live without his parents—he would miss them too much."

"So you wanted to be kind to him."

She begins to cry. Sergeant Blunt is patient and waits.

"But when Vincent came upstairs covered in blood, and he was . . . like, manic, I couldn't do it—I couldn't—but he said we had to, and there was the other boy who heard everything, and we couldn't let them live now. He yelled at me to do it. I . . . I sort of stabbed Danny in the side, and got his blood on me, and I couldn't stab again. Danny kept saying he was too young to die, and pleading for us not to kill him. Vincent ran after the other boy. I heard him doing it. He came back and he said I had to finish Danny. I couldn't. I went into the bathroom to wash the knife and Danny's blood off me. I heard Vincent . . . I heard him cut Danny's throat. I heard the gurgling. I didn't want it to happen anymore, but once it started, it couldn't stop. It had to be finished."

"What happened next?"

Silence.

Sergeant Blunt took Sophie's hand gently. "It's okay. You can tell me, Sophie. But it needs to be the whole truth. It must be the whole story."

"I got a bag of stuff, then Vincent and I left in his truck."

"You're not showing any emotion, Sophie. Does this not upset you?"

"I cried all day yesterday, but I am empty now. Does this . . . make me a horrible person?"

Sergeant Blunt asked Sophie if her parents ever abused her. She said no, they tried their best for her, and she believed they probably loved her. "Quite a lot."

Sergeant Blunt brought Sophie some paper and a pen. He asked if she wanted to write a letter of apology to her parents, and whether she might like to write a note to Vincent, too. He said he'd take the note to Vincent on her behalf. It was a tactic, something that could be used as a written confession. In the letter to her parents, she wrote:

My dear parental unit,
I am writing in response to the events at our house on Saturday. An awful thing happened and it was my fault. I am very sorry. I wish it didn't happen and that you were still with me because now I am an orphan and I have no one. I hope you can be at peace in the summerland.

To Vincent she wrote:

My dear love,
I love you with my whole heart. Whatever happens, please remember, people are lying. I feel so alone without you. Please stay strong my dear love. We might have to wait but we shall be together again, and we shall have our eternal castle and live happily. Keep hope. Believe in me. Do not trust their lies. But I know there is only so much that bonds of flesh can promise to the soul. All my kisses.

TAKEN

A True Crime Story

Vincent Ellwood told a different story to Sergeant Dave Blunt.

He said Sophie had suggested killing her parents months earlier.

"She kept on and on asking me to do it. She said I would kill them if I loved her. I said we could just run away together, but she said her parents would not stop looking for her. They would come after both of us. They had to die."

"So it was all her idea?" asked Blunt.

"I didn't want to. I mean, the idea was cool when I was high and stuff. But I was scared. I asked a friend to help me do it, and he said no way, man. I asked another and they thought I was mad."

"And they never reported to anyone that you wanted to kill Della and Mark McNeill, and Danny?"

"They didn't think I would, like, do it for real."

"So she—Sophie—pressured you? How?"

"She just would go, like, all quiet and withdraw and be sad, and it made me sad to see her like that. I wanted to make her happy. When she was happy, she loved me. We had sex. I had hope that life would be okay when she was in a good mood."

"You know she is twelve?"

"I didn't know when I met her. I thought she was, like, eighteen. She's really mature. She's so smart."

"Smarter than you?"

Vincent looked at the table and said nothing. He was a mess. Full of emotion. Unlike Sophie McNeill.

He told police he'd been drinking a lot of beer that afternoon. Then he'd gone to friends and smoked marijuana and drunk harder liquor. Then he'd done "maybe, like, five lines of coke, and then some ecstasy. I was wired. Spaced. Aggro. I went to her house with a knife."

Vincent then told Sergeant Blunt that he had entered via the basement window. In the basement he found three kids watching a video. Two boys and a girl. They saw him with his pale, kohl-lined eyes and white face makeup and black hoodie with a skull on it and the knife in his hand, and they screamed and fled up the stairs. Sophie's father came down, grabbed a screwdriver that was on the stairs, and came at Vincent.

The battle was ferocious. Loud. The mother came running downstairs, screamed. Vincent lunged at her. She raised her arms to cover her face, and he plunged the knife into her belly, then her heart. Mark McNeill was strong and a fierce family protector, but he was no match for the coked-out, ecstasy-fueled, manic Vincent Ellwood.

Mark McNeill did manage to stab Vincent above the eye and in the arm with the screwdriver. And Vincent left both Mark's and Della's blood plus his own streaked all over the walls as he staggered upstairs to find Sophie.

"She was with Danny," he said. "She had her arm around his neck, trying to strangle him, but he wouldn't die. He was begging, saying he was too young to die, and to please stop, and to help him."

"The other boy?"

"He fled into the parents' bedroom."

"What about the girl?"

"I didn't see where she went. I guess I thought she'd gotten out of the house."

"Did Sophie know about the girl?"

"No. I never mentioned it."

"Why?"

"I . . . I didn't want any more people to die."

"What happened next?"

"She told me to wait with Danny in his bedroom. She'd gone into the kitchen to get a knife while I was downstairs doing her parents. She took the knife to the main bedroom. I heard her doing the little boy. She came back, and then she killed Danny."

"You didn't kill him?"

"She killed him. She cut his throat. He was gurgling. He fought us. He . . . he tried to use his lightsaber."

Sergeant Blunt had to take a minute to collect himself. Quietly he asked, "What happened next, Vincent? I need the whole truth, understand. There cannot be partial truths. It's going to come back to bite you both."

"I freaked. She told me to go wait in the kitchen while she packed a bag."

"She wanted to go pack? While everyone in the house was dead?"

"Yeah. I . . . I tried to wait in the kitchen. I screamed for her to hurry the fuck up, but she was taking so long I flipped. I left. I ran for my truck, drove back to the trailer, and took a shower, cleaned up, started drinking more."

"Anyone at the trailer see you?"

Vincent shook his head.

"Are you certain you left without her? Because that's not what she says."

"Yeah. It happened. I was tweaking, wigging out. I couldn't stay there in that house with . . . with them all like that, with what happened."

"And what did Sophie do next?"

"She showed up later at my trailer, in a cab. She had a bag of her stuff with her, and a meringue pie that had been on the kitchen counter at her house. She said she called for a cab, then realized she didn't have money. She found her mom's credit card, ran to the local 7-Eleven down the block. It has a twenty-four-hour bank machine. She withdrew cash and then ran home to find the cab waiting. And she came here."

"And then?"

"We ate the whole freaking pie in my trailer, then took off in my truck."

LILY

THEN
Sunday. June 19.

The day she dies.

"I didn't kill them," Lily says quietly.

"A jury says you did," Arwen counters. "The jury believed the prosecutor, who said you didn't have to hold a weapon to be a murderer. You planned it. You instigated it. And at separate trials you and Vincent were both convicted on four counts of first-degree murder."

"I did my time."

"At the Margot Javinski Institute? Where you could walk around without bars? Where you were out in the community being supervised before you were even eighteen? Record expunged completely by age twenty-two? What kind of payment is that for what you did?"

"I got treatment. I worked hard—I did the work. I got well again, Arwen. I was a child. Twelve. I was confused, unwell, and I'd come under the spell of a twisted, Charles Manson–like young man. A Paul Bernardo. If I had never encountered Vincent Ellwood, none of it would have happened. And as the judge said, in this country, we don't throw children away, we don't throw them into a dungeon. And I am proof that therapy can work. I came right."

"Did you? Did you really, Lily Bradley? Or are you just a very clever con? Perhaps you learned in the institution how to refine your act, how to give everyone what they wanted to believe. Before trial you were assessed with above-average intellect, along with being diagnosed with conduct disorder and oppositional defiant disorder. Isn't that the childhood variant of sociopathy?"

"On my release the psychiatrists said I was a poster child of rehabilitation. I was no longer a danger to anyone. My recidivism potential was assessed at zero. It's why I went into the field of psychology myself. I saw how people could be helped. How important mental health and intervention can be." Lily leans forward as she sees Arwen's eyes flicker with hesitation.

"I tried to find out what happened to you, Chrissie. Arwen. I heard that your family had moved. I knew your parents loved you. I believed you would have gotten the treatment you needed, and—"

"Fuck you!"

Lily blinks.

Arwen points her glass at Lily. "You lie. You never cared about what happened to the girl you finally learned was under the bed. You have no fucking idea what I went through, or am going through. You took everything from me."

Lily swallows and tries not to glance at the door again. "I'm sorry. I truly am sorry. Tell me. Tell me what happened."

Arwen wavers. "Oh, don't go thinking your therapy shit is going to work on me now."

"I want to know, Arwen. Isn't that why you came to my practice? Even in disguise. Perhaps you don't even really know what it is you want from me, only that deep down you want me to *see* you. You want to look into my eyes. Like looking into a shattered mirror. You want to face this person who has been coupled like a dark half into your entire life from that day you brought the meringue pie to our house."

Arwen's lips begin to tremble. Her eyes turn shiny with emotion.

"Please, tell me. What happened to you after that day?"

She gets up, paces, drinks more, paces more. Rain lashes against the window. Lily feels time ticking. This woman is a bomb about to blow up her life. She needs to do everything she can to defuse it and contain the potential for damage. Any way she can. Phoebe, Matthew, Tom—no one can find out she was Sophie.

Finally Arwen seats herself in front of Lily.

"My parents moved our family—what was left of it—to Ontario. To a new town, a small one where we could start fresh. A place where they hoped I might learn to speak again. They felt it was a blessing that I had no memory at all of what happened. And they wanted to keep it that way. They kept me away from the trials, the news. They decided to call me by my middle name, Arwen, in an effort to make everything new. I did start speaking again, with help. But I did not regain recall of that bloody day. Not until much, much later in my life. After I had Joe. Because we both know, don't we, Lily, that with trauma, while the mind blocks it out, the body never forgets? It always holds the score. Eventually it all leaks out in dysfunctional ways. It manifests in behaviors like a self-destructive sex addiction—yes, that part about Paisley is true. Like substance abuse, psychotic behavior." She hesitates. "And attempts to take your own life." She drinks more deeply from her glass. Wind blows harder outside, and more debris clatters onto the roof.

Lily's gaze ticks to the scars on the woman's wrists. She's suffering. And it's all Lily's fault.

"Then when Joe was six years old, I went to see a horror movie," Arwen says. "There was a depiction of a violent stabbing. I flipped. I totally lost it—the scene triggered a psychotic episode. I didn't know why. All I know is that I was picked up by police three blocks away from the movie theater, raving and injured by broken glass, and I landed in hospital. I'd hurt myself, smashing windows, hallucinating, defending myself from people trying to cut my throat and my child's throat. I was referred to a psychiatric institution, where I was diagnosed and treated for schizoaffective disorder. Joe went into temporary foster care. He became my driver to get out. And I was lucky—if it can be called luck—to run into a doctor who believed I might be suffering from acute PTSD and not schizoaffective disorder, and that my PTSD had been triggered by the bloody scene in the movie. He worked with me, and at the same time I approached my mother, and she explained to me about my past and what happened to Harrison, my little brother. I'd never read about the 1989 Glenn Dennig murders. I'd never been told I lived in Glenn Dennig. All I'd been told was that I'd had a young brother who passed away from an illness. But after that, after I learned what happened, I began to remember, and I began to hunt for you, Sophie." She leans forward, her features suddenly turning hard and fierce and controlled again.

"I saw," she said. "I saw from under the bed what happened across the hallway in Danny's bedroom. You thought it was just you and Vincent who knew. But no, it's you and me, Lily. Because Vincent died in prison, we are the only two people left who know what really happened in that room."

TAKEN

A True Crime Story

Vincent Ellwood and Sophie McNeill were tried separately.

Sophie had trouble showing remorse and emotion in her trial. The testimony of her goth friends didn't help. They all felt Vincent doted on her and would do anything for her. Two schoolmates claimed they'd heard Sophie mention she hated her little brother and wanted her parents dead. Vincent's friends testified she'd asked him to kill her family.

The jury was additionally shocked by the brutal and bloody photographs of the familicide. They received no warning before being shown them. The jury deliberated only four hours. They came back with guilty verdicts on four charges of first-degree murder. This made Sophie McNeill the youngest person in Canada to be convicted of multiple homicide.

The maximum sentence that can be given to a child in Canada is six years in custody, followed by another four years of conditional supervision in the community. Because Sophie was diagnosed with conduct disorder and oppositional defiant disorder, she was eligible to serve her custodial time in Intensive Rehabilitative Custody and Supervision (IRCS), a program reserved for serious violent young offenders diagnosed as suffering from a psychological disorder or emotional disturbance.

By the time Sophie McNeill was eighteen, she had served her sentence. At a review before her release, she was said to be a poster child for rehabilitation. At age twenty-two, because she had committed no additional criminal offense, her youth record was expunged. And because Canada's Youth Criminal Justice Act protects offenders under the age of eighteen by ensuring their anonymity, nothing that might identify the young offender—such as the last name of a family member—could legally be publicized in the country.

As one Calgary legal expert said at the time of her release, Sophie McNeill, or S. M., as she was referred to in the media, "can now do a complete disappearing act. She will not have to reveal anything about her past unless she chooses to. She will not be restricted from working with minors. She'll be free to enter professions of trust and become anything from a teacher to a lawyer, nurse, or caregiver." Or even a therapist.

Like Dr. Lily Bradley.

Vincent Ellwood, however, was sentenced to life with no possibility of parole for twenty-five years.

It evolved during his trial that Vincent was a cutter. Not his arms, just his thighs, which he could hide from the public. He even stabbed himself once in the leg. He was twenty-three, and he couldn't hold down a job. He was intellectually challenged, lived with his alcoholic mother in a trailer on the "wrong side of the tracks," had been badly abused as a child by his mother's succession of drunk boyfriends, and had been severely bullied at school. His favorite movie was a horror flick about a bullied boy who killed and cut up his tormentors as revenge. All Vincent wanted was to be loved. Respected. To belong. The goth crowd at the mall thought he was awesome. He dressed like them, went to the punk and goth music shows around town with them. He looked arresting with his pale-blue eyes ringed in black makeup. The young girls thought he was funny, and kind, and wonderfully hyper and cool. When Vincent met young and beautiful goth Sophie McNeill at the mall, and she fell in love with him, Vincent was subsumed. As his friends said, he'd have done anything to keep the girl's affection.

After the guilty verdicts a friend of Della McNeill told reporters, "Sophie matured far too quickly. It happened overnight at age eleven. Her boobs grew, her brain changed. She became sexualized. It alienated her from the other young girls in her grade. Vincent might have been a twenty-three-year-old man, but he was like a pubescent teen intellectually. He had all the signs of someone with fetal alcohol syndrome. Together Sophie and Vincent sort of met in the middle and made strange psychological chemistry," she said.

"It was like a perfect storm of psychology. I believe if Sophie had never met Vincent, her family would be alive to this day. Would Sophie still have turned into a full sociopath? I don't know. New science says weird stuff happens to teenage brains, especially young girls who mature too fast. Can she be fully rehabilitated? I don't know. Sophie has always been smart. She knows how to adjust to make things serve her."

The police thought Sophie had been taken. But she is the taker.

She took my little brother's life. She took my life. She took my family as I knew it. She even took and ate the meringue pie my mother bought. Everything taken by a woman who now lives like a perfect, privileged princess in a lovely leafy neighborhood. A woman who wears a mask. Protected by a law that makes it illegal to name her in this country.

This woman who now tries to dig out her patients' secrets—she was the patient.

And her secret is mine.

But one disturbing question was unresolved by the trials of Sophie McNeill and Vincent Ellwood.

Neither of them took responsibility for killing little Danny McNeill and Harrison Whittaker.

One of them was not telling the truth.

And now one is dead.

But there is someone else who knows.

LILY

THEN
Sunday. June 19.

THE DAY SHE DIES.

Lily gets up. Heart beating hard, she walks to the window with her drink. She watches the rain and the trees swaying in the storm at the edge of the bluff. The ocean is shrouded by clouds. Hidden. She's scared now.

"How did you find me?"

"I located a patient who was institutionalized with you at the Margot Javinski Institute. The patient ran into you once years after your release. She recognized you on a street and called out to you—Sophie. You ignored her. But she pursued and persisted, and you spun around on the sidewalk and informed her you were Lily Marsh, and that she had the wrong person. But she looked into your eye. She knew. And she was hurt that you'd rejected her because you'd shared confidences inside. I think you started dyeing your hair after that, and you changed the cut." Arwen pauses. "This patient also told me that your champion at the institute was a psychiatrist named Dr. Deirdre Carr. I tried to find her but learned Dr. Carr is now deceased. I did learn, however, she'd lived with a partner and mentee at the time she was treating you at the

Javinski Institute." Arwen smiles slyly. "And it was he who led me here. To Story Cove."

Lily stares. Her heart beats faster. She feels herself reaching a danger point—she could snap. "What . . . what do you mean?"

"His name is Dr. Tom Bradley. He's a professor of abnormal psychology right here, at Kordel University." Her smile deepens. "Seems he and his deceased partner, Dr. Carr, shared an intellectual passion—twisted minds."

Lily's jaw drops. Nothing makes sense. She feels her brain crumpling in on itself. "You . . . you're delusional. Tom has nothing to do with this, and you cannot tell him. You can*not* tell my husband who I am or what I did. And Phoebe and Matthew—they cannot know. Please. I beg you. It will destroy them. It will destroy everything."

"But that's what I want, Lily. To destroy everything."

"Tom is—"

"You think you know him?" A snort. "You think anyone can truly know their partners? He's been aware all this time what you are, Sophie. You're his dead partner's little 'poster child for rehabilitation,' like the judge said. You, Sophie-Lily, are Tom Bradley's deviant little devil wife in a petri dish. He's been keeping his academic eye on you all this time."

Blood drains from Lily's head. Shakes take hold of her body—great big palsied shudders.

"You mean Tom never told you? He never mentioned the brilliant psychiatrist at the Margot Javinski Institute was his common-law partner . . . Oh my, what a . . . strange omission."

"Stop it!" Lily hurls her glass at Arwen's face.

Arwen ducks. The glass smashes against the wall in an explosion of glass and gin and ice and a slice of lemon. Lily, blinded with rage, fear, confusion, lurches for the woman, her hands going for her throat with the tattoo.

She is grabbed from behind.

"Lily!" Tom yells.

Lily spins around, panting, just as Arwen swipes her hand down. Tom steps in front to protect his wife, and Arwen's fingernails gouge through the skin on his neck.

Lily, shaking like a leaf, stares at the blood welling on her husband's neck. She can't seem to think.

"Arwen, stop it. Now," Tom demands.

Arwen swipes a trembling hand across her mouth. It leaves a streak of saliva. Her eyes are glassy, wild.

"Is . . . it true, Tom?" Lily demands. "Dr. Carr . . . You . . . you've known?"

Tom clenches Lily's arm in a viselike grip. His jaw is tight, his eyes enraged. "I'm taking you home," he says, voice rough. "We can talk at home."

Despair crashes through Lily. She struggles against his hold, but it only tightens. Tom points at Arwen's face.

"You—you keep your mouth shut. I will talk to you later. We'll work something out, understand? If it's money you want, we—"

"You think you can shut me up? You have no fucking idea, do you, either of you? I don't want your money. I want to be *seen*. I want my story told. You got help, Lily. You had justice and the law on your side, and what did *I* get? Nothing. What did my son get? A mom who is sick in the head and who couldn't even allow herself to love his father. What did *my* mother get? She got to grieve her little boy. She lived with guilt, with self-blame, for the rest of her life. For letting Harrison go sleep over, for asking me to take over a meringue pie in time for a massacre, for accepting a call from Della McNeill thanking her for the pie and suggesting her daughter also stay over to watch the movie. She got a husband who drowned his pain in alcohol, then died from it. And you? You . . . you fucking got to marry your doctor's partner, who has money. You get to live in Story Cove in a fucking eggplant house with green trim."

"Please," Lily says, crying, desperate now. "Please, for the children—for yours, for mine—do not do this, Arwen. Please. We can work through—"

"Fuck you," she yells, pointing her finger at Lily's face. "Fuck you to hell, bitch."

Simon enters the pool house. "What in the bloody hell—"

"It's okay," Tom says brusquely. "We're done here. Everything's fine. I need to take Lily home. I'll come back for the kids later—can you keep an eye on them?"

Simon stares at Lily, then Tom, an odd look creeping into his features. "Yeah, sure, mate. Can I . . . Is everything okay?"

"We'll talk later. Sorry about the broken glass."

Tom casts a final warning gaze at Arwen, then ushers Lily out into the pouring rain. He wraps his arm firmly around her shoulders, and he marches her up the street in the raging storm.

◆ ◆ ◆

Joe steps back into shadows behind the outdoor fireplace. His heart hammers. He heard it all. And he's read everything his mother has written about it.

He waits for Lily and Tom Bradley to depart. He came to look for his mother, leaving Phoebe in the games room with the other kids. He and Phoebe were planning to sneak into the woods later. Phoebe left a bag at his house with some vodka, a cap, a headlamp, and a waterproof sheet for them to sit on. Or under. But his mother is in trouble again. She's drunk. And she's destroying Phoebe's parents. Her family.

Joe doesn't know what to do. He stands in the shadow of the fireplace chimney, immobilized. From his vantage point he can still see in through the window.

Mr. Cody pours another drink for his mother. She downs it in one go. Mr. Cody pours another. As he gives it to her, he leans in to kiss Joe's mother.

Joe storms up the grass lawn in the pelting rain, making for the main house to get Phoebe. He sees Matthew on the patio, and another idea enters his head.

"What's going on?" asks Matthew.

"Nothing, little buddy. Nothing. Your dad is just taking your mom home because she's not feeling well. He's going to come back to get you guys. Can you tell Phoebe I had to go home? Will you do that, mate?"

Matthew nods.

Joe heads for the gate.

Matthew just stands there on the patio, looking toward the pool house while Joe goes home. And rain pours down, wind rushing through the woods nearby.

LILY

THEN
Sunday. June 19.

THE DAY SHE DIES.

Lily and Tom enter the house with a blast of rain-soaked wind. Both are drenched.

Lily spins to face Tom. His hair is plastered to his head, as hers is. She stares at him. He looks so much older with his hair like this, under the harsh hall light. A new filter has fallen over their life and it's thrown all into stark relief. Everything is discordant, off balance now. Lily has lived with this man for fourteen years, and has probably loved him from the day she listened to him presenting at the conference, then she fell deeper over dinner . . . and it's all been a lie?

"Did you know, Tom?" Her voice comes out hoarse. "When you met me? The first day—did you know then? At the conference in Ottawa, when I came to ask the fancy guest professor a question?"

He looks away.

Her heart sinks even more.

"*How* did you know?"

He swallows, says quietly without meeting her eyes, "Before Dee died in 2000—" He hesitates. "Lily, you're shivering, please, change into something warm."

"*Dee?* Dr. Deirdre Carr? You *lived* together? How . . . how could you not tell me?"

"I'm going to put the fire on. I'm going to pour us some whiskeys. Get into something dry. We need to talk."

Her eyes fill with tears.

"We *will* talk, Lily, then I will fetch the kids home, but we need to air this first, okay? You said it—we must protect the kids."

He knows she is S. M.? He knows everything that Dr. Carr knew about her? How could he have wanted to marry her, make kids with her, a family, all the while knowing what she'd done?

"Arwen cannot be allowed to let this out, Tom. We can't let her do this. What would happen to Matthew and Phoebe if the media got hold of this? What would happen to your job, to mine? To us—all of us? It's over."

"Go upstairs. Quick. Change into something warm. Lily—" He touches her face. "You need to believe one thing, and one thing only. I love you."

"You're a sick fuck, you know. Living with me all this time. For what? Twisted kicks? Some psycho thrill for the abnormal psych prof? His personal 'petri dish' wife, as Arwen called me? Some rehab project of your partner's that you can study in real time?"

He turns his back on her and shucks off his shirt as he goes into the laundry room.

When Lily returns downstairs, he's by the fire. Two whiskeys on the table. He pats the seat next to him. Lily chooses the one opposite.

"Dee—Deirdre—was three years older than me. She was forty-one when she left this earth, and . . . she was everything to me, Lily. My mentor, my lover, my friend. My confidante."

"Yet you never spoke about her. You just told me you had long-term relationships and were in one that ended a while before you met me."

"I'm sorry. With Dee and me, it was . . . more private."

"Private?"

He leans forward, his gaze tunneling into hers. "She was a brilliant psychiatrist. She graduated young, was part of a groundbreaking team at the Javinski Institute. It was she who pushed—who advocated—for you, Lily. When you were Sophie, or S. M., as the media was obliged to report about you. When the courts finally cleared you for full reintegration into society, and you were declared a poster child for rehabilitation—that was Dee and her team's doing. Her dream. To prove it could be effectively done. And when you wrote to her, and thanked her, and told her you'd changed your name, and informed her you were going into the field of mental health to help others as she had helped you, she sobbed. She told me that your success made her life work—short as it turned out to be—worth it."

"Where were you while I was in the institution?"

"Teaching. A school near the institute."

Lily closes her eyes. The weight of the deception feels unfathomable. She can't process it.

"So you knew I was this messed-up kid. You knew your partner treated me. And you said nothing when you met me all those years later?"

"When Dee died and I was going through her things, I found the letter you wrote to her. You'd signed it with your new name, and you'd entrusted she would keep that secret. Years later when you walked up to me at that conference, and I saw your name tag, Lily Marsh—it was *fate*, Lily. It was like Dee was suddenly in the room with us both, her spirit suddenly alive and shimmering over us, her two people, and I could feel her spirit was proud, and curious, and it was like her invisible, guiding hands, one at your back, one at mine, pushing us gently together. And surely you can understand that I would be intrigued to know more about you? How could I not be? I was insatiably curious to learn how you were doing, to see what of the old Sophie might linger. How could I not ask you to dinner, Lily? And you were so much more. I fell for you. Hard."

"You fell for Dr. Carr's project. Not me. You saw me as some sort of substitute, something that brought her memory close. Arwen is right. I *am* a petri dish wife. Your ex's experiment. A strange freak who murdered her family . . . who did things I can't even comprehend myself. Things I tried to bury, and now I can't. Tom, how . . . *how* can I relate to my children in the same way if they find out? How can they possibly respect and love me?"

"You're still Lily. Nothing has changed."

Tears fill Lily's eyes. Shame, disgust, self-hatred swamp her. "Everything has changed. I can't be Lily any longer. And I sure as hell can't trust you. You are just as sick a fuck as I am."

"We're just humans. Complex, complicated creatures. Every human is capable of the most heinous things, given the right set of circumstances, the right narrative. I'm not naive, and neither are you. We both know this is true."

She swallows.

He gets up and tries to put his arm around her.

"Don't," she whispers. "Do not touch me. How could you lie to me? Betray me, deceive me like this? Our marriage, our entire life, it's all built on a lie. How could you not tell me? Why?"

"Did you tell me about yourself?"

"That's different. I *became* someone else. I couldn't bring that other . . . creature into the marriage. Into our innocent, pure children's lives."

"So that was my benchmark. I decided as I fell for you that if and when you decided to confess to me who you were, I would confess in turn. We're equal in this, Lily."

She turns her head away. She can't bear to look at him. She's confused. She's Sophie again, but also Lily. She's no longer able to compartmentalize and lock her past away in the basement of her brain.

"In truth, I wanted to talk to you about it all. But I was afraid of exactly this—of what you're feeling now. I was afraid you'd quit on yourself, and on me. That bringing the specter of Sophie between us would be destructive, and that you might regress. You see, the beauty of the Youth Criminal Justice Act is that it allows young people to shuck a criminal label. They *can* bury their pasts and build anew. And society must by law let them. I didn't want you exposed unless you chose to expose yourself. I wanted you to prove it—that these laws work. That they are correct and just. That we shouldn't throw troubled children away, and that a bad kid can become a valuable, functioning member of society."

"And what of Arwen? No one helped her."

A hard look enters Tom's eyes, and a darkness seems to begin to rise around him. "She could have been helped, Lily. If her parents had sought proper treatment."

"But they were broken, too. By me and Vincent, by what we did. I am a scourge."

"Lily, I love you wholly. You must understand that. You have nothing to hide from me."

"Yet you fucked Arwen. I saw the photos Simon took. Hannah showed me."

He inhales deeply and returns to his seat. He takes a large swallow from his whiskey, and the flames flicker in the glass. "I did not sleep with her."

"I saw the photos, Tom."

"I . . . Arwen targeted me. She's cunning and dangerous and she knew how to hit my weak points, and now I know why. But I did not sleep with her. I am ashamed at my weakness, Lily. I am so sorry. But nothing went further than a kiss. Nothing went further than what you saw in those photos. You need to allow me to apologize, to atone."

She gets up, goes to stand in front of the fire, and wraps her arms tightly across her chest. She's not sure she can believe him. She no longer knows what to believe, or trust. But she's as guilty of deception.

"Give it time, Lily. We'll work through it. Bit by bit. All of it. Please, let's give it time. I know the therapist in you is capable of understanding this. Of not doing something rash."

"What of *now*, Tom?" she asks quietly, facing the fire. "What of *right now*? What of Arwen? What of the secrets she holds about us both? What would it do to the kids to find out their mother is a monster?"

"We'll find a way, Lily." Thunder crashes and rain lashes afresh at the windows. "I'm going to fetch the kids. You go up to bed and take a pill to help you sleep. Don't let the kids see you like this. There's nothing else we can do right now, but we will work it out. We'll talk to her. We *will* find a way."

JOE

THEN
Sunday. June 19.

THE DAY SHE DIES.

Joe storms around the small cottage that he keeps so neat, bumping into things, knocking things over, raking his hands through his hair. He wants to smash everything in sight. His mother's drinking, her pills, her erratic "artistic" behavior—he found a way to live with it, to rationalize it all. But this . . . what she's trying to do to Phoebe and her family, destroy them—he doesn't know what to think, what to do.

He knows from what he's read online that the kid in Medicine Hat known as S. M. did her time, and her boyfriend died in prison. She paid her debt to society under the laws that were written. She underwent rehabilitative psychiatric treatment and a graded reintroduction into society. He knows from his mother's manuscript that S. M. is Phoebe's mother. So he knows S. M. worked hard to earn a university degree. And Phoebe's mom has been working to pay back by helping others with mental problems. She's been a good citizen since, as far as Joe can tell. She's brought two lovely children into the world. She's made a nice home. She's doing her best—even if Phoebe doesn't see it. Joe saw all those photos on the wall. The family holidays, how Mrs. Bradley cares that her daughter had an empty vodka bottle. She worries that her daughter is seeing an older guy. And Joe knows why. It's personal. Mrs. Bradley is afraid the past will repeat itself. He also knows what the guys his age get up to and do to girls.

No, it's not fair that his mother suffered. But it's not fair to make Phoebe suffer now, either. It would shatter her if she learned of this shit right now.

He hears Mrs. Bradley's desperate words in his head.

Please, for the children—for yours, for mine—do not do this, Arwen. Please. We can work through—Joe clamps his hands over his ears.

His mother isn't going to protect those Bradley kids. She can't even protect her own son. The fact that Joe is sort of normal is by sheer fluke and the grace of God. His mother is going to destroy those children. She needs help. She needs to be stopped. She's dangerous like this.

Joe finds the one key he kept to her studio, and he finds a screwdriver.

He goes into her messy studio with its empty booze bottles, and using the screwdriver, he breaks open the lock on her corkboard doors. Joe flings open the doors. He rips every news article and photo off the board. He stuffs it all into a big black trash bag. Joe ferrets in his mother's drawers and finds her backup drives. He throws these into the bag, too. He scoops all her notebooks and pieces of paper off her table and into the bag. He carries her laptop and the bag back to the cottage.

Breathing hard, working fast before she comes home, Joe builds a roaring fire in the wood-burning stove. Fistful by fistful, he feeds pieces of paper and photographs from the Glenn Dennig murder into the flames. Sweat runs down his face as the fire crackles and smoke fills the cottage. He thinks of all those horrible words going up the flue, the smoke releasing them into the storm wind, blowing them far above the forest canopy where lightning cracks and thunder booms.

As the papers burn down to glowing ash, he rips pages and pages out of his mother's notebooks until his hands feel raw. Then he burns the notebook covers, watching as the metal spirals begin to glow orange. Joe throws in the backup thumb drives. He shuts the door to the fireplace, latches it, and watches the orange, pulsating glow. But he has no time to waste.

He takes his mother's laptop into the carport and drops it onto the concrete floor. He retrieves a hammer from a toolbox in the van and he smashes the computer to pieces, venting his frustration and anger and fear as the wind roars through the nearby forest and rain pours off the carport roof in a silver sheet. He can see the lights from the Cody house across the road, where just a short while ago it was all swinging lanterns and barbecue smoke and laughter and music. Before the storm hit.

"My God! Joey!"

He stalls, hammer in hand.

His mother stumbles into the carport, hair and clothes soaked. Tears burn in his eyes.

"What are you doing!"

He says nothing, gathers up the pieces of laptop, and sticks them back into the garbage bag. He carries it inside. His mother runs through the rain to her studio. Then a few moments later she bursts into the cottage, face white, eyes wild.

She stares at the fire glowing like a cauldron in the hot, smoky cottage.

"Joe?"

His jaw hardens.

"What have you *done*?"

"You have to stop."

"Joey, what have you done? What—"

"The true crime book. It's not going to give you what you need, Mom. It's not going to make you better. We can pack up and go home. Like, tomorrow. Back to your doctor. He can refer you to that guy at the institute who helped you when I was little. They can treat you properly if you let them. Yes, I read about it in your notes. I know how you had the breakdown when I was six. I never understood why I went into some kind of foster care."

"You don't understand, Joey . . . You . . ." Tears fill her eyes. She looks in desperation at the fire.

"The backups are gone, too."

She slumps into a chair, and her eyes go vacant.

"I know Mrs. Bradley did this to you when you were both little. It's not your fault. But dragging those Bradley kids through this is not going to make it better."

"Joe, this was going to be our big break, and—"

"Enough!" he yells.

She jerks in shock at his tone.

"Enough," he says again, more gently. "You are deluding yourself." He points his finger in the direction of the Cody pool house. "Did you feel better after confronting her in there, honestly?"

She rubs her wet face.

"You didn't, did you?"

"I thought I would, Joey. I thought I would feel some kind of powerful delight in seeing her crumble in front of me. I thought it would give me back something, if I could just make her *see* me, see my wound. If I could look into her eyes again, and . . ." Her voice fades and she sits, staring at him, her eyes glassy with drink and drugs, and Joe is used to that look on his mother's face. He hates this thing she does to herself, to both of them.

"I wanted her to admit it. I wanted her to look into my eyes and say sorry."

"And then?"

"Then I would write about our confrontation—blow by blow in the book. It would sell, it would, Joey. It would be like an 'own voices' thing. My story. The victim. The one who got away, but didn't. My side that got forgotten. We would actually profit something from the crime, from the havoc she wreaked."

He stares at her, long and hard. "You need to stop, Mom. For the Bradley kids. For *me*, Mom. I am your child. I am asking you, please. For me."

She stares at him for what seems an eternity. The fire crackles and the heat inside the cottage is intense. "You're like your dad, you know. All self-righteous reason."

Joe goes stone still. He doesn't dare move a muscle in case she stops talking.

"The older you get, the more . . . you look, are . . . so much like him. I loved him, you know. Truly, deeply. And that made me so scared." She drops her face into her hands and rocks. "I chased him away before he could leave me. Like all the good things in my life were always taken from me. I'm so sorry, Joey. I'm a rotten mom. I even robbed you of knowing your father, because he would have loved you, had he known about you. He . . . he would have cared for us . . ." She begins to sob. Big, heartrending, body-racking sobs. "What have you done to my work? I don't know how to start again . . . I am a failure. I have failed you as a mother."

He swallows, gets up, strokes her wet hair. "Mom," he whispers. "You can still be a good mother. The real heroes are the ones who do brave things in the face of the worst adversity. And you can stop all this. Come, let me help you back to the studio. You need some sleep. You need to get into bed."

Joe hooks his mother's arm around his shoulder, and he helps her back to her studio. He throws the piles of dirty clothes off her bed, and he turns down the covers. She climbs in.

Joe tucks his mother into her bed. He turns down the lights, leaving only her pink-orange Himalayan salt lamp glowing. He hesitates, glances at her scary paintings, whose eyes all seem to be watching him. Judging him. He feels confused. Vulnerable.

He bends down and kisses his mother lightly on her damp hair. "I love you, Mom. It'll be okay. It's going to be okay."

RIPPLE EFFECT

Later that night.

Lily wakes. Tom is sleeping soundly. She watches him a moment as the storm continues to lash against the windows.

I saw from under the bed what happened across the hallway in Danny's bedroom. You thought it was just you and Vincent who knew. But no, it's you and me, Lily . . . We are the only two people left who know what really happened in that room.

Thunder rolls into the night, but Tom doesn't stir. She throws back her duvet, gets out of bed, and goes quietly down the stairs.

In the laundry room she finds clothes. She didn't want to open the closets upstairs, so she gathers what she needs from the piles of fresh washing. She puts on leggings, a shirt, socks.

She finds a flashlight in the hall closet, finds a cap of Tom's, a rain jacket, her running shoes.

Cautiously she opens the front door. Rain drums and splashes. She listens for any sound of her family moving. Her dear family. Her family, who must come first.

Lily shuts the front door to her eggplant-colored house with the green trim and steps into the rain.

Once she nears the corner, she clicks on the flashlight. Rain glints silver in the beam.

She looks over her shoulder. Nothing stirs. Lights are all out.

She heads down the road, making for the little cottage at the end of Oak End.

◆ ◆ ◆

Joe is unable to sleep. On his phone he googles stories about S. M.—the "Mary Bell of Canada" who killed her own little brother. He wonders if his mother really did see what happened in the little boy's room, or if she was lying to mess with Mrs. Bradley's head. He wonders if his mom is going to wake with a clearer head or if she will lose her shit totally. Will she just dig all this up again and start over? Will the fallout from that awful and inexplicably tragic day in Glenn Dennig ever end, or will it just keep haunting them all down generations, until they are destroyed, one by one, in different ways? He clicks on a news story with the headline "Will S. M. Reoffend?"

> Experts are divided on whether S. M. has been fully rehabilitated and will be able to move forward with her life.
>
> "Here we have a young woman who at the age of 12 was diagnosed with oppositional defiant disorder and conduct disorder—these are two very serious disorders," said Ash Weldon, a criminal justice professor at the University of Alberta and the author of *Kids Who Kill*. "Is it possible she can change? Absolutely," said Weldon. "But we simply don't know. Every case is unique, and only time will tell in this particular instance. The upside is that S. M. was so young at the time of the attacks. This gives her a greater chance of recovery. She has apparently made progress with her

schooling and counseling, and her lawyers say she is remorseful. So those are good indicators."

Joe turns his attention to the comments beneath the article.

J Balboa: S. M. had psychopathic tendencies. Psychopaths don't "rehab" well. My guess is S. M. spent those years honing her craft at pulling off a scam and giving a s***. The caseworkers have been fooled. Psychopaths can fool anyone. Someone needs to find out her name and share it. I'd hate to think that an unsuspecting person might end up dating her or having her as a roommate. And what if she has kids? If you're in doubt, reread the portion about her brother. Sick.

RD: Remember what Wozniak said, that he'd seen lots of bad scenes and lots of dead bodies, but very few children and very few children ever in that state? That girl is sick. The father was stabbed 24 times. The boys had their throats slit.

Mary Procter: I hope that little girl under the bed and her parents find peace and can move on. But I also recall what Wozniak said at the anniversary of the murders. He said, "My biggest fear is that she hasn't been rehabilitated, that she's tricked those in the system, and that she hasn't moved forward." I think she could be a con.

Joe hears a noise. He sits upright, thinking it's another pine cone or branch debris blowing onto the roof. He hears the studio door slam.

He gets up, peers out the window.

Under the streetlamp in the street, he sees a woman with a headlamp on. *Shit!* His mother? Going for a run? Now?

Shit shit shit. She's going to get hurt.

Joe grabs his jacket. Thunder cracks. He rushes to the door. He sees the bag Phoebe left for when they were going to sneak off into the woods. He must have knocked it off the bench when he was pacing around the cottage. It's on the floor and has fallen open, exposing the cap and headlamp Phoebe brought from her house. Joe grabs them and dashes out the door.

MATTHEW

NOW
June 23. Thursday.

Matthew sneaks out of the house with his camera in his backpack. Quietly he takes the bike his grandparents keep in the garage for him.

They're having coffee in bed, and Phoebe is still sleeping. His own parents are in holding cells in the big police station downtown, which is a half-hour drive away down the Patricia Bay Highway. It's a warm summer morning, clear sky, and he cycles as fast as his little legs will carry him on the bike path that runs along the highway. It makes him breathe hard and get hot. He's tense but also excited because he has a plan.

Matthew reaches the small seaside village that is not too far from his grandparents' house. It has colorful tourist shops and a boardwalk. He locks his bike to a pole near the bus stop and waits for the bus. He looked up the timetables last night.

It arrives and comes to a stop with the usual bus noises—a sort of squeak and exhalation as if it's sighing. He climbs aboard, puts his quarters into the money jar, and takes a seat right up front near the driver. No one seems to take any notice of him, and he scoots back into his seat, his legs lifting off the ground. As the bus drives, he studies the Google map on his phone, figuring out how to get to the police station.

It's one block from the bus stop. The ride takes almost an hour because the bus stops so many times, and when Matthew steps off, his heart pounds. Cars zoom by and the buildings seem tall. But he has to push through. He's doing this for his dad, and his mom. It's his fault they have been arrested. He has to fix it.

Matthew finds the police station—a multistory concrete building with lots of glass and a totem pole outside. He enters the glass doors and goes up to the counter, which has bulletproof glass. He stands on his toes to see over the countertop, and one of the two cops behind the counter leans down to listen to him through the hole.

"Hey, young sir, how can I help you?" she says.

"Can I speak to the murder detective?"

The cops glance at each other.

"It's about the jogger murder."

RUE

NOW

Rue sticks the photos that Matthew Bradley shot of his father to a board. From the search-warrant evidence, she and her team are working to piece together an overall picture of events and a clearer timeline around Arwen Harper's murder. They're hunting for holes, avenues to investigate further. And they're waiting for the results of the RCMP DNA database search to see if the profiles from the semen or the unidentified touch DNA from the Kordel cap are in the system. The clock is ticking on how long they can keep holding the Bradleys.

Toshi combs through Harper's phone records. Georgia Backmann is viewing road cam footage from the arteries that feed onto the street that runs past the Garry Bluffs parking lot.

Rue stands back and studies the grainy photo of Tom Bradley unlocking the shed door. Another image shows him glancing over his shoulder. The dark stain on his shirt is clearly visible.

"Hey, Rue, Toshi, look at this," Georgia says.

Rue and Toshi go over to her desk. She points at the CCTV image.

"What in the hell?" says Toshi. "That's Harper's van."

Rue's pulse quickens. The van in the image is a Volkswagen, and it's painted with giant snowflakes. There is no doubt—it's Arwen Harper's vehicle.

"Watch this," says Georgia. "It blows straight through the red light at that intersection. The time here is ten eleven p.m. on June nineteenth. The night of the Cody barbecue. That's her registration."

"Can you find the van at the next cam? Is there a better image of the driver?" Rue asks.

Georgia pulls up footage from a different cam. They watch. A few minutes later, the van appears. There appears to be a lone occupant—the driver. Dark clothing. A cap and a hoodie. A headlamp that is turned off.

"Shit," Toshi says.

The door to the office opens. A uniformed officer appears. "Sergeant Duval?"

Rue glances up. "What is it?"

"Someone to see you."

"I'm tied up. Can you get someone else—"

"It's a small boy. Says his name is Matthew Bradley. He wants to speak to the 'murder detective.' He has something to show you, and he refuses to show anyone else."

RUE

NOW

Rue hurries to the reception area. There he stands. Brown hair. Freckles. Gap between his front teeth. He's frightened, that much is clear.

"Matthew, hey, buddy. Good to see you again. What's up? What can I do for you?"

"I came to show you my other photos. My dad did nothing wrong, and I—" Tears gleam in his eyes. "You have to let them go, you must."

"How did you get here, Matthew?"

"On my bike and then the bus. By myself."

"How about we go into a nice room? Can I get you something to eat? Drink?" She glances at her watch. "It's almost lunchtime. Do you like burgers? Pizza?"

"I like burgers. And fries. And pop, but my mom doesn't like me to have sugar."

She smiles as warmly as she can. "How about we keep that a secret?"

He nods.

Rue sends an officer to get takeout from the burger joint on the corner, and she takes Matthew into the interview room with the blue sofa.

He sits and immediately starts rummaging in his pack, and he takes out his digital camera.

"That's a super-cool-looking camera, Matthew."

"I got it last Christmas. I heard my gran say you took my case files and the photos I printed out of my dad after his run, but I have more photos. I heard Gran say my photos are why you put my mom and dad in prison, but I have more. And you need to see these ones. You can look on the little screen here, and scroll like this." His little finger shows Rue how to view the tiny thumbnails of the digital images stored in his camera. "I brought a cord, too." He pulls a cord out of his backpack. "So you can download them into a computer, and then let my mom and dad out of prison."

"And what am I going to be looking for, Matthew?"

"Mr. Cody."

She crooks up a brow. "Mr. Cody?"

"He . . . I think he was the last person with Joe's mom. Not my dad. Which means my dad couldn't have hurt her, right? When my dad took my mom home from the pool house, and after I saw Joe going home, I went to see who was still in the pool house. I took photos through the window. That's my specialty." His cheeks redden.

"Are you trying to show me something so that you can blame someone else, perhaps? To get your dad off?"

His face goes beet red. "You *must* let him off. Mr. Cody . . . I . . . he was in there with Joe's mom, and they were doing . . . you know."

"Not really. They were doing what?"

"Having sex. In the pool house. After my parents left. After Joe left. I sneaked up . . . I . . . I'm a stalker, you see."

"Oh, are you?"

"Like, a stealth one. Like an investigator. For my case files, you know?"

"Right. Yes."

"And I took some photos."

Rue turns her attention to the tiny images. Her heart begins to beat fast. The subjects are clearly Arwen Harper and Simon Cody. Cody has Harper pressed up against a wall, and her skirt is rucked up around her waist. They are clearly involved in intercourse. Rue thinks of the semen trace on Harper's thigh.

"Matthew, this could be very, very helpful to what is a very important investigation. Since you brought these photos in to show me, are you okay if I download them, copy them? For the investigation?"

He nods, eyes bright. "Can I see my dad and mom now?"

She hesitates. "Yes, okay. I will take you downstairs to visit your parents, but can I also scroll through the other photos you have in here?"

"Yes," he says, sitting up straighter, his confidence bolstered by her keen interest. His legs begin to sway.

Rue scrolls through the other files in the camera. Matthew has captured images of the barbecue—lanterns swinging in wind, kids playing ball, men gathered around the smoking barbecue.

"What is this one?" Rue holds the camera out to Matthew.

He peers at the image. "Oh, that's my sister, Phoebe, with Joe. Sitting on a log. I have more of them in the files. And pictures of Fi and her other friend. Phoebe was grounded that day, and she shouldn't have been sitting on the log. She gave Joe her bracelet, because he was sad."

Rue is barely listening. She's seen something that has turned her blood cold. She leans forward, urgency in her voice. "And what's this, Matthew?"

"Oh, that's . . . I . . . I wasn't supposed to be in there, but I know where Mr. Cody keeps the key in a sculpture outside the door."

"Not supposed to be in *where*?"

"His shed. It's wood and it's built into the side of the cliff. The only way to get there is down the ladder stairs. Mr. Cody keeps his trophies in there—like taxidermy birds. Eagles with glass eyes. And even a weasel. A white one. It's a winter coat. And stuff he finds beachcombing when he is bird-watching. I've seen him at Grotto Beach, picking up shells and sea glass. That's when he told me he likes to make them into mobiles. With bird feathers and bits of driftwood and stuff like that."

"And this is one of his mobiles?"

"Yes. It hangs like a dream catcher in the window and catches all the light. Some of the things he sets in resin—he told me when I found him beachcombing."

Rue's heart hammers.

She enlarges one of the items hanging from the mobile. She stares at it. Her skin goes hot. It's a green Maltese cross. Looks like jade. A tiny compass set in the middle. She scrolls the image over and studies another item hanging from the mobile. An antique-looking ring with a small silver ball in the center. There's also a hexagonal bracelet swinging from a wire. And what looks like strands of hair set in resin. Red hair. Blonde. Dark brown. The hair colors of the three Jogger Killer victims.

Her gaze shoots back to Matthew. "Matthew, can you wait here? Someone will bring your takeout. And then they will take you to your parents."

He nods in excitement.

Rue reaches for her phone as she hurries down the corridor. Her superior, Luke Holder, picks up.

"Luke—I think we got him. The JK. I need everyone in the bullpen. Stat. I think we've freaking got him!"

HANNAH

NOW

Hannah is washing dishes when she hears sirens. Joe is in the guest room and Simon is in the attic office. The kids are at school. In less than a week, they will officially be on summer vacation. She thinks of how Lily's kids are at their grandparents' and have been taken out of school early for their own well-being. She sets a plate in the drying rack. As sorry as she is for them, she's thankful it's not her kids, not her problem. The sirens grow louder. Anxiety whispers through her. Outside, the sky is bluebird clear and the sea sparkles beyond the end of the bluff. The sirens wail, louder. They sound as if they're coming closer. Hannah realizes they're on her street. Her first thought is Lily and Tom's place, like last time.

She sets down her dishcloth and is reaching for her apron ties when she hears vehicles shrieking to a halt outside their house. She freezes. Then hurries to the window. Six marked police vehicles plus a black SWAT-type van are parked at angles across the cul-de-sac and her driveway. Her heart kicks as cops in black tactical gear stream out of the vehicles. Officers wearing helmets and carrying automatic weapons come up her driveway. Others go onto their property closer to the pool house and forest. Her hand goes to her throat as another cluster of cops moves in a unit around the side of their house.

Banging sounds on their door. "Open up! Police!"

Hannah yells up the stairs, "Simon! Simon!"

He comes thumping down the stairs, sees the cops through the long window on the side of the front door, and bolts for the glass sliders in the living room.

Hannah stands frozen in the entryway.

"Police, open up!"

She hears the bash of a battering ram against her front door. But Hannah is unable to move. She is rooted to the tiles in the entryway, her hands pressed against her stomach.

Joe comes clattering down the stairs. "Hannah? What's going on?"

She still can't move, can't speak. Out of the corner of her eye, she sees her husband racing across their emerald-green lawn toward the stairs at the edge of the bluff that go down to his shed. She remembers the photos she once saw—the ones he printed out of those different female joggers. They'd been shot over a period of weeks, maybe even months, she guessed, from the different clothing they wore in the images, and the different weather conditions. And she knows. She knows that everything she has tried for years to ignore, tried to rationalize, struggled to justify and explain to herself, is about to explode into the open.

Bang. Bang. Bang. The battering against the door continues.

She remembers something Lily explained to her once. It was something the eminent Swiss psychiatrist Carl Jung had said: *People will do anything, no matter how absurd, in order to avoid facing their own souls.*

The explosive blows of the battering ram reverberate through her house, rattle the windows, shake her psyche. *Boom. Boom.*

Joe rushes to open the door, and the officers come blasting through it.

Detective Duval is in the rear, dressed in a Victoria Police Department jacket, a bullet-suppression vest, and a black cap. Her weapon is drawn. She says, "Where's your husband, Mrs. Cody? Where is Simon?"

Hannah shakes her head, her mouth open. She still can't speak.

Joe points to the open glass sliders. "He . . . went that way."

Detective Duval and the officers barrel through Hannah's white living room and out through the glass sliders that look over their magnificent ocean view.

Hannah goes to the window. So does Joe. They watch the officers in tactical gear take down her husband on the lawn near the edge of the bluff. Simon fights. But they tackle him to the ground. He struggles to his feet, but they get him down again. On his stomach. An officer presses a knee into his back, holds his face sideways in the grass. His face is red. He's screaming. Someone else cuffs him.

"What do they want him for?" Joe asks.

It's a movie, Hannah thinks, still unable to reply, unable to voice or articulate what she does not want to believe is real. It's not really happening in her backyard. It's not her husband. He never would have done those things. It's Arwen, she thinks. All this is that waitress's fault. It all started to go wrong when she blew into town in that stupid blue bus painted with snowflakes and her son riding shotgun.

Before Arwen arrived, the neighborhood was fine. Just ticking along, everyone effectively hiding their dark family secrets behind their smiling masks. But Arwen rattled their cage. The rats began running around and attacking each other.

"Mrs. Cody?" Joe touches her arm gently.

"Get out, Joe Harper—get out of my fucking house!"

He stares. His jaw drops.

"You and your damaged mother. You did this. *Get the hell out of my house!*"

RUE

NOW

"What a view," Toshi whispers to Rue. She stands with her partner inside Simon Cody's cliff-side shed. Simon has been taken into custody. She and Toshi are awaiting an ident crew.

The building hangs precariously over the sea and is reachable by steep wooden stairs that hug the sandstone cliff. Unless someone was looking right over the edge of the bluff, they would not know it was here. It's isolated, away from prying eyes. They had to breach the door with force. It was locked with a bolt.

The windows run the length of the building on the seaward side. There is a bench bed along one wall, and shelving, cabinets, a desk, and a computer printer along another. Stuffed birds observe them with sightless glass eyes, and a white weasel watches, as Matthew said.

"It's quite something all right," she replies to Toshi. Her tone is reflective of the emotion she feels looking at the sea through the mobile that hangs in the window. It turns slowly with the ocean breeze coming through the breached door. The pendants and jewels catch light and tinkle.

Toshi says, "Cody sits here, in his cabin, looking at that stunning view through resin that traps human hair, through the trophies he's taken from women he stalked, attacked, raped, and bludgeoned to death."

Rue nods. "And from the photos in those drawers, he stalked his victims for some time before he moved on them." She catches Toshi's eyes. "We got him."

He snorts softly. "A little neighborhood sleuth named Matthew Bradley got him."

Rue smiles. Then laughs. "Yeah. Who'da thunk that we needed an eight-year-old's eye." Her smile fades. "The little tyke went to Herculean effort to bring those images to us, but there's a chance Simon Cody did not work alone. He and Tom Bradley ran marathons together. They presumably trained together on occasion."

"And those Elk Lake and the Goose trails are prime training trails for long-distance runners—you think we have a killer pair? You think somehow they're both good for Harper?"

She inhales deeply, thinking of the snowflake van blowing through the red light on the night of the murder. "I'm thinking Harper might only be tangentially connected to Simon. We need the results of that DNA search."

The ident team arrives, and Rue and Toshi climb the stairs back up to the bluff to give the crime scene techs room to work.

Rue sees Joe standing on the grassy bluff near the woods. He comes over to her.

"Give me a minute with him," she says to Toshi. "I'll meet you back at the station."

He eyes her.

"Looks like he has something to say. I'll listen to what he volunteers."

He nods and heads back to his vehicle.

"Joe, what's up?" she asks as he reaches her.

"I need to talk to you. It . . . it wasn't Mr. Cody. And it wasn't Mr. Bradley. They didn't do it. They didn't hurt my mom."

Surprise washes through Rue. "What makes you say that, Joe?"

"I know. I . . . I was there."

JOE

THEN
Sunday. June 19.

The day she dies.

Joe rushes out the door wearing Phoebe's dad's Kordel cap and his headlamp, but as he reaches the carport, he realizes he doesn't know how far into the woods his mother has already run, and if he charges along the path after her, in the dark, in this storm . . . He's seen her like this before. When she's borderline psychotic. She hears things, sees things that are not there. And if she took some of her pills after he tucked her into bed, she could be in a serious way. It could explain why she went into the woods in the dark.

He could call for help, but it might not come soon enough, and tons of people and sirens descending on her in the woods with lights from all directions, it could trip her out. Mostly Joe is worried about the cliffs where the trail comes out along Garry Bluffs. He needs to head her off before she gets out onto Garry Bluffs.

He sees the van in the carport.

If he takes the van, he can drive quickly around to the parking lot on the other side of the woods. She'll have let off some steam by the time she exits the trail there. She'll be tired, more manageable. If he parks at the bluffs and enters the trailhead from the parking lot, he can approach her head-on and wait for her, instead of scaring her by chasing after her.

Joe rushes back inside to get the spare set of van keys.

He starts the van, backs out of the driveway, and roars down the road in the pouring rain, wipers whipping back and forth.

He blows through a red light at an empty intersection.

When he reaches the parking lot, it's empty. He screeches to a stop right in front of the trailhead. Joe finds a flashlight in the glove compartment, and he switches on Mr. Bradley's headlamp.

He gets out of the van into the storm, and he runs into the moaning and groaning forest. Thunder grumbles over the ocean.

About a half kilometer along the main trail, Joe glimpses a light bobbing through the mist and trees.

He stands still, breathing hard, waiting for her.

As she comes closer along the trail, he calls out to her. "Mom!"

She stalls.

"Mom—wait up!" He goes toward her.

She spins and darts into the bushes and starts crashing through the undergrowth. Joe sees the beam of her headlight bouncing off fog and between trunks. He aims his flashlight into the woods, trying to see where she is going. Panic strikes a hatchet into his heart.

She's making for the cliffs on the other side of those trees.

Joe hurries into the bushes after his mother, following her bobbing light. "Mom! It's me! Joe! Please stop!"

Her light keeps moving, tunneling through the mist. He hears her fall, and he can hear her crawling. His heart hammers. He doesn't know how close to the cliff she is. He moves faster, calling after his mother.

She goes down again. Her light goes out.

Joe stops. "Mom?"

Just the pattering of rain and the whoosh of wind through the trees. Thunder cracks and branch debris comes hurtling down. Joe inches forward, carefully panning his light over the ground. He sees her footprints in the mud.

"Mom?" he calls tentatively. Lightning cracks and thunder booms. Suddenly she lurches up out of the ferns, and like a wounded deer, she bashes and crashes toward the cliff edge. Fearing for her life, Joe chases after her.

He pops out of the woods, and she's there, right at the very cliff edge. His heart freezes. He can't breathe. He briefly shines his light in her face and sees she's been cut. Panic wars with caution. He can see she's in one of her delusional, manic phases.

He raises his hand. "It's okay, Mom, it's me, Joe, it's okay. Take my hand." He reaches it out to her.

She lunges at him like a wild animal, hitting him across the face. It knocks the cap and hood off his head. The light of her headlamp shines in his face. For a moment she stalls. "You?"

Emotion burns in his eyes. "Yes, yes, it's me, Mom. It's okay. Give me your hand." He holds it out again.

Wind gusts suddenly. Trees bend and a loose branch crashes down and hits the side of her head. She screams and steps backward. He lunges to grab her, but she fights him off, ripping Phoebe's bracelet off his wrist as the crumbling sandstone gives out under her shoes. She windmills her arms as she goes over. Joe hears her scream and a gut-sickening thud. She screams again, then the wind snatches her voice and thunder growls, drowning the sound.

Joe stands in shock. He inches to the edge, peers over into the dark abyss. He can't see a thing. All he can hear now is wind and rain.

He races as fast as he can back to the trail. He runs for the bluffs. He crosses the parking lot and hurries down the slippery stairs with his handheld light because the headlamp got knocked off.

When he finally finds his mother on the stone beach, she's gone. She is bashed and broken and bloodied on the stones. Joe sits there and sobs into the storm and wails.

And then he gets scared.

RUE

NOW

Rue sits on a bench beside Joe, listening quietly as he confesses his story.

She is silent for a while. They watch the water.

"Why, Joe?" she asks quietly. "Why didn't you just come to us and tell us what happened?"

"I . . . I was scared. I . . . She was so messed up, and I was scared. Alone. I have no one. I . . . didn't know what would happen to me, and I didn't want to go to prison. I also didn't want to have to tell anyone what she was working on, because I wanted to protect Phoebe. But then you arrested Phoebe's parents, and it's hurting them all anyway."

"I don't understand."

He inhales deeply. "Please, you can't let Phoebe or the media know. I read up about it. Under the laws, a young offender who has had a record expunged like that—she can't be named publicly. Not even by the police."

"What are you talking about, Joe?"

"She was the child killer."

"*What* child killer?"

"Mrs. Bradley. She was the child who murdered her own family with her boyfriend in Medicine Hat in 1989. Mrs. Bradley was Sophie McNeill."

RIPPLE EFFECT

NOW
September 4. Sunday.

After church, Lily, Tom, and the kids walk home and stop to buy ice cream cones from a food truck near the water. Lily glances at her husband. Tom's eyes smile as he hands her a rum and raisin cone.

"Don't know how you can stomach that flavor," he says.

"Yeah, it's blech," says Matthew around his mouthful of chocolate chip ice cream.

"Ditto," says Phoebe.

"Well, it's a good thing you guys don't have to eat it, then," says Lily, taking a lick.

She and Tom walk slowly side by side while the kids run ahead to feed the ducks in a pond. The sun is warm on Lily's shoulders. Flowers erupt in a riot of color along the verges. And best of all, the Bradleys are no longer being tailed by the media. All the frenzy was immediately redirected toward Simon Cody, who has been charged with the murder of three women and named as the Jogger Killer. There is speculation on talk shows from retired law enforcement experts that Simon could be linked to a lot more cases. Lily thinks of what a criminologist said on television last night.

A sociopath, a serial sexual predator like Professor Simon Cody, doesn't suddenly get up one day and do this. It takes practice. Refinement. He's done this before. I have no doubt there will be more.

Tom was released shortly after Simon Cody's arrest, and after the semen DNA trace from Arwen's body came back as a match to the other jogger victims. Hannah was questioned, then the very next day she flew with Jacob and Fiona to Winnipeg, where she is staying temporarily with her parents. The Cody house, grand upon the bluffs overlooking the sea, stands empty and sealed off.

Ironically—but perhaps not surprisingly—Dianne Klister, like a heat-seeking rocket, stepped into the media glow and offered to represent Kordel professor Dr. Simon Cody, the Jogger Killer.

"Did you see it—did you have any inkling at all about Simon?" Lily asks Tom again. "Because I didn't. I just thought Simon was odd in the way a philosophy professor can be odd. But you—you drank with him, you trained with him, ran races with him. You *knew* him."

"Maybe in retrospect cracks were showing. The way he was with Arwen, and with me . . . the way he sat on his boat taking those photos, things he said to me. I . . . There was a dark side to him oozing through."

"Devolving?"

"Conceivably. It's how these things usually go. He was probably ready to kill again and getting antsy for the fix, trying to figure out how to do it."

"Do you think he'd have hurt Arwen, given the opportunity?"

"Simon was pragmatic. He wouldn't have hunted right in his backyard," says Tom. "He's smart, a calculating predator. A survivor. If I was a gambling man, I'd bet Detectives Duval and Hara have already found evidence in his shed that he was stalking and setting up for a fresh victim, but farther afield."

She shivers as a breeze ripples over her skin. "But then Arwen arrived and messed everyone up in the neighborhood. Including the killer across the street."

Tom gives a wry smile and takes a mouthful of his cone.

"I think Hannah knew about him," Lily says. "At least on some level. I believe it's why she showed me those photos and took them to the cops. Denial. Deflection."

They stop and sit on a bench, thighs touching. She's still processing the fact that Tom has known all along she was Sophie. That he married her and made a family with her and lived with her all these years and kept his silence. He's told her again that he *wanted* her to be the poster child for rehabilitation. He wanted Dee's work to count. He remains a student of disordered minds, and he's always been a fierce mental health advocate. It's all his way of continuing the fight against the stigma, he told her.

I believe in restorative justice, Lily. I believe people can become better versions of themselves if they are not forced by society to wear a negative label.

As Lily believes the restorative justice program can work for her patient Tarryn Wingate.

As she believes Garth Quinlan could be a better father and positive member of society as long as he could keep his own dark past buried.

For a while Lily really feared that Tom might have hurt Arwen. She thinks Tom feared it could have been her. They both had opportunity. They both had motive. But Lily had gone down the road that night in a last-ditch effort to try to talk Arwen out of the book. She wanted to convince Arwen that therapy could still help her, and that it would be better for their children if this did not go public. But when she reached the cottage, no one was home. At the time, part of Lily was relieved. She didn't entirely trust herself *not* to hurt Arwen. Perhaps she *could* have been driven to kill if Arwen had refused to listen to reason.

If Lily really thinks about it, at the bottom line, she *did* kill Chrissie-Arwen. It was all her fault, going all the way back to that day in Glenn Dennig. If it weren't for her actions, Chrissie-Arwen might still be alive right now.

She glances at her husband. His eyes meet hers, and her heart squeezes with a strange emotion.

Perhaps she and Tom are just a perfect match. He's twisted. Like she is. As he said, human beings are terribly complex creatures. And sometimes there are no simple textbook answers. Sometimes human chemistry just coalesces in a perfect storm. As it did with Sophie and Vincent.

And all marriages have their secrets.

"I do love you," she says.

He stares at her. Ice cream drips down his fingers. He looks as though he's going to cry.

Matthew's ice cream is finished, and he's throwing the last pieces of his cone to the ducks.

"It's not good for them, you know," says Phoebe. "It's got sugar and crap."

He pretends he doesn't hear. He throws another crumb and glances at his mom and dad sitting on the bench. Close. Touching. His eyes go hot. His chest fills with a funny mix of pride and love. The murder detective said he'd make a brilliant investigator and that he should stay in touch. She'd give him a tour of the station and stuff if he wanted to visit her and Detective Toshi Hara again. Matthew thinks Detective Hara is cool in those clothes he wears. He didn't know cops could look like that. Detective Hara said Matthew should get a medal and that he was brave. His dad and mom hugged him so tight and sobbed and said he was a wonderful boy and that he had "saved the day." Even Phoebe reluctantly said he was a pretty cool little brother.

Phoebe is sad, though, because Joe is leaving. He came to say goodbye. After everything that happened with his mother, he's going back to Ontario.

"I'm sorry about Joe," he says quietly, and he throws another crumb.

Phoebe looks at him. He can see she's trying to scowl, but she can't get it right today. Her lip quivers instead. His sister looks pretty—none of that weird makeup. It's as if she's not trying so hard to be a freak at the moment.

"It's okay," she says. "I . . . I'll see him again, maybe."

"Or maybe not."

"Whatever. I'm glad the police never pressed charges, and that the coroner ruled it was an accidental death. I'm glad the cops helped him find his bio dad."

Matthew nods. It's good to have dads, he thinks. He doesn't know what he'd have done if they hadn't let his dad out of prison.

Rue and Eb go up to the airline check-in counter with Joe.

Joe carries on his back a big backpack that Eb gave him. He stops, inhales.

"You going to be okay?" Rue asks. She's in casual clothes. She and Eb have been spending quite a bit of time with Joe, renting kayaks, paddling up the gorge and out to sea, going on hikes. It's helped take her mind off Seth moving out. It's helped Eb and Joe, too.

Joe nods. "He's going to be waiting. Shit . . . I'm nervous. I . . ."

Rue touches his arm. "It's okay, one step at a time. Go easy on him, too. He never knew he even had a son."

"I don't know how to thank you," Joe says, his glance going between Eb and Rue. "Both of you. For all the gear, for letting me stay at your place." His eyes pool with emotion, and his hands tremble a little. "For helping me navigate this, and in dealing with what will still come. But mostly for finding him. My father."

"Police tools can come in useful," Rue says.

"But you did more—you used a private investigator on the other end."

"Only to speed things up. It wasn't hard, Joe. You would have gotten there on your own once you started the process, I know you would have. It's not like he was hiding or anything—he just didn't know about you. And your father sounds like a good, kind man. I'm just sorry he missed out on the life of a very, very special young person. I'm sorry for your mother, too, that she missed out on sharing you with him."

He struggles to keep it in. Eb glances away out of deference to Joe, giving him space to not feel embarrassed.

Rue hugs him and holds him tight, and she feels a ridiculous swell of emotion and affection for this boy. She feels him. She understands what it's like to want to belong to people who look the same as you, who share your blood. She pats his shoulder and says near his ear, "You're a really special person, Joe. Remember that. The Bradleys are lucky. Phoebe and Matthew especially. You spared those kids a lot by doing what you did to all that material of your mother's. You won. And so did I. I got my bad guy. You protected your friend."

"For now."

She steps back. "Yeah. For now. You take care, Joe. We'll always be here if you need us. Call, or visit, anytime."

"Bye, Detective. Cheers, mate," he says to Eb.

Rue and her son stand shoulder to shoulder as they watch Joe go through the check-in and then into the security area. He waves, then vanishes from sight.

Quietly Rue says, "Well, it's just you and me now, kid."

"I told you, Mom. I'm okay with that." He hesitates. "I still love Dad, even though he's a loser. It's not like he's going far away or anything."

"Yeah, well, just don't go following his girlfriends and giving me a heart attack, okay?"

He hooks his arm in hers and they head back to the car. Rue notices he's found his save-the-rhinos bracelet and is wearing it again. She doesn't mention it.

◆ ◆ ◆

That night Lily sits at her desk, writing in her journal. She's following her own advice to Garth. She's documenting her past for her children in the event of her death. One day they will find out, even if it's after she is gone. And when they do want to know, when they're ready, it'll be here. And it will be *her* narrative, not someone else's. Her version. Not Vincent's. Or Chrissie-Arwen's. History, after all, is told by the survivors. And Lily is the only survivor here, orphaned by her own hand. Meanwhile, she will protect her own children's innocence. She'll do her best to nourish them and grow them strong and resilient. She reminds herself that having children is a hopeful and redemptive act. It's a chance for reinvention. Parents generally do what they can to make the world a better place for their progeny. It's the nature of the human condition. And she *will* be a good mother. The courts gave her that opportunity. So has Tom. She's not going to waste it. Neither will she allow anyone to take it from her.

At the top of her notes, Lily copies the artist's statement from one of Arwen's paintings, which Joe gave to Phoebe, and which now hangs in her daughter's room.

> *It's best not to resist the change the "Death" tarot card brings. Resisting will make transition difficult. And painful. Instead one should let go, embrace the necessary change, see it as a fresh start. The Death card is a sign that you need to draw a line through the past in order to move forward. It says: Release what no longer serves you.*
>
> *—Artist's statement. Death. 36 × 48. Oil on canvas.*

AUTHOR'S NOTE

In my preface to *The Patient's Secret*, I note that the story idea grew around a core of true crime. Lily's background was inspired by a shocking familicide that occurred in the Medicine Hat area on April 23, 2006. And while there is no real S. M., there is a real J. R., who cannot be identified under Canadian law, although her name does appear in content generated outside the country.

Like my Lily, J. R. was driven in part by forbidden love to kill her family with the help of her then-twenty-three-year-old boyfriend, who can be named—Jeremy Allan Steinke.

J. R. became the youngest person in Canadian history to be convicted on multiple counts of murder. In 2016 she was set free. The maximum possible sentence for a child under fourteen is ten years.

J. R. was called a poster child for rehabilitation. Others—including the officer who first responded to the scene—were not as convinced.

While many of the murder details in my fictional Lily's past have been drawn directly from the facts of the true crime, there was no Chrissie equivalent to witness the horrific events, and other aspects, including Chrissie's little brother, are entirely fictional.

But one disturbing question indeed lingered after the trials. Neither J. R. nor Jeremy Steinke took responsibility for the death of J. R.'s little brother.

Only those two know what really happened in that house, and one of them is not telling the truth.

ABOUT THE AUTHOR

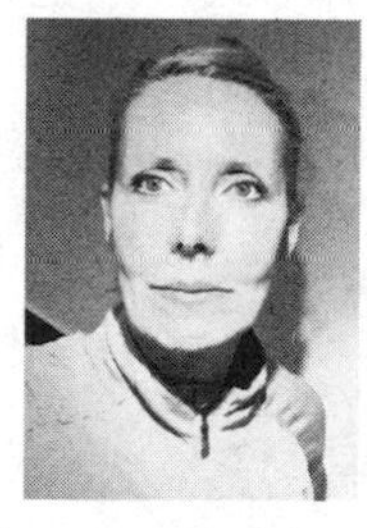

Loreth Anne White is an Amazon Charts and *Washington Post* bestselling author of thrillers, mysteries, and suspense, including *Beneath Devil's Bridge*, *In the Dark*, *The Dark Bones*, and *A Dark Lure*. With well over two million books sold around the world, she is a three-time RITA finalist, an overall Daphne du Maurier Award winner, an Arthur Ellis Award finalist, and a winner of multiple industry awards. A recovering journalist who has worked in both South Africa and Canada, she now calls Canada home. She resides in the Pacific Northwest, dividing her time among Victoria on Vancouver Island, the ski resort of Whistler in the Coast Mountains, and a rustic lakeside cabin in the Cariboo. When she's not writing or dreaming up plots, you'll find her on the lakes, in the ocean, or on the trails with her dog, where she tries—unsuccessfully—to avoid bears. For more information on her books, please visit her website at www.lorethannewhite.com.